Dance Down the Mountain

Dance Down
the Mountain

RICHARD HAMMER

Franklin Watts · New York · Toronto · 1988

Library of Congress Cataloging-in-Publication Data

Hammer, Richard, 1928–
Dance down the mountain.

I. Title.

PS3558.A4485D3 1988   813'.54   88-20686
ISBN 0-531-15098-4

To
Arlene
AND
Emily

I'm the king of the castle
And you're the dirty rascal;
On my head I wear the crown,
You can never push me down.

Old Nursery Rhyme

When you do dance, I wish you
A wave o' the sea, that you may ever do
Nothing but that.

Shakespeare, *The Winter's Tale*

Part One

*

1 The first time Charlie Stuart took me up to the top of his mountain, he told me it was sacred and it was haunted. I laughed and began to say something about Hollywood being filled with sacred places that were a hell of a lot more accessible, and if the ghosts were looking for spots to haunt, they were hardly likely to pick some godforsaken mountain top; if you were looking for ghosts, you'd be a lot more likely to find them in one of the palatial old mansions or maybe somewhere around Grauman's or the Pantages. Then I realized he was serious. Some amateur archeologists grubbing around under the rocky outcroppings, he said, had unearthed and managed to identify stone altars and, from their location at the rim of the steep, perilous precipice, had theorized that whoever had built them in that particular place had done so to worship whatever gods they prayed to and to propitiate the wrath of those gods in bad times by throwing their young virgins from the altars down the cliffside. The ghosts of those who had practiced those ancient rites were as old as the Chingichnich, maybe even older, maybe as ancient as the first people, whoever they were, who fled south ahead of the advancing ice sheets, or north ahead of whatever or whoever was chasing them, and proceeded to take up squatter's rights along the Southern California coast.

The day we went up there was a perfect one for all that Stuart wanted to show me. The night before, a Santa Ana had howled off the desert and ripped away the yellow sheet that had coated the city, filled the air, and blocked out the sun for weeks. By noon, the winds had died, and the air was calm, clean, and brilliant. Stuart had dropped by about then and hauled me away from work, insisting that he had something important he wanted to show me and it couldn't wait. "I don't care what you're doing," he said. "Get your ass out of that chair and come on."

"Charlie, Charlie," I said, "I'm right in the middle of this thing. I've got it moving, finally. Don't break the line, for chrissake."

"Screw the line," he said. "Maybe it'll move faster when you get back. Maybe you'll get inspired."

"Later, Charlie. Another time."

"You want to argue?"

"I want to work."

"Who the hell's paying you, anyway? If I say it's time to take a break, it's time to take a break."

So I took a break. We got into his Cadillac. "Why the hell should I drive a Mercedes or a Rolls," he said just about every time we got into that car. "A Caddy's good enough for Charlie Stuart. Believe me, if you're American, then, by god, you ought to buy American." We headed west on Sunset, made a turn into one of those twisting streets just before the Beverly Hills line, and started spiraling up into the hills, higher and higher, turning a dozen times back on ourselves until we were three or four ridges up from the strip, which had long since vanished from sight and sound. At the crest, more than a thousand feet up and, though you'd never know it, only about a mile from the turn, Stuart pulled the car to a stop, threw open the door, and got out. The wind was still blowing hard, strong enough so that I had to brace myself against it, certain that if I relaxed, it would hurtle me over the edge, straight down the steep, dry brush-encrusted slope a hundred feet or more into a caldron of ripping mesquite and rocks, among which, I was sure, rattle-snakes and centipedes and a lot of other unpleasant creatures were waiting.

"Okay, kid," Stuart said, making one of his all-enveloping gestures to encompass in one movement everything in every direction. "You ever see anything like it in your life? Tell me, wasn't it worth the drive?"

I looked. I nodded slowly. "Never, Charlie. Never in my life."

"Will you take a look at that." He pointed excitedly. A stag, a doe, and two fawns were picking their way along a narrow ledge far below. They didn't pause, didn't look up, didn't take flight, ignored our intrusion, if they even noticed it. "You see 'em all the time from up here," he said.

"I'm sure that's not all you see," I said. I didn't mean what he thought I did.

"You can say that again."

We were on the highest point of one of those ridges that contort in folded corrugations ever higher up from the coastal flats. From where we stood, the view was the kind that some natives, but more especially the newly arrived, who have become more native than the indigenous Californians, are always dreaming about and bragging about to newcomers and visitors, though they rarely see it themselves except on picture postcards. From Malibu and Topanga Canyon in the north, where a spur of the Coastal Range touched the sea, to the Palos Verdes Peninsula in the south, Los Angeles spread out like a toy city, set there not to be peopled, not to be believed in, but only for the aesthetic pleasure of whoever happened to be standing on this mountain peak, looking down. It was like standing over one of those train sets they used to set up in the department stores or in the Lionel showrooms when we were kids, everything almost but not quite real, but close enough so that you might imagine you were some Gulliver looking down on a world of Lilliputians. There were rows upon rows of orderly miniature palms lining thin ribbons of pavement and miniature houses with miniature blue dots of glass shimmering in the backyards reflecting brilliant points of light. We looked down on the towers of Century City, flashing blinding sparks of sun, looked down on the spire of the Mormon Tabernacle beyond, and beyond to Santa Monica, and beyond to the Pacific, flat and blue, and in the far distance, rising soft and misty blue-gray, a specter in the ocean, Catalina. On a clear day, we had heard a hundred times about a hundred different places since arriving, you can see Catalina. I hadn't see it before, either because the days had never been clear enough or I hadn't been in the right place. But on this day, from this spot, there, indeed, was Catalina.

"You like?" Stuart asked when he was sure I had taken it all in, though all I'd really gotten was an image burned into my eyes. There hadn't been enough time to absorb it all. No matter how long you stood there and stared, there probably wouldn't ever be enough time.

"It's incredible," I said.

"You know it," he said. He was a small, pudgy man, not much over five feet six or seven, but he seemed to grow then, to puff up, and his voice got too loud, reverberating off the hollows and the ridges. "It's mine," he said. "I own it."

"You what?"

"I own it."

"Nobody could own this."

"Maybe nobody. But Charlie Stuart's not nobody."

"What are you going to do with it?"

"What the hell do you think? I'm going to build up here,

of course. One of these days I'm going to build up here, and it's going to be a house like nobody's ever seen before."

"You're crazy." The only thing I could think of was that you'd have to be a madman or a fool or a dreamer of impossible dreams to even contemplate building a house on the top of this mountain. It would be like playing Russian roulette with a bullet in every chamber. One false step and it was a drop, a sheer drop, more than a hundred feet straight down, and if that didn't kill you and if the brush and rocks didn't tear you to shreds, then whatever was lurking down there would sure as hell finish you off. There were enough signs posted along the roads down below forbidding smoking or even lighting a match, even in a closed car, to let you know that the danger of one of those sudden, all-consuming hillside infernos lay always just beneath your feet, and if one started, the mountaintop would be nothing if not a death trap. And if the fires didn't come, there was always the potential of a mud slide during the rainy season, which meant taking a roller-coaster ride with the house right down into the gully below. And then there was the fog. When it rolled in, it would be so thick anyone up on the mountain would begin to think he was alone in his own private universe with no way down. About the only advantages I could possibly imagine were the view and perhaps that you'd be above the smog most of the time. But that was small comfort.

So I looked at Stuart and shook my head and said, "You're kidding. You're not really thinking about building a house up here?"

"Damn right," he said. "I know, you think I'm one damn fool. Hell, lots of guys have thought that about me, and they've had to change their minds pretty damn quick, let me tell you. A fool? Not Charlie Stuart. A dreamer, maybe, but no fool. I'm a dreamer, sure, and this is some kind of dream, let me tell you."

"You really are serious."

"You know it. Hell, Harry, I bought this damn piece of land a lot of years ago, a couple of years after I came out here. Before the war. My war, the real war. Paid peanuts for it. The guy I bought it from, he couldn't wait to unload. He thought I was nuts. Told me so, for a fact."

"Maybe he knew what he was talking about."

"No way. He was the one was nuts. He couldn't see no farther than the door to the bank. Me, I knew this was special the first time I ever stood here. It was back in forty. I was driving back from the studio, cruising along Sunset when I got this feeling, like it was life or death. Right there was this turnoff, this little road, so I swung into it and started heading up. I didn't know if that goddamn beat-up Ford was going to make it, the road was winding like a snake almost straight up and there were times I was sure the car was going to flip over like a sommersault. Pretty soon, the road turns to dirt, hardly wide enough for the car. They hadn't got it paved back then. They didn't know how to build up in the hills so nobody wanted to live up here but some stinking hermits in tents and cardboard shacks. Finally, I got to the top, right here, and I got out and, Jesus, you could see to kingdom come. They didn't have Century City back then, it was Twentieth and if you had a pair of binoculars, you could have looked down into the back lots and watched a dozen movies being shot. Standing up here, it was like all the blinders came off my eyes and I could see the whole fucking world for the first time. It was the top of the world. I knew I had to have it. It belonged to me. So, I found out who owned it and I asked him how much he wanted and I didn't even try to haggle, I just paid his price and it was mine."

"You've owned this for more than thirty years?"

"Damn right."

"And all you've ever done is come here and look?"

"Yeah. But that was all right. It was here and it was mine and I knew that someday I'd build my house up here. All those bastards down there on the flats, they think that's the place to be. Well, that's not for me. I'll build my house up here and I'll be looking down on them. But it's got to be a special house, the right kind of place for me and for this mountain, and maybe, just maybe, for somebody who understands what I'm getting at. Christ, two wives, two exwives, and neither one of them had the foggiest idea what the hell I was talking about. Well, one of these days it's going to happen and I'm going to find that person who gets it. And then the time's going to be right. It's coming real soon. I can feel it." He stared hard at me, perhaps waiting for a challenge. I said nothing. He swung around suddenly and started back to the car, calling over his shoulder, "Okay, come on. You've seen it. Now, let's get moving. Like you said, you've got a shitload of work waiting."

For another moment, I stood on the edge, staring out from that mountain toward the sea and beyond. Maybe Charlie Stuart was something of a fool, and maybe he was a madman, and maybe this was an insane dream, like so many others he had had all his life. But maybe there was nothing wrong with a dream, nothing wrong with building castles in the sky. So often, dreams are what keep a man going if he believes he can make them come true. And, I thought, nobody gets hurt in dreams.

I looked down, hoping to get one more sight of those deer on the ledge below. But they had vanished long since. I turned away then and walked slowly back to join Stuart at the car.

So this is Charlie Stuart's story, and mine and Katie's, and of the journey we all made to that mountain peak of his and the price we paid to reach it.

2

I can't say that I had any great affection for Charlie Stuart or even that I considered him a friend. But in those days there was little I wouldn't have done for him. I believed he was our savior, that he had rescued us from the edge of disaster, that he had kept the wolf away from the door.

We had come out from New York six months before, filled with high hopes and bright prospects. Through all the years since, I have looked back, as one inevitably does on decisions that radically altered the course of life, and wondered not if the decision was a wise one but, rather, what might have happened to us had we not made it. There are, of course, no answers, and the wondering is useless, the kind of intellectual game we all play yet which merely abrades the mind with the sands of bitterness. Much as it might have been nicer not to play that game, it was a thing I could not avoid. For what had begun so brightly and with such promise turned into a nightmare from which there seemed no prospect of awakening. There was no way we could have known or anticipated that, of course, when we made the decision to leave New York and head west. At that moment, Katie and I were sure that we were doing the right thing, the best thing, and were making no mistakes.

Katie was a dancer, which is a bland way of saying it, like saying Renata Tebaldi was a singer or Georgia O'Keefe was a painter. True, but hardly enough. Better, Katie was born to dance. It was there in the way she held herself, in the way she moved, in everything about her. It was impossible to miss or ignore. Her mother warned me just before we married that Katie's first steps had been glissades and her first words an announcement that when she grew up she would be not a ballerina but a prima ballerina, and so I had better be prepared to accept that I would have to share her with the ballet and could not always be certain of holding first place or even equal status. She had never wavered from that early determination, and at eight she was dancing in the children's corps in the Christmas productions of The *Nutcracker* at Lincoln Center, and that was just the start. She knew her destiny, and others who saw her knew it, too.

She was nineteen and in her first season dancing featured roles the first time I saw her. I had just returned from a time in the Deep South, writing about a lot of bad times and a few good and hopeful ones in Mississippi and Alabama, Georgia and Louisiana, and those other then unpleasant and a little unhealthy places. I had written well enough and observed deeply enough so that people who tended to be suspicious of and secretive with all whites, reporters or not, Yankees or not, had come to trust me some, and so I had gotten stories that others had not and won a few prizes and a little praise. When I got back to New York, though, what awaited me was precisely what awaited every reporter who had been out on his own, away from the day-to-day control of the paper's editors. I was given a desk about halfway back in the long main room filled with reporters assigned to the metropolitan staff and forced to compete for assignments, to compete for front-page bylines with a half a hundred other hungry reporters, thrown the small stories that might be turned into something a little more important with some digging. It was, I understood, and others before and after me had and would come to understand, New York's way of saying we were not independent, that no one of us was indispensable, that we were part of a whole and the whole was more important than any of its parts.

It was not to be permanent. Dave Goldberg, the assistant managing editor, told me that. I just had to relearn that old discipline (my place, perhaps). When I did, he said, what would I like to do? Perhaps it was time to move on and up. There was an opening as an assistant metropolitan editor. Would I like that? It was time, he said. You could remain a reporter all your life and just be a small cog no matter how important you thought you were. Or you could become an editor and start on the ladder to real power on the paper. The time was now to make that decision, he said.

If there was one thing I knew, it was that I didn't want to edit what other people wrote. I wanted to do the writing. And I had no desire to become part of the power struggle and the choosing of sides that was unrelenting among those on their way toward the top.

He was disappointed. He told me I was making a mistake. Writers were a dime a dozen, but editors were something else. If you had ambition, you became an editor.

I didn't have that kind of ambition.

Then what would I like? I could go to Washington. The bureau in the capital had put in a bid for me when the time was right. The national desk wanted me; it had liked the way I had covered the South, and there were plenty of stories all over the country, and anything outside New York was its province. I could stay on the metropolitan side and, perhaps, get ever more important local stories. And the foreign desk had expressed an interest in me.

I knew what I wanted. There was only one story then, and I wanted to see it. I said, Vietnam.

He said it would be a year before a spot in the bureau there opened up.

That was all right. For that assignment, I'd wait the year. So I stayed in New York and wrote local stories, and a book, which not many more people read than had read my first one.

And I met Katie. About seven one night, my story handed in, waiting for the loudspeaker to crackle the essential "Thank you, Harry Miller, and good night" so that I could leave, I was at my desk, reading. Nick Janovsky, the dance critic, wandered by, waving some tickets. "Anybody interested in the ballet tonight?" he asked everybody and nobody.

I had nothing planned, nothing better to do, and though I knew little about the fine points of ballet, I enjoyed it, its blend of music and theater and dance. I flagged him. "Worth my time?"

"Shit, yes," he said. He talked a hell of a lot less couth than he wrote, but who doesn't? "Good program. New kid. A comer."

I took a ticket, went, sat a couple of seats away from Nick, and watched a flame blaze across the Lincoln Center stage. It was more than the fire of her hair that drew and held the eye. She had that aura it was impossible to miss or ignore. She was something special. A comer, as Nick said. For me, even then, more than a comer.

I grabbed Nick at the intermission. "You know her?"

He looked at me and grinned. "Who?"

"Cut the shit, Nick."

He grinned wider. "You want to meet her?"

"Yeah."

"Everyone wants to meet her."

"Am I everyone?"

"Harry, you've been down in dear old Dixie too long."

"What's that got to do with anything?"

"She's a kid."

"All I want is to say hello and I think she's great."

"Sure. You and everybody else." Still, he did something he almost never does. He took me to a joint where the ballet kids hang out after the curtain (he wasn't reviewing, so he didn't have to worry about a deadline), and we had a drink, and the kids came in, and he went over and said hello and then brought Katie over and introduced her, and she sat down, and he vanished, and we went on from there.

We saw a lot of each other after that, when we could, and pretty soon I wasn't seeing anyone else, female, that is, and she wasn't seeing anyone else, male, that is, and I suddenly didn't mind that the three desks couldn't make up their collective minds whose Kewpie doll I was going to be. It was all right with me if I hung out in New York and got to see a lot of ballet and learned something about that art form.

Katie was dancing a lot then, and she was getting reviewed, and the reviews were almost always not just good but wonderful, filled with those hyperbolic phrases about effortless grace and distinctive line and deep involvement and probing interpretation and all the rest, all of which she laughed at, since, like most performers, she didn't have a terribly high opinion of the knowledge or judgment of critics. Audiences adored her; the applause and cheers and the bouquets, not just roses (which I sent) but a botanical garden of flora, washed over her in waves. After she danced *Raymonda* on an hour's notice, Nick, whom I called when I found out and who, at my urgings, went and watched, wrote, in the next morning's paper, at the end of a lyrical review, "Miss Summers gives every indication that she is a candidate to inherit the crown worn so gloriously in years past by Maria Tallchief, Melissa Hayden, and their like. It will come as no great surprise if, before too long, we see her in ballets choreographed for her talents, which are many."

It didn't happen. The talent was there and never vanished, but by the time she was twenty-five, the promise had not been fulfilled. Now and then she danced a lead, but her career seemed frozen on that rung just below the summit, on that rung of second leads and last-minute substitutions. I went to Nick one day and asked what the hell was happening. She had the talent, she had more than talent. What the hell was it?

"I hear stories," he said. He knew I was seeing her. He didn't know, very few people did, that it was more than now and then.

"What kind of stories?"

"I hear she's a smartass, talks back, asks too many questions, thinks she knows too many answers, and doesn't take orders. I hear she doesn't want it bad enough. You know what that means, Harry? She doesn't stab people in the back, she doesn't stomp on people, and maybe she lets them stomp on her. I hear she's screwed up and not dedicated, which means maybe she thinks that ballet ain't the end of the world, after all. I hear all kinds of things. Like I hear you're going to Nam. But, shit, Harry, she's a nice kid, and she's bright, maybe too bright, and maybe that's one of her problems. She ought to be at the top. But she ain't."

She was, indeed, a nice kid, and she wasn't on top, not where she thought, and a lot of other people thought, her talents and a few other things ought to have put her. But she was still very young, and she had lots of time.

Nick had heard right, and I went off to that dirty little war that wasn't a war to write about it, and when I got back a year later, Katie was right where she had been when I left. She had begun to believe that she had gone as far as she would go, at least with that company and probably in New York. What she couldn't understand or, if she understood somewhere inside, couldn't accept was why she had not gotten to the place she believed she belonged. There were a lot of reasons, of course, and if what I heard and Nick Janovsky heard and told me were anywhere close to the truth, talent, or lack of it, had nothing to do with it.

The world of the ballet is possibly the narrowest and most insular of any of the arts. A company is closer and more intimate than a family, and most of its members have little interest other than ballet. It is filled with unconcealed ambitions and naked passions and volatile temperaments. Gossip, often mean and spiteful, echoes backstage and spills over into private life, though for the dancer there is little to separate company life from private life; for most, they are the same. Petty jealousies explode into violent feuds, and minor misunderstandings become bitter wars. There is little opportunity to draw back and gain perspective, and so the antipathies and misapprehensions grow ever deeper until they become frozen in an unthawable ocean. Katie and her promise and her career were, in some measure, locked in that ice.

Everyone knew, a dancer told me one night, and I heard variations on the theme on other occasions, why Katie had lost her chance to dance the pas de deux from *Sylvia*. "It happened just before she met you," she said. "Todd's a cherry picker, and when Katie said no, there went the chance. He wasn't even subtle about it." Todd was the company manager. She might have worked through that in time, but not through the antipathy of the chief choreographer and artistic director, Walter Berenyi. He refused to give her leads because, he said, she wasn't dedicated and single-minded enough. He was incensed when she took a week that was coming to her to fly to Hong Kong to be with me; he had raged at her when we married, shouting that great dancers must choose between their art and the "mundane" world and it was obvious that she had made her choice and it wasn't for art; that she spent what little free time she had trying to get through school and earn a degree, was clear and incontrovertible proof, he stormed, that no matter her talent, she would never be great, would never merit a place in the pantheon. When she had begun to think about and explore the possibilities of going with another company in New York, he had passed the word that she was unreliable and not truly dedicated, and then he accused her of disloyalty. There were these reasons, and there were probably others, but whatever, she was not where she wanted to be and had expected to be as a dancer, and she knew that if she stayed with Berenyi and his company, she would never get there.

And then Terry Markoff reappeared. He had been one of the company's older soloists when she was first starting, had broken away to do his own choreography for a couple of companies in Europe, had returned finally and settled in Los Angeles. Now, with what seemed good financial backing and good management, he was about to start a company of his own on the Coast. He appeared in New York, watched Katie dance, and was convinced that those early appraisals of her talents, which he had shared, were more than justified. He offered her a leading place in the new company, promised her prima-ballerina roles in half a dozen productions, some old ones that every classically trained dancer dreams of doing, *Swan Lake* and *Giselle* and *Les Sylphides,* and some new ones that were just emerging from his fertile creative mind. He went on a campaign to woo and win her. Maybe he wasn't offering her New York, and maybe his new company wasn't one of the great ones, but if she joined him, she would finally get to dance those roles that had filled her dreams, and she would get to create new roles, and it might, just might, be a way to get to where she was sure she belonged.

If it was what Katie wanted, it was fine with me. There was little holding me to New York. I was free-lancing then, and so the ties had loosened. I had covered my wars, and when I returned, I had turned down another foreign assignment because of Katie and had settled in. Too soon I had grown bored, not caring; which is the worst and most destructive, covering and writing about where the streetcorner peddlers went in winter, about Christmas with the hookers on Eighth Avenue and New Year's Eve with the homeless on the Lower East Side and Thanksgiving with the new immigrants in Queens, about small murders in Harlem and drug deaths in Bed-Stuy, and a lot of other minor episodes in the never-ending serial of New York life. Maybe they were all good stories, and maybe they were what really interested newspaper readers, and I was told I wrote them well, but after a time of seeing men die and people, children especially, starve and die, and a country ravaged, they had come to seem something less than of greatest moment to which I wanted to devote all my energies. For years I had spent my nights and free time writing, had published some books that had been well received by the critics and ignored by the book-buying public. If it seemed the time, then, to try it on my own, without the daily distractions and frustrations, then the time was now, for I managed, on the strength of a couple of chapters, a sketchy outline, and a reputation, to talk a publisher into a good advance on a new novel. With the money from that advance, with the money we had saved, and with the salary Katie would be earning from Markoff's company, we figured we'd have enough to see us through. I was sure I could write the new book just as well in an apartment in Los Angeles as in an apartment in New York, and perhaps better and quicker, because there wouldn't be any friends calling and asking to meet at the White Horse or up at Elaine's or at Joe Allen or at any of the bars over on Third and Second avenues, irresistible requests after hours of staring at pages on which words didn't want to appear.

We left on one of those bright, bitter winter days when the sun's rays are stinging darts driving angry pellets into the skin. We had spent the previous days packing what we decided to take along, though really doing more drinking with old friends than packing, which is why it took so long. In the morning, a couple of those friends, mine and Katie's, came by to help us load the U-Haul hitched to the rear of our old Plymouth. There were some tears and a lot of warnings about the dangers of Lotus Land and advice not meant to be taken seriously about not falling into the trap, about staying out of the sun and not breathing the smog or drinking the water and all the other clichés spoken to those on their way west.

When the van was loaded and it was time to leave, somebody said, "You guys take care of yourselves out there," and it didn't come out as light and free as he meant it.

"Don't worry," I said. "We'll make out all right."

"Get that goddamn book written."

"That's what I intend to do."

"Dance a storm, Katie. Then Balanchine will come begging."

She laughed. "We can all dream."

"You'll be back."

"Sure we will. You just wait."

We found a small, cheap apartment in one of those slightly seedy pink frame houses that couldn't make up its mind whether it was supposed to be Mexican or Colonial or modern, off Fountain along the border between West Hollywood and Hollywood. I set up my typewriter on a table in one corner of the bedroom and quickly discovered that the blank pages stayed just as blank in California as in New York. The words came just as slowly and just as hard, only now there weren't any of those late afternoon calls to take me away and ease the anxieties over a couple of drinks and some inconsequential talk.

But it was working for Katie. She liked the company.

Terry had rounded up a lot of talented dancers, some the equal of any she had known in New York below the first rank. If there was a little jealousy at the arrival of a New York dancer without one of those awesome reputations as prima ballerina, still Terry grew ever more convinced that she was all he had expected and hoped for, that she was the unrecognized talent he would spring on the public to vast acclaim, for her and himself. And the more she danced in rehearsals and the more she revealed of her talent and dedication, the greater the respect and affection she earned from the company.

It lasted little more than a month. I was sitting at the typewriter late in the afternoon, words and ideas at last beginning to flow, the fallow period at an end, the pages beginning to fill. Beside the typewriter a pile began to grow as my mind found twists and turns and complexities I hadn't sensed before. The phone rang. I ignored it. It continued to ring, insistently, demanding an answer. I turned off the typewriter, went to it, snapped something impatiently into the receiver, then stopped and held on, listening and trying to understand the words.

It was the hospital. Katie had been in an accident.

What kind of accident?

It took a little time to piece it together. She had left rehearsal with a couple of the other dancers and had stepped off the curb with the light when a car, trying to beat the changing light, had come charging through the intersection. It hit her.

How badly was she hurt?

I'd have to speak to the doctor about that.

God. Was she alive?

Yes, she was alive.

Get me the goddamn doctor.

The doctor was busy. I ought to get down there as soon as possible. He'd be available to speak to me when I arrived.

I called a cab and then stood at the curb for ten minutes

waiting for it to arrive. Those ten minutes seemed more like hours. It was another fifteen minutes in the hospital emergency room before anyone could locate the doctor, whose name I can't remember, if I ever learned it. He appeared, a young resident, looking harassed, exhausted, emptied of any emotion. He steered me into one of the cubicles. Katie was lying on an examining table, her red hair fanned out damply around her head, and seeing it, I had one of those odd thoughts: What had happened to the white ribbon she always wore to tie her hair back? Her face was so pale that the sprinkling of freckles across her nose, usually nearly invisible, appeared as small blotches. Her eyes were swollen and closed. There were bruises, turning purple, on her cheeks and her arms. She was out. She had been heavily sedated, the doctor explained.

He motioned toward her right leg. It lay on the table, twisted, turned at a grotesque angle, swollen, discolored. She had a compound fracture of the leg, the doctor said. They'd X-rayed it. It would be set when the orthopedic resident arrived; the X rays had shown that the breaks were pretty clean, and there didn't seem to be any bone fragments floating around, so she probably wouldn't require major or prolonged surgery. Once the leg was set and in a cast, she'd be into an upstairs room. She'd be there at least three weeks with the leg in traction. Other than the leg, he said, she was in pretty good shape, considering—probably looked a lot worse than she really was. There were the multiple bruises and contusions, of course, but fortunately there were no internal injuries. She was lucky. She might have been killed.

Lucky. Just a fractured leg. For a dancer. I said that to him. He tried to look sad, to look as though he understood and cared. Maybe he did, but he was too tired and had seen too much to show anything. I asked if she'd be able to dance again. He shrugged. He said he didn't know. It was too soon to make a prognosis. It would depend on how everything healed, and even then, nobody would know for quite a while. In any case, she couldn't even think about trying for some time. She'd need a lot of physical therapy, and then we'd just have to wait and see how things developed. If he were to make a guess, though, he'd have to say the odds were less than fifty-fifty.

What about the goddamn driver? Where was he? Did he have the slightest idea of what he'd done?

The doctor didn't know. That wasn't his business. His business was treating emergency cases when they were brought in, and that's what he'd done.

What about the driver? Where could I find out?

He gestured toward two cops standing off to one side of the emergency room. They'd been the first cops on the scene, had summoned the ambulance and then followed it into the hospital.

I went over to them. Hit-and-run, they said. It happened so fast and the car sped away so rapidly without stopping or even pausing that nobody had thought to get the license. All they knew for sure was that it had been a Volkswagen. There wasn't much chance they'd learn any more. One Volkswagen looked pretty much like another, and there were thousands in the city, probably half of them with dented fenders. They'd do what they could, but I shouldn't hope for much. I ought to be grateful for one thing, at least. It had been a Volkswagen that hit her and not a Cadillac.

Grateful I was not. I swore about the son of a bitch who'd been driving that Volkswagen and raged about what I'd do if I ever came across him (though what I actually would have done, being essentially a nonviolent man, I haven't the least idea). And I raged at the cops for standing around and not being out trying to find the bastard, which they should have been doing, told them I'd been around cops long enough to know they'd always find some excuse for not doing what they ought to be doing. They looked at me with pity and tried to calm me down. I turned my back on them and walked stiffly away and back into the cell where Katie was lying. It was all so useless and frustrating, and what people say about letting the anger out because it helps is wrong. It doesn't help.

So Katie was in the hospital, her leg in a cast from ankle to hip, the leg and the cast lifted, stretched, supported by a maze of wires and pulleys. The room filled with flowers from the company, and most of the other dancers kept showing up to see her, and Terry Markoff came once and looked at her and tried to smile and say something comforting and optimistic, though to me out in the hall he just shook his head and looked ready to cry. Everybody tried to be cheerful and tried to convince her that it wasn't as bad as it seemed, that she'd make a complete recovery and would be back dancing before she knew it and the whole thing would be only a bad memory. She didn't believe them, and she could read in their faces that they didn't believe it, either. She spent a lot of time just lying on that bed staring at the cast and the pulleys. Now and then she talked to me, if not to anyone else, about the future, or lack of one. A future? Not for a dancer with a crippled leg, not for a dancer who'd never wanted to do anything but dance, who didn't know how to do anything but dance.

I tried to tell her we were all positive she'd dance again. She just had to hold that close, know that it would just take time.

She told me to stop lying. Even if her leg healed completely, she'd lose at least a year. And a year without practice, a year without dancing, was a lifetime to a ballerina. She wasn't sixteen, with time to spare. It had to be now or it wouldn't be. She'd never make it back, not even to the second rank. She should never have come to California. She should never have reached for the star. She should have recognized what she was, known her limitations and been satisfied.

I kept saying she was wrong. I kept trying to convince her

she would dance again. And when that got too hard, I tried
to tell her that if, somehow, it didn't work, there was still
plenty she could do.

Like what?

She wasn't like so many others, I said, who knew nothing
but dance. She'd made sure of that. She gone to school, she'd
gotten her degree. There were other things. Maybe not
what she dreamed about, but still, other things.

She laughed at that, but without any humor. A degree was
just a piece of paper, she said. It didn't qualify her for anything. She supposed, she said acidly, that I thought that as
long as we were in California, she ought to think about the
movies.

I hadn't thought that at all, but she'd said it, so I said,
"Why not?" She was beautiful. She was talented. She knew
how to move. She had the grace that couldn't be taught.
Maybe. Who knows?

Hollywood was filled with pretty girls who thought they
could act, she said, dismissing the whole idea. They all
thought they could be in the movies. Well, she didn't happen to be one of them. There just wasn't anything she could
do now.

"If you keep on like that," I said, "then there sure won't
be any hope for anything. You used to believe in yourself,"
I said. "My god, you had an ego," I said. "You used to
believe you were the best, that there wasn't anything you
couldn't do. You just have to keep on believing that. Because
it's true."

She was just feeling lousy, she said.

A hospital's no place to make plans for the future.

Those days, I spent most of my time in the hospital with her,
even sleeping on a cot in the same room during the nights
when she was torn by pain. There was no way I could work
or even think about work. That would have to wait. As I was

leaving after her third day, one of the nurses stopped me and said that the business office had asked if I could come by before I went home. I went by. A nice lady took out some papers, spent some silent time going over them, then looked up and said there seemed to be some problem about the insurance. I said I didn't know what she was talking about, that Markoff's company had a policy that was supposed to cover Katie and me for any illness or accident. She said well, there seemed to be some question about that, and would I please check and get back to her so she could straighten out the records.

There was a message on our service when I got home. Please call Barney Gallagher. The name jogged nothing in my memory. But the number was that of the ballet company. I called. I got Gallagher. He started by saying how sorry he was, how sorry everyone was about what had happened to Katie.

I said that Katie would be glad to know that. I still didn't know who he was.

He said that I probably didn't recognize his name unless I'd happened to look at Katie's salary checks. He was the treasurer of the company.

I said, "Oh, yes," and waited. I had the feeling I wasn't going to like what I was going to hear.

He said he had some bad news.

I didn't say anything. I waited.

He said was I aware that the company had been going through a hard time, financially, that is.

I said no.

He said well, that happened to be true. In fact, for a number of reasons he didn't want to go into then, it had overcommitted itself, on talent, sets, designers, and just about everything else. It had overcommitted itself to such an extent that it had been forced to go through its reserves just to keep afloat. It had run out of money, and its sponsors and patrons, who had already contributed extensively, had refused to ante up anything more. To put it bluntly, he said, the company was broke.

I listened. I asked into his silence what did that mean, exactly?

He said what it meant exactly was that the company was folding, even before the season began. There just wasn't any more money and no hope of any more money, so it was closing down. That was hell for everyone, he knew, but there weren't any alternatives. What it meant, in practical terms, was that everyone was being let go as of the end of the week. He knew it was going to be especially hard for us, since with the accident and all we were going to need every penny we could scrape up, but that was the way it was, and there wasn't anything he could do about it. Katie would get paid for the week, but that was the end of the money in the till.

I took a deep breath, told him that since I couldn't argue with reality, I guess we'd have to accept that. There was just one thing. I'd just been told by the hospital that there was some question about the medical insurance. I said I was sure it was just a mistake, but I wished he would straighten that matter out.

He didn't answer at first; then I could hear the hesitation and the embarrassment in his tone. The whole thing was so unexpected, he said. It was going to mean a lot of trouble for him and the others who'd been handling the finances. But they hadn't had any way of knowing something bad would happen. Oh, they had been told that dancers have accidents, but they didn't think it could happen to them. If you don't think anything is going to go wrong, you don't prepare for emergencies. He had to admit now that what they had done was inexcusable. (Also illegal, I was tempted to say, and I was also tempted to say he'd hear from our lawyers in the morning. Only we didn't have any lawyers or know any who would take a case on spec when the people we would be suing were about to go out of existence and so there was nothing we could collect even if we won. So I didn't say anything, just listened.) But they had tried to cut every corner they could think of just to try to stay afloat. They had put off payments as long as they could, hoping to find a way to raise money. One of the payments they hadn't made was the premiums on the medical insurance. By the time they realized the policy was about to lapse, there wasn't any money left. And so, just the week before Katie's accident, the insurance policy had been canceled. Katie was, thus, not covered by medical insurance. He was sorry, but that was they way it was.

Trouble seems always to come in multiples, never in singles.

Katie healed rapidly and well. The bruises faded and were gone within a week, and the X rays showed that the bones in her leg were knitting as they should, that there were no major complications there. By the time I brought her home from the hospital, her leg was in a new and lighter cast, which would remain for at least another month, and she was able to move about on crutches with increasing agility. Physically she was getting better every day. Psychologically she remained trapped in depression, which was, of course, understandable. And the depression was not helped by the state of our finances. We had gone through just about everything we had. There had been the usual bills, and now there were the hospital bills and the doctor bills, and as the money went out, there was nothing coming in. The doctors and the people at the hospital had been sympathetic and understanding when I tried to explain, but sympathy and understanding don't last long in the face of reality. Demands and then the threats about prompt payment had to be dealt with as best we could.

In desperation, I called New York, talked to Sy Marshall, my editor, and tried to tell him what had been going on. I asked if he thought it might just be possible to get the next installment on the advance.

"How's the book coming?" Sy asked.

"It was coming until Katie got hurt. Since then I haven't been able to think about it."

"That's understandable," he said. "But I'm sure you'll get back to it now. When am I going to see some pages?"

"Soon."

"How soon is soon?"

"I don't know, Sy. I can't give you an exact date. About all I can promise is you'll see pages pretty soon."

"You get me some pages, Harry, and I'll see what I can do about getting you some money," he said.

"No pages, no money?"

"You got it."

"How many pages?"

"Half the manuscript."

"Jesus."

"I'm sorry, Harry, but you have to understand my position. I spend half my life trying to get manuscripts out of overdue authors. I wish I could help, but the people upstairs scream bloody blue murder anytime I try to get something with nothing to show for it."

The last thing we needed then was more trouble. But that's exactly what we got. We should have expected it. Even before we left New York, we had been in the middle of a struggle with the IRS. Our accountant, wise in the ways of tax loopholes, had figured out a few years before what he claimed were some nice deductions, legitimate according to his reading of new tax statutes. They reduced our tax liability to the point where that year we owed almost nothing. At least that's what the return we filed said. We didn't argue, of course. Who argues when told they don't have to pay taxes? He was supposed to know his business. The only thing was, the IRS didn't happen to read the tax laws the same way he did. They looked at the deductions, said no way, and then proceeded to add on interest and penalties and told us to pay. The accountant said, "Pay. Don't fight it. You can't win. Nobody beats the IRS when they decide you owe them. The longer you wait, the more it's going to add up." That was very nice advice, and we probably would have taken it if we could have. We couldn't. We'd committed ourselves to the move and to the new life and to the costs they would entail until it all started to pay off. That, however, is an explanation the tax people didn't want to hear and certainly weren't about to buy. In the middle of everything else, we got one of those official letters in the long envelopes demanding payment within ten days. I called the IRS and tried to make the lady who answered understand why it was impossible for us to pay. She cut me off, said it would be better if I came to her office and talked to her in person.

I went downtown. She sat there and listened while I told her about the hospital and the accident and the doctors, about the closing of the ballet company, about all the rest.

"We'll have to garnishee your salary," she said.

There wasn't any salary for her to garnishee, I said. Katie's job had come to a sudden and unexpected end, and I was, as they say, self-employed with no regular income.

She didn't quite understand that. She said we must have some income.

I explained that my income came from advances and royalties.

She said then I could just assign those advances and royalties to the government.

I said that would be nice if it were possible. Only it wasn't. First, the money all went through my agent, when there was any money. And, second, there wouldn't be any money until I finished the book I was writing.

She looked as though she didn't believe me. She said why didn't we borrow?

I said if we could borrow, it would be money to live on. We'd like to be able to pay the taxes, but those immediate necessities came first, at least the way I looked at it.

She said they'd have to move and seize our bank account.

I laughed and told her if they did that, they wouldn't find much in it, hardly enough to buy her a pack of cigarettes.

What kind of real property did we have?

"Our clothes," I said, "a little furniture, my typewriter, and the car." I couldn't think of anything else.

She said she was very sorry, obviously we were having a lot of trouble, but she was only an employee trying to do her job, and her job was to find a way to collect what we owed the government. It would be very difficult for us, especially living in Los Angeles, but she was going to have to have our car seized.

Three days later, a tow truck appeared in front of the house and, as I watched from the doorway, hooked up the car and took it away.

The wolf was at the door. His name was Wolf Rabinowitz, and he was the landlord. We were two months behind in the rent by then. He rang the bell and stood in the doorway, a tall, fat man with a fringe of white hair around a freckled red scalp, his shirt-sleeves rolled up against the heat so the faded blue tatoo on his forearm was clearly visible beneath the slick of sweat. He looked at me. "Mr. Miller," he said.

"Hello, Mr. Rabinowitz."

"I have come for the rent," he said.

"I know. I'll have it for you soon." I was getting tired of giving that response, but I didn't know what else to say to anyone. I was getting tired, too, of the next question.

"When is soon?" he said. "You tell me last week, you will

have it soon. You tell me the week before, last month, too. You tell me soon, but the rent I don't see. So please tell me today, Mr. Miller, when is soon?"

"Soon, Mr. Rabinowitz. That's all I can say. I'm trying to raise it."

"I'm sorry for the trouble you are having, Mr. Miller. I'm sorry for what happened to your wife. That beautiful girl. It is terrible. A tragedy. I understand. But a charity home I don't run. People, they live here, they pay the rent. That they understand. They don't pay the rent, they don't live here. You understand?"

"I understand, Mr. Rabinowitz. Just give me a little more time. I promise you, you'll get paid. Just give me a little more time."

"So I ask you again, how much is a little more time?" He sighed. He was a nice man, not belligerent, not angry, not even threatening, just a man who happened to own a few houses where the rent allowed him to live comfortably. In other circumstances, I probably would have liked him. Certainly I could have sympathized with him. But at that moment he was just another of the threatening shapes that inhabited this unending and worsening nightmare.

"I wish I could give you a definite answer," I said. "I'm trying. God knows, I'm trying. I'll pay the minute I can. What else do you want me to do?"

"You would like me to tell you what you should do?" He looked at me and shook his head. "You would listen to Wolf Rabinowitz? Then I will tell you. What you do is get a job."

"I've got a job."

"You've got a job? The clickety-clack of the typewriter? That's a job? They pay you for this job? Then you should pay me. They don't pay you, it ain't no kind of job and you should get a real job. You think I want this? You think I should come knocking on your door all the time to get my money, which belongs to me and which also I need? You think I want to throw you into the street, you and that beautiful wife who has had such bad trouble? I would let you have the apartment free, no payment, no rent until you could pay. That I would do. I cannot. The bank, they won't let me. My wife, she won't let me. My children, they won't let me. The grocer, he won't let me. Nobody, they won't let me. They say, Wolf Rabinowitz, you are a fool. The money for the rent they owe, you should collect, or they should go so you can have somebody will pay and not owe. You think I can answer? You think they care if I tell them you are nice people and one day you will pay? You think a choice I have? Get a job, Mr. Miller. Get a real job which pays you real money. Then you can pay and we have no more of this *tsuris.*"

"I have a job. I'm writing a book. That's my job." Perhaps if I hadn't heard much the same arguments from relatives when I first began writing and talked about going on my own, I wouldn't have gotten stiff-necked with him. But those words rang such a familiar galling note that the response was almost automatic.

Rabinowitz shook his head sadly. He sighed. He said, "You are writing the book. I know. You tell me and I hear the typing, so I know it must be so. But, Mr. Miller, you understand, everybody they are writing the book. They are making the movie. They are composing the song, the symphony, the concerto. They are painting the picture. Everybody, they are creative, they are geniuses. Only if they don't pay the landlord, what are they? You want to create the book, go and create, Mr. Miller. I will not stop you. Only you should first get a job so you can pay. Then you can create what you like and there won't be no more trouble."

"Just what kind of a job do you think I ought to get, Mr. Rabinowitz? Have you got any suggestions?"

"What kind of a job? You think I care? Dig a ditch, Mr. Miller. Sell a pair of shoes. Wait on a table. Do what you must to earn the money. There are jobs. Find one. But you,

you are an artist, Mr. Miller. So tell me, why you, why the artists, they all think they should do only what it is they feel here, inside? They should do only what it is they say they have to do? Mr. Miller, you think the man who collects the garbage, that is what he wants to do? You think the Mexican who picks the vegetables in the valleys, that is what he wants to do? You think all the people, they do what they do because it is what they want to do? Look around, Mr. Miller. You will see all the people everywhere. They do what they must do to earn a living. You think all of them are in love with what they do?"

Maybe Rabinowitz had read Thoreau and maybe not, but he was throwing at me a paraphrase: "The mass of men lead lives of quiet desperation." I started to feel sick inside. Maybe I whispered those words. Rabinowitz heard something, shook his head angrily, and said, "Yes, Mr. Miller. Yes. It is the world. You think I like what I must do? You think it is what I dreamed when I was a boy in Poland, before the monsters, God curse their souls, came with their camps and their furnaces? You think I dreamed I would grow old and die in Los Angeles and my life would be collecting rents? I do what I must do so my family may eat the food and wear the clothes and be human beings. I do the things most people do, Mr. Miller, to earn the money so we may live. If God said, 'Wolf Rabinowitz, you could do whatever you wanted in this life,' I tell you it would not be collecting rents. But I do it. I am not an artist, Mr. Miller. I create nothing, no books, no movies, no music, no paintings, nothing. But I give the artists a place to do the creating. That I do. And the artist must pay for what I give. That is the world. You understand?"

"I understand, Mr. Rabinowitz. Of course I understand."

He sighed. "I give you two weeks more, Mr. Miller. Not a day longer. Two weeks. It pains me in my heart, I have a terrible ache to say it, but then, if you do not pay, out you must go."

I couldn't blame him. In his place I might have done the same, probably wouldn't have been so patient. But I wasn't in his place. I was in the nightmare, not knowing what to do or where to turn, not knowing how to keep this particular wolf from coming through the door.

3 It had all come down around us so fast and so without warning that there had been no time and no chance to doing anything to turn aside the onrushing and crushing avalanche. One day it had been the springtime, with all we had planted and tended beginning to grow. The next day a winter storm descended in an instant, wiping away and destroying it all. We couldn't pay the rent, and we couldn't pay the ever mounting doctor bills, and Katie's cast was coming off, and she'd have to begin physical therapy, and there was no way we could afford that, and no way we couldn't, not if her leg and body were ever to have a chance to regain strength and agility. We were in a trap, the lines tightening, strangling. During all the five years of our marriage, we had had no secrets, had shared everything. Now I kept secrets and tried to protect her from finding out just how bad things were. Bills came, and I didn't open them, just tossed them into a dresser drawer. I fielded the increasingly angry and threatening phone calls from creditors, murmuring promises that I could see no way of keeping.

But such secrets can't be held long, certainly not after the IRS came and towed away the car. Katie went searching, found the bills and opened them, went through the checkbook and looked at the minuscule balance, looked at me helplessly, and her depression deepened.

There had to be a way out, and I would have to find it. I had heard of guys who, in dire emergency, could sit down and crank out a book in a week, driven by desperation. I wasn't one of them. There was just no way I could finish the book I was supposed to be working on and on which hardly a word had been written since the accident, no way I could write enough to get some money out of it. What was needed was a quick, even if temporary, answer. So one morning I took the bus downtown, to the *Times,* and the next day, to the *Herald-Examiner.* There were guys on both papers I had known over in Asia or someplace else where our paths had crossed during an assignment and some kind of friendship had grown. They all acted as if they were pretty glad to see me and surprised to find me in Los Angeles, and even more surprised to hear that I was in Los Angeles trying to write a book. Nobody comes to L.A. to write a book, they said; nobody in L.A. writes books. We talked about the old days and laughed some about things that hadn't seemed particularly amusing when they were happening, and there was a lot of surprise when I said the main reason I'd dropped by was that I was looking for a job. When they got over the surprise, they introduced me to the right people. I got a couple of pleasant lunches and some more pleasant conversation and the sad tidings that things were pretty tight at the moment for a guy with my background, that there was a hiring freeze, but maybe in a couple of months things would loosen up, and when they did, they'd sure as hell would be back to me. A couple months wasn't soon enough, though I didn't tell them that, just thanked them and said I'd be looking forward to the call when it came.

I had always sworn that I'd never borrow, that I'd always pay for what I wanted and if I couldn't afford it then, it would have to wait until I could. But this was different, and so I swallowed a couple of times and got up the courage and started calling everyone I could think of who'd ever asked a favor from me or who had ever seemed to give a damn about us, and I managed to borrow a couple of hundred here and there, enough to buy starvation rations and pay the utilities, but not much more, not enough even to pay Wolf Rabinowitz. I called Frank Lester, my agent, in New York. He sympathized, as everyone did, reluctantly agreed finally to send me what he could, maybe a couple of hundred. But where the hell was the manuscript? Or at least a couple of chapters.

I'm working on it, I lied. But we had to have money fast, and it would really have to wait until there was a little daylight. How about getting me an advance on a quickie book? I didn't have any ideas for one, but maybe he did, or maybe an editor somewhere did? Or how about a couple of quick and easy magazine pieces?

Out of the question, Frank said. Not when I already had an advance on a book and the promised first chapters were already late. People in the business knew about things like that, and they wouldn't buy. It wouldn't do my reputation one bit of good. And he wouldn't even ask. He had his own reputation to think of.

He had to know somebody, I said, anybody, who might need a guy who could do a good job fast. I wasn't proud. I wasn't particular. I didn't care what it was, just so long as it paid. If he could just think of somebody. If he could just drop a word during a casual conversation. He would have my eternal gratitude.

I don't think he had ever heard me beg before, and I was begging then. He said, reluctantly, that he'd think about it and if anything developed, he'd give me a call. Then he said, "Why don't you come back to New York? If you were in

New York, maybe we could work things out easier than by long distance."

I laughed bitterly. That would be nice, but you had to have money to get back, and we didn't have any.

"What are we going to do?" Katie said. The cast was off. She was using a cane now, was beginning to walk a little, though the limp was bad. Her face was gray with the pain that was constant and with the strain of a session with the therapist and of the agony of trying to persuade him to accept partial payments out of the money we managed to borrow, with the promise of the rest soon.

"I wish I knew," I said. "I'm running out of ideas."

"We've got to think of something," she said.

"And fast. We're running out of time."

"If I could only walk," she said, "I could try to get a job."

"But you can't walk yet. Not enough."

"Maybe I ought to try. I can get around now. And I get stronger every day." She paused, shook her head. "If only I hadn't had that accident."

"Sure. And if only the company hadn't gone under."

"If only they'd paid the medical insurance."

"And if only that fucking accountant hadn't had bright ideas."

"If only we'd stayed in New York."

"If only I stayed on the paper."

"If only I'd been satisfied to dance second leads."

"Sure. And if only if onlys were dollars, we'd be millionaires."

We both started to laugh. It wasn't very funny or very witty, it was old and trite and dumb, but there hadn't been much to laugh at over the last months, and so we looked for humor anywhere we could find it. When we stopped laughing, Katie said, "Think of something, Harry. You always used to be able to think of something."

"The only thing I'm capable of thinking is that I love you."

"There's that," she said.

"It'd be a hell of a lot worse if you weren't around."

"There's that," she said. "Only if I weren't around, it wouldn't have happened, and you wouldn't be in the middle of this."

"Don't say that," I said. "Don't even think it."

"I know," she said.

"The only other thing I can think of," I said, "is that I want to make love to you."

"I'm glad," she said.

We made love then, on the floor in the living room, not bothering to go into the bedroom, and for a little while there was something else, something pleasant and more than pleasant, to obsess us. But even then the troubles intruded, for the leg throbbed when she tried to use it, so even making love wasn't as good or as all consuming and world obliterating as it had been before. When we finished, we lay there looking at each other and trying to pretend it had been good as always, each of us knowing the other was lying.

The next morning, I started looking through the want ads in the *Times.*

She watched me. She said, "What do you think you're doing?"

"Looking for a job."

"You won't find your kind of job in the want ads."

"I'm not looking for my kind of job. I'm looking for any kind of job."

"That's no good."

"Maybe it's no good, but I have to do something. I have to earn a buck. Any way I can."

"You can't," she said. "It would be better if you just sat down and tried to finish the book."

"I have. I can't write. And I can't not do this."

For the next couple of days, I went around with the paper

folded open to the classifieds, went to Bullocks and Robinson's and the Broadway and May and the other department stores, went to the discount houses, went to the supermarkets, went to the clothing stores, went down the list and went everywhere. And everywhere there was some personnel manager who laughed and told me that I didn't have the right qualifications or that I was overqualified for the kind of openings they had or that they knew I wasn't and couldn't be serious or that they were looking for permanent employees, not for somebody who'd leave five minutes after he was hired.

The phone rang. It had to be another bill collector. I went for it. Katie beat me to it. She listened, then held the receiver toward me. "It's for you, Harry."

It had to be a bill collector or somebody with some more bad news. I didn't want to talk to anybody like that. I started to tell her to say I wasn't home. But why should she be stuck with that? I got up and went to the phone. A woman's voice said, "Harry Miller?" I said yes. She said, "Just a moment, please. Mr. Philip Garland would like to speak to you."

Phil Garland. We'd worked on the paper together back in New York, in better times. He was about ten years older, had been around a lot longer, but we became friends, had gone out on stories together, had done some drinking together. He had gone out to write about the war, and I'd replaced him when his time was up. The last time I'd seen him was that week in Saigon when he was going and I was arriving, and we'd shared the rooms that had been his and were about to be mine and would later be somebody else's. We sat around nights that week smoking a lot of dope and listening to the Stones and the Jefferson Airplane and the Beatles and some hard-rock groups whose names I no longer remember and some good jazz from the collections he'd brought with him. We listened to the records one at a time

before he put them in the crates to ship home and even at
three in the morning, when all the crazy photographers and
the other reporters who seemed to congregate in those
rooms that week, maybe because the music was good and
loud and memory blocking and the dope was plentiful and
strong, and it was time to say good-bye to a guy going home,
had gone and we were alone, to the Beethoven Rasou-
movsky quartets, which somehow seemed infinitely more
appropriate to the hour and the heat and the dark and everything else. During the days, he took me around to meet the
right people at MAC-V and the right, and the wrong, people
at the temples and in the government and the military and
told me he'd let me meet the grunts on my own out in the
field because he was damned if he was going to leave Saigon
again until it was time to get on his PanAm flight for home.

His last day, he walked into the office, dressed as always
in stained khakis and a faded knit polo shirt, carrying a pair
of old mud-caked combat boots in one hand. He walked into
the bathroom and tossed the boots into the tub, on top of the
dozen other pairs that were relics of a dozen other guys who
had been there before us, laughing about not breaking the
tradition. (I sometimes wonder what ever happened to all
those boots, Phil's and mine and the others, thrown onto the
pile by the all the guys who moved in and out of that office
just off Tu Do during all those years.) He said good-bye
then, "Good-bye, suckers, enjoy the war," and he'd try to
avoid us when and if we ever got home, and we'd damn well
better avoid him, and his taxi was waiting down on Tu Do
with all his luggage, and you know how far you can trust
a Gook driver with your luggage when you're not watching, so he couldn't hang around and listen to all our sad
farewells, and then he was gone. By the time I got home a
year later, he was gone from the paper and from New York,
too. A book he'd written had been picked up for a lot of
money by the movies. He'd quit then and gone to the Coast
to work on the screenplay, had stayed on and found a per-

manent place not as a writer but as one of the rising executives at a major studio, and he'd gone on rising.

So much of all this flooded me during that interval between the mention of his name and the sound of his voice. And so, too, did the thought. Why hadn't I called him? I had seen his name often enough in the papers, so I knew where he was and how to reach him. I had talked about him to Katie. But I hadn't called. There wasn't any reason except, perhaps, pride, and I thought I'd run out of that.

His voice came through the phone. "Harry. For chrissake. I didn't know you were out here. How long have you been around?"

"Hell, Phil," I said. "Oh, four or five months, I guess."

"You son of a bitch. And you've never called."

I made some feeble excuse, said something about remembering the last thing he said in Saigon.

He laughed. "I hear you quit the old mother."

"Everybody has to one day."

"You know it. You writing another book?"

"Trying to."

"Trying don't mean doing, old son," he said. "You having trouble filling the blank pages, hunh?"

"You could put it like that."

"Why the fuck did you come out here to write a book, anyway? Don't you know nobody writes books in La-La Land?"

"Actually, we came out because Katie got offered a job."

"Katie?"

"My wife."

"Not the redhead? The one you couldn't stop talking about that week in Nam? The . . . the what? . . . the dancer, right? You went and married her?"

"Right after I got back."

"Good marriage?"

"The best."

There was a little more, and then his voice grew serious.

"I was talking with Frank Lester the other day. That's how I found out you were out here. He told me you were having a little trouble."

"He told you true."

"So tell me. Maybe I can help."

"You don't want to hear my tale of woe."

"Shit, I hear fifty tales of woe every day, from guys I hardly know, from guys I met maybe one time at party. The phone doesn't ring it's some guy with trouble. For a buddy I can listen."

So I told him. Not all of it, but enough.

"Shit," he said. "They really came down on you with both feet. With all four feet."

"Eight feet. Maybe ten."

"You fell into a bucket of shit and came up smelling like shit."

"We haven't come up yet. But the stink's there."

"You need help." It wasn't a question.

"We need help. And that's putting it mildly."

"What are you willing to do?"

"Anything. You name it, I'll do it. You want somebody to sweep out the joint, I'm your man. I'm not proud."

"You mean that?"

"Damn right. You got something?"

"Maybe. Not me. But maybe I know about something. I don't have the foggiest what it'd pay. But you could work that out."

"Tell me, for chrissake."

"Look, you guys can probably stand a decent meal. Why don't we have dinner and talk about it. Bring your wife. Damn right, bring her. I want to see if she's as good-looking as that damn picture you wore out."

"When?"

"When are you free?"

I laughed sourly. "When aren't we free? Name the time, name the place. The sooner the better."

"It's that way, hunh? Okay, let me check the calendar."
I heard paper shuffled. He was back on the phone. "I can
switch things around. It's not that important. I can put the
guy off a couple of days. It'll be good for him. What do you
say to tomorrow?"

"Tomorrow it is."

"About seven? I'll make the reservations. At the Bistro.
What say if I pick you guys up about then? Okay with you?"

"We'll be ready."

He rang the bell a little after seven. He had changed. I
suppose he had gone Hollywood, but in his own way. He
was dressed in a three-piece business suit, dark gray; it had
the look of Brooks Brothers, custom-made. He wore a white
shirt, button-down, and a striped tie. He had on highly
polished black shoes. His hair, if not short, was on the short
side, and there was a distinguished touch of gray at the
temples. Parked at the curb was a Jensen Excalibur. I was
impressed, by the car, by him, by the look and aroma of
success and satisfaction.

We greeted each other like the old friends we were, but
also like old friends who had gone different roads, one up-
ward and the other the reverse. "You've changed," I said.

"Changed?" He looked puzzled.

"Not the way I remember you from Saigon. Or from
New York."

"That was in another country," he said, "and besides, the
wench is dead."

There was still some of the old Garland there. I grinned.
"Mr. Marlow, I presume."

"Philip," he said. "Never Christopher."

"Either way," I said, "you're looking good."

"I'm feeling good."

"You should," I said. "From what I read, you're sitting
on top of the heap."

"From what I hear," he said, "you're sprawled down at the bottom." His eyes went over me, nothing escaping them; he hadn't lost that, either. I still owned some clothes from the better times, and they hadn't deteriorated yet. And that evening I had put on one of the good suits. "The suit looks good," he said, "but you look terrible."

"I feel terrible," I said.

"Well, maybe we can change that."

Katie came out of the bedroom. She could make even cheap clothes look expensive, but what she was wearing wasn't cheap; it was one of the extravagances from our last days in New York. She was wearing a white silk blouse and dark green silk skirt. Around her neck she had a single strand of lustrous pearls, and dangling from her ears were drops of dark jade, both from a small, out-of-the-way shop in Kowloon, bought during that week we had together. She looked beautiful. Her long red hair wasn't gathered tightly behind with the usual white ribbon; she let it flow loose around her face and over her shoulders. Even the cane and the limp didn't seem to detract.

Garland stared. He nodded slowly. "You ought to have better pictures taken. The one Harry carried didn't half do you justice."

Katie laughed, one of those laughs that says, I know you're lying, but I like it, anyway.

He looked at the gold watch on his wrist. "You guys hungry? I know I am. What say we get moving." He took Katie's arm before I could move and escorted her with elaborate care out of the house, down the stairs, to the car, guiding her over obstacles, real and imaginary, seating her carefully in the backseat. "I'd rather have you up front, next to me," he said, "but you'll be a hell of a lot more comfortable back there. You can put your leg up. Harry, up front with me." Once we were all in the car and he had pulled away from the curb, he glanced over his shoulder at her and demanded that she tell him about the accident. She demurred. He insisted. She told it shorthand, but enough so that he swore about hit-and-run drivers, about injustice, about bad things happening to nice people. "What are you going to do now?" he asked.

"Have therapy," she said.

"Are you going to be able to dance again?"

"I don't know," she said slowly. "Ask me in three months, in six months."

"Are you good?" he asked.

"When I could dance?" she said. "Yes."

"Better than good?"

"Yes."

"Good," he said. "No false modesty. I like that. Out here, if you don't blow your own horn, it won't make a sound. Because nobody else is going to do it for you. Actually," he said, "I know you're good. I know just how good you are."

"I suppose you can tell that just by looking at me," she said.

"I suppose I could," he said, "but that's not the way I work. I check. Ask old Harry here. That was one of the things about me. I always check with the people who've got the inside facts. They tell me you're not just good, you're fantastic. You like to hear that?"

"Of course," she said.

"You don't think they were feeding me a line?"

"No," she said.

I was enjoying this. It was nice to hear Katie's ego re-emerge, nice to hear that confidence about herself in her voice again.

"I like that," he said. "You and me, we're going to get along just fine." He looked across at me and grinned. "What do you say we dump old Harry here off on the next corner and the two of us go off and make beautiful music together?"

She laughed.

"Okay," he said, "so you won't. I knew you wouldn't. You see, I know a lot about you. Not just from Harry and his big mouth back when. I hear you got a temperament big as a house and wild as a hurricane. I hear you're a dream to work with, never make trouble. Which is it?"

"I'm easy to work with," she said, "when I get my way."

He liked that. "You want a job?" he said suddenly. He took a quick look back at her. So did I. She was sitting absolutely still, staring at the back of his head.

"Ask me again in three months," she said finally.

"I'm asking you now," he said.

"I can't dance," she said. "Not now. Maybe never."

"I'm not asking you to dance," he said.

"I don't want charity," she said.

"I'm not offering charity," he said. "I'm asking you if you want a job?"

"Yes," she said, "I want a job. But it depends on what kind of a job."

"Can you help teach girls who don't know the first thing about dancing to at least look like they know their right feet from their left? Can you teach them how to pretend they know how to dance? That kind of thing."

"I've never taught."

"I'm not asking if you ever taught. I'm asking if you can do this."

"Yes," she said. "I ought to be able to do that. It never occurred to me."

"Well, let it occur to you now."

"All right," she said. "It occurs to me."

"Would you like to do it?"

"For money?"

"Of course for money."

"Then I'd like to do it."

"Okay. You're hired." He turned in the seat and grinned back at her.

"Just like that?" she said.

"Just like that."

I watched her closely. She exchanged a glance with me,

then looked away. A dozen emotions passed over her face: bewilderment, uncertainty, eagerness, sureness. She looked at the back of his neck, at the side of his face as he turned slightly. "Did you just make this up?" she asked.

"Let's just say it occurred to me."

"When?"

"What difference does it make? We're starting a new musical, and half the bums on the lot want their girls in it, in the chorus, for chrissake. The trouble is, most of those girls can't even walk, let alone dance. We need somebody to make them look good."

"You don't have anyone at the studio who can do it?"

"Screw the people at the studio. I decided I want you. Make up your mind. You want the job or not?"

"I want the job."

"Okay. You got it. We'll talk money later. You just show up in Burbank at eight o'clock tomorrow morning."

She smiled a little, nodded slowly; then her face got serious. "There's just one thing."

"There always is."

"My leg. I still have trouble getting around."

"For chrissake," he said, "if you could dance, I'd cast you in the picture. You can't dance, okay, so you'll teach the dumb bimbos. When the leg's better, we'll see what we'll see."

"My god," she said to me, "you didn't tell me he was like this."

I was just as stunned as she was. "He didn't used to be," I said. "Or maybe he just never showed it."

"You just never saw my good side, Harry," he said. He looked back at Katie. "Okay, so you'll be on the lot at eight. I'll get word out so they'll be expecting you."

"There's a problem," I said then.

He looked at me wearily. "Don't make more problems, Harry. I'm doing my best to solve your problems as it is."

"Maybe," I said. "But Katie hasn't got any way of getting to Burbank."

"Get up early and drive her, you lazy slob," he said.

"I would," I said. "But we don't have a car."

"How the hell can you be in L.A. without a car?"

"The IRS," I said.

"Screw the IRS," he said.

"That's only one of the things I like to do to the IRS."

"What the hell," he said, "so I'll send a car. It'll be at your door at seven-thirty. Now, no more problems."

We pulled up in front of the restaurant. Somebody rushed out and opened the doors, helped us out, greeted Garland by name, took the car, and drove away. We walked into the restaurant, threaded our way through the mob that swarmed around the entrance. The maître d' saw Garland and moved quickly toward him with a broad smile. "Mr. Garland," he said, "how nice to have you with us. If you'll just follow me, your table's ready." He led us past the impatient crowd, ignoring those in it, to a table near the center of the first floor room. "This will be satisfactory?" he asked. "Or would you prefer more privacy?"

"This will be fine," Garland said. He reached out and shook the maître d's hand.

Phil Garland was in his element. It was a lot different from what we had shared, but he was at home here now. There was no way to doubt that. People made detours by our table to say hello. People got up from other tables and came over to say hello. Phil introduced them all, quickly, and some of the names and some of the faces were familiar, but they were interested in Phil Garland, not us, though more than a few eyes lingered a little too long on Katie. Waiters hovered. Garland ordered drinks, and they arrived almost as though they had been made and were ready before he ordered. He ordered dinner for the three of us without looking at the menu, and the maître d' took the orders and

complimented him on the choices. He talked about the movies, and we talked about the old days on the paper and the
changes he'd noticed since he'd left, changes he said sure as
hell weren't for the better. He talked about a lot of things,
everything but what he'd invited us to dinner to talk about,
and he was constantly interrupted by people coming by to
say hello and ask when was he going to find a minute to sit
down and have a talk. He left us only once. A tall, heavy-set
woman, overdressed in too many gems and an expensive
gown that didn't quite become her ample body and with a
little too much makeup layered carefully on a plain, strong
face, swept in, trailed by a handsome couple whose faces
were instantly recognizable from a dozen films. The maître
d' hurried just a step behind them, and seated them along the
wall in one of those spots that gives the appearance of privacy but actually is designed to draw focus. The woman was
impervious to everyone and everything, but there was
hardly a head that didn't turn toward her. Garland excused
himself, rose and walked over to her, greeted her warmly,
and they talked for a few minutes. Garland laughed a couple
of times, though from where we were, it seemed that the
laughs were more than a little forced. Finally, he turned and
came back to us. "Sorry," he said, "but I had to talk to her."

"Who is she?" I asked.

"You don't know?"

"No. Should I?"

"If you're planning to stick around here and have anything to do with the business, you damn well better know.
That's Winnie Argoth."

I looked at Katie. She looked blank. I thought I'd heard
the name. "An agent? Isn't that right?"

"Old buddy," he said, "agent ain't the half of it. You just
stay on the good side of Winnie and make sure you don't
cross her."

"Like that," I said.

"Like that," he agreed.

We finished dinner. They brought the coffee. He took out a cigar and lit it. Back in the old days, he used to chain-smoke cigarettes. He leaned back, took a deep drag, looked at me, and said, "You ever hear of Charlie Stuart?"

It was dropped into the middle of nothing, not even a non sequitur. It was just there. I shook my head. "Charlie Stuart? Rings no bells."

"Of course you never heard of him," he said. "You'd have to be in the business a while to know him, or know about him. Unless you're a buff of old B-flicks, and I take it you're not."

"I'm not. They were part of the Saturday matinees when I was a kid. But all I remember is a lot of cowboys shooting up a lot of Indians."

"That's all anybody remembers," he said. He took a sip of the coffee and made a face. "It's one thing they do lousy here," he said. "About Charlie Stuart. He made a lot of those B-flicks back in the old days, before either of us had ever dreamed of Hollywood, buddy. He was at Monogram, at Republic, then at some of the majors. Columbia, Metro. You name it, he was there. You've heard of the yes men? Well, Charlie was the epitome. I don't think he ever said no in his life, at least not back in those days, from what people say. He said yes to Louis B. Mayer, and he said yes to Harry Cohn, and he said yes to just about anybody who'd let him say yes. And he said it so often and so well that they used to throw those three-day B-flicks to him just to make him feel good. Who the hell cared? They had to fill those double bills somehow, and one piece of garbage was as good as another, but somebody had to make the garbage, and Charlie Stuart was one of the somebodies. You dredge 'em out and you'll see 'Produced by Charles Stuart' in big letters. King Charles, some guys used to call him, the king of the Bs. Of course, those days are long gone and probably better forgotten. But King Charles hangs on. He's somewhere in his middle fifties now, I'd guess. It doesn't matter. What matters is what I'm about to tell you. You a member of the guild, Harry?"

"The guild?"

"Yeah, for chrissake. WGA. Writers Guild of America."

"No."

"That means you never wrote a screenplay. Right?"

"Right."

"No sweat. I never wrote one, either, until I came out here. You can write. That's what's important."

"You've got a screenplay you want me to write?"

"Not me, old buddy. Charlie Stuart. You believe in ghosts?"

"Ghosts? What the hell does that have to do with it? You're leaving me miles behind."

"It's got everything to do with it. Charlie Stuart needs a ghost."

"Let him go to the cemetery."

"Not that kind, dumbhead. The kind of ghost that writes, only doesn't have a name."

"Oh."

"Yeah. Oh. Charlie Stuart has a story. Shit, everybody out here has a story. He's sure his story is the winner of all time. That's what everybody thinks. The thing about Charlie is, he won't turn his idea over to somebody who might be able to turn it into something. Maybe it's good. Maybe it stinks. Nobody's going to know for sure until it's down on paper. But Charlie won't give it to somebody who could put it down on paper, not if it's going to end up 'Screenplay by Joe Smith.' He's going to produce the damn picture, if it ever gets done. That's what he wants, and who the hell cares. If it's good, he can produce it, and somebody with balls can sit on his ass and make sure it comes out right. But the first thing is, it's got to get written. Charlie's going to write it himself. That's what he tells everybody. That's what he's been saying for god knows how long. He's got this great idea, this blockbuster, and he's going to write it, and when we see it, we'll shit in our pants for a chance to put it on the screen, with the solo logo 'Written and Produced by Charles Stuart.' You getting the drift? The only thing is, the son of a bitch can hardly write his own name. And somewhere inside he knows it. He won't admit it. But he knows it. What he really wants, when you come right down to it, is a ghost. He won't say it out loud, but that's what he wants. Now, for chrissake, that's against guild rules. You write something, you get credit, or maybe the guild has to arbitrate to decide who gets credit. If you want, you can even use a phony name, just so long as the guild knows. But, you don't write, you don't get credit. It's as simple as that. If the guild finds out a guy's ghosted a script, his ass won't be in a sling; he won't have an ass. And if the guild finds out I'm telling you about this, it'll be my ass, too. But, what the hell. What have you got to lose? The way things are with you now, what have you got to lose?"

"Let me get this straight, Phil. Are you speaking for this guy Charlie Stuart? Do you want me to ghost a screenplay for him?"

"Shit, Harry, I don't want you to do anything. You're interested, I'll put a flea in Stuart's ear, and then you and he can take it from there."

"That simple?"

"Hell, no. It won't be simple. You don't know King Charles Stuart. You do it, you'll curse the day you ever met me and I mentioned it to you. But, what the hell, you need the bread, and Charlie's got bread to spare, and if you can work it out right, he'll give you enough to put you back into the sunshine. The only thing you won't have is a name. As far as the world will know, you won't ever have existed."

"Right now I couldn't care less."

"Then you're interested?"

"Just lead me to him."

Katie had been listening in silence, her face growing more and more distressed. She spoke then. "You don't have to do it, Harry."

"I have to do something," I said. "It might as well be this. About the only thing I know how to do is write, so why not?"

"You don't have to," she said again. "We'll have some money now. I've got a job."

"Sure," I said. "But it won't be enough and not quick enough."

"Listen to her, Harry," Garland said. "It's a long shot. I don't even know for sure if he'll agree. There are no guarantees."

"But he'll put money up front?"

"If he wants you? Yeah, he'll do that. I'm sure of that."

"Then I want to do it. Not just that, I have to do it."

"Your choice," he said. "Just remember. You're the guy who said yes."

4

A couple of mornings later, I hitched a ride out to Burbank in the car that came for Katie. Charlie Stuart had an office on the lot, paid the rent, showed up every morning, and left after a few hours. Once in a while he was thrown some consulting work by old friends from palmier days. Aside from those sporadic diversions, nobody seemed exactly sure how he filled his days.

Since I was very early, I went with Katie to the rehearsal studio to watch her work, stood well off to the side while she went into the changing room, and studied some of the early arrivals who were beginning to warm up at the barre. Katie was back in a few minutes, her hair pulled tightly back, dangling through the white ribbon, wearing old black leotards, a cardigan around the top, heavy wool leg warmers around her calves, ballet slippers, and, incongruously, the cane in one hand. She ignored me and advanced toward the dancers, most of whom were dressed as she was, except for the sweater.

The night before, when she arrived home late and exhausted, exuding an aura of barely contained excitement, there was little doubt that this was working well for her. "It's marvelous to be doing something again," she said.

"Can they dance?"

"Some of them. There are a few from the company and a couple of others."

"As good as you?"

"When I could dance?" She shook her head. "No."

"Not one?"

"No."

"What about the others?"

"They're beautiful."

"Naturally. What else would you expect? But can they move?"

"Not yet."

"Can you teach them?"

"That's what I'm getting paid for."

"And you like it?"

"Yes, I like it. I feel like a grandmother sometimes. They're so young, and most of them know so little. It would be so much simpler if I only had my leg back. But I like it. It makes me feel worthwhile. I can give them so much."

"What's the choreography like?"

"I don't know yet. I haven't seen it. All I'm trying to do now is teach them what first position is, just the basics. There'll be time enough for the rest when they learn how to move a little."

Later, we made love, and for the first time since the accident, since the beginning of the troubled times, it worked, and we lost ourselves in the lovemaking, and when it was over, she opened her eyes, stared into mine for a long time, held on to me, and whispered, "Oh, that was good."

"Better than good."

"Better than better than good. Can we do it some more?"

"Anytime."

"Now?"

"Now."

On our bed, our bodies illuminated by the eerie glow of the moon from outside and by something indefinable from inside, she had time for me, and we had time for nothing but each other, and there was nothing outside to intrude or break the spell.

In the rehearsal studio, she had no time for me. She was all business, all the professional, dedicated to what she was doing, but glowing, too, with an eagerness and an exhilaration. She moved along the row of dancers at the barre, straightening a leg, aligning a back, adjusting a head, positioning an arm, tapping with her cane someone who seemed to be slacking off. She took them through the barre exercises, the demi-pliés and pliés, the battement, the port de bras, the ronds de jambe, the frappé, in all five positions. She was demanding, insisting, driving, ordering, unwilling to accept less than a strive for perfection. "That's right. . . . Now again. . . . Once more. . . . Don't stop. . . . You're beginning to get it. . . . Now reverse. . . . Slowly, slowly, slowly. Everything should be in one movement, everything together. . . . Don't rush it. This is not an exercise class. This is ballet. Remember that. Don't forget it. Ballet. Ballet. Slow. Easy. It has to look effortless."

This must have been the way she had been driven when she was learning and through all the years and the endless hours of every day at the barre, watching herself in the mirrored walls, and on the floor, practicing, practicing until she could move without effort, fly without wings, become the swan, the princess, the fairy, anything she wanted, anything she was asked. She couldn't do it herself now, but she could at least try to drive and inspire and teach these others to do it for her. Some might learn, and some others might learn enough to get by, to pretend they knew what they were doing.

There were a few, I thought as I watched, who would never be able to move across a stage without tripping over their own feet. I watched one girl down at the end of the barre. You couldn't miss her, for a lot of reasons. She was struggling, sweating, her movements were jerky; she couldn't dip lower than a demi-plié no matter how she tried, and she was trying. And she was always at least half a beat behind everyone else. It was obvious she didn't know the first thing about dance and had no talent for it. But she was spectacular in other respects. She was built like a top-heavy hourglass, with enormous breasts that stretched her leotard to the bursting point, that looked as if they must have been given at least one silicone injection, her body curving down to a narrow waist and swelling from there into round and sensuous hips, and she had one of those faces, under short dark hair, in which every feature was perfect, maybe a little too perfect, except that the eyes weren't blank, the eyes were sharp and seeing. She wasn't, then, built like a dancer. But she tried. She swore, she groaned, she persisted until, at last, she grabbed the barre with both hands, leaned her head against the mirror, and said angrily, "It's impossible. I can't do it."

Katie moved over beside her. "Don't give up, Suzie," she said. "You're making progress. Try it again. You can do it."

"I can't."

"It takes practice, that's all. It will come with practice."

"Not with me," she said. "I'm no dancer. I'm not built that way. He said it would be easy. He said it would be fun. Like hell."

"It is fun when you know how," Katie said. "Here, let me show you." Katie dropped her cane, moved to the barre, straightened her back and head, and dipped slowly and effortlessly into a plié, so slowly it was almost impossible to follow the changing movement, everything linked, moving as a unit. But it was the right leg that was bearing her weight, and as she dipped lower, a spasm of pain passed across her face. She held the position, almost but not quite a grand plié in fourth position, waiting for the spasm to pass, and when it did, finished the bend, rose slowly, and turned back to the girl. "You see," she said. "Like that. Or something like that, anyway. It's not that hard with practice. I used to be able to do it a lot better, but with this—" She moved away, picked up her cane, and tapped her leg with it deprecatingly. "Look, Suzie," she said, "if I can do it with this thing, then so can you. Just keep trying."

The girl, Suzie, had watched her with wide, almost frightened dark eyes, was staring at the leg and then up into Katie's face. She nodded slowly. "Okay," she said. "I'll give it another go. I don't believe it, but I'll try." She grasped the barre, struggled, and managed to get almost down into a grand plié, though still with effort and jerkiness.

Katie watched, nodded, and smiled encouragement. "Good girl," she said. "If you keep working on it, it will come. And when you can do that, you'll see how much easier everything else will be. You'll see how easy it will be on the floor." She passed on down the line, watching, correcting, helping.

"Isn't she marvelous?" a voice said from just behind me. I turned. It was Terry Markoff. "Isn't she just the greatest?"

"I'll buy that," I said. "How are you, Terry?"

"Just wonderful."

"We haven't seen much of you since the accident." He had come to the hospital that one time, had called a few times, and then there had been only silence.

"Oh, I couldn't," he said. "It was so tragic. It was such a dreadful thing. I couldn't face it."

"I suppose not," I said, and having gotten to know Terry, I realized he was speaking the truth. "I didn't know you were working here."

"Oh, yes," he said. "I'm choreographing the picture."

"Katie didn't tell me."

"I don't think she knows yet. I wasn't here yesterday."

"But you knew she was working here?"

"But of course, dear boy. I absolutely insisted that Katherine had to be my assistant. I had to have someone I could trust to work with these . . . these . . . Well, they are cows, aren't they?" He shook his head. "Katherine is such a talent. She'll inspire them. If only she could dance again. Well, she will dance. I feel it."

"You really think so?"

"Think so? Dear boy, I know so. I'm positive. She has the gift. She would have been my star. She will be my star. I can see it already." His eyes studied Katie, studied the line critically even as he talked. He nodded approval at something she was doing. He said, "I must be going. I certainly do have my work cut out for me." He glided across the floor toward the dancers, shouting, "Katherine, my love . . ."

She looked up. "Terry." They came together in a laughing, delighted embrace. I looked at my watch. It was time to be going. They didn't look in my direction as I went out the door.

I wandered across the lot, asked some directions, found the building at last, and went up to the second floor where Stuart had his office. I knocked at the door. A voice told me to come in. He was holding the phone. I thought I heard the hum of the dial tone as I started across the room. Maybe not. He put his hand over the mouthpiece, nodded toward me, motioned toward a chair on the other side of the desk, then said into the phone, "Yeah, well, you tell that no good son he'd better do it if he knows what's good for him. . . . What? . . . No, no, of course, not. Don't take any crap from him. . . . Look, my appointment just walked in. I got to go. I'll be back to you later." He put the receiver back in its cradle.

If he had been trying to impress me, I wasn't impressed. Though why he should have tried a snow job then was beyond me. I was, after all, only a ghost, or a would-be ghost, and a ghost is a disembodied spirit, so why bother to make pretenses around one. Or maybe it was just his way; maybe he was the kind of guy who was always onstage, who always had to put on a show for whatever audience was around.

He looked at me, grinned, and reached over the desk to take my hand. "Hi," he said. "You must be Harry Miller."

"Right," I said. The grip was firm, the hand dry. After the briefest shake, he released his grip.

"Call me Charlie," he said. "Everybody does. We don't stand on New York formalities around here."

His office was not large, but it was cluttered. There was a desk, big, curving, modern, rosewood, and he sat behind it in a large high-backed saddle-leather chair, executive style. There were a couple of other, lower backed, armchairs, leather, not plastic, and an upholstered sofa that looked as though it had rarely felt the weight of a human backside, a coffee table with some expensive, massive stone ashtrays, some lamps on end tables, a couple of filing cabinets, a bookcase filled with bound scripts and a shelf of books, a thick neutral-shaded carpet. The desk held the telephone, the usual collection of pens and pencils in a leather container, a couple of yellow legal-sized pads with scratching on them, a lamp, and a desk calendar, open to today's date, with, I could make out upside down, my name entered opposite the time and the rest of the page blank.

Charlie Stuart was a pleasant-looking man with a kind of nervous energy he appeared to have trouble containing. As I would soon learn, he moved constantly, getting up, jittering across the floor, around the room, sitting down in one chair or another, getting up again, unable to stay for long in one place. His hands were well manicured, with a shine on the nails that said colorless polish. He was, as Garland had estimated, somewhere in his middle fifties, though he made an effort to look younger. He was short and a little paunchy, with thick arms and, I noticed when he stood, legs a little short for his body. His face was open and seemed guileless, the brown eyes friendly and only a little wary, and he had a full head of wavy, carefully groomed, and stylishly barbered black hair with graying temples and sideburns; the black, I guessed, was probably proof that Grecian Formula worked. He was dressed the way some people thought Hollywood producers ought to dress, in a bright yellow polo shirt with an alligator on one breast, lavender golf slacks, beltless, black socks, and shiny white loafers.

I was dressed in a suit. It had been a deliberate choice. He leaned back in his chair and studied me. "For chrissake," he said, "you look like some kind of fugitive from Madison Avenue."

Only later, when it was too late to use it, did I think of a good riposte. Then I only shrugged.

"Nobody out here wears a goddamn suit. Not during the day, for chrissake."

"I do," I said mildly.

"Yeah. You and your buddy, Phil Garland, who thinks he's God almighty. Who else? Jesus, you guys from the East give me a swift pain in the rectum."

I got up. "It was nice meeting you, Mr. Stuart."

"Hey, for chrissake," he said, "where the hell are you going? You got no sense of humor?"

I hesitated.

He laughed, waving me back into the chair. "Sit down, for chrissake. Sit down. Me and my big mouth. That's my trouble. I always say the first thing comes to my mind. It don't mean a good goddamn."

I hesitated.

"Hey, sit down. What do you want me to do? Say I'm sorry? Kiss your ass? Come on, sit down, sit down. Let's talk."

I slid back into the chair.

"No hard feelings?" he said.

"Of course not."

"Good. You play golf?" He made a gesture, and I followed it, to an expensive set of clubs in an expensive black leather bag leaning against the wall in the corner.

"Not in years," I said. "I played a little when I was a kid. But not since. I play tennis these days, when I get the chance."

"You ought to take up golf," he said. "Great game. Frees the mind for a couple of hours. You ride around in a cart out in the great fresh air, and it helps you think, helps you solve all your problems. You ought to play. You'd love it."

"If I ever have the time."

"Make the time. I'll tell you what. We'll make a date. Right this minute. I'll take you out to the club, and we'll play a round. Here, let me take a look at the calendar." He bent forward and flicked through the pages. There were only a few entries. He scratched something on one page. He looked back, smiling. "Week from Sunday. I'll get us a tee-off time and let you know."

"I don't have clubs," I said.

"No sweat," he said. "They've got a shit load out at the club. You can borrow some, rent some if you have to. You'll love it. And it'll give us a chance to really get to know each other."

"Whatever you say." I shrugged, certain it was all talk.

"I say we play some golf." He straightened up. "Okay, now let's get down to business. I haven't got all day." He glanced down at the blank page on the calendar. "Got a date later to play some golf out at the L.A. Country Club. (I was supposed to be impressed, I guess, but I wasn't; I didn't know the L.A. Country Club was supposed to be something special.) That's how come the clubs are here instead of out at my club." He laughed. He got up, strode around the desk, skittered across the room, sat for a second on the sofa, leaving a virgin mark, got up again, and stood looking down at me. "I was talking to your friend Phil Garland. He mentioned you."

"He said he would."

"He says you can write a shit storm."

"I write."

"I know that. He didn't have to tell me. I've read your stuff."

"Really?" I was sure he was lying.

"No bullshit. I never bullshit. I read the stuff you wrote from over there. Don't remember much about it. But I remember the name, and I remember it was damn good. Read your books, too." He named two and proceeded to summarize the plots. "You think I picked that up out of some review? Had a reader tell me?" He went over to the bookcase, bent, pulled out a book without even searching for it, and held it out. It was one of mine. It looked as though it had been read. "You believe me now?"

"I'm impressed," I said. "You must be one of the few people who's ever read it." But maybe it wasn't so surprising after all. If he was going to hire me and pay me good money to, as Garland said, put his ideas onto paper, he'd have been a damn fool not to have read something of mine to find out if I could write. And then, as I had discovered during an hour in library going through old clips and packaged studio bios, he'd begun as a reader for one of the major studios right after he arrived on the coast, one of those guys who reads the books and plays and other stuff somebody up there thinks might make a movie or somebody on the outside thinks ought to be a movie, and then synopsizes them for somebody a rung higher who can't be bothered reading a whole book. He must have read a couple of a hundred books during those first years and perhaps he still read; reading is a habit that's hard to break, it lasts a lifetime.

"Shit. More people should've read it. It's damn good. They should've made a movie out of it."

"They didn't."

"Well, they should have. One of these days, maybe I will. Who knows?"

"That would be nice."

"You ever write a movie?"

"No."

"You think that's bad? Hell, no. That's good. Means you don't have anything to unlearn. Means you come to it with no preconceived ideas. Means I can teach you the right way."

"I'm sure you can."

"You don't believe me? You think I'm some old Hollywood fart talking through his hat? Listen to me, kid. Before I came out here, I used to teach a course in journalism at City College. And that's the god's honest truth. I can still teach you young guys a thing or two. And you'd better believe it."

"I believe it."

"Okay. We got that out of the way. What did Garland tell you?"

"He said you had an idea and you needed somebody to turn it into a screenplay."

"Shit. How wrong can you be? I don't need anybody to turn my idea into a screenplay. I could do it myself if I had the time, which I don't. What I'm looking for is a guy who ain't got some great big fucking ego, like most of the goddamn writers in this town. What I'm after is a guy who's willing to work with me on my idea, my story, which belongs to me, which I've lived with for as long as I can remember. What I'm looking for is a guy who's willing to do it my way, the way I want it done, so it'll come out big, big, a goddamn blockbuster at the box office. You understand? I'd do it myself if I had the time. But the thing is, I can't sit still long enough. My brain's always working. I'm casting the damn thing in my head, picking the right director, drawing the budget, a million things. I've always got something going, a million different things. So I just don't have the time to sit at the typewriter and let it go. What I need is a guy to do some of the dirty work. You understand?"

"Of course." I knew exactly what he meant by the dirty work.

"You work with me, right? You do it the way I say, right? You check every fucking word with me, right? Every fucking scene, right? And you never forget it's mine, it belongs to Charlie Stuart, lock, stock, and barrel. Right?"

"Right."

"You want to do it?"

"Sure."

"Shit. You haven't asked what it's all about."

"I'm sure it's great."

"Goddamn right it's great. Here, let me show you." He walked back behind the desk, pulled open one of the drawers, took out a manila folder, opened it, removed some type-written pages, and handed them to me. There were three pages, single-spaced. I read them. They contained a summary of the plot. The idea wasn't bad. It had the elements of what I imagined went into a big picture. There was action and adventure and suspense. There was love and hate and in-between. There was boy gets girl, boy loses girl, boy gets girl back. There were some nice twists and surprises, and the possibility of some nice relationships between characters, if those characters could be made believable and complex and given elements with which an audience could identify and empathize. There wasn't all that much original in it, but then, there usually isn't. A lot had been stolen from Shake-speare and the Greeks and dozens of others, but then, who hadn't stolen from them? There was a lot of crap in it, too, but that could be tossed on the scrap heap and nobody would ever miss it. What it was, finally, was the hint of an outline and not much more, and hardly complete. But there was enough to see that it had possibilities.

He watched me anxiously while I read, trying to decipher what I was thinking. I kept my face blank. A couple of times, he interrupted the reading to ask what I thought. I waved the questions away. He came around from behind the desk, stood over my shoulder, reading along with me, chuckling a few times at what he must have pictured as potentially funny scenes. I finished and put the pages back on the desk.

"Well," he said, "what do you think?"

"It's got possibilities."

"Possibilities? Shit. Who're you kidding? It's all there, and you know it. All you have to do is fill in the blanks. And I'll help you do that. For chrissake, all you have to do is sit at the typewriter and type."

"Maybe a little more than that."

"Not much more. You can do it?"

"I think so."

"Great. When can you start?"

"Anytime. Tomorrow, I guess."

"Why not this afternoon?"

"Sure. This afternoon."

"Great. You go home and start working on it, and then you check with me in the morning."

"I'll do that."

"And we'll start working together, right away."

"Anything you say."

"One thing," he said.

"Yes?"

"On the title page. You write, 'Original story and screenplay by Charles Stuart.' Right?"

"Right."

"Because it belongs to me."

"Right."

"Because all you're going to do is write what I tell you to write."

"Right."

"And you're not going to go around telling anybody what you're doing. And I mean nobody."

"Right."

"Will you, for chrissake, stop saying right?"

"Right."

We both laughed. "Okay," he said, "we got ourselves a deal."

"We've got a deal."

"Okay. Now beat it and get to work, and get back to me first thing."

"Just one thing."

"Yeah?" He looked impatient.

I took a breath. "We haven't talked money."

He laughed. "It clean went out of my head. My mind was going a mile a minute in a million directions. You got a figure in mind?"

Negotiating about money was not one of my stronger points. When I did, I usually put on too low a price tag, undervaluing myself. I knew what I needed. I hoped for more. I said, "Not really. I'm kind of new at this business. I'll leave it to you. What are you thinking of?"

He named a figure. It was low. Even I knew it was too low. "I was hoping for more."

"What the hell," he said, "why argue?" He boosted the price by a couple of thousand. What I didn't know then, what I learned later when I checked, was that the figure was five thousand under the guild minimum, and a lot more under when you realized he was saving on the mandatory pension and welfare contributions and other guild requirements. Still, his figure would pay off what we owed and leave us a couple of thousand in the black. And we would have Katie's salary to add to that. Because my mind was exploring it and I didn't answer immediately, he must have thought I was going to ask for more. So he quickly added, "Of course, I'll cut you in for a piece of the action. I'll give you, oh, let's say, two and a half points. That satisfy you?"

I was ignorant and naive then. I didn't understand that the points could add up to something, or more likely nothing, and it depended on whether they were gross or net, what kind of gross or net, and whose books were used to figure it out. I was naive enough not to know that I didn't know. I said, "That sounds okay to me."

"Okay. So now we're settled."

"Well, just one more thing."

"Okay, for chrissake. Shoot."

"Could I have something up front? To seal the deal."

"Why not? It's expected. How much do you need?"

I took another breath. "Half."

"Half? I was thinking more like a third. But, what the hell, what's a couple of grand, more or less? You want half, you got half." He reached into the top drawer of the desk, pulled out a check ledger, opened it, calculated, wrote out a check, tore it off and handed it to me. "Now beat it, kid," he said. "And when you call in the morning, I want you to tell me you got ten pages done. At least." He laughed. I hoped he wasn't serious.

I got up and started for the door. He called after me. "Hey, you forgot this." He was holding out the three pages. "You'll need this."

"Of course." I took the pages from him. As I was going through the door, I glanced back. He was sitting behind the desk, holding the manila folder open, reading a duplicate of the pages he had given me, smiling, chuckling aloud.

5 When I got home that afternoon after a long, circuitous bus ride that made me, for the first time, think fondly of the New York subways, I called Phil Garland. A colorless, formal voice told me he was in conference and couldn't be disturbed. Would I care to leave a message? I would. I said to tell him that Harry Miller had called and that everything had worked out. He would understand. When she heard my name, the voice warmed a little. "Oh, Mr. Miller," she said, "you're on my list. Mr. Garland is having a small gathering at his home on Saturday evening. He wondered if you and Mrs. Miller would be free to attend."

I said we would be.

"Then I can put you down. It will be at seven." She gave me directions to the house. About an hour later, she called again, this time to tell me that she had spoken with Mr. Garland and that he was pleased everything had gone well and that he would send a car for us on Saturday.

A day or two later, as promised, Wolf Rabinowitz turned

up. I heard the bell and went to answer it. He stood in the doorway, a melancholy look on his face. He expected the worst and wasn't looking forward to what he would have to do. "Mr. Miller," he said.

"Mr. Rabinowitz."

"I heard the typewriter. I do not like to interrupt when you are creating."

"That's all right."

"Glad I am that you are writing. The last time, all was silence. You know why I am here."

"Of course. Come on in."

He looked as though he didn't know whether to laugh or cry. "You have the rent?"

"You bet." I led him into the living room and handed him the check I'd already prepared, for the back rent and the current month.

He looked at it suspiciously. "If I drop it on the floor, it will stay and not jump back into my hand? If I deposit it, it will not be like the rubber ball?"

"No way," I said. "It's good. Just go and deposit it."

He smiled happily. He put the check into his pocket. He said, "Now friends we can be again. No more angry landlord and tenant."

I called Charlie Stuart and he called me, and we talked every morning and every afternoon and sometimes in between over the next days. Naturally, I hadn't written ten pages the first day, had barely gotten into the first scene after a couple of days. Beginnings are always the hardest, but then, middles and endings aren't that easy, either. He was disappointed. He'd expected much more rapid progress; everything was there in the outline; all I had to do was type it out and fill in the blanks. Maybe he was right, but the thing was, there were mainly blanks, huge ones. He said that maybe the thing was to start really working together. He'd put everything else to the side. Then we could make it move. Unfortunately, he was all booked up for the rest of the week, but bright and early Monday morning, we'd begin in unison, a real collaboration, he called it. Of course, we'd work at my apartment, not in his office. In the first place, he didn't have a typewriter there, though he could certainly get one if he had to, but, more important, he was sure I'd be more comfortable working at home. And he hoped I'd have a lot to show him when he arrived.

Phil Garland was living well. That, of course, was to be expected. He'd bought one of those big houses that date back to the thirties on one of the winding streets a couple of blocks north of the Beverly Hills Hotel, where the flats just begin to give a hint of turning into the hills. He sent a Mercedes limousine for us, and when we arrived at his house, the street was already lined with Mercedes and Rolls and Cadillacs and Lincolns, Ferraris and Maseratis and Jaguars, and an assortment of expensive esoteric models. The lights were blazing in the house, and over the house it was possible to see the glow from lights in the backyard, and the sound of loud voices and laughter echoed into the street. A small party, his secretary had said.

A butler in white jacket greeted us at the door and checked our names off on a list. Garland passed by from some other room, saw us, and detoured in our direction. He was wearing a dark suit, white shirt, and striped tie. I was wearing a dark suit. Katie was wearing a long black dress, the pearls and the jade earrings. (We'd debated about what to wear, had decided that with Garland, even if it was a small gathering, a little formality wouldn't hurt.) He smiled, welcomed us, bent and kissed Katie on the cheek, held her off and told her she was ravishing, told her that every time he saw her, she was more beautiful than the last time. "Every woman in this place is going to fade into the woodwork beside you," he said. "And I'll tell you something else. Before the night's out, half of them are going to back you into a corner and ask where you get your hair done and where the hell you got that color."

She laughed. "I'll tell them the truth. From my mother."

He laughed. "Never tell anyone around here the truth. They'll be sure you're lying." He held her off and looked at her again. "I like the jade," he said, "and the pearls. I liked them the other night. You should always wear them."

"They are lovely, aren't they," she said. "We bought them in Hong Kong."

"When were you there?"

"When Harry was in Vietnam."

He looked at me and grinned. "Nice way to spend R and R, old buddy. How come it never happened to me? Don't tell me. There's no Katie in my life." He made a sad face. He said, "You and me and the bankers, old buddy."

It came out of nowhere. "What?"

"The suits. Don't you know yet, nobody wears suits out here. It's not fashionable."

"Who the hell wants to be fashionable?"

"We set our own style, right?"

"Right." We both laughed. He led us into the living room, the size of a hotel ballroom. There was hardly room to move. People drinking, picking food off trays passed around by waiters and waitresses in uniform, smoking, dropping ashes on the thick blue carpeting, talking, laughing. At one end were wide French doors opening out onto a patio that fronted on a brightly illuminated pool and where there seemed even more people congregating. There were, I guessed, at least a hundred people in the living room and out on the patio. Half a dozen older men were in suits, and they were with older women in long, quite formal and conservative gowns. Garland's bankers. There were a lot of younger people, and there was no pattern to their dress. Some, both men and women, were in designer jeans or casual slacks, very tight, with shirts and blouses opened almost to the navel. Some of the women were in long dresses, though they were cut more to reveal than conceal. You name it, they were wearing it. I recognized some of them, the new stars and the would-be stars of tomorrow from movies and television, the new Hollywood elite. There was a smattering of middle-aged and slightly older men and women, dressed a little more circumspectly, though there wasn't a tie to be seen on any of the men. They were the old Hollywood, a little uncomfortable with and a little removed from their successors in the hierarchy of stardom. They were there because Phil Garland had asked them, and when he asked, it was more than a request. Among them were those faces we had seen and loved or hated, cheered or hissed, up there on the big screens all our lives, and from a distance across the room and through the haze of smoke, they looked as though they'd hardly changed with the years; up close, I discovered, the ravages of age and time were there, and even carefully applied makeup couldn't quite conceal them, and I realized that the right makeup man and a good cameraman and lighting designer could take years off anybody, could make a woman of sixty or more look twenty-five, could make a man of sixty-five look still the dashing cavalier of romance and adventure capable of any exploits.

Garland got us drinks, cornered one of the waitresses and insisted we sample the food, then led us slowly through the room. He stopped to introduce us to a lot of people, some of whose names I would remember because I'd seen them in films and most of whom promptly forgot mine when they realized I wasn't anyone important or likely to be and so couldn't do them any good. Nobody forgot or ignored Katie. Garland held her arm protectively, almost possessively, casting his own aura around her, and if I hadn't realized she was enjoying it and was being amused by it and deprecating of it at the same time, it might have burned a little hole of jealousy in me. But I had grown used to men acting like that around her and understood exactly her reaction. Again and again, when he stopped to introduce us, he would say, "This is the beautiful Katherine Summers," and the way he said it, you knew he thought she was something special. The eyes would pass over, stop, return, and hold, and Garland would laugh. "You can look, but don't touch and don't get any bright ideas. She's taken." And the eyes would go down to her hand and fix on the wedding ring. You could almost hear the disappointment and then the calculation in a mind that said, What the hell, marriage doesn't mean anything these days. After a few moments and a few words, somebody would spot the cane, and there would be a question or a look. "Don't give it a thought," Garland would say. "She had an accident. But she's on the mend. That thing will disappear any day."

And the inevitable question: "What kind of accident?"

"I was hit by a car," Katie answered.

"My god. I hope it wasn't serious."

"Broken leg."

"Christ. I hope they got the bastard."

"They didn't. It was hit-and-run."

"Christ." And then, "But you're all right now? I mean, once you get rid of the cane and all that."

She shrugged and didn't respond.

And then the next question: "It was just the leg? I mean, nothing worse?"

"No, just the leg."

"Well, you have that to be thankful for. I mean, once you get rid of that thing, you can still work. You can even work with it. My god, I can see it now. Phil, what a great idea for a picture."

"It's been done," he said. "A thousand times."

"Everything's been done. So you just do it again, with a new twist."

"I don't act," Katie said simply.

"You don't act?" Surprise. "You're not in films?" In that crowd, everybody was in films; they all acted or directed or wrote or had something to do with the movies, even the bankers who put their money into them.

"No, I was a dancer."

"Not a hoofer," Garland interrupted. "Ballet. You should have seen her. She was going to be one of the great ones. A real prima ballerina. Hell, you will see her. You can bet the house on that." He had never seen her dance.

"Oh." Commiseration. "And the leg. How awful. But you will be able to dance again. Once you're completely healed."

"I don't know," Katie said.

"You can bet on it," Garland said, riding over her.

"You're going to put her in a picture, Phil? With those looks. With that hair. With that body. My god, she'll be dynamite."

"I'm thinking about it," he said.

"If you're thinking about it, it's as good as done."

"I just have to find the right property."

"She'll make the property. You can count on that."

"I don't act," Katie said.

"Not yet, you don't. Just wait."

It went on like that, all across the room, out onto the patio. After a while, it was even funny to notice the eyes following her, the women's calculating or examining, envious or attempting to ignore and dismiss and unable to do so, and the men's admiring, a lot more than admiring. It wasn't just that she was beautiful, which she was; there were plenty of beautiful women in that room and on the patio, and most of them with a lot more in the breast and hip department than Katie, who was built like the dancer she was. Maybe it was just that she was new and unknown and so mysterious; or that there was something, the something that had always been there, so vulnerable about her that you wanted to go to her; or there was that other thing nobody could ever define but which I had noticed the first time I ever saw her; or maybe it was that people saw that Garland had a particular interest in her, that she might well be his protégée, not necessarily in the Hollywood sense of the word but in some real sense, for he acted toward her not as a lover or a would-be lover but as a protector, even as a parent.

Someone brought her a dinner plate from the buffet. Someone else found her a seat on a chaise out by the pool. A crowd, mostly male, gathered. I was gradually elbowed out of that closing circle and stood on the outside, watching. Garland hovered for another moment, looked across heads toward me, and made a don't-blame-me gesture. He bent and said something to her, edged his way through her new admirers, and paused as he reached me. "I ought to see to some of my other guests," he said. "Circulate, Harry. You can take care of yourself. You won't get near Katie for the rest of the night." He laughed and went through the French doors.

For a few moments more, I watched. Katie was having fun. She was enjoying the attention, was amused by it, and I could see she didn't really believe or understand it; but then, she had never seemed to understand that she could draw men that way, never believed the compliments. She had said to me more than once, "It's ridiculous. My breasts are too small, my hips are too narrow, I'm too tall and too skinny, my legs are too long, and I've got too many freckles. If I cut my hair short, people would think I was a boy." Nobody would ever make that mistake.

I wandered away, found the buffet, filled a plate, and went looking for a place to roost. I found one on a sofa in a sitting room off the big room. A couple of other people were there, eating and talking. His face was vaguely familiar, from some television series, I thought. She looked like a dozen other blond, big-breasted, good-looking girls at that party and in that city. They talked, ate, and ignored me. Unlike Katie and a lot of other people I know, I have rarely been able to start a conversation with strangers. (Going after a story for a newspaper is, of course, different; you are forced to approach strangers, and while it may be difficult, you do it because you have to.) I felt constrained, was seldom the first one to say the first word. Sometimes, though, there isn't a choice. I didn't realize it at first, but they were talking about Katie.

"He's got a new girl," he said.

"He's always got a new girl," she said.

"Sure. But he usually likes them with a lot on top."

"Like Suzie."

"Like Suzie. Like you. Like a dozen others."

"I wonder how Suzie's taking it. I haven't seen her around."

"Maybe he told her it was time to take a hike."

"Just when he put her into that new picture?"

"It could have been the kiss-off. Payment for services rendered and good-bye. It's been done."

"I know," she said. "What do you suppose it is? I mean, she's pretty enough and all that. And that hair. I wonder who does it. Whoever he is, I wish she'd let me in on the secret."

"Somebody said she was some hot young kid from back East," he said. "You know, off-Broadway or something. But I never heard of her."

"I suppose you've heard of everybody."

"I get around."

"You don't have to tell me. Maybe it's the cane. It gives her a kind of look, you know. Exotic or something."

"It's phony," he said with absolute assurance.

"You mean, like an eye patch or something? To attract a lot of attention?"

"Right on the button."

"I wish somebody'd think of something like that for me," she said.

"It's not a phony," I said.

The stopped, stared, annoyance across the faces and in the attitudes. "You say something?" he said.

"I said the cane's not a phony."

"How the hell would you know?"

"She happens to be my wife."

It took him just a moment, enough to understand, to take that in and find a way to deal with it. He leaned back and grinned cynically. "If she's your wife," he said, "I sure as hell wouldn't be sitting around in here. Not when Garland's on the make. He'll have her in the sack before you finish that plate."

"Not likely," I said.

"Don't doubt it, man," he said. "You don't know him."

"Oh, I know him," I said. "And I know my wife. And if I were you, I'd try to think of something better to talk about than a lot of bullshit. I'd find something I knew about. Or maybe that's too hard." I got up, left the half-empty plate on the sofa, and walked out. They had gotten to me. If they were beginning to speculate like that, then certainly others were or soon would be, and the stories would start to build and grow a lot seamier and a lot nastier. But I couldn't think of anything that could stop them now. We'd have to learn to live with them, as we lived with so much else.

I wandered over to the patio entrance and stood in the doorway, watching. Katie was still on the chaise, still in the center of a crowd, though it had grown larger. She was talking and laughing and often turning to a very spectacular, very buxom girl with short dark hair sitting next to her. It took me a moment to recognize her. She was the clumsy kid who couldn't do a plié. Someone had just left the crowd and was coming through the door. I asked, as he was about to pass me, who she was. He said, "You mean the redhead? Everyone wants to know that." I said no, the other one. He laughed. "That's Suzie Willens. Hands off. She belongs to Garland."

I got another drink and roamed, nodding to some people I'd been introduced to. They nodded back absently but didn't break their conversations or invite me in. An older woman whom I hadn't met was standing alone. She smiled at me. I smiled back. From the way she was dressed, I guessed one of Garland's banker's wives. She took a step. I took a step, and we were together. "It's a very nice party," she said.

"Yes," I said.

"But Philip's parties are always nice. So many interesting people."

"I suppose so," I said. "But this is the first one."

"Oh," she said. "You're somebody new. How nice."

"Actually," I said, "Phil and I are old friends."

She looked at me. "From the East?"

"That's right."

"How nice to find an old friend when you're in a strange city."

"Isn't it," I said.

"Are you in the movie business, too?"

"No," I said. "I write. Books."

"How interesting. Would I know anything you've written."

I mentioned a couple of books.

She shook her head slowly, sadly. "I'll have to get them from the library," she said. She looked at me again. "But I've seen you," she said.

"Hardly likely," I said.

"Yes, I have," she said. Her face worked, brightened. "I know. You were with that gorgeous girl. How can you possibly leave her alone with all these—Well, when I was a girl, we called them wolves?"

I laughed. "She can take care of herself. She really can. Besides, you know what they say. There's safety in numbers."

She laughed at that. "I don't think I've seen her before," she said. "Is she a new actress?"

"No," I said. "She's a dancer. Ballet."

"Oh, I just love the ballet. You must introduce me."

"I would," I said, "if we could ever get through the crowd around her."

She laughed. "Do you know her well?"

"Yes," I said. "She's my wife."

She smiled. "You lucky man."

"I think so."

We talked some more, and then her husband joined us and we talked, and then they slowly drifted away, her last words, "Now, don't forget, you said you'd introduce me to your wife."

"I won't forget."

I went looking for a bathroom. I don't know how many there were on the first floor, but they were all in use. I went up the stairs to the second floor, found a vacant one, used it, started out, and turned the wrong way, wandering down a hall. About halfway down, there was a door slightly ajar, a dim light beaming out from inside, some murmured conversation. I glanced in, got a whiff of a once-familiar aroma, but not as strong or all enveloping as I remembered. It might have been possible to get a contact high just standing there and breathing. Half a dozen people, men and women, all in their early to mid-twenties, were sitting on a bed, passing joints back and forth, drawing deeply, holding, exhaling with loud sighs. One of them looked up a little blearily, noticed me, and made a vague gesture.

"Hey, man," he said, "come on in. Join the party." I walked in. He stared at me a little suspiciously. "Do I know you?"

"I doubt it," I said.

"You ain't the fuzz?"

"No way," I said.

"I mean, the suit and all. You know. Only the fuzz wears suits."

"I wear a suit, and I'm not the fuzz."

"You say it, I'll buy it," he said. "Come on in, join the fun, split a joint."

I walked in, took a drag on the joint he passed to me, and passed it on. It was not very strong, not very good, not the way I remembered from a long way away and what seemed a long time ago. He watched me, grinned when he saw I knew how, and said, "Good stuff, right. The best."

I nodded. "Good stuff."

"Straight from Mexico," he said. He lit another joint, taking it from a cigarette case, already rolled and packed. It seemed too easy; we used to roll our own. The joints kept being passed. Pretty soon, I could feel that little buzz in my head. Even enough of weak grass will give you that. A girl kept looking at me. She seemed about eighteen, a redhead, only the red didn't come from her mother. "You're cute," she said.

I laughed. "Nobody's called me that since I was a kid, and then it was my mother."

She laughed too loudly. "I like older men," she said.

"Well, I'm an older man." In that group, I felt like a grandfather.

She suddenly stripped off her blouse. She wasn't wearing a bra, but then I don't think any woman under forty was wearing a bra that night. She thrust her chest out at me, the nipples bright red as though she'd smeared them with lipstick. The nipples were large, but then so were her breasts, enormous. I wondered why every woman out there seemed to think silicone was as necessary as food. She said, "You like my tits?"

"They're very nice." Nobody was paying any attention to her, or to me.

"Let's go find a room and fuck," she said.

"I don't think so," I said.

"You like it better with people watching? Great. We can do it right here." She started to pull down her jeans.

"No," I said. "I mean, I don't think so."

"You don't want to fuck?"

"Not really," I said.

"You queer or something?"

"No."

"You don't like me." She started to cry.

"It's not that," I said. "I'm here with my wife."

"Shit," she said, "everybody's here with a wife or a husband or a something. You think anybody cares?"

"Are you married?" I asked.

"Shit, no," she said. "I'm just a something. You know, I'm living with a guy." She looked around. "Anybody seen that fucker Donnie?" There were no answers. Nobody was paying any attention. "If I know him," she said, "he's off someplace screwing his cock off." She looked at me again, thrust the chest out, and pulled the pants a little lower; she wasn't wearing underpants. "You sure you don't want to fuck?"

"I'm sure."

She shrugged. She didn't bother to pull up the pants or put the blouse back on. She grabbed a joint, took a deep drag, and leaned back against one of the other guys. He fondled her breasts absently. She said, "Freddy, you want to fuck?"

He looked at her, took a drag, and muttered, "Later."

She said, "Nobody wants to fuck. What kind of party is this?" She took the joint and inhaled.

Pretty soon, I got bored, with these kids and with the conversation, or lack of it. Listening to them, I wondered if one of them could speak an intelligible English sentence. The poverty of language and thought made me think, Probably not. I got up to leave. Somebody started to protest. "Hey, man, where you goin'?" He had trouble getting the words out.

"Time to move on," I said.

"Hang around," he said. "You're a nice guy even if you are an old fucker."

"Thanks," I said, and started for the door.

"Hey, man," somebody else said, "stay put, stay cool. The best is yet. My man'll be here. With the best. Blow your mind. Prime coke."

I declined. "Got to be moving." I walked out into the hall and steadied myself against the wall. Outside that stifling room, so filled with the sweet smoke, even the stale air of the hall tasted good. The buzz started to disintegrate, vanishing rapidly. With good grass, the buzz lasts. I wove down the hall, trying to find the stairs, realized I was still going the wrong way, turned, and stumbled against another door. It opened. Two couples were sprawled across the bed in there, clothes strewn haphazardly around the floor. It was an interesting sight. One of the girls lifted her head and grinned. "You want to join the fun?" she said. I backed out. She went back to what she had been doing and muttered, "Shit, for a second I thought it was my husband." I closed the door, found the stairs, and went back down to the first floor.

I got another drink at the bar, was cornered just as I was turning away. The guy had had a little too much to drink. But by then there weren't many people there who hadn't had a little too much to drink or a little too much of something else. "I met you," he said. "I know you."

"You don't know me," I said. "But we met."

"You're Garland's friend."

"That's right."

"You in the business?"

"No."

"What the hell do you do?"

"Write."

"I thought you said you weren't in the business."

"I'm not."

"Then how come you say you write? Everybody writes is in the business. You workin' on a flick now?"

"I write books," I said.

"Shit," he said. "I read any?"

"I doubt it."

He accepted that. "How come you're a friend of Phil Garland?"

"From the old days," I said.

"The old days?" He looked as though there couldn't possibly have been anything before that moment.

"We worked on a newspaper together."

He brightened suddenly. "That's right," he said. "That's what he used to do. Before he got honest." He laughed. "I suppose you were over there with him."

"I was over there," I agreed.

"Shit," he said, and his face flushed angrily. "You're one of the bastards who's making us lose the goddamn war."

I turned and walked away from him, through the room, which seemed as full as ever. Nobody ever went home from those parties; nobody ever even thought of leaving, I guessed, until somebody threw them all out. I crossed to the patio, looking for Katie. She was still on the chaise. She glanced up, noticed me, smiled and waved. It wasn't a signal for me to rescue her, just recognition and a message that she was still having a good time.

I wandered back through the room, leaned against a wall off to one side, and watched the faces, trying to see how many of them I recognized. More than half. A hand suddenly gripped my arm. It was Charlie Stuart. He was wearing pink slacks, a white shirt with no tie, open a couple of buttons down his chest so that graying hair showed, a black silk jacket, black socks, and shiny black slip-ons. "Jesus," he said, "I wondered if you'd be here."

"I'm here," I said.

"Why the hell aren't you home working?"

"Even a dog's entitled to a night out," I said. I didn't say ghost.

He laughed. "Fantastic, isn't it?"

"I guess so. I haven't been to one of these before."

"Nobody throws one like Garland, believe me. Right out of the old days, only better." He backed off and looked at me. "How come you're all alone? Aren't you having a good time?"

"That's the host's question," I said. "But yeah, I'm enjoying myself."

"Just wait. You ain't seen nothing yet." He tugged at my arm "I'm about to make your evening."

"Really? How?"

"Don't ask. Just come with me. I want to show you something. I want you to meet somebody, absolutely incredible. I never met anybody like her in my life, and you'd better believe it." He dragged me across the room, out through the French doors onto the patio, across the flagstones toward Katie. I started to laugh. He stopped and said sharply, "What the hell's so funny?"

"Nothing," I said. "Not a thing."

"Okay," he said, and started to move again, pulling me with him. "Wait'll you meet her," he said. "She's got every guy in the joint comin' in his pants." He clutched my arm tightly and pulled me into the crowd, forcing an opening, propelling us both until we were standing right in front of Katie. She looked up and smiled. I grinned back. Stuart didn't seem to notice. He was obviously too obsessed with what he imagined as his discovery, too obsessed with introducing one discovery to the other, though his manner was that of the proud lover wanting to show off the object of his love.

"Hey, Katherine," he shouted, trying to make himself heard over the cacophony that ringed her. "Miss Summers." She looked toward him, nodded vaguely, pleasantly, trying to place him from among all the men she had met and who had swarmed around her that night. He said, "I want you to meet a friend of mine. A very close friend. A talented guy. A real talent, not like some of the jerks around here. This guy writes books. I mean, real books, terrific books." He shoved me forward. "Miss Katherine Summers," he said, formally, "I want you to say hello to my friend, Harry Miller."

"Hello, Miss Summers," I said. "It's nice to meet you."

"Hello, Mr. Miller," she said, keeping a straight face, as I had done, "it's nice to meet you."

I bent down, took her head in my hands, and kissed her. She put her arms around my neck and kissed me back. The noise around us evaporated in an instant, became total silence. We both started to laugh. I looked back at Stuart. He was pale, aghast, staring at us with disbelief.

"It's all right, Charlie," I said. "I know Miss Summers. We've known each other for a long time."

"Yes," she said. "Actually, you see, we're married."

Charlie stared, grinned, then burst into a loud roar of laughter. "Son of a bitch," he said. "And I thought I was doing you a favor." The looks on the faces of some of the others in that circle were not quite so amused.

We left a little while later, searching for Garland first, finding him at last in a small room, talking quietly to two of the men in business suits, the bankers. He saw us, excused himself, and moved forward, smiling with pleasure. We told him it was late and we were leaving. He tried to talk us into staying. We were tired, we said. It was really time to go. He walked us out to the waiting Mercedes, turned us around before we got in, and made us look back at the brightly lit house, up at the stars dimly speckling the sky, almost lost against the reflected glow. He looked at Katie, and his face stopped laughing, became serious. He waved an arm. "Look at it," he said. "Take a good look."

"I'm looking," she said.

"If you want it," he said, "it can be yours. All of it, and more."

She looked at him. "What do I have to do to get it?"

"Just be," he said.

"That's all?"

"That's all. Whatever it is, you've got it. I saw it the first time I met you. Everybody here tonight saw it. You can have whatever you want."

She stopped smiling. She looked straight into his face, knew this was no joke, knew he was telling her something he completely believed. She shook her head slowly. "Not whatever I want," she said, becoming just as serious as he. "Not what I really want."

He looked at her, shook his head, smiled again, and bent and kissed her lightly. He turned and went back into the house.

We sat in the back of the limousine without talking for a time on the ride home. Both of us, I think, were trying to sort out all that happened. Finally, I asked, "Did you have a good time tonight? Or don't I need to ask?"

"It was incredible," she said. "I feel like a fairy princess, like Cinderella."

"Isn't that what Phil said? That's certainly the way everybody acted around you."

"Do you think all the parties out here are like that?"

"I seriously doubt it."

"I know what a flower feels like," she said.

"What?"

"You know, when all the bees are swarming around. It doesn't have to do anything, and it doesn't understand why."

"Just be careful you don't get stung."

She laughed. "It was fun," she said. "Even if it never happens again, it was fun. I'll always remember it."

"For you," I said, "it'll happen again, and again, if you want it to. Didn't you understand what Phil was trying to tell you?"

"Don't get serious," she said. "Not tonight. You. Did you have a good time? I didn't see much of you."

"I couldn't get near you," I said.

"Did you have a good time?"

"An interesting time."

"You're being serious again. You won't commit yourself?"

"A lot of images," I said. "Too many to sort out right now. But it was interesting. You can say that."

"Are you jealous?"

"Should I be?"

"Never."

"No?"

"No. You're the only one who matters. I love you, and that's all that counts."

"There's an echo in the car."

She moved against me and kissed me, then was silent again. Suddenly she laughed. "Who was that little man, the one who tried to introduce us?"

"That, my love, was our benefactor. That was Charlie Stuart."

"Really?" she said. "I thought he was nice. A little foolish, but nice."

"He's all right."

"I like him."

6 We stayed in bed through noon the next day, making love with an intensity and a kind of desperation that hadn't been there since those weeks when we had first lived together, the weeks before I had gone to Asia to cover a war and she had gone on tour with her ballet company and we had known it would be a long time before we would be together again. Now it was as though we were trying to wrap ourselves in our private world, keeping the outside at bay for just this moment. We had come through a bad time, but now it seemed that forces were gathering around us to propel us into something strange and out of our control.

Between times, we talked, trying to sort out and put together the disparate pieces of the night before. She made light of it all, deprecated what had happened to her, but inside she had begun to sense it could not be dismissed, even if she did not fully comprehend it. I mused about the scenes, separate and isolated and unlinked, trying to see them as part of a whole.

The car arrived early to pick up Katie on Monday and

ferry her out to Burbank. A few hours later, as promised or threatened, Charlie Stuart turned up. I let him in. He looked around eagerly, then sagged with disappointment. "Where's your wife?" he asked. "Where's Katherine?"

"In Burbank," I said. "Working."

He looked surprised. "Garland's got her cast already?"

"No." I shook my head. "She's working with the dancers on a new musical. That's what she does."

He accepted that, drank some coffee that I made, then rose and said, "Well, it's time to go to the mines. Time's wasting, and time's money."

We went into the bedroom. I sat down at the typewriter and lit one of the dozens of cigarettes I light when I'm trying to write, though most of them burn down in the ashtray, forgotten after the first puff so that sometimes there are five or six going at the same time. Stuart stood over me and began to pace. And so we began.

Those sessions every morning from then on lasted two or three hours, until noon or a little after, when he finally left, saying he was late already, he had a million things he had to do, and I had the drift. The sessions were not easy. They were trying and exhausting. He had been around films so long that he was sure there wasn't anything he didn't know or couldn't do. And there was a lot he did know, instinctively by then, especially on the technical side, where I was ignorant. He could rattle off all the technical terms and details that were necessary to turn a script into workable form: how to indicate close-ups and long shots, intercuts and dissolves and fades and crosscuts and all the rest. Out of that long experience had come, too, a well-developed sense of timing and pace; not that he could do it himself, but he knew just how long a scene could be stretched without losing the audience; he knew what could be done with the camera alone and what required dialogue, and that's an area where anyone who hasn't written scripts treads on treacherous turf; he understood the necessity of building tension to create drama and crises; he had a visual mind, so he could look at a scene on paper and see it played on a big screen inside his head; he had some abilities as an editor, so he could look at dialogue and know when it was right and when it rang false; he could look at a scene and sense whether it worked or didn't and have some idea of where it was going wrong; he could see where characters were moving nicely and where they were straying along faulty paths into dead ends. He had these attributes and a lot more, and these were the good parts, the parts I welcomed.

But there was a lot he didn't have and never would, but which he thought went along with the rest, naturally, and which he was certain he was just as much a master of. He might have a sense of what was good or bad dialogue, but he couldn't write it himself or speak it; he didn't seem to have the foggiest idea of how people really talked. He might know what was good or bad with a scene, but he hadn't a clue as to how to construct one. His concept of characters and how to develop them and give them complexity and shadings and inner motivations was, at best, rudimentary.

He had, then, all the learned technical expertise and none of the more indefinable, innate, and infinitely more necessary and elusive abilities to create. That didn't stop him from thinking he had them. He would stand over my shoulder, pace back and forth, trying to dictate dialogue, trying to construct a scene, as though I were a secretary who would write down verbatim everything he said. Of course, he would inevitably break somewhere soon after beginning, saying, "Well, you know what I mean. You get the drift. Now, you just take it from there."

He would be back the next morning, and the next and the next. Immediately, he would take the pages I had written and go over them, scrawling and scratching with thick black pencils. He was good at that, very good. He caught quickly where I had gone wrong, and sometimes, his suggestions about how to fix the problem areas were on the mark. If what I wrote bore little resemblance to what he had tried to dictate the day before, or a few days before, it didn't seem to matter if what I'd accomplished worked in his eyes; it mattered only when what I'd done didn't work, and then he would become furious, ordering me to do it the way he'd told me and not try to get fancy on my own when I didn't know my ass from my elbow about films.

Much as I detested those mornings, dreaded Stuart's coming, cursed silently his presence, exhilarated in his leaving, somewhere inside I understood that this was not time wasted. For his presence, his enthusiasm, which abounded, his demands, even his ideas and suggestions, even when inappropriate and appalling, propelled me forward, gave me the motivation and the impetus and even the necessary discipline to give some shape to what had been, until then, only an amorphous dream of his. If progress was slow, if we advanced only by inches, only a page or two at a time, still we advanced.

Katie was growing stronger all the time. Working, being driven to demonstrate to the dancers, helped a lot, and an hour every afternoon with the physical therapist helped even more. She was walking better, the limp hardly noticeable, and she was relying less and less on the cane, even forgetting it at times, needing it only when she was tired and the leg ached and the limp became pronounced. I could sense in her the growing hope, if not belief, that things would work out, after all, that maybe she would actually dance again.

A couple of Sundays after Garland's party, Terry Markoff turned up about one in the afternoon, bearing under his arm a large ballet pad on which he had sketched some of the preliminary choreography for the film. He had talked often with Katie about his ideas and his plans, had demonstrated steps and patterns for her, had listened to her suggestions and adopted some of them. That day he wanted to talk in detail, to argue and listen, to find if there might be alternatives for the difficult movements he wanted that were beyond the capabilities of most of his dancers.

They sat together on the couch and went slowly over the sketches, which only a trained choreographer or dancer could possibly understand and follow. I went into the other room and tried to work for a while but didn't have much success and so gave up, went back into the living room, and sat off to the side, reading the paper and trying, at the same time, to listen and understand them, to cut through their private language. After a time, Terry rose and unwrapped a thin square package he had brought with him. It was a private pressing of the still uncompleted, or at least unpolished, music for the film, only the piano and not a full orchestra. He put it on the stereo, went out onto the bare floor, and began to demonstrate some of the moves. Katie watched intently, and I could see in her the desire, the straining, the old feelings, coming alive. She rose suddenly, leaving her cane by the couch, joined him, and together they moved into a gliding, effortless pas de deux. It lasted only a few minutes. She pulled away, stopped, glared angrily down at her leg, put her hands on her hips, and stood, staring at him.

"I'm terrible," she said.

"You're wonderful," he said, but it was obvious that he didn't really mean it.

"You're lying," she said. "I can hardly dance a step, even when I've got you to help."

"You're coming along," he said. "You can't expect miracles. It takes time."

"Time. Time," she raged. "Everybody says that, give it time. I go to the therapist every damn day, and he says it takes time. You say it takes time. There isn't enough time in this world. It's not going to happen. You know it. I know it."

"Don't be silly, Katherine," he said. "You're doing beautifully. It won't be long."

"It'll be never," she said. "Watch. Just watch." The music was still playing. She spun out alone. She was going to dance a pas seul, and we would see. The glissade was nice, effortless, and for a moment it seemed that Katie was wrong. Pas de bourrée. Easy. An arabesque, and now there was a slight wavering. She couldn't hold it as she once had. With the music, she tried a pirouette on her good leg, and something was missing. Back to glissades, and then she did what she should not have tried. She lifted off into a jeté and landed on her right leg. It buckled, couldn't sustain her. She collapsed and lay sprawled on the floor.

Both Terry and I ran to her. "Are you all right? For god's sake, did you hurt yourself?"

She was sobbing, in anger and pain and frustration, though more in anger and frustration than in pain. She pounded the floor with her fists. "No," she said, her voice muffled and broken. "I'm not all right. I'll never be all right."

"Are you hurt?"

"Yes, I hurt inside. That's where I hurt. I can't do it. Not anything. I'll never be able to do it again. Not ever like I used to."

There was nothing we could say. We both believed her then. We both knew it, and we knew there was no way we could lie to her and make her believe she was wrong.

She lay there, and we stood across her body, looking at each other, Terry about to cry. He turned away so she wouldn't see him. She got up after a while, felt her right leg, stretched it, and limped back to the couch. She bent over the sketches, pointing things out to Terry as though nothing had occurred, taking a pencil and redrawing some of the steps, some of the moves. He nodded approval. She sighed. "I suppose I can always teach," she said. "I think I'm a good teacher. Maybe in time I can even learn to choreograph."

"You have the feel," Terry said.

I felt awful. I went into the kitchen and made some coffee

and sandwiches. They took a break, and we ate. We carefully avoided talking about what had happened. And we felt stifled. We had to get out of there, out into the air. Terry suggested a ride. Just drive around on a beautiful Sunday afternoon. So we got into his car and started heading nowhere. And then I said, suddenly, on a whim, "We need a car."

Katie turned, looked at me, and nodded. "We need a car. Can we do it?"

"We can do it," I said, and believed it. "We've got some money now. And out here you have to have a car. We can't keep sponging off Phil."

We would have an adventure, at least. We would spend the rest of the day car shopping, and if we were lucky, we would find something cheap and drivable.

Terry drove, and we cruised along Olympic and Pico and some of the avenues heading out toward the airport, stopping at used-car lots wherever we saw them. We saw a lot of cars that should have been put through the compactor. We drove a few that looked all right on the outside but didn't sound or drive all right on the road, cars where it was obvious nobody had bothered to touch anything under the hood and where somebody had certainly turned back the odometer.

Early on, we had seen one car at a foreign-car lot on Olympic. We had looked at it briefly, decided it would be too dumb and frivolous to even consider, and had gone on. Two or three times, we had driven past. It was always there. Late, when it was dark and the lots were beginning to close, we passed again. What the hell, I said, let's at least take a look. We haven't seen anything we'd want to buy. It won't hurt. It might even be fun.

It stood there on the lot. An MG-TD. British racing green. A few dents, but not many. The tires looked new. The leather seats were a little worn, but soft and not cracked, obviously cared for. Under the hood, the engine was a little dirty, but not too dirty, no sign of an oil leak or a cracked block or anything, nothing visibly wrong. In the boot, there was a canvas top in fair condition. The price scrawled in white crayon across the window didn't seem that outrageous. We looked at each other. Skeptical. Shook our heads.

"Dumb," Katie said.

"Dumb," I agreed.

"Smart," Terry said. We looked at him. He was smiling, delighted.

A salesman, hot, tired, wanting nothing but to go home unless it was to make a quick and effortless sale, and sure we were only browsing, not buying, watched us from a distance. The longer we stood over that car, moved around it, examined everything about it carefully, the harder he watched. Finally, he shrugged, sighed, and walked slowly toward us. He asked if he could help.

I asked if we might test-drive the MG.

He said, "Why not?" He went to the shed that was the office and returned with the keys, flipped them to me, and climbed into the passenger seat, the left side. I got behind the wheel. He asked if I knew how to drive an MG. I assured him I did. We took off and drove a couple of miles through the area. He yammered away about the sterling features of the car and was so insistent that I was sure there must be something wrong with it. But I couldn't find much. And by then I didn't really care.

When we got back to the lot, I handed the keys to Katie, kept a straight face. She saw my eyes. She got in, drove away, was back in about fifteen minutes. Her face was sober, but she had that look in her eyes.

The salesman watched us, couldn't read us. He asked what we thought.

I said it seemed a nice enough car. But it had a lot of mileage, and given the car's age, I was sure this must be the second time around.

He swore those were the original miles. Nobody had ever touched the odometer.

There was a little ping in the engine, and second gear seemed to stick.

Nothing to worry about, he said. The mechanic could fix that in no time.

The engine looked pretty dirty.

If we really wanted the car, he said, they'd steam clean the engine. They'd go over the whole car from stem to stern. They'd replace the plugs and points. They'd tune the engine. They'd change the oil. They'd put in coolant. They'd do everything that had to be done. They'd fix those little dents I pointed out. Hell, they'd even simonize the car so it would look like new. But we'd have to make up our minds now. It was getting late. It was about time to close up. If we'd buy now, they'd do it all. But if we waited, he couldn't promise, he couldn't even be sure the car would still be there another day.

I looked at Katie. She looked at me. He still couldn't read what we were thinking. He got anxious. He said, "Look, let me go talk to the boss. Maybe I can persuade him to knock five hundred off the price if you buy right now." He walked away, went back into the shed, and returned immediately with an older man, the Smiling Jack whose image, giant sized, loomed over the lot. He talked fast, and most of what he said I couldn't understand, and I was sure I'd seen him giving the same pitch on one of the local television stations. He started to sweat. The salesman was sweating even more. Terry said it was getting late and maybe we ought to be going. We could always come back another time.

Smiling Jack said when we came back, if we didn't make a deal right then, a lot of the promises would be withdrawn, and the car certainly was going to be gone.

Terry asked if he'd like to make book on that.

Tears welled in Smiling Jack's eyes. They flowed down the salesman's cheeks. Smiling Jack sighed. He said we

looked like a nice couple. He said he was going to do a favor
for us. He said how could he not do a favor for such a
beautiful young lady who had obviously been in an accident
of some kind, what with the cane and all. He said he'd cut
the price by three hundred. He looked at us. Katie looked
at me. We hesitated.

The salesman broke in. He told Smiling Jack he'd told us
maybe he could get the price down by four hundred.

I said, "You said five hundred."

He sighed. He said, "That's right, I promised five." His
cheeks were even wetter.

Smiling Jack glared at him. Smiling Jack said it would
come out of the salesman's pocket. Smiling Jack said, "A
promise is a promise." Smiling Jack asked did we want the
car or didn't we.

We both took deep breaths. We both grinned. We both
said we'd take it. Everybody smiled. Everybody shook
hands. We went into the office. We signed a lot of papers
as Smiling Jack filled them out. We wrote out a check as a
down payment. He didn't even ask that it be certified. He
asked if we wanted to get our own financing for the balance
or would we like him to finance it.

I figured our credit rating must be zero then, and so we
told him what the hell, he could do all the paperwork if that
would speed things up. He smiled broadly at that. He did
some figuring and showed us some numbers. I wasn't dumb
enough not to see that he was going to get a couple of
percentage points more than a bank would charge, but since
we wouldn't be able to borrow from a bank, anyway, what
the hell. I reminded him of the promise of a tune-up, a
checkup, a simonize, and all the rest. He swore it would be
done. He said they'd arrange for the license and registration
and all the rest. We shook hands. He told us we wouldn't
be sorry. I asked if there was any kind of guarantee; his
eagerness had sowed a little doubt, and I was wondering just
what was really wrong with the car; as we later found out,

there wasn't anything wrong, not that we ever discovered.

He said of course there was a guarantee. All his cars were guaranteed for thirty days.

I asked when we could have it.

He looked at the check. He looked at us. He looked at the salesman. He said, "Thursday."

"We were dumb," I said when we were back in Terry's car.

"We were stupid," Katie agreed.

"You were brilliant," Terry said. "It's a darling car. It was made for Katherine."

We decided to go somewhere to celebrate and stopped at a steak house along LaCienega. When Katie was dancing, she could eat about twice as much as anyone else. Since the accident, she had hardly eaten at all. That evening, she devoured her steak and then ate some of mine.

7

On Thursday, after Stuart departed, I did not go back to the typewriter as usual. I walked down to Olympic and then took the bus to Smiling Jack's, signed some more papers, shook hands with the smiling one and the salesman, watched the mechanic screw on the license plates, opened the hood and looked at the engine, and walked around the car. As far as I could see, they had done everything they promised. I was surprised. I thanked everyone, got into the car, and drove away.

I had to drive it a little, enjoy it for a time. I drove out to the beach at Santa Monica. It was a cloudy day, a little chill, and there weren't many people on the sands. I sat in the car and looked out over the Pacific. You couldn't see Catalina; you couldn't see much with the lowering clouds. I drove on up the Pacific Coast Highway to the end of Malibu, unable as always to understand why houses practically touching each other were so dear. I turned and headed back, crossed the mountains through Benedict Canyon, slid down into the valley, and finally arrived at the Burbank lot. I parked in the visitor's lot.

It was still early, so I wandered around, came to the administration building where Garland had his office. He was in conference, his secretary said. She couldn't possibly disturb him.

That was all right. I'd just taken the chance he might have a minute since I was on the lot, anyway. I told her to tell him I'd stopped by and would be in touch later.

Just as I was turning to leave, an inner door opened, and he appeared, in his shirt-sleeves, his tie pulled down, bending to talk to a smaller man who looked familiar. Garland glanced up, saw me, waved, and said, "Harry, for chrissake, what the hell are you doing out here?" He came forward with the other man and made a brief introduction. I knew why the face was familiar; he was one of the most successful and most sought after directors of the moment. Garland nodded to him and said something about how he'd bear that in mind, turn it over, and then get back. He shook hands, then took my arm and led me into his office. His secretary started to protest. He had another appointment in ten minutes. He waved that away.

If the office was not up to the photographs one has seen of the lairs of the old-time movie moguls, it was, nevertheless, impressive in both size and furnishings. But what particularly intrigued me, though I made no comment, was that, on a larger and grander scale, it could have passed for the office of the publisher back in New York. Some things don't die, or if they die, they die hard.

He smiled at me, motioning to a chair. "Not going formal today?" he said. I was wearing old khakis and a plaid shirt, what I usually wear when I work. "What brings you around?" he asked.

I said I had come out to pick up Katie.

He looked at me narrowly. "Since when do you have wheels?"

"Since a couple of hours ago."

"Why the hell didn't you tell me you were in the market? I'd have gotten you a deal."

I said we hadn't thought we were in the market. We'd just gone out Sunday afternoon on a whim and had ended up buying.

"Where?"

I told him where.

He said, "Smiling Jack's? Are you out of your head? Don't you know that guy's the biggest crook in town?"

I said I thought we'd actually gotten a pretty good deal. He'd knocked five hundred off the price.

"That means he only made twice what the car's worth and what he expected. Are you sure it's got an engine?"

I said I'd driven it for a while that day and it was running fine.

He said, "Wait a week. I hope the bastard gave you some kind of guarantee."

"A month," I said.

"Well, there's that. But I'll make book that on the thirty-second day the damn thing'll fall apart. What the hell is it, anyway?"

I told him.

He said, "An MG? No wonder you guys don't have a pot to piss in. I suppose you're going to let Katie drive it."

I said of course, so she wouldn't need his car and driver any longer.

He sighed. He asked me to give him the license-plate number. I dug through my pockets, found the registration, and read it off to him. He jotted down the numbers, then flicked a switch on the intercom. When his secretary responded, he told her to have a parking permit issued to the MG, read her the license number, and said the permit should be ready and waiting by the time we left. "And, Mary," he said, "have somebody find a good spot for it by Building Four. Have them mark it reserved for Katherine Summers.

I want it there when she gets here in the morning." He flicked off the intercom, then looked at me and grinned. "Okay? Satisfied?"

"Sure," I said.

"Power and position have their rewards."

"Not like the old days."

"In the old days," he said, "we didn't have position, and we sure as hell didn't have power."

We talked for a few minutes about inconsequentials. He looked at his watch a few times, and I started to get up to leave. He asked, without too much interest, how things were going with Charlie Stuart. I shrugged and said they were going. He laughed and said Stuart had told him they were going beautifully and as soon as the script was done, he'd give Garland first crack. "I can hardly wait," he said.

We were both standing, starting for the door. He suddenly laughed. I asked him what was so funny. He said did I know that Katie had an admirer?

I said that after his party I was sure she had plenty of admirers.

He said, "One in particular. And you know him."

I looked at him. I said she hadn't mentioned anything. Who was he?

He said, "Charlie Stuart." He said Stuart was following her around like a pet dog. He was hanging around the rehearsal studio every afternoon, running into her as if by accident. He'd even taken her to lunch one day.

I said she hadn't mentioned it.

He said no reason to. It obviously didn't mean a thing. Besides, a lot of guys had fallen for her, and I'd better get used to it. And then he added, by the way, when were Katie and I free, because he wanted us to come to dinner.

I said, "You mean like the last time, with a hundred other people trying to monopolize her?"

He laughed, said, "Not this time. Just you and Katie."

I said, "That would be fine. Give us a ring. We're usually free."

He said, "Why not make a date right now?" He walked back to the desk, flicked the intercom, and asked his secretary to check his book and see what nights he had free. She paused, came back, and said he was booked every night but a week from Wednesday. He looked at me. I nodded. He said, "Put the Millers down for that night." She said his next appointment was waiting.

He came out from behind the desk, put his arm around my shoulder and led me to the door, opened it, and said good-bye and he'd see us soon. Then he moved quickly to welcome the next appointment. She was an old-time star who hadn't worked much lately. She looked a lot better and younger on the screen than close up.

Katie drove home. It had begun to drizzle, but we didn't put the top up; we left it in the boot. I suggested we get it out. She refused. The fine mist sprayed across her hair, darkening it, dampening it, making the fine strands cling like silk to her wet face. Every once in a while, she wiped them away with an impatient hand, but otherwise ignored them, seemed to enjoy the rain. And she enjoyed the driving. She was exhilarated. She drove with sureness and speed and laughter. She was as happy as I had seen her in a long time.

On Sunday, I played golf with Charlie Stuart. He had put it off a couple of times, and then I was sure he had completely forgotten. At least I hoped so. But the Friday before, he reminded me, and so there was no way out. He picked me up before eight that Sunday and drove us out to the club, where he arranged for me to borrow a set of clubs and a pair of shoes. We went over to the practice tee, and after he'd watched me swing ineptly a few times, he walked away, came back with an assistant pro, and then stood back and watched while I had a half-hour lesson. It was rudimentary, the pro trying to teach me how to stand and how to hold the club and swing, telling me to keep my head down, my left arm stiff, stay down to the ball, move through it, swing easy, don't try to kill it. He said I ought to take a series of lessons, because I had a feel for the game. I doubted that. I only hoped I wouldn't make a complete ass of myself and that Stuart was as much of a hacker as I thought he probably was.

We teed off. Stuart's drive wasn't long, but it was right in the middle of the fairway. My drive was a lot longer, but it hooked deep into the rough, and it took five minutes to find the ball while an impatient foursome back on the tee glared and, finally, played through. That's the way it went for eighteen holes, until we finished early in the afternoon. I, at least, got some exercise. I walked, and I swung the club a lot. Stuart rode the cart. He wasn't very long, but he was straight, and he had a touch around the greens. I hooked and sliced, was all over the course, lost a half-dozen balls, and grew increasingly frustrated. He laughed a lot. About the only positive note was that I managed to hit the ball, didn't whiff at it. Stuart shot an 83, which, he said, was right on his eleven handicap. I stopped trying to keep score about the fourth hole and wouldn't let him keep it for me, so I have no idea what I shot and certainly had no desire to know.

"I'm humiliated," I said on the way home.

"Bullshit," he said. "You did okay for a guy who hasn't played since he was a kid. You should see some of the old farts around the club, and some of them ain't so old, either. You could beat the pants off of them, even today."

"That'll be the day," I said. "But you're damn good."

"For an old man?" He laughed. "Yeah, I'm pretty good. But let me tell you, it cost a bundle to be able to shoot a decent round. I can't begin to tell you the lessons. But I love

the goddamn game, and I play it a lot. That's what it takes.
Lessons and practice and playing. We got to do this some
more."

"Never."

"I'll change your mind," he said, grinning.

To be polite, I asked him in when we reached the apartment. He agreed immediately. The moment we were
through the door, he looked around eagerly, then smiled
with obvious relief. Katie was on the couch, going through
choreography diagrams, pencil in her mouth. She looked
up, smiled at me, smiled at him. There was a difference in
the smiles.

She got up and made some coffee, and we sat around. She
asked about the day. He said it had been just great. He said
I was a natural golfer, just needed a few lessons and some
practice. I told him he lied through his teeth. We all laughed.

He stayed for about an hour, until even he couldn't miss
that Katie was becoming impatient, her eyes straying to the
diagrams littering the couch. He got up then, started for the
door, said how great it had been, and then paused and looked
around. "You know," he said, "this place is a real dump, a
shit hole, if you'll excuse my English. I don't know how you
can stand it."

I looked at him, surprised. "It's not so bad," I said.

"I wouldn't wish it on my worst enemy," he said.

"We're happy here," Katie said.

"You can be happy someplace else," he said. "Someplace
fit for humans. You want, I'll find you a nice place, maybe
Beverly Hills, maybe Westwood, maybe West Hollywood,
someplace worth living in. You'd like that."

"Thanks, Charlie," I said. "We appreciate it. We really
do. But I don't think so."

Katie turned slowly and looked at me. I couldn't read the
expression, and this time I couldn't read the eyes.

Stuart was amazed. "Why not?" he demanded. "You in
love with this dump? I'll find you something ten times, a

thousand times, better, and it won't cost you an arm and a leg."

"It's not that," I said. I was watching her, not him. The way she was standing, the way she was watching me, I had a very uncomfortable feeling.

"Then what?" he demanded.

"It would be senseless," I said. "When I finish this thing for you and when Katie finishes working on the picture, we're going back to New York." I hadn't said that before. I hadn't said it to her. But I had been thinking about it for a time and had grown convinced it was something we had to do. Very little right had happened to us since we had been here.

"I don't believe it," he said. "Why would you want to do a stupid thing like that?"

Katie wasn't saying anything. I didn't like that. I said, "I don't know whether I can explain it. I just don't feel we belong out here. We miss New York. We miss the East. It's where we belong."

"That's what you say now," he said, and he looked angry, disbelieving. "You'll change your mind."

"I don't think so," I said.

"I know so," he said. "And when you do, all you have to do is whistle and I'll work something out for you. Because I mean it. Maybe you don't think so, but you kids belong out here. This is where it's happening. And if you're going to be out here, you got to have a decent place to live. But, what the hell, I won't argue now. Let it lay. Think about it. The offer's always open."

He left a few minutes after that. I walked him out to his car. Katie stood in the doorway, silently watching us, then turned away. When I got back into the house, she was on the couch, going through the sketches. For a few minutes she didn't say anything. Then she looked up at me. She stared. She said, "Did you really mean that?"

"Mean what?"

"About going back to New York."

"Of course."

"Why?" she asked.

"Don't you know?"

"No," she said slowly. "I don't know. What do you think is in New York?"

"Whatever it is, it's better than here."

"For who?"

"For both of us."

She looked at me. She shook her head very slowly. "Not for me," she said.

I started, looked hard at her.

"What would I do if I went back?" she said.

"What you always did."

"Not anymore," she said. "I can't dance anymore. So what would I do back there?"

"It seems like a good idea," I said. "It's what I want to do. I think it's best for both of us. Like I told Charlie, we don't belong out here. This isn't our kind of place, whatever that means. I can't explain it. But I think you understand."

"No," she said, "I don't understand. What would you do back in New York that you can't do here? Go back to the paper?"

"No," I said. "That's done with, even if they'd have me back, which I doubt. You know how they feel about guys who leave."

"Then what would you do that you have to go back?"

"What I do. Write."

"You can write here. You can write anywhere. All you need is your typewriter and a place to work."

"That's what I used to think. I'm not so sure anymore."

"What about me?"

It was a question I hadn't thought about, really. I had just assumed it would be as it had been. That was wrong, of course. It couldn't ever be that way again for her. I said, "What about kids? We've talked about it. Maybe we ought to."

"If we want kids, we can have them here. We don't have to be in New York to do that."

"Are you saying you want to stay here? You really want to stay out here?"

"Yes," she said. "I want to stay. I'm doing something now, and I'm good at it. It's not dancing, but I'll never dance again. I know that. But I like what I'm doing. And everything's just starting for me out here. It's all new, and I like it, I'm excited by it. I'm having a good time. Maybe I'm even starting to believe the things Phil Garland and others are telling me. But that doesn't make any difference. I just know I want to stay. This is where I belong. So I want you to tell that man, Charlie Stuart, to do what he offered. You tell him to find us a nice place to live."

I bristled. I glared at her. "You want me to ask that man for a favor? Bullshit. That I won't do."

"Then I'll do it," she said.

"Like hell."

We had had our arguments and our fights and our battles before. Everybody does. They had generally been over unimportant things, things of the moment that passed quickly, and when they did, we always seemed to emerge stronger and surer. But in this there was a sense that we were dealing with something radically different.

She stood there, hands on her hips, unmoving, immovable. There had always been steel beneath that soft, seemingly vulnerable, glowing surface. She could never had done the things she did, have been so dedicated and sure and driven, have gotten as far as she had, if it hadn't been there. Now it was out in the open, unconcealed, in her eyes, in her face, in the rigid posture, in everything about her.

We glared at each other from opposite ends of the room. There was, at that moment, nothing more to say. I turned, slammed out the door, and began to walk. It was still light, and I walked a long way for a long time, into the dark and the night, not knowing where I was going, where I was, not caring, walking into exhaustion. At intervals, patrol cars passed, slowed as the cops inside took long, examining looks, then cruised past. Pedestrians on deserted streets at night in that city were not a common sight, and so I was somehow suspect.

We had, I came slowly to understand during that walk, been fighting and arguing not about a choice between New York and L.A. That had been a surface thing, though it had brought into a sharp focus the differences between us, differences we had known and recognized and understood before but which had always united rather than divided us, which had complemented each other. I am a private man working alone in a lonely profession. There are times, at the end of long days bound to a typewriter and chair, staring at pages on which words come slowly if at all, when the loneliness suddenly becomes intolerable. It is then that I seek out people I know in the watering holes, share a drink, share some talk, about shared loneliness, about anything or nothing, and in those moments the despair of the anchorite is briefly allayed. But, as I have said, I do not make friends easily, and so those I make I come to treasure. The friends I had made, with whom I felt a closeness and an ease, with whom I could talk and reveal even small pieces of myself, were mainly in the East, and I missed them. I had made few friends in the West who shared that common bond with me. Those I knew, mainly on the papers downtown, I felt a deep reluctance to see because of what I imagined as my failures. So I saw regularly only Stuart during the day and Katie later, and if Katie was everything to me, she was still not enough; she could not fill that empty place.

But Katie was gregarious. Her days were filled with people who shared interests and careers and dreams and talents with her. She made friends easily and attracted strangers with a facility I envied and could not find in myself or completely comprehend. She could be anywhere and within hours would know everyone and they would know her, and there would be a dozen strangers who were strangers no longer, who considered her a close friend and even a confidante. As long as she was fulfilled in what she was doing, the place did not matter, nor, perhaps, even the people, for there were always new people to captivate her interest and attention; the life of the performer, dancer, actor, whatever, is, after all, a life of constantly changing circles, of a steady parade of new people and new friends.

That was the surface, and we had long recognized it and, certainly back in New York, had come to terms with it and seen how we could both use what the other had. But now we were facing something deeper and potentially destructive. Without our sensing it, it seemed that our values and our goals were beginning to change and we had begun to drift along diverging paths. If unchecked, if not sensed and dealt with, that drift could turn into a race, and the paths would veer ever more sharply away from each other. We had all that we shared, and we had our love, to turn the paths back toward each other, to stop the drift. We would have to fix firmly on that. It had to be enough. I could not imagine, and I could not abide, the thought of a life without her. I did not think it possible to exist separate and without her.

The house was dark when I got home. She was in bed, huddled on the far side, at the very edge of the mattress. I undressed. I reached out to touch her. She did not move.

8 Resolves made in the dark of night are often put aside in the light of day. We think then that perhaps it is better to do nothing, to let time and events heal the wounds, than take a chance by precipitous action. So it was with me. I did not know what, if any, resolves Katie had made during that long night. She said nothing. If we did not pretend the next morning that nothing had happened, still we did not act toward each other as though the issue had been a serious one, had been anything more than one of those minor disturbances that would heal itself and vanish. But there was a constraint that had never been there before. I felt it, and I was sure so did she. There were moments when I felt an aching desire to reach out to her, to say something. I kept my silence.

A few days later, when Stuart arrived for our morning's labors, he announced, with a kind of strained casualness, that he had run into Katherine (he always called her that, never Katie) at the studio the afternoon before (and he always referred to it as the studio, never the lot, which may have been the term reserved for the newer breed; they were separated by so many things, the old wave and the new, even by terminology). I did not smile; he was, after all, always running into her out there, and not by accident. She had even begun to tell me of it, finding it humorous, not annoying, he was so ingenuous. But this was the first time he had mentioned it.

"She said it would be okay if I went ahead," he said.

"Okay about what?"

"About looking for a new place for you kids."

I could feel the ice in my face, my body stiffening. "Go slow, Charlie," I said.

He looked at me for a long moment. "You mean it ain't okay?"

"Just go slow, that's all."

"Me and my big mouth," he said. "It's always getting somebody into hot water."

He dropped it then, did not return to it, and whether he did anything about it in the weeks to come, I never knew.

We went to work after that, but it was not a good session; he left early, and I had a lot of trouble concentrating the rest of the day.

We had a dinner invitation. The phone rang while I was working. The voice on the other end was a woman's, sounded middle-aged, sounded vaguely familiar, though I couldn't place it, and the name initially meant nothing.

"Mr. Miller," she said, "this is Helen Fitzmaurice. I hope you remember me."

I murmured something vague and noncommittal.

She said, "Of course you don't. You must have met so many people that evening. We met at Philip Garland's party. For a few moments we were a small island in the midst of that very large ocean of people. I thought we had a very pleasant conversation."

"Oh, yes," I said. The banker's wife.

She said, "I went to the library. They had only two of your books. I could hardly put them down."

I thanked her. I was also amused. I didn't think I wrote books that were unputdownable.

She said, "The reason I'm calling is that Mr. Fitzmaurice and I are having a few friends in for cocktails and dinner on Friday. Very informal. I know this is short notice, but we were hoping you and Mrs. Miller might be able to join us."

I hesitated. I said I thought we were free but I'd have to check with my wife.

She said she understood and could we let her know as soon as possible.

I said we certainly would.

Katie was dubious. She was working hard, and the hour with the therapist was a strain, and so sitting home and doing nothing in the evening had an irresistible attraction. She asked about the Fitzmaurices. I said all I knew was he was probably a banker, one of Garland's bankers. I had met Helen Fitzmaurice at the party, when she was otherwise engaged, and we'd had a nice casual talk.

"Why do they want us?" she asked.

"Your guess is as good as mine."

"Do you want to go?"

"Not if you don't. We can always beg off."

"But you do want to go, don't you," she said.

"I suppose so. It'll sure be a change. We haven't met people like that before."

"All right," she said. "We'll go." She went to the phone, called and accepted, and received directions to a house in Brentwood.

Mrs. Fitzmaurice had said it was to be informal, but I had a feeling that informal with them meant not wearing tails or evening gowns. So I got out a suit again, and Katie put on one of the skirts and blouses from the wardrobe she had carefully accumulated back in New York. The skirt was soft and swirling like gossamer; it swirled ever more from the tight waist, made even tighter and smaller by a wide black belt, and she looked not only as if she were floating but as if she were so fragile a breeze might lift and waft her away. The only debate was whether or not she should take her cane. She wasn't using it much any longer, didn't need it most of the time, but after long, hard days when fatigue sent spasms of pain shooting down her leg, it seemed almost indispensable, and that had been one of those long and hard Fridays. She held it, looked at it, sighed, and finally decided she ought to take it.

On the way to Brentwood, she said, "The Fitzmaurices are collectors."

I glanced over at her. "Really? What do they collect?"

"Suzie wouldn't tell me. She said we'd find out soon enough."

"What else did she say?"

"Nothing."

Despite the rather detailed directions, we managed to get lost, made a few wrong turns, finally retraced our route, and found the house on the second try. It was a large antebellum mansion, white pillars and all, set on a rolling lawn. I suppose it might have looked just right at Tara or on some southern plantation. The inside of the house matched the outside, so you had the feeling that if only you were dressed appropriately, you could have been in the Tidewater about 1850. Helen Fitzmaurice collected American art of the first half of the nineteenth century; there were portraits and landscapes everywhere, mainly southern in motif. She also collected early Wedgwood, and there was a lot of that around.

We were the last of the four couples to arrive, and we were by decades the youngest. The others were all in their mid-fifties to early sixties. Of the men, Fitzmaurice was a senior vice-president of Bank of America, another was his counterpart at Crocker National Bank, one was senior partner of a major downtown law firm, and the last was president of an aerospace company out in Pasadena. The woman were all what could only be defined as housewives; they had married young, had raised their children and sent them to the best schools and then out into the world, and now they spent their days on charities and culture and other good works. Being among them, I felt I had stepped back in time, to another era, to the years when I was growing up and people were sure they knew what and who they were and what was expected of them. They believed in the old verities and the old ways; they were comfortable and satisfied and wanted nothing more than what they had attained; and somehow they had managed to escape or ignore the dissatisfactions and urgencies and drives as well as the changes that have filled our decades and our lives.

The men drank martinis and the women Manhattans or whiskey sours, mixed and served by an elderly, unobtrusive black man in a white jacket. A young black woman in a white uniform-dress served hors d'oeuvres. The cocktail time lasted an hour, and then we moved into the dining room and ate a pleasant enough dinner, served by the same black pair.

There wasn't much talk about the movies, because nobody seemed very interested. Except for Katie and me, who were peripherally involved, and Carleton Fitzmaurice, who put his bank's money into films as an investment, nobody had any connection with the business, and they seemed just as happy about that. The men talked business and they talked politics, and they were all conservative Republicans. So there was a lot of praise heaped on Richard Nixon, whom apparently they all knew personally, and how he was finally putting the country back on the right road and undoing what Johnson and Kennedy and Truman and FDR had done to wreck the country. It had been a long time since I had sat in on that kind of conversation, and since it was obvious by the look on my face that I disagreed with just about everything they said, they kept piling it on and kept trying to draw me in and, I thought, see just how long it would be before I exploded. I managed to hold myself, though, and I think they were disappointed.

As conversations invariably did in those days, the talk naturally turned to the war. There wasn't a man in the room who didn't believe, and say, that if you got yourself into a war, then you damned well ought to fight it to win, and if you weren't going to do that, then you damned well ought to get out and save what you could, though you had to make sure you got out with your honor intact. Nixon, they proclaimed, was on the right track, at last, in getting us extricated from the mess in the Asia. They all, however, would have wished it another way. As the lawyer said, "What we should have done in the first place was what somebody suggested, I think it was Ron Reagan. We should have paved over the whole damn place and turned it into the world's biggest parking lot."

I said, mildly, "Actually, if you've been there, you begin to think that's precisely what we've been doing."

The look they turned on me said they all knew I had been there and just what I had been doing. But the aerospace guy said, "You were there?"

I said yes.

He asked if I'd been in the army.

I said no, I'd been a reporter.

And, of course, they began to talk about reporters and the press and the garbage that was being fed to the public. Somebody said, "I suppose when you went over there, they told you exactly what you were supposed to write."

I said yes, they had; they had told me to write what I saw and what I learned. That was all. And that's what I had done, and as far as I knew, that's what everyone else had done and was still doing.

The lawyer got a little testy and said one of my problems, and obviously the problem with most of the reporters, was that we never took the larger view. We didn't understand what was at stake. We concentrated on the little things and the little people and ignored all the major issues, and so we distorted what was really going on.

I said maybe he was right, but I had always thought that what happened to people in a war somehow transcended the larger issues. If there wasn't anybody left when a war was over and everything had been destroyed, then what was the use of the war? We argued about that until the women decided it was time for us to stop and join them.

Katie's cane, of course, had been noticed as soon as we arrived, but she passed it off as only an affectation these days, a hangover from an accident she'd had. Helen Fitzmaurice kept watching her. Sometime during the evening, she said, "My dear, I know you. I mean, I've seen you before. And I don't mean at Philip Garland's party."

Katie smiled, shrugged, and said she didn't think that likely since we hadn't been in California long and we hadn't circulated much.

Helen Fitzmaurice said, "No, no. I don't mean out here. Now, let me think." Her face worked; everyone waited. Her face brightened. I remembered what she had said to me at the party. She said, "Of course. I've seen you dance." And then she rushed through an explanation. She and Carleton made trips to New York several times a year. She was a devotee of the ballet; Carleton, of course, really didn't care much for dance, but then, most men don't, do they? (He snorted agreement with that.) So while he was busy in the evening, she always went to the ballet. "I saw you in *The Fire Bird*, last year, I'm sure, or the year before. Oh, other ballets, too. Remember, Carleton," and she turned to her husband, "I came home and said I'd seen this exquisite dancer with red hair. I told you I couldn't understand why she wasn't dancing the lead, she was so much better than—Oh, what was her name? Don't you remember?"

He shrugged. As she had said, he wasn't much interested

in ballet. He had an opinion about the kind of men who were, and he obviously never listened when his wife talked about dance. But the way his eyes kept roving over Katie, I had the impression that for just once, he thought he might have missed something. He smiled at her. He said, "Are you dancing now? If you are, I think I might even be persuaded to attend."

"Carleton," Helen Fitzmaurice said, a warning in her voice.

"I don't dance anymore," Katie said.

He stared at her, and so did everyone else. Even Helen Fitzmaurice, who had noticed the cane, was shocked. "Oh, my dear," she said, "but you must."

"I was in an accident," Katie said. "I broke my leg."

"But it's healing. You said the cane—that you were nearly well."

"Yes," Katie said. "But not for dancing."

"But of course that's only temporary."

"No, it's permanent."

"Oh, my dear. What ever will you do now?"

"I'm trying to do some choreography," Katie said.

"How nice," Helen Fitzmaurice said. The way she said it, you knew she was sure choreography had ended with Diaghilev and Fokine, though maybe Tudor and Balanchine may have added a few modern tricks. Then she brightened. "Of course, you must fill your time. But now, if you're not dancing, you should have children."

Carleton Fitzmaurice laughed a little too loudly. "That's Helen's solution to the problems of the world. Children."

"There's nothing wrong with children," she said. "You ought to know. You have three of your own."

"Don't remind me," he said.

There was a lot of talk about children for a while, and then about other things, and a lot of quizzing of us about dance and books and more, and by about eleven, as though someone had rung a bell, everyone started to move toward the door. We thanked the Fitzmaurices and said we'd enjoyed ourselves.

Helen Fitzmaurice bent toward me and said, "Did I mention that I took your books from the library?"

I said she had.

"I liked them very much," she said. "I could hardly put them down. I hope you're writing another one."

I said I was trying.

She said I must promise to let her know as soon as it was published and she'd be sure to buy a copy if I promised to autograph it especially for her.

She turned to Katie and, with intimacy, said she hoped Katie would really consider what had been said. Children, she said again, can fill your life and make you forget all the things you once were so certain were important.

We got into the car and drove away from antebellum and Brentwood. "I'm proud of you," she said. "You didn't lose your temper."

"I did," I said. "A couple of times."

"It didn't show."

"You weren't close enough."

"At least you didn't shout."

"No, I didn't do that." I sighed. "My fault."

"Why?"

"I was the one who said we ought to go."

"I didn't say no." She suddenly started to laugh. "I know what Suzie meant."

"About what?"

"Collectors."

I laughed. "I suppose they can hang us on the wall, too."

"Along with the paintings and the Wedgwood." She choked on a laugh. "Did you see the one in the bathroom?"

I could hardly control the car. "The couple?"

"Their eyes followed you."

"I know. I was sure they were watching me."

"I didn't know they painted things like that back then."

"They probably didn't."

"You know," she said, "if I ever considered having children, and, Harry, I've been thinking about it, what that woman said to me tonight would be enough to banish the idea forever."

"Not quite forever, I hope."

She smiled. "No, not forever."

"You must let them know when you dance again."

"Of course. And you must autograph your next book especially for her."

"Naturally. Maybe I'll even dedicate it to her."

"You said it would be a change. You said we hadn't met people like them before, not out here. You were right."

"Yes, I was right."

"If she calls again—"

"We'll be otherwise engaged. Of course, what makes us think she'll call again."

"She'll call," Katie said. "Because we're so bright . . ."

"And entertaining . . ."

"And different . . ."

"And collectible."

It was all so nasty. It was the most fun we'd had that night.

9

Phil Garland kept his promise. When we reached his house the following Wednesday evening, in our MG this time, not in one of his limousines, owned or hired, there were only Katie and me and Garland and Suzie Willens. She was, as I was discovering through Katie, a lot smarter and a lot sharper than one would have thought looking at her.

Katie didn't bring her cane. It had gone into the closet the night we got home from the Fitzmaurices', and she had sworn it would never come out again, even if she had to crawl from one place to another. Garland spotted its absence immediately. "Where's the ubiquitous stick?" he asked.

"I've given it up."

"For good?"

"For good and all."

"Let me see you walk," he demanded.

She shrugged, then walked across the room and back.

"Okay," he said. "I can't even spot a limp."

"It's there," she said. "I'm just learning to hide it. But it will go, too."

"Dance?"

She shook her head. "No," she said. "Not again. Never again. I'm trying to get resigned to that, so I keep saying it to myself. 'Katie, you're not going to dance again. Forget dancing. It's not for you.' It's hard. But I have to do it." She smiled at Suzie. "Suzie can always dance for me."

Suzie laughed sarcastically. "Fat chance," she said. "You picked the wrong number. I may be a lot of things, but a dancer sure isn't one of them." She looked at Garland. "And you're the one who told me it was going to be a breeze. Just follow directions." She looked at me. "Do you know what that guy said? He said I'd fade into the bunch. The way I move, I'd fade into the bunch like an apple fades into a bunch of bananas."

I looked at her. "That," I said, "is not the only reason you stand out."

She grinned at me. "You think I didn't notice you that one time watching me?"

"How could I help it?"

"Because of this?" She tapped her chest. "No way, man. It was because I was so lousy." Then suddenly she grinned. "You know, we've never even met. I'm Suzie."

"And I'm Harry. And I've heard about you. In fact, I keep hearing about you."

"Not as much as I hear about you. And I'll give you odds on that."

I liked her. The better I got to know her, the more I liked her, and the more I wondered whether Garland knew what he had living in his house with him. She could be fun, and she could be funny, serious and sardonic, wise and foolish, depending on the moment and the relevancy. Her judgments of people, including herself, were sharp and insightful. She understood her own limitations, but that didn't stop her from trying to overcome them, witness that she was, as she had said, still basically inept as a dancer, but she kept on trying, never gave up, and improved steadily; she would never be very good, but she would no longer be the worst, either. Perhaps, most important, was that she had come to adore Katie.

That evening, though they had left each other only a few hours before, they immediately went off into a corner and fell into the patter of shop talk. And Garland and I talked old times, through drinks and on into dinner prepared by his extraordinary cook; just how extraordinary I had no idea until I tasted her food. She had made a cold soup with just a hint of saffron; a salad of five different kinds of lettuce with a dressing she called vinaigrette but that was like no vinaigrette I had ever tasted; lobsters flown in from Maine that morning, shelled and steamed with oysters in a broth of wine and herbs, then put back into the shell; succulent berries with a flavor that defied taste, floating in a liqueur; and coffee from the Blue Mountain of Jamaica. A different wine was served with every course, from a small, exclusive California vineyard that he, Suzie noted, and he dismissed, owned a piece of and which catered to only a few very select customers.

We talked and we reminisced, and Suzie said with a resigned sigh, "It happens all the time. Whenever he's with somebody he used to know back then, all they do is talk about the good old days. You'd think they missed them and wanted them back."

"Not a chance," he said.

"Never," I agreed.

"Who'd want to go through all that crap again?"

"Nobody in his right mind."

"Long hours, hard work, lousy pay."

"Never sleeping in the same bed twice, if you even had a bed."

"Always on the move, rotten food when you had a chance to eat, and that wasn't often."

"New York never satisfied, demanding changes, more copy, answers to impossible questions, always five minutes before deadline."

"Being chased down a Mississippi highway by a pickup truck with five guys carrying loaded rifles, wondering if you'll get to see the sun rise."

"Being told by an Alabama sheriff you have five minutes to cross the bridge into the next county."

"Hiding behind a cop car on a Bed-Stuy corner in the middle of the night while some nut is sniping from a rooftop across the street and the whole damn place is burning down."

"Counting the body bags coming off a chopper on the pad at Chu-Lai."

"Trying to find someplace to hide from the incoming at Khe Sanh."

"Stumbling over what was left of a grunt who'd stepped on an APM near Cambodia."

"Who the hell would want to go through that again?"

"You'd have to be nuts."

"You're both nuts," Suzie said, "and you miss it."

"Right," Katie said. "They'd do anything to have it back."

"You're both crazy," we both said. And if we didn't mean it, still we meant it.

It wasn't until the coffee that there was any talk of business, and then it was Suzie who started it. Out of nowhere, into a momentary silence, she said to Garland, "Katie ought to be in a film. She's good. I can feel it. Everybody feels it. She'd be a natural."

"Her choice," Garland said. "She's been asked."

I looked toward her, and so did Suzie. She didn't look at either of us. "I can't act," she said.

"What difference does that make?" Garland said.

"If I can dance," Suzie said, "you can act."

"I won't do something I'm not good at," Katie said.

"Good? What the hell are you talking about?" Garland demanded. "Half the girls out here, half the guys, too, they can't act their way around the corner. Does that stop them? Like hell."

"It stops me," she said. "I won't do what I don't know how to do."

"A load of crap," he said. "This is the movies we're talking about. We're not talking about Broadway, off-Broadway, the goddamn legitimate theater. We're talking about the movies. A good director can make Sadie Klutz look like Ingrid Bergman. A good director, a good cutter, that's all you need. You want me to tell you how many Oscars have gone to fruitcakes with the talent of a dead lobster? It would take me all night."

"I'm not a fruitcake," she said, "and I've told you before, and I told Billy Fielding when he asked me, I'm a dancer—I was a dancer. I am not an actress, and I have no desire to be an actress."

"Do you think being an actress is so different from being a dancer? What do you do when you dance? You act, for chrissake."

"It's different. Yes, I act, with my body, with everything. But I do it as a dancer. I don't know how to use my voice like an actress. I don't know how to move or do anything like an actress. I'm not an actress."

"How do you know if you won't try?"

"I know. And what I don't understand is why you're trying so hard."

"Why? Because you've got something. Don't ask me what it is, but it's there. I know it. Suzie knows it. Everybody knows it. We all see it."

"I don't know what you're talking about," she said.

"You don't have to. All you have to do is believe it."

"Do you really think it's that easy? Do you think being a dancer is easy? Do you think anyone is born knowing how to dance? It takes work—my god, the work, the years of it, and the training, all your life, the training. You have to want it so much that you're willing to give up everything for it."

"Really?" he said. "Look at you. Everyone I've talked to says you were one of the best. And you didn't give up everything. You got married, didn't you, and I don't see that you've quite given up old Harry here."

"Yes, I fell in love, and I got married. And didn't I hear that I wasn't dedicated enough? And did I ever get the roles I should have danced?"

"Do you regret it?"

"That I didn't dance what I should have danced? Yes, I regret that. That I married Harry? No, I'll never have any regrets about that. I thought I could have both. I still think I could have had both."

"Okay. But now you say that part's over. The dancing. Okay. So now we're offering you another option. Take it, Katie."

"How can I possibly even think about it? I don't know if I have any talent that way. I certainly don't have any training. I know that being an actress, a good one, takes training just as it does to be a dancer. You can't do it in a week. And I won't make a fool of myself. Not for anyone."

"That's the last thing you have to worry about."

"It's the first thing."

"Then learn to act, for chrissake," he said. "Get yourself a coach. Go enroll in some classes, some good classes with the best people, if that's what you think you need. We'll even pay for it."

She stared at him, her face, her eyes, intense. She said very slowly, "Do you really mean that?"

"Damn right I mean it. And in the meantime, take the goddamn part in the goddamn picture. I've read it. You could do it in your sleep. Only you won't have to, because you'll have one of the best goddamn directors in the business to help you every step of the way. You can learn by doing."

"Listen to him, Katie," Suzie said. "Do it."

I could feel Katie wavering. "I don't know," she said, but in her voice there was the thing that said she did know.

"What's to know?" Garland persisted. "Let me put it another way. Let's be a little crass about it. Don't tell me you can't use the dough? I know what you're getting paid. And I know what Harry's getting for what he's doing. That and two fifty will buy you a ticket to the movies, if you pick one where they're showing reruns." He pressed at her. "A flea couldn't live on what the two of you are taking home."

"Say yes, Katie. For god's sake, say yes," Suzie said.

Say yes," Garland said, "and I'll get the word to Billy in the morning and he'll dance a goddamn jig."

"What about my dancers?" Katie asked then. "I'm good with them. I think I'm good for them. They're learning, and I want to stay with them and see them through."

"So, there's nothing to stop you from staying with them. You can pull down both jobs. It's been done. And you'll get to see your name up there on the screen, twice."

"I don't know," she said slowly. "Let me think about it."

"All right, so think about it. And you'll let me know in the morning. First thing."

"I will," she said. We knew, Garland and Suzie and I, the thinking had already been done and she had made her decision even if she wasn't ready to speak it at that exact moment.

"Jesus Christ," Garland said. "Can you really believe all this crap? Every day I've got a thousand girls and a thousand guys beating at my door begging me to give them a break, give them anything, a walk-on, a one-line bit in a film, anything to get them started. All I ever say is don't call me, I'll call you if and when I have something. This is the first damn time since I've been out here that I've had to practically get down on my knees and beg somebody to take a part. I ought to have my head examined. But you know what the shrink would say? Garland, you're one smart bastard."

We left soon after. When we reached the car, Katie held out her hand. "Do you mind if I drive?"

"Go ahead," I said, and handed her the keys. I've always thought of myself as a good driver, but she was better, and driving that car every day over the mountains, she had come to know all its idiosyncrasies, of which she had discovered more than a few, and how to deal with them. She started the car, pulled away from the curb, and drove expertly, obviously trying to free her mind of everything but the driving, concentrating intently on the road.

I sat beside her in silence, studying the expression on her face. It was absorbed, perhaps even angry, working. After a while, I said, "You didn't tell me." I didn't have to explain.

She was silent for a moment. Then, still not looking at me, staring straight ahead, she said, "There wasn't anything to tell. I didn't think they were serious."

"They were."

"I know. Now."

We didn't speak again until we got home, and then we didn't talk about the evening or what had happened or what it might mean for her and for us.

10 In the days and weeks that followed that evening at Garland's, we did not see much of each other, and when we did, Katie did not have much time for me. She left early for Burbank; I managed to get up before she left so we could at least have coffee together and a word or two. She spent her mornings with Terry Markoff and the dancers. Instead of lunch, she spent the noon hour with the acting coach the studio provided, who not only tried to teach her how to use her voice and how to act like an actress and not a dancer but also how to stop walking like a dancer, with her feet always in first position. Part of the afternoon was devoted to Terry and the musical arranger and director, working on the choreography as more and more of her ideas were finding their way into the dance sequences; the rest of the afternoon she worked on her scenes with an assistant director, and sometimes with Billy Fielding himself, and with other members of the cast. (She didn't know it, and I found out only later when Garland told me, but her part had not existed in the original screenplay. Fielding had seen her one day when he happened in on a dance rehearsal, had watched her and not the dancers, had gone to John Bedoric, the producer, and then to Garland and insisted that he must have her, that a role had to be written in for her. He had spelled it out, a small role with a crucial dramatic impact; since the film centered around the world of the ballet, the idea had not seemed outlandish, and so the role was written in, of a dancer who dies after a tragic accident on the eve of what would have been her first major triumph, her place then taken by the young star of the picture, who proceeds to dance her way to glory. It was, in variations, the theme of a hundred films, and as Garland had said, it was a role Katie could have played in her sleep, since it was, after all, not too far distant from real life.) From the studio, she rushed to her physical therapist and from there to acting classes at a laboratory in West Hollywood that theoretically permitted entrance only after lengthy interviews and auditions and then only to the most dedicated, the most talented, and the most promising, though on occasion exceptions were made when enormous pressure was brought to bear. Katie laughed about that and said in her case the only thing she had going for her was the latter. It was always late when she got home, and convinced that she would not have thought about eating, I had dinner ready. Even then, there was little time for talk, no more than a few tired, mumbled words; she had little time even then for anything but the books she pored over as she ate and later on into the night. They piled in an ever mounting stack, spilling over onto every available space: Stanislavsky and a lot of others and their disciples and commentators; theories and practice of film acting and stage acting; plays and film scripts and scenes for study and a lot more. She should have been exhausted, ready to drop, but she was not; the adrenaline was surging, and instead of fatigue, she appeared bright and exhilarated, unable to stop. When I went to bed, she would still be engrossed, would barely raise her head from the page, would say, "Not now. I'm too busy. I've got to finish this. I've got to understand it." Most nights, I would be asleep by the time she crawled into bed, and if I was not, if I turned to her and fumbled toward her and began to try to make love to her, there would be a perfunctory acceptance on her part, as though for this she did not have time then. As she had said, she couldn't learn to act in a week. But she was going to make the effort, was trying to absorb as much as she could as fast as she could, was trying to make acting as much a part of her as dancing had been. It was, of course, not possible in that time, might never be possible. She was aware of that. If it did not come, it would not be for want of trying.

In those weeks, I tried to bury myself in my own work, become obsessed with it, as I had been in the past writing books—the book I was supposed to be writing put aside for now—use it as a means of blocking out the growing frustration and bitterness, and not a little envy and jealousy. She was embarking on something that, if Garland and the others were right in their gut reactions, could lead to a future almost without limits. She was embarking on something she had initially resisted but which now she appeared to relish and seemed to have some natural talent for, and more and more it began to seem to her perhaps a viable alternative to what was forever denied her.

I was happy for her and proud of her, and yet I was also envious and jealous. For she so obviously liked it all. And though I was rapidly becoming adept at the work I was doing, was becoming ever surer of myself and my instincts, was certain I was making fewer and fewer false starts or going off in wrong directions (though I knew I wouldn't really be certain of any of that until I had finished a draft and had a chance to read and think about it), there were nagging dissatisfactions. The line seemed to have become clear, and what had once been Stuart's idea and Stuart's project alone had now become at least in part mine, as well—in some ways, more mine than his. Still, I knew that this was not really for me; it was not the kind of writing I wanted to do or that could ever satisfy those deeper needs. Even as I sat and felt a scene flowing, my mind turned to the unfinished manuscript that lay in an old cardboard box in one of the drawers across the room. A few times, I stopped, pulled it out, reread what I had written, saw where I had strayed, knew I could fix that, knew what would follow and how to take it there. And I knew that when I was finished with Charlie Stuart, that was what I would turn back to.

If Stuart noticed my sometime distractions, he never commented. He seemed pleased that I was taking his dictation so well and was now making such good and rapid progress. After he had gone through some pages one morning, he told me he was sure that at last I understood exactly what it was he wanted, that I had begun to anticipate him, as though I could read his mind, that we had become, in his phrase, "so to speak almost like twins" in our thinking. He was so convinced of that, he said, that he had begun to think we didn't really need these morning sessions any longer. I should just keep working the way I was. If I got stuck, I could always call and he'd come running to help me out, of course. In the meantime, what he'd do was come by every couple of days and pick up what I'd written, take it away, go over it at his leisure, and then we'd get together and talk about it. What he really wanted to get busy doing, he said, was drawing up a budget, putting down some ideas for casting, thinking about the right director, and beginning to let the word leak that he was about to finish what was going to be the hottest property in town.

That suited me fine.

A couple of weeks later, Suzie called late in the morning. She asked me to come out to the lot and have lunch with her. Her voice was serious. I said I'd love to but we'd have to make it another day or another place because sorry, I had no car, so no could do.

She said that was all right, she'd forgotten we only had one and Katie was using it. She still wanted to have lunch. She'd drive in, pick me up, and we could have lunch someplace along the Strip. Maybe Scandia.

I said Scandia was way out of my budget. If she wanted to make it Hamburger Hamlet, the one on the corner of Sunset and Doheny, which was closest, that would be just dandy.

With all the starving actors? she said. Those days are over for good. If we made it Scandia, she could put it on Phil's charge.

I said let's make it the Hamlet, which may not be in the expense-account league but which the starving actors still couldn't afford. Besides, since the only reason she could possibly want to have lunch with me was because she wanted to talk about something, and probably in private, the Hamlet would serve a hell of a lot better than Scandia, where everybody knew her.

She agreed, a little reluctantly.

She picked me up about one, and we headed west toward the Hamlet. It was obvious that Phil appreciated her a lot and was treating her well. She was driving a Porsche, and the pants and knit sweater she was wearing couldn't have come from anyplace but one of those shops on Rodeo I had never been inside. We talked about nothing but the weather and how everybody she knew and thought I knew—and some of whom I may actually have met, though could barely remember—was, and we didn't talk about anything more consequential until we were at the restaurant and we had our drinks and they'd taken our orders. Then she leaned forward, stared at me over her glass, and said, "What gives with you and Katie?"

"Beats me," I said. "What makes you ask?"

"You think I'm dumb?"

"That's the last thing I'd think," I said.

"Thanks for nothing," she said.

"What makes you think something gives?"

"I've got big brown eyes," she said, "and my ears hear. And Katie's my friend." She paused for a moment, looked a little to the side, missing my eyes, and added, "And so are you."

"I believe it," I said. "But I still don't know what you're getting at. What is it you think you see and hear?"

"That's just the trouble," she said. "It's what I don't see and what I don't hear. It used to be Katie talked about you all the time. Now she hardly mentions your name. I ask, and all she says is you're fine and working hard."

"She speaks true."

"Don't shit me, Miller," she said, and her voice got very tough. "All a jackass would have to do is take one quick look at you and he'd know you're not fine. And that goes ditto for Katie."

"She's just working hard, that's all," I said. "Too damn hard, as it happens. She doesn't have a minute for anything else. And you'd better not forget, you're one of the people who pushed her into it."

"We didn't have to push hard," she said. "It was there waiting. All she needed was a little nudge."

"More than that."

"Okay, so more than that. But it's the right thing for her."

"Maybe."

"No maybes. But that's not it. And you know it. It's something else. You guys love each other. My god, Miller, I've never seen it the way it is with you two. You guys give marriage a good name, for god's sake. Even for Phil. He watches you and he starts thinking maybe it's not such a bad idea, after all."

"So when's it going to happen?"

"Never," she said. "With him, it's all just talk. He doesn't love me. I'm just a convenience. Until the next one comes along."

"Then why stay?"

"Why the hell not? You got a better idea? He's good to me. He got me started. I know where I stand with him, which is more than I can say about a lot of people I know, or used to know. I'll ride this train to the end of the line, and then I'll get off."

"Just like that?"

"Just like that," she said. "But screw me. I didn't come here to talk about me. I came her to talk about you and Katie."

"There really isn't anything to talk about, Suzie."

"There's plenty to talk about," she said. "But you guys won't talk. That's the trouble."

"I wouldn't know what to say."

"That's your problem. You always have to put it into words. Goddamn writers. Do something, for god's sake. Just for a change. You two guys need each other."

"I'll buy that," I said. "At least that I need her."

"You think she doesn't need you?"

"I'd like to think she does."

"Don't you know you two guys keep each other sane in the middle of this loony bin. Can't you see that?"

"It's nice to think so," I said. "But she's a tough lady, Suzie. She may not look it, but she is. She'd always make out."

"Don't you believe it," she said, "not for one goddamn minute. Haven't you learned yet what this business is like?"

"I suppose not," I said. "But then, I'm not really part of it. I'm just sort of way out on the fringe somewhere, maybe not even close enough to be an observer."

"Then it's about time you make it your business to find out. Garland told me you were a goddamn good reporter. You could find a story under a rock if you had to. Well, you better start looking under the rocks. This place is a fucking zoo, that's what it is, and all the animals are just waiting to pounce the second somebody unlocks the cages. Katie's choice meat, Miller, and don't you ever forget it. You should see the animals looking at her. And what the fuck is that fat little bastard doing always hanging around for, with the drool dripping out of his mouth?"

"Who are you talking about?"

"The King of the B's, that's who. That little toad, Charlie Stuart, that's who."

"I wouldn't worry about him."

"Yeah? The cemeteries are full of guys who said that."

"Katie can take care of herself."

"Maybe. But if I were you, I'd do some of the taking care."

11

Near the end of the first month's shooting on Katie's picture, as I had come to think of it, I finished the first draft of Stuart's screenplay. I didn't read it then. I took it over to a Xerox place on Highland, wandered around while they made a copy, took it and the original home, and called Charlie Stuart to tell him it was done. He danced across the phone lines, shouted that he was leaving that minute and would be with me as fast as he could get across the mountains. He showed up in less than an hour, so over-flowing with anticipation and excitement that he could not stand still. He grabbed the copy out of my hands and said he'd start reading as soon as he got back to the office and then we'd talk and he'd begin planning the next move.

When he was gone, I went into the living room, sat down on the couch, and started to read. Until that moment, all I had ever read, and I think all that Stuart had really ever read, had been the individual scenes as they had come through the typewriter. Neither one of us had ever read it whole, from beginning to end, or from beginning through any long stretch, without a break. I read slowly, trying to free my mind from the words on the page, trying to hear the words spoken, trying to see the action played out on the screen, trying to visualize the thing whole. I even forced myself to read aloud, to slow down the tempo of the mind racing through words.

When I finished a couple of hours later, I sat without moving, holding the script in my lap, staring at it. Maybe I was wrong. I went back and started at the beginning, read it again, slowly, carefully, forcing my mind to visualize. The feeling of depression deepened.

It was not that there were not good things in it. There were, and I recognized them and remembered how I had felt when I had written them. If some of the dialogue was a little too literary, that was probably to be expected and wouldn't be too hard to fix. If there were places where I had tried to use words instead of letting the camera and the director tell the story without words, that, too, was to be expected and could be fixed without much trouble. If I'd tended to rely too much on words in dialogue and description and so not give the actors and the director the necessary freedom to explore and develop and find their own meanings and their own motivations and their own ways, that, too, was a hang-over from writing books, was to be expected and could probably be taken care of. Piece by piece, scene by separate scene, it probably wasn't too bad. But, taken as a whole, viewed that way for the first time, it didn't work, it didn't hang together, it didn't move, it was too much on one emotional and dramatic level. The essential peaks and valleys, slowly building tensions, weren't there. And there were other problems I saw, as well. The first third of the script seemed to work reasonably well; the trouble began about there. The mood darkened, and a different picture and a different concept and design began to emerge, but never stayed, shifted and veered at places back toward the original line.

Before, in writing, I was able to divorce myself from the world around me and lose myself in the characters I was trying to create, in what they were doing and where they going, so that they seemed to have lives of their own and often surprised me when they did the unexpected, what I had not planned. Thus, at the end of a day, it was as though I had spent the hours far away with people who had different cares and concerns, different motivations and solutions, from mine in my world. I had not been able to do that with this script. The divorce had not been total, had sometimes not even been partial. I tried to force the people in this make-believe world to bend to my will, to do what I wanted them to do, or what Charlie Stuart wanted them to do, or what he or I or both of us thought they ought to do. That element of spontaneity that is life was lost; they had not, as actors often describe the way they want to work ideally, moved from moment to moment never knowing what the next moment would be or where it would all lead; everything was predictable, and because it was predictable, it was lifeless.

I read it a third time, watching now for the signs, spotting where I had forced, where I had pulled back, where I had not allowed a free play. Could it be fixed? I hoped so, for both Stuart's sake and mine. I got out a yellow pad, sharpened a dozen pencils, opened the script to the first page, and began to make detailed notes. I went page by page, line by line, word by word. I was intent on missing nothing that was bad or ill conceived, or even what might be good in itself but that didn't work here. That was the easy part. The hard part, what seemed almost the impossible part then, was to explore, begin to try to develop and weave the radical changes and new directions that were essential. After a few hours, I thought that maybe, just maybe, it could be done. It wouldn't be simple; it might even be harder than what had preceded; it would be a lot of work, a lot of blocking out what had already been done.

But, if Stuart wanted, I thought it would be worth the try. And we did have one thing going for us. We wouldn't be dealing with blank pages now. We had pages filled, and even though much of what was on those pages would have to be junked, still some kind of framework existed, no longer just in somebody's mind.

Katie got home late, as usual, and sat down to the dinner I had prepared, not with much enthusiasm or care this time, though she didn't notice that. She opened one of her books and read a page or two while she ate the food she never tasted; she probably had no idea what she was eating. As always, I asked how the day had gone. As always, she mumbled something noncommittal, something indecipherable. Suddenly, she put the book down, looked up, and said, "I heard you finished the script today."

"Charlie's got a big mouth," I said.

"I know. He should have waited to let you tell me. But he was excited."

"That was then. Before he read it. I don't think he's quite so excited by now. It stinks."

She didn't argue. One thing about Katie, she trusted my judgment about things she thought I knew something about, as I trusted hers in her areas. She said, "I'm sorry. I know how hard you worked. What are you going to do?"

"Try to fix the damn thing."

"Can you do it?"

"Maybe." I had a sudden idea, and I knew it was not just a good one but a necessary one. "Let's get the hell out of here."

She said, "It's late."

I said, "I don't mean now. I mean, let's go away. Let's go someplace for the weekend."

She thought about that for a moment. She said, "Where?"

I said, "I don't know, and I don't care. Anywhere. Let's just get in the car and drive and see where we get to."

She nodded. "All right. When do you want to leave?"

"The sooner the better. Tomorrow morning. No, you can't. You have to work. Friday night."

She thought for a moment then shook her head slowly. "We can't," she said. "We're shooting late on Friday."

"Okay. What about Saturday morning? Early. Very early."

"Saturday morning," she agreed. "Very early."

Stuart called the next morning. I could hear it in his voice. "I read it," he said. "I read it four times. It's not bad." He didn't mean that.

I said, "It stinks."

He said, "No. It's got some good things in it. The first third. That's great. With a few changes, it'll play."

"Maybe," I said, "and maybe not. But not the rest, Charlie. Not the rest."

"I should have seen it," he said. "I should have stayed around and made sure. I never should have left you alone. I should have been smart enough to see it."

"You couldn't," I said. "You never really saw it whole before."

"I guess not," he said.

"Don't show it to anybody, Charlie."

There was gloom in his voice. "I didn't know," he said. "I thought—"

"Oh, shit," I said. "Who did you show it to?"

"Phil Garland," he said. "I mean, I'd promised him first crack. I made a copy and gave it to him."

"Before you read it?"

"Yes," he said, and the tone said it all.

"Shit," I said. "That'll do it." Garland was, after all, the only outsider who knew I'd been writing the damn thing. He was my friend. He thought he knew what I could do. He had recommended me for the job. I sure as hell didn't want him to see what had come of it.

"Don't worry," Stuart said, trying to sound confident. "Maybe he hasn't read it yet. You know him, he's got a million things on his desk. He probably wouldn't get to it for a week. I'll give him a call now. I'll tell him to forget it, forget I ever gave it to him, and to give it back. I'll tell him it's just a rough, it was just to give him a rough idea, but after you and I talked, I realized he ought to wait until we get the revise done so he'll really see what we want to do. He'll buy that. Believe me, he'll buy that."

I said I hoped he was right.

He said, "You got any ideas?"

"Plenty," I said. "I spent the afternoon making notes."

"We go back to square one, I guess," he said.

"Just about," I said.

"Well, we got to get together," he said. "Right away, start working together again, like we did at the beginning. I mean, that's when it all went sour, when I stopped coming around. I mean, I can find the place with my eyes closed. It stands out like a sore thumb. What we got to do is we got to be like twins again."

"If you say so."

"I said so, didn't I. And I say we start now. Not today. Shit, I'm booked today, or we could start now. We start on the weekend, and we work straight through. We don't take one fucking day off until we get it right."

"Not this weekend, Charlie," I said. "Let it ride until Monday. We'll start fresh then."

"What's wrong with the weekend?" he demanded. "The sooner we start, the sooner we get it right, the sooner we get it done."

"Let's think about it for a few days," I said. "You don't want to go off half-cocked. Let it sit and ferment. Monday's plenty of time."

"Shit," he said, "it's been fermenting. I want to start this weekend."

"Not possible," I said.

"What do you mean, not possible?"

"Katie and I are going away for the weekend."

"Screw that. Put it off."

"Sorry, Charlie, not this time," I said. "We both need it. If we don't go, I won't be any good, anyway. We'll all be better on Monday."

He argued for a while, but it didn't do any good, and eventually I just said good-bye, I'd see him on Monday, and hung up.

The first rays of the sun were just breaking over the mountains to the east when we left that Saturday morning. Katie had gotten home very late the night before, and she dozed on the seat beside me while I drove. There wasn't much traffic that early, and I decided to ignore the freeways, taking the coast highway north instead. I had no idea of where we were going except north, no plan, just to drive until it seemed we had gone far enough and it was time to stop. Nobody in Malibu was awake when we passed through. On the road heading south there were trailer trucks and some of those battered old heaps carrying fresh produce into the city but few other cars moving in our direction. We went through those little towns that dot the ocean, passed through Santa Barbara, and kept going. Katie woke, sat up, said nothing, just watched the passing scenery. A distance north of Santa Barbara, in one of those small towns that seemed to have been put there a long time ago for no particular reason, we passed an inn overlooking the sea. It had a pleasant, worn look about it. I glanced at Katie. "It looks like a nice place," I said. "What do you think?"

She glanced back over her shoulder. "Whatever you say," she said. "You make the decisions."

"Okay. Then I decide we stop."

"Then we stop."

I made a U-turn, backtracked, and pulled in beside the

inn. It had obviously been some years since it had been painted, but it had the look that said somebody cared and took pains with it and made all the necessary repairs and wanted people to like it. And they had rooms. We got a big one with a view out over the Pacific.

We ate lunch there, in a small dining room on the first floor, against a wide window through which we could see the ocean and the sand and the blue, the clear bright blue of the sky. Everything had a fresh look, an untouched look. The food was wholesome and well prepared, and if not in the class with what Garland served or what we might have gotten in a good, expensive restaurant somewhere, it still tasted good, and we had no desire to move. After lunch, we went upstairs, changed into bathing suits, and carrying a blanket with us, went down to the beach. It was practically deserted; just a few other people, and they were far away. We spread the blanket and then left it and walked, wading along the edge of the gentle breaking surf, stopping every once in a while on rock jetties so that Katie could rest her leg; it still throbbed a little when she tried to do too much.

We went swimming, and the water was warm and healing, washing away remembered pain. And then we lay on the blanket in the hot sun, dozing.

I opened my eyes, and she was on her elbow, looking down at me. "I love you," she said.

"Yes," I said. "I'd like to make love to you," I said. "Right now. Right here."

"Yes," she said.

I reached up and pulled her down against me and kissed her. She kissed me back. I said, "What would they say?"

"They'd come and watch," she said.

We both laughed and lay there, holding each other. I said, "I thought actresses weren't supposed to get sunburned."

"They're not," she said.

"You're getting sunburned."

"I'm not an actress," she said.

"I don't know about that," I said.

"Not yet, anyway," she said. "Besides, they have good makeup people." Then she pulled away and sat up. "But maybe we ought to go in. You're not looking like old pale-face himself right now, you know."

Upstairs, when she took off the bra and pants of her bikini, the sunburn was already visible, bright and glowing brighter against the whiteness of her breasts and loins, making what was always so startlingly pale seem even paler and more translucent. "Does it hurt?" I asked.

"Not yet," she said.

"It will."

"I know."

I suddenly laughed, staring at her.

"What's so funny?" she asked.

"Your shoulders, your legs, your face, your stomach, everything, they're practically the same color as your hair."

She took a strand of her hair and held it against her shoulder, trying to match the color, then went over to the mirror and stared at herself; her eyes went down to the red curls at the base of her stomach, comparing them critically to the redness of her thighs and lower belly. "A different red," she said. "They clash." She turned toward me. "Do you like my body?" she asked suddenly.

"Of course," I said. "I love your body."

"No," she said. "Seriously. Do you like my body?"

"You have a beautiful body, Katie."

"I never thought so," she said, and she turned back and studied herself in the mirror. "I always thought it was just a body. It served me well because it was right for a dancer. But that's all. But now people keep telling me I have a beautiful body."

"They tell you true," I said, "and if they could see you now, they'd tell you even truer. And they'd want to do something else to prove it."

She looked past her own image in the mirror toward me.

I had taken off my shorts. I had a sunburn almost as bright as hers. That wasn't what she was looking at. She said, "I'd love it if you'd prove it, Harry."

We were on the bed, and I held her and she held me, and we made love then, gently at first and then more violently, more desperately.

"Do you remember what we used to say?" she said at some point, then or later.

It had been a long time ago, at the beginning. But I remembered.

"What does the miller do in summers?" she whispered.

"He grinds exceedingly fine," I answered, as softly as she.

"Oh, Miller," she said, "grind me exceedingly fine, exceedingly, exceedingly fine."

She held on to me then, or another time, pressed me as close to her as she could, and whispered, "Hold me, my love. God, I love you. Hold me. Never let me go."

Those days were our idyll. We left the room only to go downstairs to the dining room for meals or out onto the beach, though the next day we coated ourselves with lotions and did not remain long in the sun. We left late on Sunday, looked back as we turned on to the highway, knowing this was our inn, our private place that we could never share with anyone. I drove back down the coast highway, not hurrying, retracing our route and, for one of the few times, wished the car had bench seats instead of buckets so that she could have been closer to me.

It was midnight when we walked through our door. The phone was ringing. I shrugged, sighed, and went to pick it up. It was the answering service. They had been trying to reach us for two days. There was a message from Philip Garland inviting us to a small gathering at his home on Monday evening. The operator said she had taken the message personally and Mr. Garland had said it was very important that we attend.

12 There were about a dozen people at Garland's that Monday evening. Suzie saw us when we arrived, came forward quickly, stood back and looked at us, and grinned happily. "My god," she said, "you both look marvelous. Absolutely incredible. You must have gone away."

Katie nodded. "We took the weekend," she said. "Up the coast."

"Thank god," Suzie said. "Phil had a fit when he couldn't reach you."

"We didn't tell anyone we were going," Katie said.

"And you didn't leave a message where," Suzie said.

"Because we didn't know where when we started," I said.

"That's the best where," Suzie said.

"What's the occasion, anyway?" I asked. "What's so important?"

"You'll see," she said, and the smile was secretive.

"I had to give up a class for this?" Katie said.

"Yes," Suzie said. "You sure did. But I'm not going to tell. It's a surprise."

Katie knew or had at least met some of the other men in the room, if not the women, though most of them were strangers to me. Billy Fielding, a man in his late sixties, was there with his wife, a surprisingly plain, if pleasant, woman at least thirty years younger. So was John Bedoric, the film's producer and his wife; and Karl Vogel, the president of the studio, with his wife, and some others from the lot. And then there was a woman I seemed to recall having seen before, and I suddenly remembered her from the restaurant where Garland had taken us that first evening. She was Winifred Argoth. There was something about her that instinctively turned me off. It was not just that she was unattractive and a little too heavy and that she dressed in clothes that did not suit her no matter how expensive and well made or that the carefully applied makeup was a little too thick and did nothing to make her feminine. I know people like that and have been comfortable with them, and they have been my friends. It was not just that she dominated a room with an outsized and imperious manner and that her eyes passed over and immediately dismissed anyone who didn't interest or concern her. It was not even her reputation, that the road she had traveled to the throne of Hollywood agentdom was paved with dismembered bodies. It was all that and something more, something indefinable. I formed an instantaneous dislike, the kind of thing that comes up unbidden at first meeting or even at first look and floats ever after like flotsam along the surface of the emotions. So I saw her opaquely, as though through a distorted lens that magnified all her faults and concealed all her virtues. My view of her, then, and my reactions to her were forever colored darkly. Close at her side, looking at her with adoration, was a small, effeminate young man whom everybody ignored. He wasn't the only one others ignored. I was pretty much in the same category, though Suzie paid attention to me, and Garland did on occasion. Mrs. Fielding was cordial, if a little distant.

Garland served a good dinner, though not as good as the

one he had served when there had been only the four of us. When we finished, he rose and ordered everyone downstairs, to his private screening room. When everyone had found seats, he announced that we were about to see some of the rushes from the new musical. "Only Billy and John have seen these," he said. "Even Karl hasn't had a look yet."

Winnie Argoth groaned, said that she'd seen too many rushes in her time and what she liked was the finished product. She looked as though she were getting ready to leave.

Garland told her to sit tight. She had never seen rushes like these, he said. In fact, he was showing them especially for her. She groaned again, but her face showed a little interest, and she gave a resigned sigh and settled back. The lights dimmed.

The first clips were dance sequences, and they lasted about ten minutes. I recognized the choreography that Terry and Katie had developed, saw the changes Katie had made, which worked even better than Terry's original concept, and it was obvious that her touch was in the way the dancers moved; it was like watching an imitation of her, though a pale imitation. I glanced over at her. She was smiling and nodding. She was pleased with what she was seeing. I looked back at the screen. Somewhere near the middle of the corps was Suzie, and she was moving as though she knew what she was doing. If she didn't have the fluidity and the grace of a born or trained dancer, she held her own and didn't look too out of place. I touched Katie, leaned toward her, and whispered, "I didn't think you could do it."

She whispered, "She worked hard, and when she puts her mind to it, she learns fast."

The dances ended, and Winnie Argoth made some sarcastic comment that went unremarked. The screen lit up again, and there was Katie. If I held my breath, it was only for an instant, and if I was sweating, it was out of a combination of joy and amazement. Garland had been absolutely right.

It wouldn't have made one bit of difference whether Katie could act or not; nobody then, and perhaps not until a second or third viewing, if even then, would ever notice or care. If there had been a murmur of talk during the dances, now there was total silence; everyone in that room was watching the screen with complete concentration. Something was happening up there that defied explanation. She glowed on the screen, dominated it without knowing it, and you didn't notice anyone else, didn't care what anyone else was doing. You couldn't take your eyes off her.

There were three scenes in which she appeared that were shown that evening. In the first, she was just off to one side, talking softly, the words indistinguishable, just the murmur of her voice. She was with another dancer, both in leotards, a background, supposedly, for the two stars in the foreground. But Katie, doing nothing but standing and talking quietly, drew the eye, caused you not to look at the stars.

The second was her scene. She was alone on an empty stage, practicing steps for the ballet in which she was to become a star, only the music of a rehearsal pianist filling the soundtrack. It was a brief scene, carefully done to avoid putting any strain on her leg, and she was not asked to do anything exceptional or difficult, any of the things she once could have done without thought or pause or effort. Watching her, you knew not only that she could dance, that you were watching a dancer of extraordinary talent, but that who you were really watching was a star.

The last scene was her death scene. She had been hurt in an accident outside the hall (that would be filmed later, and if it was all shades of *The Red Shoes,* nobody cared) and was being carried in and set down carefully on that empty, dimly lit stage. She died just before the doctor arrived. She didn't have a line, only a look, but it didn't matter. Somebody was crying, and I could hear the broken sobs. Other than that, the only sound was the whirring of the projector. Then it stopped, and the screen went blank, and the lights came up.

For a moment nothing happened, nobody moved. I looked at Katie. Her eyes were still fixed on the now empty screen. She turned and caught my expression. "It was the director," she said. "That wasn't me up there. It was Billy."

The noise started. Fielding was shouting, to no one and everyone, "Was I wrong or was I wrong? Didn't I tell you? For god's sake, didn't I tell you?" John Bedoric was shaking everyone's hand and grinning and sweating, and Garland was euphoric. Winnie Argoth was glaring. "You goddamn motherfuckers," she said. "Why didn't you warn me? Who the hell is she? Where is she?"

Only Suzie came to Katie then. She put her arms around her, tears running down her cheeks, and she didn't seem to care or notice. "Let's get the hell out of here," she whispered, "before they start looking for you."

We got out of there fast and went upstairs. Suzie made us drinks. "It starts," she said. "Brace yourself, you guys, because now it starts."

We could hear them coming up the stairs, Winnie Argoth's loud bellow riding over everything. They came into the room, saw Katie, moved to her, surrounded her. The women cried and told her how wonderful she was and looked at her with a kind of startled awe. The men hugged her and shouted at her, each trying to make himself heard. She was marvelous. She was incredible. She was going to be a star. She was going to be bankable.

Winnie Argoth, her flunkie following behind like a remora, shoved her way through, glared at Katie, and demanded, "Who are you?" Without a break, without even looking, she continued, "Nicholas, get me a drink."

"Right away, Winnie," the flunkie said, and headed for the bar.

Winnie Argoth repeated her question.

"I'm Katherine Summers," Katie said.

"I know your name, for chrissake," she said. "That's not what I asked." She looked at Katie. "Come over here with me. I want to talk to you, in private."

Katie looked at me. Winnie Argoth followed the look, took me in with total indifference, and dismissed me. "Get lost, creep," she said.

"He's my husband," Katie said.

"I don't care if he's your goddamn jack-in-the-box." She looked at me again. "Get lost, husband," she said. She put her hand on Katie's arm and forced her to move, propelling her off to a corner of the room and ordering everyone else to stay clear. Even from the distance, she was loud enough so nobody had to strain to hear what she had to say, which was undoubtedly her intent. She told Katie she was going to be a star. She told Katie she was not going to be a star, she was going to be a superstar, a goddamn nova (and I had one of those odd thoughts; in this realm of stars and super-stars and ever bigger and brighter stars, whatever happened to twinkle, twinkle, little star?). She told Katie she could have the sun and the moon and everything else she wanted. She asked Katie who her agent was, because Winnie Argoth was prepared right then and there to go to the phone and work out a deal to buy out her contract. Katie must have said she didn't have an agent, because Winnie Argoth started to roar with laughter. Katie sure as hell did have an agent, as of that minute, she said, and if anybody wanted to talk to her from that minute on, they sure as hell had better do their talking to Winnie Argoth.

She glared around the room, focusing on Bedoric and Garland and Vogel. She shouted, "What are you creeps doing to promote my girl?"

Karl Vogel said mildly, "It's a little early for that, Winnie."

"Bullshit," she said. "You just get your asses out of your goddamn chairs for five minutes and start the ball rolling."

"Whatever you say," Vogel said softly. He looked at

Garland. Garland shrugged. Vogel said. "You invited her, Phil."

"Wouldn't you?"

"Hell, yes."

Suzie came over to stand by me. "You need another drink?"

"I think that would be a very good idea." We went to the bar and made drinks.

Suzie said, "The cages are open, and the animals are loose."

"And Katie's the morsel?"

"They sure as hell think so. You'd better watch it, Harry."

"I'll be sure and do that." But I wasn't sure exactly what it was I could do.

"Watch out for the bitch more than any of the others," she said.

"Oh?"

"She'll cut your balls off if you give her half a chance. And she'll use a dull knife."

"What makes you think so?"

"She doesn't like husbands," Suzie said. "She doesn't like lovers. She doesn't like boyfriends or girlfriends. They get in her way. She's sure she owns Katie now, and she'll bury you in an ant hill and cover you with honey if she thinks she has to, to keep on owning."

"Nobody owns Katie," I said.

"Don't tell that to the bitch."

Garland came over then and asked if we could talk privately for a minute. He led me into a small room nearby. He said a few inconsequential things. Then, "Look, I don't want to spoil the evening."

"That's all right," I said, and knew what was coming.

"Charlie Stuart gave me a copy of your script."

"He told me. He shouldn't have."

"Maybe. But he did."

"And you read it?"

"I read it. I'm disappointed."

"To put it mildly?"

"No. Disappointed is enough. You've got a germ there. It's just that it should be a hell of a lot better. It can be a hell of a lot better. And you can write a hell of a lot better than that."

"I know."

"I wish he'd listened to you and not shown it to me."

"You and me both. I told him. But you know Charlie."

"Yeah," he said. "I know Charlie. Look, Harry, it's buried in there, what you're trying to do. Can you dig it out?"

"I'm going to try."

"You do that," he said, "and then let me see it again when you're satisfied. Remember, not until you're satisfied."

"It's Charlie's script," I said. "It's up to him."

"Of course," he said. "That's right. By Charles Stuart. But what the hell. At least you made a few bucks."

"You think that's the end of it, don't you, Phil?"

"You never know, do you," he said. "Maybe. Maybe not. I got faith in you, Harry. Why don't we just wait and see? Anyway, I thought I ought to say something to you. Now, let's forget it. I've put the whole thing out of my mind. Anyway, this is Katie's night. Let's go celebrate."

13 We had begun again, Charlie Stuart and I, from, as he said, square one. For three days, he stood over me, paced back and forth, dictated, tried to read what I was writing as I wrote. It didn't work. He said that was the way it worked in Hollywood, that was the way movies were written, and maybe he was right. He said that was true collaboration, and maybe it was. I suppose there are guys, a lot of them, who can work that way. God knows, a lot of damn good screenplays have been the result of collaboration, and so have books and plays and more. So it must have some validity, and it must work for some people. But it wasn't working for me. It was impossible. By the end of the third day, when the efforts, the combined efforts, of the two of us had resulted, as far as I could tell, not only in nothing but in a deadening of even the effect and drive that had existed in those first original scenes, I looked up from the typewriter, shook my head, and said, "It won't work, Charlie."

"What do you mean, it won't work?" He was shocked. "You're crazy. We're really starting to roll."

"On square wheels, backward," I said. I pushed my chair away, turned it, and leaned toward him. "Look, Charlie, I want to make a suggestion, and I don't want you to take it the wrong way. Please. This is your thing. It always was, and it always will be. I know it, you know it. Without you, it never could happen. All I'm trying to do is some of the dirty work. Okay?"

"Sure, okay," he said. "You're not telling me anything I don't know already. So what's the big idea of yours?"

"What I'm going to suggest is this: You go into the other room, sit down, read the papers, read a book, watch television, only keep the sound low. I don't care. Do whatever you want. Go for a walk. Go play golf. Anything. Only leave me alone for a while. Let me play with this thing on my own. I know what you want, so you don't have to worry that I'll go off in some oddball direction. I just want to see what happens when I don't have anyone standing over my shoulder. God knows, it can't come out any worse. I'll give it to you page by page, as soon as a page comes out of the typewriter. You can have it any way you want. Page by page, scene by scene, whatever. You read it. If you don't like it, if you think I'm going off in the wrong direction, we'll talk it about right then. I'll stop right there, and we'll talk about it. We'll fix it. And we'll keep going back to the beginning to make sure the whole things stands up all the way along. It's the only way, Charlie. As things stand now, nothing's going right. I can't work with you pacing back and forth behind me, with you reading over my shoulder, with you dictating to me. I can't do it that way. I never could. I'm sure there are guys who can, and maybe you should have gotten one of them. But you didn't. You got me, and now you're stuck with me unless you want to say good-bye right now and start over with somebody else. I have to

do it the way I do it. It's the only way. I hope you understand."

He objected strenuously and vociferously. He accused me
of trying to steal what belonged to him. He said I was trying
to make it mine and take all the credit, that I was trying to
cut him out of what had been his from the beginning and
always would be. I did my best, reasonably and with a
degree of calm I found amazing in myself, to assure him, to
convince him that he was wrong, that what he was accusing
me of was the last thing I would ever do. Only Katie and
Garland knew what I was doing; I hadn't told anyone, and
I knew Katie hadn't, and I was sure Garland hadn't, either
(from the things Suzie had said, I knew she didn't know,
that she thought I was working on a book), and I'd bet he
hadn't. So when it was done, if it was any good, everyone
would believe that it was Charlie Stuart's work and Charlie
Stuart's alone. It took most of the rest of that day before I
could convince him. And when he finally realized that I was
adamant, that as long as I was involved, it just wouldn't
happen any other way unless he sat down and wrote it
himself, which deep inside I was sure he understood was not
a possibility, he agreed, reluctantly, sourly, and with a lot of
warnings.

But he agreed, and he did as I asked, and then we were,
in his words, indeed on a roll. I wrote slowly and carefully,
considering, turning over, rejecting a dozen ideas, a dozen
words, a dozen twists and turns of dialogue and action, a
dozen possibilities before fixing on one and adopting it. I
never lost sight now of the line we had to follow, knowing
that no matter how good an idea or a piece of dialogue, how
dramatic and moving a scene, if it strayed too far from that
line, it was no good. All around me, on the table, on the
floor, all over the bed, was the litter of the pieces of the
original script, dissected and torn to shreds, slashed with
deletions and notations, the litter of my notes and Charlie's,

with my hastily penciled starts for new scenes and revised scenes and restructuring, my handwriting indecipherable to anyone but me, and sometimes not even to me. It looked like an impenetrable jungle, and I don't think anyone but me could have found what he was looking for in that chaos no matter how long and hard he searched. But this was the way I had worked for years under pressure to revise and change, and I could always find what I was seeking within minutes. I was now blocking the world out, was retreating into the new and private world coming to life in my mind and on the pages, was allowing the characters to play their lives from moment to moment, never knowing for sure where the next moment would take them.

Within days, I was certain I was moving not only well but in the right direction. If this new version when it was finished was not completely right, it wouldn't be so wrong, either, and it would be good enough so that what would follow would be comparatively simple, would be, in essence, only a polish. Every fifteen minutes or so, I felt his presence in the doorway, watching anxiously, waiting. I never looked up, never acknowledged that he was there, and, indeed, most of the time I was probably unaware of his presence. I ignored him until a page was done, and then I called, "Charlie . . ." He'd come dashing into the room, grab the page, and go off to read. He made no comments, offered no criticisms or suggestions, only read and stacked the pages in a growing pile and waited for me. There wasn't any need for him to say anything. It prickled along his skin; it was obvious in the flush of his face when I chanced to look his way. He believed it was good. He was growing ever more convinced that at last he was getting all he had ever hoped for.

In my obsession, and such it surely was, to finish this thing and finish it well and, perhaps, because I was tiring of him, see the last of Charlie Stuart (though I knew it would not be the end; I had committed myself, without really under- standing I was doing so, to staying available to help as long as he needed me), I was able to block out almost everything. There was just one disturbing intrusion. Winnie Argoth was trying to take over Katie and her career, and probably her life, too.

The day after we had seen the rushes at Garland's, Katie arrived home, sat down to dinner, started on another book, closed it, and wanted to talk. Winnie Argoth had called that day while she was in a session with her acting coach, had ordered the session interrupted, and had demanded that Katie be summoned to the phone immediately. Katie had gone, not knowing then who it was, sure that because of the urgency of the message, there must be trouble somewhere, probably at home.

The voice on the other end of the phone line had blared at her, "Where the hell were you this morning?"

Katie still wasn't sure who it was, and she asked.

The voice said, "Who the fucking hell do you think this is? It's Winnie Argoth, and you were supposed to be in my fucking office at ten o'clock."

Katie was learning, she was becoming adept at mimicry, and the voice that emerged from her mouth as she repeated what had been said to her was a pretty fair imitation of Winnie Argoth, and at that moment, even the words didn't sound that strange or out of place. There are some people, both men and women, for whom profanity is as natural a part of their vocabulary as the use of the personal pronoun, who use it so regularly and insistently as modifiers in almost every sentence that the words themselves become only meaningless adjectives, come to be expected and eventually ignored by the listener. You accept the fact of them as part of the person, understand that they no longer even think about what they are saying and wouldn't realize what they had said even if it were pointed out. Winnie Argoth was such a person. She had probably used the words originally for effect, to shock, to call attention to herself. But by now they had become just one part of her character that you accepted and expected. I know a lot of other people who are the same. Katie was not one of them. It was certainly not that she was a prude or even looked with disdain on the use of those words. She used some of them sometimes, of course, but they always sounded alien coming from her mouth. Perhaps it was because she had been raised in a family that eschewed them, that did not permit their use by the children, and so she had never learned to speak them cavalierly and without thought, and now it was too late to learn.

She tried to tell Winnie that morning that she hadn't realized they were supposed to meet, and besides, such a meeting would have been impossible. She was working, and that took precedence.

Winnie told her a meeting with Winnie took precedence and that she should just march in and tell them she was due at Winnie's office. "Then you get your ass over here."

Katie turned her down. She said that was something she not only couldn't do but wouldn't do. Winnie yelled, threatened, and badgered. Katie told her she had to get back to her acting class. That was what was important. Winnie calmed down then and made a date for lunch the next day. She, Winnie, would drive over to the Burbank lot, and they would have lunch there, in one of the private dining rooms. Just the two of them. "And I'll bring the fucking papers and you sign them."

Katie had trouble understanding it. Why would Winnie Argoth want her for a client? Winnie had power, enormous power, too much power, and she knew how to use it, how to reward her friends and punish her enemies or those who had given her slight. She relished that power, relished her reputation as a vindictive bitch, someone to be wary of, to walk carefully around, never to cross. She controlled the destinies of some of the biggest names in the business—stars,

directors, screenwriters—whose very appearance in or connection with a film, if it didn't necessarily ensure quality,
though that often went along, guaranteed a huge budget and
millions pouring into the box offices, and whose collective
salaries and fees and cuts and splits and points must have
approached the size of the national debt. She had been at
Garland's for the screening, I learned from Suzie, though I
don't think Katie knew it then, because Garland and Vogel
were trying to negotiate picture deals with a number of
Winnie's clients and Winnie was being tough and they
thought maybe they could ease their way with her if they
gave her first crack at an unknown they were convinced was
about to rocket into the movieland stratosphere.

So when Katie said she couldn't understand why Winnie
Argoth was after her, I said, wearily and cynically, "Come
off it, Katie. It's time to stop playing little Miss Innocent.
She saw what everybody else saw last night, and she wants
to cash in."

For the first time, she didn't argue. She accepted that. And
then, for one of the few times since all this had begun, she
asked what I thought. Should she do it? Should she sign with
Winnie? It was flattering to be wanted by someone with
Winnie's reputation for making deals and careers.

I was a hell of a one to ask, and I told her that.

She said, "You're the most important one to ask. You're
the one person I can depend on."

I said, "You know I don't like her."

"Why?"

"Instinctive. You know the feeling you sometimes get."

"No other reason?"

"Her reputation and all that. But that's just rumor. So I
suppose it's just that."

"But you don't think I ought to sign with her?"

"I didn't say that. You have to have an agent now. And
she sure has clout. But look, Katie, you ought to talk to other
people, people who know this business. I'm the wrong guy."

She had already talked to others, she said. To Billy Fielding. Of course, he was one of Winnie's people. And she had talked to Phil Garland and John Bedoric and even to Karl Vogel.

What had they said?

"They all said I should do it. They said it would probably make a lot of trouble for them when they wanted me for another picture. But I should do it, anyway, for my own sake. They said if Winnie wanted me, I ought to jump at the chance. They all said that."

"Did you ask Suzie?"

"Yes. Suzie's like you. She doesn't like Winnie. She wouldn't tell me why. She just said she didn't like her."

"Did she tell you not to sign?"

"She said I could have any agent I wanted. She said I ought to take my time. But it was my decision."

"She's right."

"But you think I shouldn't sign with her? You agree with Suzie?"

"Look, Katie, I just met the woman for the first time last night. It would be stupid of me to give you that kind of advice."

"Harry, you have instincts. You have good instincts. I trust you."

My instincts, of course, said don't do it. My instincts agreed with Suzie, that there were plenty of important agents and any one of them, once they got a look at Katie on the screen, would start a campaign that would make a lover's wooing look like child's play. But against my instincts was the advice of the people who had started her, who were fostering her new career, who were telling her to do this thing even if only to protect their own interests in other directions. If I said no and she listened to me and I was wrong, I would have to take the blame for misdirection and for an aborted career. She had already suffered enough, I thought, with the loss of the career she had wanted more than anything else. I couldn't say no. I said, "It has to be your decision, Katie. You have to make it. If you think it's the right thing for you, then do it."

She signed with Winnie Argoth the next day.

Then I began to hear a lot about Winnie and what Winnie said, for Winnie called her on the lot every day, Winnie showed up unexpectedly to take her to lunch, Winnie asked her to drop by the office on her way to the acting lab after work for a quick chat. Winnie even started to watch her language a little around Katie; Winnie told her that, told her she was being careful because she thought maybe Katie didn't appreciate some of the things Winnie said, and Katie laughed when she told me that. And Winnie told her a lot more, about what she was and about what she was about to become. And Winnie repeated it often enough so that maybe Katie was beginning to believe it, just a little. Winnie told her she was something that comes along maybe once in ten years, if that. Winnie said, "There was Garbo and there was Bergman and there were the Hepburns, both of them, and maybe a couple of others. All you had to do was take one look and you knew they had it, though what the hell the it was beats the hell out of me. But you knew it. Go look at their films, and I don't mean the ones when they got big, really big. I mean the early ones, when they were just starting, before anybody knew who the hell they were. It was there. You could see it and feel it, and you can still see it and feel it and know. You could be looking at yourself, baby. That's you. You've got the same fucking thing, whatever it is."

Winnie did more than talk. She put pressure on Bedoric and on Garland and on Vogel. She told them they were a bunch of fucking cheapskates who didn't know what they had or what it was worth and they'd be goddamn sorry if they didn't do something to correct it before the sun set.

Katie got a raise, a huge one, and now she was making more than twice what I had ever pulled down on the paper, and I was not the lowest-paid newspaper guy in town.

Winnie said it was time to start preparing the public for Katie. They said it was too early; the picture wasn't even finished yet. Winnie said it was never too early. She wanted to start reading about Katie, in the trades at the very least. Within a week, there was a story in *Daily Variety* and another in the *Hollywood Reporter* about a wave of excitement that was racing through the Burbank lot. Insiders who had seen the rushes of a new musical, both papers reported, in just about the same words, were not even bothering to whisper; they were shouting that a new star was about to be born. Katie didn't tell me about that. Charlie Stuart did. Reading the trades was part of his daily ritual, of course, as it is with most people in the business, and so he arrived one morning, flushed with excitement, and thrust the papers into my hands, demanding that I read before I did anything else.

Winnie did a lot of other things, too, and some of them I didn't like very much. She said it was important for Katie to be seen. People had to get to know who she was; they had to get to recognize her on sight even before the picture was done and released. And it was essential that Katie be seen with the right people, with the important people, so that the world would know she was important. She wanted Katie to go to dinner with some of the important male stars. That Katie refused to do. She was married, Katie said, and if she was going to go out to dinner with any man, it was going to be with her husband. Winnie argued and insisted, but Katie wouldn't budge on that. So Winnie found another way. She took Katie to the Polo Lounge a couple of times at the right hours. She set things up with men Katie couldn't very well refuse. Karl Vogel, who was old Hollywood, took her to dinner at Perino's, an old Hollywood standby. John Bedoric took her downtown to the Windsor, not necessarily for the steaks but so people would see her with one of the top producers. Billy Fielding broke his habit of rarely dining out and took her to dinner at a new "in" place in Westwood. Garland took her to the opening of a show bound for Broadway at the Music Center; Suzie and I went along on that one, though we sat two rows behind. Most of the time, I stayed home and wrote. I was not invited, or when Katie suggested I come along, I turned her down, knowing that she was the only one who wanted me and if I went it would not sit right with anyone else.

About the only times I was invited with Katie were to parties on the weekends, and now there were parties almost every Friday and Saturday night and Sunday afternoon. Winnie was at every one, ignored me, made sure I was shunted off into some corner when she took Katie around by the arm and introduced her to everyone who was anyone or who might someday be someone, introduced her with a proprietary air.

Maybe it was going to help Katie's career. Winnie certainly insisted it would. And we had all, certainly, read enough about how such things do, about how necessary they are, especially for someone just at the beginning. Maybe. And maybe I was dumb because I resented it and I didn't really see what it had to do with what she was trying to do and become, which was to grow into a good actress, if that was possible, which it seemed to be, and to get there through the things she possessed, that were inside her, not by extraneous nonsense.

I wasn't sure whether Katie liked it or not, whether Winnie's sharp and so authoritative tongue was really convincing her it was necessary. I asked now and then and got mixed responses. She was, naturally, flattered by the attention. And she was given little chance to think or to stand back and gain any perspective. After some of her evenings out with important people alone or with important people at parties, she would tell me it had been fun and she had had a good time; sometimes she would say it had been a total bore and all she had wanted was to leave and come home, to get back to the real world to studying and working with other actors at the lab. When she had begun, she worked at the lab five nights a week. Under Winnie's pressure, she had cut back to three, and some weeks to two, so that there would be nights when she would be free to be seen.

One afternoon, after Charlie had gone and I was written out and was trying to come down with a drink and a book, the phone rang. The voice on the other end said, "Is this Mr. Summers?"

I said no, it was not Mr. Summers.

The voice sounded puzzled. Isn't this the residence of Katherine Summers? it asked.

I said yes, it was.

The voice asked when Mr. Summers would be home.

I said there was no Mr. Summers as far as I knew. I said that my name was Mr. Miller and that Katherine Summers' name was Mrs. Miller.

The voice apologized, but there was no apology in it. The voice said could I wait a moment, Miss Argoth would like to speak with me.

I waited. Winnie Argoth's too loud, too strident voice blasted into my ear. I held the phone away. "Is that you, husband?"

I said it was indeed me.

"I want to talk to you."

"All right, I'm listening." I don't usually answer that way. I may not be very great on the phone, but usually I'm at least polite. Winnie Argoth brought out something else.

"Not on the fucking phone," she said. "I want to talk to you where I can see you. Come to my office. Tomorrow. At three."

"Impossible," I said. "I'm busy."

"Fuck busy," she said. "Unbusy busy. Whatever it is, it can wait. Be here at three." She hung up.

I didn't tell Katie she had called. I don't know why. Maybe because there really wasn't anything to tell yet and maybe because I wanted to see what it was all about before I said anything. But I thought about it and wondered about it all the next day; the gnawing and twisting disrupted the pattern of my work, so that what I wrote wasn't much good. Stuart recognized it, looked worried, and asked if something was wrong. I said no, it was just one of those days. They happen. You expect them and you get used to them. By the middle of the afternoon, he realized it was useless hanging around, and he left.

I took a shower, changed my clothes, called a cab, and rode to Winnie Argoth's office in one of those tall buildings along Sunset in West Hollywood, buildings I always thought incongruous in that setting, surrounded as they were by mountains on one side and dipping into valleys on the other and ringed by small buildings and houses from another time. Her office was on the top floor, one of the five floors occupied by the agency of which she was one of a dozen vice-presidents, though the title hardly indicated her power in it and in the business. I arrived just before four. She kept me waiting another half hour, then sent her flunky, Nicholas, out to fetch me. Her office was in the southwest corner, so she had a view out over Beverly Hills to the ocean far beyond. On a clear day she could see Catalina, but not so clear as from Charlie Stuart's mountain. Her office was vast. Her desk was a thick glass slab set on marble pillars. Papers were strewn all over it. There was a thick red carpet. Chairs were arranged around a low marble table, and there were two couches fronted by marble-and-glass tables. The fabrics were delicate and feminine, and I was sure she hadn't picked them out herself. Big as the office was, it appeared too small for her, seemed unable to contain her.

Nicholas had knocked at the door, opened it at a peremptory call, held it open while I entered, and closed it noise-lessly behind me so that Winnie Argoth and I were alone. She sat behind the desk, glaring at me. I wondered if she ever did anything but glare. She said, "You're late, hus-band."

I said, "I told you I had work to do."

"You made me wait," she said. "Nobody makes me wait."

I shrugged. "You wanted to see me?"

She gestured toward one of the chairs lined up in a row before her desk. "Sit down," she ordered. I sat in the chair at the end. She said, "What the fuck is it you do, husband?"

"Would you mind not calling me that," I said.

"What the fuck should I call you?"

"My name is Miller. Harry Miller. You can call me Mr. Miller. You can call me Harry. You can call me Miller. You can call me hey you. I don't give a shit. Only don't call me that."

She laughed. It had a nasty edge. "I ask you again, what-ever your name is, just what the fuck is it you do?"

"I write."

"What the fuck do you write? I've never heard of you. And I know the name of every piss-ass writer in this busi-ness."

"I'm not in the business."

"Then what the fuck do you write? Letters?"

"Books."

"Books? Shit. Nobody writes books out here. They write movies. They write for the tube. Nobody writes books."

"I write books, and I'm out here."

"Shit. The only reason any asshole writes books is to sell 'em to the movies. How many you sold to the movies?"

"None."

"That figures. I had you marked the first time I saw you. Strictly small-time. Strictly a nobody."

"Your judgment," I said.

"You can kiss my ass on that," she said. "What is it with you?"

"You tell me. I suppose that's why I'm here."

"You along for the ride? Is that it? You figure you'll pick up the chips when they fall off the table? You figure you got yourself a gold mine and you're going to ride it as long as it lasts?"

I thought about making a comment about mixed metaphors but decided not to. I said, "I wish I knew what you were talking about."

"Come off it, husband," she said. "You ain't that dumb."

"Oh, you don't know," I said. "I can be very dense at times. Just ask Katie."

"That's what I'm talking about, husband."

Oh, so now we come to it. Suzie had warned me. I just hadn't believed it would ever be this direct. "What about Katie?"

"You're in her way."

"Really?"

"Don't play your fucking games with me, husband. She's about to get on a fucking skyrocket. It's going to take her to the goddamn moon if I have anything to say about it, and you can bet your ass I do."

"Oh, I believe it," I said. I didn't say which part I believed.

"So what are you going to do? Hang around and pick up the fucking crumbs? Riding the fucking gravy train? Hang on to her fucking coattails? Be Mr. Summers? You do that and you hold her back. Believe me, husband. I know."

"I have no intention of holding her back," I said. "Why would I? If I wanted to ride the gravy train, as you so crudely put it, then I certainly wouldn't do anything to hold her back."

"Just hanging around, you're holding her back."

"Personally, lady, if I may call you that, I think you're wasting my time and yours. What we do with our lives is strictly up to Katie and me. To use your terms, it's none of your fucking business."

"Fuck you, husband," she said. "It is my business and don't you ever forget it. That girl belongs to me."

"You couldn't be wronger. She belongs to herself."

"Husband, you give me a stiff pain in the ass."

"The feeling is mutual." I didn't know why I continued to sit there and listen to her, engage her. Maybe it was only to hear if she had anything else to say or to learn how long I could take it.

"You know her trouble?" she said. "She's too fucking loyal."

"I'd say that was one of her good points. Among many."

"She won't tell you what she knows."

"And just what is it she knows that she won't tell me?"

"She's taking off, husband. She's leaving you behind, in the fucking shit, that's where. Maybe one time you had a thing going with her, when she didn't know what she was. Maybe one time she thought she needed you, when she didn't know where she was heading. But that's all over, husband. All over. She doesn't need you anymore. You're just in her way."

"I suppose you think she needs you."

"Fucking A. I'm the one's going to get her where she's going. I'm the one that's going to see she gets what she ought to have, everything, all of it. I'm the one. And I'm the one that's going to make damn sure nothing gets in her way."

"And you think I'm in her way."

"Bet your ass. So take a hike, husband. Do it now, before she wakes up and takes a good look and throws you out on your fucking keester. Do it now and maybe we'll even make it worth your while. Wait and all you'll get is shit. Believe me, I'm telling you the fucking truth." She glared at me.

I had neither the need nor the desire to sit there and listen to any more. It was all becoming repetitious, and the sound of that grating voice was pounding inside my skull like a migraine. I sat for one more minute, staring back, trying not to let all that was boiling up inside me explode through the surface. I was probably not very successful, but then, I'm not an actor. I got up. I said, as mildly as I could, "I think I'll take your advice. I think I'll take that hike."

I turned and walked out of that office, trying to move with slowness and deliberation, but once I was through the door, I hurled it back with as much force as I could, heard the loud reverberation, saw the flunky's startled expression, and walked rapidly back down the corridor toward the waiting room and the elevators.

14 I never told Katie about that confrontation in Winnie Argoth's office, and I'm sure Winnie Argoth never mentioned it, either. There was no reason why she would have. Such skirmishes were, for her, just one facet in taking over the career, and life, of a new client, and she never had any doubts that she would win. She had never lost. Most of her victories were quick and decisive and met with only token resistance, and if I had put up a brave front before her and indicated that I was not about to capitulate, still she believed that in the end the result would be no different from any that had gone before.

I said nothing for other reasons. There were moments when I did frame the words to set it all before Katie, but the words never came. What would I have said? The scene had been so baroque as to be not only unbelievable to anyone who had not been there but nearly unreportable. Katie was, after all, only too aware of my instant antipathy toward the woman, and had I said anything, I'm sure she would have thought I was exaggerating, that it could not possibly have been that way. As Winnie Argoth so rightly said, Katie was loyal, and one thing I did not want to do at that point was to divide that loyalty, to make her choose. It would have been one thing had she still been dancing; in that world, she knew herself and knew her abilities and talents, had a clear and objective sense of what she could do, and so while she enjoyed praise and flattery, she did not need it. The world of acting that she now inhabited was something else. She had no clear view of her talents and her potential, was struggling and uncertain and filled with doubts and questions. She needed the praise and she needed the flattery and ego massaging not so much from me as from those who knew that business and were not just in it but at the top of it. To cast doubts on Winnie Argoth, then, would have been to cast doubts on what Winnie Argoth was telling her, and that would have seriously weakened her still tenuous belief in herself. I held my silence.

And I heard the stories of the victories that Winnie had won for her that she could not have won for herself, that she would not even have thought of seeking. Winnie thought Katie deserved special billing in the credits for the musical. Without discussing it with Katie, Winnie had gone with her demand to Bedoric, who, according to Winnie, had hemmed and hawed and wouldn't commit himself, so she had gone to Garland and then to Vogel. Her pressures had forced them to capitulate, and they had finally agreed to give Katie a single card at the end of the cast credits reading: "And introducing Katherine Summers as Melissa."

A long time later, during a rambling conversation, Suzie and I began talking about Winnie Argoth, began trying to come up with some of the good things she had done. We laughed a little at how short the list was and how hard it was to find anything to pad it out. I mentioned the matter of the billing. Suzie looked at me cynically. "The bitch actually took credit for that? Jesus, Phil told me they were planning on doing that right after they saw the first rushes."

"I suppose they were planning on giving her that raise, too," I said.

"No," Suzie said, "give the bitch that. The card didn't cost anything. Money's another matter. That was Winnie."

After that meeting with Winnie Argoth, I made it a special point to go to all those weekend parties without complaint. They bored me, most of them, and I had heard all the stories before, a dozen times, and I really didn't care what kind of a deal Burt or Jack or Scott or somebody else had just made with Metro or Twentieth or Columbia or whoever, and I wasn't really interested in who was sleeping with whom, of either sex, and who was swinging both ways, and who was coming out of the closet, and I was getting a little tired of finding out who was the best source for coke or grass or whatever else was the "in" drug of the moment. And most of the people at those parties didn't know who the hell I was and didn't especially care, and all I did was get a drink and stand off to one side, usually alone, and watch Winnie Argoth hover over Katie and make sure she had long conversations with all the important people. I went because I knew Winnie Argoth didn't want me to go. She made that abundantly clear. A few days after our meeting, which it took me more than a few days to recover from so that I could begin to work freely again and allay Charlie Stuart's growing worry that had begun to appear almost a frenzy, Katie laid out the weekend party schedule as given to her by Winnie. Though she was getting invitations on her own by then, Winnie insisted that before any were accepted, they had to be checked and okayed. "Winnie says you don't have to go if you don't want to," Katie said. "It's just people from the business, and you probably won't have much fun. But she says I ought to go because it'll be good for my career," and she made a face and laughed deprecatingly.

"What the hell," I said. "I'd rather stand off and watch you than sit around here alone."

So I went, and Winnie Argoth would see me, hold herself and not say anything, and just take Katie away in an instant. I never had anything to say to her, of course, and we'd both make sure to avoid each other all through the evening.

Katie noticed, naturally, but she just put it down to my dislike of Winnie and Winnie's preoccupation only with things that concerned the business. I don't think anyone else noticed, or cared if they happened to notice. Anyone else, that is, except Suzie, who was, as I have said, a lot wiser than anyone suspected. There was one night when was I standing off to one side, alone as usual, with a drink in my hand in somebody's backyard in Bel Air, watching the crowd collect around Katie. She was still new enough, I suppose, to be something of a novelty. The old stories were whirring around me, and I wasn't listening to them, any more than I was listening to the gossip of some other people about Katie, which bore about as much relation to reality as green cheese does to the moon. I sensed somebody watching me. Suzie was standing a half-dozen yards away, her own drink in her hands, measuring, calculating. There was an open lane between us. She walked down it.

"Hi, Miller," she said. "You alone?"

"All alone. Where's Phil?"

"Off somewhere trying to come on with some kid whose tits are bigger than mine, I suppose. That's where he usually is." I looked hard at her; there was nothing in the face. She swallowed her drink and thrust the empty glass toward me. "Get me another."

"Sure. What are you drinking?"

"Vodka," she said. "Russian. With one ice cube."

"Got it," I said. "I'll be right back. Don't go away." I

went off to the bar, got her the refill, got a refill for myself, and returned. She hadn't moved. She took the drink, nodded, and took a swallow. She drank it as if it were water.

"How you doing, Harry?" she said.

"Okay."

"The book coming along?"

"Coming along."

"When you finish, you'll autograph a copy for me?"

I laughed. "Somebody else asked me the same thing."

She looked blank. "Who?"

"A Mrs. Fitzmaurice."

"Oh, her. I mean it," she said. "I'll read it."

"Sure thing, Suzie."

She took another swallow, looked at me briefly, then out over the swarm around Katie, laughing, talking too loudly. She looked back, her eyes measuring. "The bitch got to you, did she?"

"What bitch is that?"

"Don't play games with me, Miller," she said. "You know exactly who I mean."

"I assume you're referring to Winifred Argoth."

"Assume? Assume? What kind of bullshit language is that? You know damn well I'm talking about that bitch."

"Maybe. But I still don't know what you mean."

"Bullshit. You think I'm blind or something? I've been watching. You go past each other like one of you's got poison ivy or something."

"You've got us wrong, Suzie. I don't mean anything to her, and she doesn't mean anything to me."

"She called you in for a little talk yet?"

I looked at her. "Why would she do that?"

"Because that's the way she is. She does it all the time. I told you, she doesn't like husbands of her people, she doesn't like wives of her people, she doesn't like whatevers of her people. Remember, I told you that."

"I remember."

"She wants to run everyone's life. She doesn't want interference. Husbands, wives, whatevers, they're interference. They make trouble. They get in the way of her power and control, and if there's one thing that bitch loves, it's power and control, and if there's one thing she can't stand, it's anything that gets in her way. She does things then."

She took another swallow. I looked closely at her. "Did you get in her way, Suzie?"

She didn't answer right away. She kept turning the glass around and around in her hand. She looked into it, then took a last swallow. "Before Garland," she said into the empty glass, "I was with a guy. You wouldn't know him. You probably never heard his name. He had a shitload of talent, that guy. Not like Katie. She's something different. But this guy, he could act a storm. He was just beginning to go places. Winnie saw it, and she got her claws on him. I suppose she would've made him big-time in the end, but the stupid motherfucker liked to fly, only that was one thing he wasn't very good at. But by then it didn't mean a thing to me. The bitch called me in and we had our little talk, and I got the fast kiss-off. I wasn't the first, Miller, and you won't be the last, not unless somebody throws the bitch on her back and rams it into her, which is what she needs, that is, if she even has one to ram it into, which I doubt."

"I'm sorry, Suzie," I said, ignoring the rest, the jumbled syntax and all.

"Screw sorry," she said. "Fight the bitch. You got to fight her. Maybe you won't win. Nobody ever does. But you got to fight her. And maybe you and Katie, maybe you can win. Somebody's got to."

"Right at this minute," I said, "Katie's convinced she needs her. Winnie tells her that, and everybody tells her that."

"Sure they tell her. Why not? They all think they need the bitch. But let me tell you, Katie needs her like a virgin needs Casanova." She looked into her empty glass, put it to her mouth, got nothing, and said, "Get me another drink, Harry."

"I think maybe you've had enough."

"Screw enough. There's no such thing as enough. Get me another drink. Be a little gentleman, like you are, you poor jerk, and get me another drink."

I sighed and took her glass and started away. She looked after me. She said softly, "You and me, Miller. We got no chance. You won't know how it happened, but one of these days we're going to be on the outside looking in. Only not like now. Then it's going to be through the bitter tears."

I finished the second version, handed the pages to Charlie Stuart, told him to sit down and start reading from the beginning, and then I went back into the bedroom and did the same. Before he had half finished, I could hear the noise, the gleeful little shouts, from the living room. I ignored them. I read slowly, not pausing until I'd turned the last page. I was pretty satisfied. We were almost there. Not quite, but almost.

I went into the living room. Charlie was grinning, nodding, as he turned through the last pages. I sat down and waited. He finished. He jittered out of his chair and started to dance a little jig around the room. "Son of a bitch," he shouted. "We got it! We got it!"

He was infectious. I grinned back. I said, "Not so fast, Charlie."

"What do you mean, not so fast?" He was incredulous. "I tell you, it's here, right in my hand. We did it, you son of a bitch. We did it." When he said "we," I was never sure whether he was speaking in the royal sense or whether he meant the two of us.

I said, "I want to make a few changes."

"What changes, for chrissake? They'll buy it just the way it is, let me tell you. They'll crawl all over themselves to get their mitts on this. I been around this business a long time, maybe longer than you've been alive. I know. I can feel it. You want to make changes? Shit. The director's going to want changes. The stars are going to want changes. Let them ask for them. That's the way we do it. You don't have to make it perfect. It won't ever be perfect, because other guys get involved and all of them got big ideas."

"Look," I said, "just sit tight, Charlie. Give me another week, another ten days at the outside." I flipped open the script, turned pages, stopped, and pointed out a dozen scenes I thought ought to be tightened, ought to be reworked to make them sharper. He read through them again.

He looked up. "Maybe you're right," he said. "Why take any chances now when it's all going to fall into our laps, anyway."

Why take chances, indeed?

It took me another week, and then the last page, the last reworking, was gone, into Stuart's hands. I felt drained, the emptiness that comes when you've finally finished something you've spent a long time doing and you've given it to somebody else and there's nothing more for you to do. Somebody once said that finishing was like giving birth to a child. I wouldn't know about that.

It had fallen just at the right time. I knew I had to get away then, get away from everything and not think, not do anything. And that was the week Katie finished her work on the picture. The dance numbers were all in the can, and so were her scenes. There was still a little more to be done on the picture (and then, of course, there would be the cutting and the editing and all the rest once the set was struck), but none of it involved her. She was free, or as free as Winnie Argoth would let her be.

There was no dinner for her when she got home that night. I hadn't bothered to cook, hadn't felt like it, hadn't had the patience even to think about it. As she came through the door, I said, "Let's go out and get something to eat for a change. Maybe someplace close, down on LaCienega."

She said, "Wonderful. We can celebrate. We can even have champagne. I finished today."

I said, "Fancy that. So did I."

She hadn't known I was that close. She stared at me and started laughing, and then we were both laughing and hugging each other, and then we decided, what the hell, we wouldn't go out, we'd just fish around in the refrigerator and eat whatever happened to be there, which happened to be eggs, and maybe have a couple of beers, if there was any beer around.

While we were eating, I said, "Let's get away." I didn't tell her that we'd had a call earlier, just before she got home, from Karl Vogel's wife, inviting both of us to dinner on Saturday. Mrs. Vogel seemed a nice lady, and I hated to disappoint her. She called me Mr. Miller and asked if Mrs. Miller and I were free. I was very regretful and very polite, and I said we'd love to come but, unfortunately, we had already made plans to go away for the weekend. She was warm and understanding and said she understood and we would certainly make it another time, very soon.

Katie said without even thinking, "Let's. Where?"

I said. "Where would you like to go?"

She said, "North. Back north. Up the coast highway, past Santa Barbara. There's a little inn on the ocean."

"An excellent choice."

"I'll let Winnie know in the morning," she said.

"Why?" I asked. I felt suddenly very cold.

"Oh, you know, she likes me to tell her what I'm doing."

I said, "If you feel you have to, then I guess you have to. Only don't tell her where we're going."

She looked surprised. "You know I wouldn't do that," she said. "That's our private place."

So she called Winnie Argoth early the next morning. I was in the other room, but even over the distance I could hear the bellow of outrage. Winnie told her she couldn't go.

Katie said that was ridiculous. Of course she could go. She was finished with the picture, and so there was nothing to hold her back. Besides, she was tired and needed to get away.

Winnie said something might happen in the next few days. She was already talking with people about another picture for Katie. Katie had to be around just in case.

Katie said whatever it was, it could certainly wait until Monday.

Winnie said there was a very important party on Friday night.

Katie said she'd been to enough important parties and it wouldn't hurt to miss one. If she missed one, maybe that would make people talk about her even more.

Winnie said Karl Vogel and his wife were having a small private dinner on Saturday and she was trying to wangle an invitation for Katie.

Katie said that was too bad, and Winnie should stop trying and then nobody would be disappointed. But Katie just had to get away.

Winnie said, "It's that husband. He's talked you into this."

Katie said nobody had talked her into anything. We'd made the decision together, as we made most decisions together. It was something we both wanted and needed.

Winnie kept at it until at last she realized that nothing she said, no matter how loud and insistent she was, was going to change Katie's mind. She took another tack. She demanded to know where we were going just in case she had to be in touch.

Katie said she was sorry, but we didn't know where we were going. We were just going to drive and end up somewhere.

Winnie said, "You won't tell me?"

Katie said no, she wasn't going to tell her.

Winnie said, "You have to call as soon as you know where you are. I'll give you my private home number."

Katie said she'd call Winnie on Monday when we got back.

Winnie said, "No, you have to call as soon as you know where you are." And she started to rattle off her private number.

Katie said she didn't need the private number because she wasn't going to make any phone calls over the weekend. She said she hoped that Winnie would have a pleasant weekend herself and she'd call on Monday when we got back. And then she hung up.

Over the next hour, while we threw things into suitcases and got ready to leave, the phone kept ringing. We let the answering service pick up, which it did every time after the third ring. As we were walking out the door, I grinned and said, just for the hell of it, "Let's find out." I went back to the phone and checked. There had been five urgent calls for Katie from Winnie Argoth. There had been one urgent call for me from Charlie Stuart. We laughed, and I told the service we'd be away and unreachable, and then we carried the suitcases out to the MG, tossed them into the boot, and headed north.

They remembered us at the inn. They welcomed us back as old friends, even gave us the same room we'd had before. We arrived on Thursday afternoon and didn't leave until late Sunday evening. It was the longest time we had been away and alone together since either of us could remember, probably not since that week in Hong Kong. We swam and walked the beaches and waded in the ocean. We ate at the inn and in a few places nearby that the people at the inn recommended, though we could never remember just what we ate or whether the food was any good. We got sunburned. We slept a lot. And we made love a lot.

We got home late Sunday night. We didn't bother to check with the service. That could wait until morning. We fell into bed, tired, not from exhaustion but with that good feeling that comes from pleasure and liberation.

15 The phone woke us early. We lay in bed and let it ring the three times until the service picked up. It rang a few more times before we finally got out of bed, and we still didn't answer. While Katie made breakfast (cooking was one skill she had never mastered, probably because, like most dancers, food was something that didn't interest her that much, was just something necessary to stoke the body; but then, pouring juice, filling bowls with cereal, and pouring boiling water through a coffee filter aren't especially difficult things to do), I finally got around to checking with the service. The list of calls was long. There had been several from Charlie Stuart for me, one that morning. There had been a dozen from Winnie Argoth for Katie, two that morning. There was one for me from Phil Garland and one for Katie from him. Two different messages. There was a call for Katie from Suzie. There was a call for Katie from Terry Markoff, not important, just return it when she got around to it. There were four or five calls for Katie from people she'd met and become friends with on the picture.

We ate breakfast and tried to decide where to begin. "I suppose," Katie said, "I ought to call Winnie. I did promise."

"Or I ought to call Charlie Stuart," I said. "Or we both ought to call Phil. Why don't we just put slips of paper in a hat and let the fates decide?"

"Between us," she said, "we don't own a hat." Which was true.

We never got around to making the decision. The phone rang again before we had to. I answered, and the voice said, "Just a moment, please. Mr. Garland is calling Mr. Miller."

I waited. Phil's voice came over the line. "You bastard," he said. "Why didn't you return my call?"

"We were away. We didn't get back until late last night."

"You had to pick this weekend?"

"What did I do now?"

"Do? You bastard, I'll tell you what you did. Charlie Stuart came waltzing into my office Thursday morning. Without an appointment. He just breezed past my secretary and marched in on me, and I was right in the middle of a meeting with Winnie. He looked at her, and he grinned this shit-eating grin like even Winnie could wait for him to speak his piece, and he gave me some of the same. And then the little son of a bitch dropped a package on my desk. He looked at me and he said, the little prick, 'Garland, I like you, so I'm giving you first crack. But you've only got till Monday.' And then he turned around and walked out, and I'm sitting there with my mouth hanging open like some goddamn asshole. And Winnie's sitting there watching the whole goddamn performance."

He went on nonstop, and there was no way to stop him or break in to ask a question. Winnie asked him what that was all about, and since he was damned if he knew, he told her she knew Charlie Stuart as well as he did, and maybe he's got that damn thing he's been talking about all these years finished at last and he decided he was the guy to read it.

She asked whether there was anything in it for any of her people, and Garland said how the hell should he know, since he hadn't read it himself and for all he knew maybe there wasn't anything in it for anybody because maybe it was a stinkeroo. She said, "You never know," and why didn't he just have a Xerox copy made for her to take along when she left so she could see for herself. When Winnie asked, you did.

All he had given her was a copy of the screenplay. But there was more in the package than that. "You sometimes forget," he said, "how much guys like Charlie Stuart know about this business. They've been around so long you take them for granted." All through the time I had been working, and maybe from long before that, and certainly during that last week, he had been doing his own kind of work. Drawing on his experience and his knowledge of changing times and trends, he had figured and calculated and drawn up a complete detailed budget for the film, the over-the-line costs and the below-the-line, breaking down every item, marking the ones where costs were solid and those where he had been forced to estimate. He had penciled in cast suggestions for all the major roles and some of the smaller ones; he had penciled in a director and a chief cameraman, a cutter, lighting designer, scene designer, costume designer, and a lot of other major technical people. It was all there for Garland to see.

"I took the script home," Garland said, "and I read it Thursday night. Let me tell you, Harry, I didn't want to. Not after the first one. But Winnie had it, and I knew she was reading it, so damn it, I had to. You dirty son of a bitch. You did it this time. You really did it. I didn't think you could, not after that first bomb. But you did."

He went on in that vein for quite a while. I listened. Finally, I said, "I'm glad you like it, Phil."

"Is that all you have to say? Like it? Didn't you hear me? I'm nuts about it."

"I'm happy for Charlie," I said.

"You can bet your ass you should be happy for Charlie. I talked to Karl Vogel on Friday. He read it. I talked to him on Saturday. He's even crazier about it than I am. I talked to Charlie yesterday. I told him we want to do it. I told him we wanted to go into preproduction as soon as possible, like yesterday."

I said that was wonderful. I probably meant it. I'm sure I meant it. But what I really felt was just an emptiness, the nothingness that follows the end of something when you know you won't have anything more to do with it.

He said, "I'm going to talk to Charlie about giving you a screen credit. You know, screenplay by Charles Stuart and Harry Miller."

"Don't do that, Phil."

"What do you mean, don't do it? Are you crazy? It's your goddamn screenplay. You earned the goddamn credit. And it'll be money in the bank. You'll have to fight off the offers."

"Don't do it," I said again. "It belongs to Charlie. It's his, and his name is the one that's on it. That was our agreement."

"Shit. Agreements are made to be broken."

"Not by me."

"You're an asshole," he said. Then, "Look, if you won't budge, then maybe I'll just spread the word around, very quietly."

"I don't want you to do that, either," I said. "Just leave it the way it is. I'll feel better that way."

"For chrissake, why not even let me do that little thing?"

"It's not so little. And I owe Charlie. I owe him at least that. He was the guy who saved us. Remember? It wasn't so long ago."

"He's not Jesus Christ, you know."

"Phil, just drop it. Let Charlie have his dream. I don't need it."

"Then what the hell are you going to do now?"

"What I should have been doing all along. Get back to my book."

"You want to write another screenplay? I can set it up."

"No, thanks."

"What's the matter? You think it's beneath you or something?"

"It's not that. It's just not my thing. I guess there are plenty of guys who love it and who wouldn't do anything else. I don't happen to be one of them, that's all."

"Your choice," he said. "You change your mind, you let me know."

"Sure thing."

"Okay. Now, is Katie around?"

"She's right here, trying to figure out what we've been talking about."

"Give her the phone," he said.

I handed her the phone. She looked at me with a question. I shrugged. She put the phone to her ear, but her eyes stayed on me. She listened. She said a lot of yesses and some noes. She said no, she hadn't, but she would. She said no, she didn't. She said yes, she'd like to. She said she was sure Winnie would have no objections. She said she'd talk to her. She said no, she hadn't talked to her yet. She said yes, she was glad Winnie liked it. She said yes, she'd be there tomorrow morning and they could talk more about it then. She hung up.

Her eyes hadn't left my face. She said, "Could I please read the script?"

I said, "Of course. I thought you'd never ask. I'll get it for you."

She said, "Phil thinks there's a part in it for me."

That surprised me, but not for long. While I was writing, I had not had any particular actors in mind to play the roles. I had only been trying to write characters an actor could play, characters who were alive enough on the page so that an actor could put the spark into them and give them dimensions and complexities that were only implied. Now I knew precisely the role Garland had in mind for her; it was really the only one that would suit her. It just happened to be the female lead. After seeing her on the screen in those first rushes and in another group another evening where she had some lines, I thought she could probably do it, certainly could do it if she had the right director and was surrounded by good professionals.

I handed her the script. She sat down on the couch, curled her legs under her, and read. She didn't look up once until she was finished.

Charlie Stuart called while she was reading. Like everyone else who called that morning, he demanded to know why we hadn't returned his calls and didn't want to hear the explanation that we had been away and out of touch. I should have called him, anyway, he said, because he had terrific news.

I said I knew. Garland had called and told me.

He went on and on, and I hardly listened. He said I'd better free myself and keep free and available, just in case.

I said I'd be around, just in case, because I had some things I had to do. I wasn't planning on going anywhere.

He said maybe he ought to get me a job on the picture. As script supervisor or something that didn't mean much but that would make sure I was available when he needed me.

I said no thanks, I was satisfied with things as they were.

He said he owed me some money.

I said yes, he did.

He said he'd send off a check right away, and maybe he'd even throw in a few thousand extra for good measure, to show his appreciation.

I said thanks, I could use the money.

He said he'd like to drop it off personally but he was going to be very busy from then on. What he'd do was send it over by messenger.

I said that would be nice.

He said he had to run.

I went into the bedroom and took out the unfinished manuscript, put a piece of paper in the typewriter, and started to move into a different world. It wasn't easy. The phone continued to ring, and every time it did, Katie called and asked me to please answer it and if it was for her to say she was busy and couldn't come to the phone just then but would call back later. I did.

I couldn't do that, though, when it was Winnie Argoth. It was her voice, not the flunky's, and she was not pleased to hear mine. She made some comment, which I ignored, and demanded to speak to Katie immediately. I said Katie was busy and couldn't come to the phone. It was nice to say those words. She filled my ear with some of the choicest examples from her extensive vocabulary and told me I had better let Katie make that decision. I sighed, looked over at Katie, and told her who it was. She looked annoyed, put her finger in her place in the script, and carried it with her to the phone.

"Yes," she said. She listened. She said she knew she had promised but the phone had been busy all morning. She listened some more. She said would it be allright if she called back a little later. Winnie obviously wanted to know what was so important that she couldn't talk then. Katie said Phil Garland had asked her to read a script and she was in the middle of it. She listened. She said yes, that was the script. She said yes, she knew Charlie Stuart, he was a friend of Harry's. She said could they please talk about it later, after she'd finished reading and had done some thinking. She hung up and went back to the couch.

Sometime in the middle of the afternoon, I sensed her presence. She was standing in the doorway, the script in her hand, watching me. She had an odd expression on her face. I pushed back away from the typewriter.

She said, "I've read it. Twice."

"Yes?" I said.

"It's wonderful," she said.

"Do you know what part they want you for?"

"I think so," she said, but I could tell she wasn't quite certain. "For Sarah." Sarah was a nice role and in the overall scheme a not unimportant one. But still, it was a minor role. With the right actress, it might draw a lot of attention, but it would never take major focus, and it was not meant to.

I said, "I think you're wrong. I think they want you for Marianne."

She started. She stared, not believing. "I couldn't," she said.

"I think you probably could."

"But it's the lead. It's for a star."

"That's right," I said.

"You can't be serious."

"I'm very serious. It's time you woke up and took a look at yourself, Katie. That's how they see you."

"I think I'd better call Winnie," she said.

Winnie didn't ask. Winnie told Katie that Katie loved the script, just as Winnie loved it. Winnie said she found it hard to believe that a fat little pimp like Charlie Stuart, who'd never accomplished diddley-squat before in his life, could have written it, but his name was on it all alone, and in this town, nobody who'd written something like that would let somebody else take the credit all by himself. Well, she said, in this business you learned never to be surprised. Stranger things had happened. Charlie Stuart had certainly been talking long enough about this thing he was going to spring on everybody one of these days. So maybe this was the day. There was one thing certain, Winnie said. The lead, that girl, Marianne, was perfect for Katie. It read as though it had been written for her and only her, as though Charlie Stuart had had her in mind from day one. But, Winnie said, if those bastards out in Burbank thought they were going to get Katie just because they had the right role for her, they'd better think twice. If they wanted her, they'd have to come up with the right kind of deal. She and Katie had better talk in the morning, early. They had better have breakfast together, because there was a lot to talk about and they were due at Garland's office at eleven. She'd meet Katie at the Polo Lounge at eight-thirty. There was one thing that Katie shouldn't forget; she should drum it into her brain before she went to sleep: She was to keep her mouth shut and not utter a sound unless Winnie gave her a nod.

They had their breakfast at the Polo Lounge, and then they drove out to Burbank together and arrived at Garland's office precisely at eleven. When something important was brewing, Winnie was never late. The reports I got of that meeting later, first from Katie and then from Garland, told me that this time, at least, Winnie earned her money. This time, at least, Winnie was really working for Katie.

Garland was not alone, of course. Charlie Stuart was with him, but, naturally, he would be, for this was his thing. And after the first fifteen minutes, Karl Vogel walked in. It was all very warm and cordial at the beginning, everyone telling Katie how marvelous she was in the musical, how the public was going to devour it and her like they were everybody's favorite dessert, and how even the critics were going to be snowed, and if they weren't, then there had to a lot more wrong with them than everybody already thought, and who cared about the critics, anyway, it was the public that counted, and the public was going to line up around the block three times even in a blizzard. Vogel said the important thing now was to strike while the iron was hot. It was essential to get Katie into another picture, a big picture, as soon as possible and have it ready while she was still riding the crest.

Winnie agreed. Did they have a particular project in mind? She assumed they did, since Charlie Stuart was there and, of course, they had all read his script. Wasn't that what they were here to talk about?

That, Garland said, and a few other things. They had some other properties they thought might be just right for Katie, too. One thing follows another. What would Katie think if they offered her a three-picture contract? He looked at Katie.

Winnie said, "Look at me, don't look at her. I do the talking for her around you sharks." She said did they think they were playing tiddlelywinks with babies? There was no way on God's green earth that she was going to let her Katie get locked into a deal like that.

Not even if the money was right?

What kind of money were they talking about?

Garland mentioned a figure. Not for all three pictures but for each picture individually. Katie couldn't believe what she heard. "If I'd been there alone," she told me later, "I'd have said yes that second and thought I was a thief."

"If you'd been there alone," I said, "they'd never have made that kind of offer." Give Winnie her due.

Winnie laughed. It was not a pleasant sound.

Vogel said he thought it was a generous proposal. More than generous. After all, Katie was just a beginner. She'd only made one picture, and that hadn't been released yet. Nobody knew her. Nobody knew what she could really do. Nobody knew if she had staying power. They were taking a big gamble with no assurance of a pay off.

Winnie laughed some more. If they thought it was such a gamble, she said, they'd never have made the offer in the first place. If what they were trying to do was cheap her down and lock her in, then she and Katie were going to walk out right that minute. The word was out. She knew it and they knew it. There were plenty of people in town who'd be willing to take a gamble on Katie sight unseen, right that very day, only they wouldn't consider it much of a gamble.

It went back and forth that way for a long while. Winnie was good at this sort of thing, very good, but then this was how she had made her real reputation, how she won and kept her clients. She had walked into that room knowing what she was after, and she had no intention of walking out without getting it. To Winnie Argoth, negotiations were an art, and they often meant setting a position and not moving from it, or not seeming to move from it, and letting the other side do the caving. She had what they wanted. They'd have to meet her terms to get it.

By lunch, nothing had been settled. They broke, went to Vogel's private dining room, and chatted about everything but the business they were supposed to be doing. Katie noticed that nobody had a drink, though drinks were offered. Perrier was the drink of the day.

Back in Garland's office after lunch, the preliminaries over, the hard bargaining got under way. Winnie had dozens of questions, and before she would discuss anything, let alone agree to anything, she wanted answers. Some of the questions, obviously, were none of her business, but she asked them, anyway, and expected to hear the answers. She wanted to know what the budget for the picture was. They told her, using the figures Charlie Stuart had prepared. She said it sounded a little low. They said it wasn't carved in granite and could always be changed if necessary. She said it was going to have to be changed. They didn't argue.

She wanted to know about the financing. Vogel said the studio would advance half the budget, would release and distribute the film. Winnie asked who was putting up the rest. Vogel said private sources. Winnie said what private sources? Vogel said it was complicated. Winnie said uncomplicate it. Vogel said, well, since this was Charlie Stuart's project and since he and Phil Garland had brought it to the studio, the film would be made by an independent producing company they were setting up under the studio's aegis. It was going to be called Stugar Productions. Stugar would be responsible for raising the other half of the capital. Garland said the money was already promised; he arranged that with some of the bankers he knew over the weekend. Winnie asked what kind of interest he was paying on the money and how many points he was giving away. Garland told her. She said he must have something on those guys. You couldn't buy money at those rates these days. Garland only smiled.

Winnie asked who was going to direct. Stuart said he'd given the script to Walter Frank over the weekend and Frank, who already had two Oscars on the shelf and was salivating for a chance to win a third, had called early that morning and said he wanted to do it. Winnie said he wasn't a bad choice, even if she didn't happen to represent him. But had they thought about Billy Fielding? He'd already worked with Katie, and she trusted him. Garland said Fielding wasn't right for this kind of picture. Winnie said Fielding was right for any kind of picture and if anything happened with Walter Frank, they ought to keep that in mind. Garland said he'd make a note of it.

Winnie asked who they had in mind for the major roles and the more important featured ones. Stuart said they hadn't contacted anyone yet; they wouldn't get around to that until later in the week, at the earliest. Winnie said if they were that close, they must have some names in mind. Stuart looked at Garland, and Garland nodded. Stuart mentioned some names. Winnie listened. She objected to a few; they weren't strong enough or good enough, or they were too old or too young, or they just weren't right, not the way she saw the picture. She offered some suggestions of her own. Some happened to be her clients, but others weren't. Garland said she had good judgment and they'd consider them carefully. She said they ought to do more than consider.

She wanted to know when they planned to go into production. Garland said that preproduction would start that week and if everything went according to plan, they thought the cameras could start to turn in forty-five to sixty days. The shooting schedule would be sixteen weeks, though they might have to extend to twenty. He looked at Winnie and said, "You know, Winnie, you're sitting on the wrong side of the table. You ought to be sitting here, running this damn company."

Winnie laughed and said, "Someday, buster. Someday."

Winnie took it all in, turned it over, digested it. They waited. She had some more questions, and they were answered. Finally, she said, "Okay, now we can get down the business we came here for. You want my Katie for the lead, for this broad Marianne, right?"

They agreed. And, of course, they would like a commitment for another two pictures after this one.

"Bullshit," she said. The most she'd give was an option for a second, with terms to be negotiated, but not less than 25 percent more than Katie would get for this one.

They argued about that. Vogel said she was asking for the moon. She said no, just the sun. It went back and forth until they finally agreed that Katie would give them the option for the picture after this one with a salary boost of at least 10 percent. Winnie added, however, they should never forget that the 10 percent boost was just the place where they were going to start talking; it was just a floor.

"The usual perks, of course," Winnie said. "Limo. Unlimited expenses at all times on location, within reason, of course, personal dresser, personal makeup man, all that crap."

No arguments there.

Billing. Winnie wanted a single card for Katie, and it had to be the first one, before the titles, before anyone else.

They argued about that, and the voices got louder and a little angry for the first time, and Vogel and Garland wouldn't give in on this one. There were going to be other stars in the picture, at least two others, and they would be a hell of a lot better known and bigger box office than Katie. If they gave the first card to Katie, they'd never get the picture made. Everybody would want first card, and they'd never be able to sign first-rate people. But before that argument was over, Winnie got what she really wanted, which was that nobody would get a single card and that Katie's name would appear before the titles on the same card, on the same line as the other stars, and in the middle of that line. ("That's the important spot," she explained to Katie later. "Because when they cut off the sides to fit the picture on the goddamn tube, the only name anybody can ever read is the one in the middle.")

"Okay," she said. "Now let's talk money."

They made an offer, and it was a lot bigger than the one Katie had heard during the morning. Winnie snorted and doubled it. They argued. They resisted. Winnie said, "If you want her, you got to pay for her. What she's worth. The question is, how much do you want her?"

They argued some more. Figures flew about the room. At last, they reached a compromise. It was not what Winnie had asked, but it was higher than they had offered.

Winnie had one more thing. "Now," she said, "how many points?"

"Winnie," Vogel said, "haven't you gotten enough. Do you want the sun, the moon, and the stars, too?"

"You bet your ass," she said. "How many points. And I don't mean net. I mean gross."

Before it was over, Katie had two points, and when they finally walked out of that room, Katie had become a very rich young lady.

16

Winnie Argoth was not, of course, only storm and vitriol. She had not gotten where she was merely by inspiring fear and ladling acid. There was guile in her, and she knew how to use it when she had to. She understood the value of flattery, especially when it came to nurturing the fragile egos of her clients. She could be devious and subtle and insidious when she thought it necessary. She was adept at reading people and gauging how best to deal with them to win what she was after. If she had misread me, and to a lesser degree Katie, it was, I think, because we were outside her experience. The world of films was her world, the only world she really knew, and so she tended to see people and things in terms of that world. But I was not of it, and didn't want to be in it, and Katie was only beginning to be part of it. In Katie, she recognized the uncertainties, the doubts, the hesitations, about her own talents and abilities, and so she set about to do all she could to convince Katie that she was far better than she knew and that in Winnie's hands and under Winnie's tutelage she would attain more than she had ever dreamed possible and would deserve it all. If Katie had once had another dream and if it were now forever denied her, Winnie bent her energies on convincing her that there was nothing second-best about a new dream, that it could be the equal, and more than the equal, of the old one, and that Katie could achieve as great, if not greater, inner gradification and fame by succeeding here.

But to do this, Winnie had to strip Katie of all the impedimenta of the past. She believed that completely. That had been her way with most of her people, anyway. With Katie, she was convinced it was even more urgent. I was, of course, part of the impedimenta. If Winnie had any sense of the bonds between Katie and me, she was not troubled by them and believed she could snap them with only a little effort; she had done that before and so was convinced that marriage or any relationship was, at best, a tenuous and impermanent thing. I was in the way, I was a reminder of a dead or dying past, and so I must go. If, in some ways, I was different from the others she had dismissed, she didn't care and made no effort to find out why. She had no desire to find out who I was or what I did or whether I might have some value. I was simply "husband," and if she had her way, I would soon be the forgotten ex-husband. With me, she used the storm and the vitriol. With Katie, she used subtlety and guile. I don't think she ever launched a direct attack on me to Katie or ever revealed what her plans for me were. And if Katie saw, or sensed, she tried to ignore, out of that loyalty to those who were close to her and out of a belief that she could right anything through her own efforts.

Winnie was good. If there was antagonism between us, she said, she couldn't really understand why. Obviously, for some reason, I had taken an instantaneous dislike to her. That was my problem, not hers. If she didn't particularly care for me, and that was just too apparent to miss, it was simply because the business was her life and so she had little time for or patience with people who had nothing to do with the business. Actually, I didn't concern her at all except as I affected Katie. If Katie wanted to keep me, who was she to say nay? Of course, I probably resented the fact that Katie was increasingly turning to her and leaning on her for advice. But it was only natural that Katie should. What else was a good agent for, an agent who knew the business as well as she and who had the kind of power she had? Of course, I must resent the fact that they talked so often and in a language I didn't understand and about things that couldn't possibly interest me. She never could understand why I insisted on going to all those parties. They must bore me. I was an outsider who had no sense of what was going on or how important those occasions were. Maybe I resented the fact that Katie was becoming such a success and was becoming famous and was leaving me behind and I blamed it all on Winnie. Whatever it was, it wasn't Winnie's doing.

After the triumph in Garland's office, Katie was inside a euphoric dream, and she didn't want to wake. She couldn't comprehend what was happening to her, couldn't believe it, could hardly accept it. She had heard, as we all had, the tales of the others to whom much the same had happened. But they were someone else, not her, and they had dreamed this dream and striven with everything in them to attain it. For Katie, it had been something she had never even considered. What was happening was pure accident, and she wasn't sure she deserved it or had earned it. It was all an illusion, but at that moment she didn't want it to go away; she wanted to enjoy it as long as it lasted.

I spoiled that moment for her, with a little help from Winnie Argoth. In her elation, Winnie wanted to take Katie to dinner to celebrate; she had found a special place in Santa Monica that hadn't been discovered yet. It would be perfect. This would be their night. But for Katie victories to be real meant sharing them with me. Winnie tried to talk her out of that. This was their victory and theirs alone. I wouldn't understand, would probably be bored by the things they had to talk about. Katie said that was silly. Of course I'd understand. Of course I'd want to be with her and share it all with her. They'd have plenty of time to talk later. She wouldn't be able to talk, anyway. This was a night just to glory in it all, and she couldn't possibly do it without me.

It was a miserable celebration. We drove out to Santa Monica in Winnie's limousine. Winnie insisted that Katie sit beside her in front while she drove. (It might be a block-long limousine, but I couldn't imagine a chauffeur driving; Winnie always had to be at the controls.) I sat in back. Winnie talked nonstop, to Katie, and pretended I wasn't there. In the restaurant, where the food was mediocre enough so that I was sure I knew why it hadn't been discovered and probably never would be unless people went because Winnie went and they wanted to be in the same place, we ignored each other, though there were occasional digs. Winnie monopolized Katie, and when Katie turned to me to say something, Winnie invariably had something to say to distract her. The tension and the barely concealed hostility at that table were as thick as the fog outside. Even in her euphoria, Katie couldn't miss it, and this time she couldn't completely ignore it. Her eyes kept flicking between Winnie and me, and there was a worried look in them.

After Winnie dropped us off and we were in the house, Katie said, "You two really spoiled my evening, didn't you."

"I guess we did," I said. "I'm sorry."

"Will you please tell me what it is with the two of you?"

"Winnie doesn't like me, and I don't like her. And that's probably putting it mildly."

"Well, I don't like any of it," she said. "I want you to stop it. You're the two most important people in the world to me right now. You'd both better learn to get along."

"You'd better tell that to Winifred Argoth."

"I intend to," she said. She shook her head angrily.

"Sometimes, Harry Miller, you give me a swift pain in the ass."

Within a week, the contracts were drawn and signed, and Katie had more money in the bank than either of us had ever seen or imagined could be in one place at one time. She wanted to deposit it in our joint account. I told her that was dumb. She had to open a separate account in her own name. We argued about that until she finally agreed, but only after I agreed that the money was there for both of us.

She had a lot of free time then. It would be weeks before any real work on the picture began for her, though out on the lot, the preproduction work was racing. She had some meetings out in Burbank with Walter Frank and with Garland and Charlie Stuart, had some initial sessions and tests with the technical people in lighting and costuming, met and talked with the other actors, worked daily with her acting coach, and spent a lot of time at the acting lab. There were meetings with a financial wizard Winnie recommended about investments and taxes and the other things you have to worry about when you have a lot of money and know there's going to be a lot more. It might have seemed a full schedule, but for someone who had been working as long and hard as she had, it make her feel that time was empty. There was no way I could share those hours, though. I was writing, and the words were coming, and the book was taking shape at last. So she filled the idle hours with shopping, which she hadn't done in a long time, coming home with boxes filled with clothes, for herself and for me, and she had lunch and afternoon cocktails (which, for her, meant mainly sipping a glass of wine) with Suzie and with some of the dancers from the first film, with Terry, with some of the new friends she made, and, of course, with Winnie Argoth.

She did something else. In the middle of one afternoon,

she came bursting into the house filled with excitement, came into the bedroom, standing just inside the door. "Are you working?" she asked, and I knew she wanted me to stop.

I said, "Yeah, but I'm just about ready to quit for the day."

"Good," she said. "Can you stop now and come with me? There's something I want you to see."

"What?"

"I'm not going to tell. You'll just have to wait until we get there."

We went out to the car. She drove west on Sunset, made a turn a little before Beverly Hills, and drove a little way up into the hills before pulling to a stop in front of a house set just a little way back from the road. It was a nice-looking house, perhaps a little smaller than some of its neighbors, sided with California redwood, the roof a darker, rougher shingle. I knew why we were there.

"Do you like it?" she asked.

"It looks okay from the outside," I said.

"You have to see the inside," she said. She walked up to the front door, took a key from her pocket, inserted it into the lock, and pushed the door open. She stood aside and made me go first. The inside was furnished, and the furnishings were obviously not cheap. They were modern and they were tasteful and they fit. Whoever had done the decorating had to know what he was doing. Katie took me around. The house had two floors and a basement that, I found out when we went down there, had all the usual stuff plus a laundry. On the ground floor there was a large living room, a dining room, and a big kitchen with a glass-enclosed breakfast area. The rear wall of the living room was sliding glass, opening on to a flagstone patio and then to a small pool and beyond, just before a high fence of closely joined logs, the bark dangling roughly off them, a handsome flower garden. Upstairs, there were two bedrooms, one large with a dressing room and private bath, the other a little smaller and also with bath. The smaller room had been set up as an office, though it contained a convertible sofa just in case you had guests who were going to sleep over.

"What do you think?" she asked anxiously. "Do you like it?"

"It's very nice," I said.

"It's ours," she said.

I nodded slowly. "I thought you were going to say that."

She looked at me carefully. "Are you angry?"

"Why should I be angry?"

"Because I did it without telling you."

"You wanted it, and I guess you can afford it."

"I didn't buy it," she said. "I only rented, with an option to buy."

"I see."

"Are you mad? You look mad."

"I'm not mad."

"Yes, you are. You wanted to go back to New York. You said so. But don't you see, we can't now."

"I suppose not."

"And the place we live in—"

"You're right. It's a dump."

"We can't entertain there."

"I suppose we can't."

"And we've made lots of friends. It's time we started paying them back. They've certainly entertained us enough."

"Of course."

"Harry?"

"Yeah?"

"It's the right thing. We can be happy here."

"If a house can make you happy, I suppose this is a good place."

"It is. I know it is."

"I didn't know you were looking."

"I wasn't. Not really. I mean, Suzie said we ought to. She said we could afford it now. She said we'd earned a nice place to live. She took me to a few places. But I wasn't really looking. And then we found this. I fell in love with it the minute I saw it, and when I walked inside, I knew it was us."

"Whoever did the decorating did a nice job," I said.

She smiled a little shyly. "I did it," she said. "Suzie helped, but I did it."

"Oh," I said. "So you've known about it for a while."

"Yes," she said. "But I didn't want you to see it until I had everything just right. Isn't it wonderful?"

"You're right, Katie. It's wonderful. And you deserve it. You deserve only the best."

So we moved and in that way made a commitment that I had not wanted to make, had resisted making but had known we would have to make, had known it really since that day in Garland's screening room.

We needed only a small van to transport the things we had brought from New York and still wanted to keep and the few things we had acquired along the way. As the loading was just finishing, Wolf Rabinowitz turned up. He had dropped by, he said, to collect the keys and return our security. I told him that hadn't been necessary. I would have dropped them off at his office, and he could have mailed us the security.

He said no, no, he had been in the neighborhood as it was, and besides, he had wanted to see us one last time and wish us good-bye and good luck. We had been good tenants. We had never made any trouble. I was a nice man. My beautiful wife was a nice lady. She always had a smile and a friendly word for everyone. He was sorry that we were going, but he could understand. He wished only that we would have a wonderful life in our new home. After all the trouble we had had when we first arrived, it should be so, because we deserved it.

I thanked him and we shook hands, and Katie kissed him on the cheek, and he blushed, and then he turned and walked away down the street. We waited until the van had pulled away, went back and checked to make sure we had left nothing we wanted, then got into the MG and drove away. I looked back once. It was, indeed, a dump.

And the new house, on its plateau a little way up the hill, was, indeed, a nice house. It was nice to live in a place that was clean and where there was green and where the smell was not of rotting garbage that nobody bothered to collect but, rather, of the faint spicy aroma of growing things in the backyard, the scent always drifting through the open windows. It was nice to live in a place where the furniture was new and good to look at and not old and shabby, with the padding bleeding through holes in the upholstery and with the wood scratched and dented and warped. It was nice to have room to spread out, to have a kitchen big enough and modern enough and equipped enough so that if you felt like it, and I often did because I liked to cook, you could experiment and try almost anything. It was nice to have a pool where you could swim and relax when you'd dried out at the typewriter, where the two of us could sometimes take our clothes off and swim together and make love on one of the lounges out in the air and not worry about shocking the neighbors, because nobody could see in over that high fence that surrounded the property. It was nice to have a room to work in, a room to which I could go in the middle of the night and work for a couple of hours when the solution to a problem suddenly woke me, knowing that I could go and write and not disturb Katie. It was nice to have a home where Katie could bring her friends and talk or do whatever it was they did and not have to worry about disturbing me. It was nice for a thousand reasons. And, except for a vagrant sense at odd moments that we had made a commitment I was still dubious about, a feeling that I, or we, had spread a net to trap us, I had a nice feeling about that house.

A week or so after we'd moved, I called my agent in New York to tell him we'd moved. He said, "So you've decided to stay in Lotus Land, after all."

I said not necessarily, but the house was a lot better than where we had been living and it was time for the change.

He asked, "Have you been doing something I don't know about?" Which meant, of course, had I been doing something and not paying him his 10 percent.

I said no, but that Katie had gotten a start in the movies and it was beginning to look as though she might have a career.

He asked about the book.

I said I was really working on it at last, and I hoped, since I thought I was working well, that if everything continued on this course, he might see a complete manuscript in a few months.

He said great, and it's about time and what the hell have you been doing all this time, anyway, and you'd better call Sy Marshall and tell him, because he's been on my back and I've been trying to get him off.

I called Sy. He said that was the best news he'd had all day, because the business people were on his ass about all the advances he had outstanding to authors who weren't turning in manuscripts and maybe it was getting to be time to think about suing a few of them. He asked whether the book was any good. I said I thought so, but who was I to judge? He said he couldn't wait, and damn it, keep in touch and let him know the progress.

Those first weeks there were a lot of people around a lot of the time. Katie was paying back favors, and I didn't mind, since I could go upstairs and lock myself in my own room and work and nobody bothered me. If I decided to go downstairs to get some coffee or something, nobody paid much attention, and I don't think half the people there knew who I was or really cared much, which was all right with me. We even had a few parties in the evening, and they weren't too bad, because Katie made sure to invite at least a couple of people I knew, which meant I didn't spend the time always on the outside looking in.

Suzie was there a lot, and the second week we were in the house, she came to stay. She moved into my office, on the sofa bed, which she abandoned early in the morning so I could work. If I couldn't go to it during the night, and there were nights when I wanted to, that was all right, too, because Suzie was Suzie. Whatever the trouble was between Garland and her, she wouldn't tell me, though I'm sure she told Katie, who didn't repeat it. Whatever it was, it passed after three or four days, and Suzie left and moved back into the big house in Beverly Hills, and all seemed well there again.

Perhaps the best thing was that I no longer had to deal with Winnie Argoth. I didn't have a phone in my office, and if it rang in another part of the house while I was working, I ignored it, knowing that if she was home, Katie would answer, and if not, then the service would pick up. If Katie still talked about her a lot and saw her often, too often as far as I was concerned, at least she didn't turn up at the house. When we did run into each other at a weekend party, there seemed to be some kind of truce. I guess Katie must have said something to her, because at least she nodded, if she didn't say anything, before she led Katie away.

I heard from Charlie Stuart seldom and saw him hardly at all, which bothered me not in the least, since I had my own work to concentrate on. He sent us a huge plant as a housewarming gift, so huge there was no room big enough to contain it and us at the same time. We put it out on the patio, and it flourished. The first time Suzie saw it, she said, "What is it with that guy? Does he owe you guys something, or is it just that he's in love with Katie? That thing must have set him back two, maybe three, hundred bucks." We both assured her he was just a generous man and a good friend. She laughed loudly at that. Katie wrote him a nice note of thanks and then thanked him personally when she ran into him on the lot.

She invited him to dinner, casually and without much thought. He accepted eagerly, made a date right then, and arrived at our door wearing a suit; I hadn't known he even owned one, and he shamed both of us, since I was in old chinos, just having finished work, and Katie was in jeans. But he didn't seem to mind. He was filled with pleasure at being with us, or, rather, her, in the new house. He told us how great we both looked, how great the house was, how great everything was, but mainly he spent the evening staring at Katie, the kind of look boys used to give girls in school, the girls they were always afraid to talk to. Katie was amused. He left early, and I'm sure he had no idea what we fed him. Other than that, he called me about once a week to tell me how hard he was working and how fast and smoothly everything was going. They were making such rapid progress, he said, that it looked as though they'd probably push up the starting date for the production by at least a week.

As that day drew closer, Katie spent more time with the script, marking it, trying to explore character and meaning with her coach and at home with herself. A couple of times I would look up and find her standing in the doorway, waiting. She'd say, "Do you mind if I interrupt you for just a minute? I mean, is it really okay?"

I'd tell her it was, and she'd come in with the script open, a puzzled look on her face. She was having trouble with a scene. She wasn't exactly sure of the motivation, of what I had been trying to do there. (When that happened, I made mental notes, certain I'd probably have to make a change at some point, though I sure as hell wasn't going to do it until I was asked.) We'd talk about it for a few minutes, and then I'd grin and say, "You know what they say. Unless he's James Joyce, never ask a writer what he was trying to do, because he can't tell you because he doesn't know. Only the critics know."

Stuart was right. They breezed through preproduction. But then, he'd laid it all out beforehand, like a master technician. He knew precisely what locations he wanted, and he knew the best way to get them. He had formed mental images of sets and costumes, and he sat down with the designers and explained his ideas, and they were usually pretty good, usable with some modifications. He had his hands in every area. But then, this was his dream, it had been his dream for nearly as long as anyone could remember, and he had filled it to the last corner and wasn't going to let anything damage it.

Rehearsals began early on a Monday morning. The limo Winnie had demanded for Katie arrived at six to transport her out to Burbank, the hour she would be leaving from then until the picture was finished. She came home tired but elated. Things had gone very well. Some of the actors were a little too temperamental, but Walter Frank, who could be even more temperamental when he wanted to be, knew how to deal with that kind of thing. He was a good director, as his record proved. He knew what each scene needed, and he strove for it tirelessly, but he never lost sight of the total pattern and plan. He drove his people hard, but his demands were rarely outrageous. He wanted results, that's all, and he was going to get them. Toward Katie, he was as patient and understanding as Billy Fielding had been; he was filled with suggestions and insights, told her to take her time, not to rush things. He guided her, and every day her confidence grew.

A few times after that, Charlie Stuart came by with a copy of the script and pages of suggestions from Walter Frank. The director wasn't happy with this scene. He thought this particular piece of dialogue didn't ring true. When that happened, he turned to Stuart, writer of the screenplay, given access to the sound stage because he was the producer, and asked him to please make the necessary fixes and have them ready by morning, if possible. Stuart, of course, brought them to me, and while I read them over and played with the ideas, none of which required any major effort, he'd go off and spend the evening hours waiting and talking with Katie.

They had been shooting for three weeks, had been on location for one (an empty week for me, with Katie away, but I was well aware that it wouldn't be the last one; there were six more weeks on location scheduled, and three of those weeks would be in a row, in an isolated place in the Colorado Rockies from which weekend travel home would be difficult if not impossible), and they were back on the lot for interiors. Stuart called in the middle of the afternoon, in what sounded like growing panic. There was trouble with two scenes, and it looked to him as though the trouble might be major, not something easily repaired. One of the stars had gone into a temperamental fit. He was making threats. He was demanding changes, complete rewrites. Worst of all, Walter Frank seemed to be leaning in his direction.

I sighed and told Stuart to bring me his notes that night and I'd see what I could do. He seemed uncertain about that. He wasn't sure that would do it. He said he thought the best thing would be for me to come out to the studio and watch. If I saw it for myself, maybe I'd see what they were talking about.

Going out there was something I had no desire to do. I wanted to stay as far away from the making of that picture as I could. And I thought Stuart would want me to stay far away, for obvious reasons. But he waved that away. He said I could just show up as a visitor who wanted to see how they made movies. There were often visitors on the set, and I was, after all, Katherine Summers's husband, so why shouldn't I come around now and then to see what she was 'oing?

With that excuse, maybe he was right, and maybe it wouldn't hurt. Certainly I'd have a better idea of what was getting actors into a swivet, and that might make it easier for me than just trying to figure it out from Charlie's notes. And it was not a bad time for me to be doing it. I'd finished the first draft of my book that week and had sent it off to New York, and now I was waiting to hear the reaction. That's not the best time to be wandering around alone in an empty house with no place to go.

I had the MG now, and I drove it out to Burbank the next morning. Stuart had a visitor's pass and a pass to the set waiting for me at the gate. I picked them up, asked some directions, and found my way. The red light was on over the door, and I had to wait until it went off before I could enter. The sound stage was one of the big ones. It was filled with the interiors of several rooms in several different houses, with a thousand lights overhead and everywhere, with an impenetrable maze of wires and lines and cables, with cameras, with deck chairs, and with people all moving, obviously not blindly, obviously knowing exactly what they were doing and where they were going.

Charlie saw me. He had been waiting. He hurried over with a copy of the script in his hands. It was open to one of the scenes that Katie had been having trouble with one afternoon. This one, he whispered, and he flipped through the pages, and this one. Both scenes took place in the same location, though at different times. He suggested that maybe I ought to go and stand off to one side and watch. See what I could see.

I moved well into the shadows. I looked around for Katie, but I didn't see her. Under a bank of lights, in front of several cameras, before one of the interiors, Walter Frank was in an argument, and it didn't appear to be a mild one, with one of the actors. Stuart joined them, and they both turned on him.

Frank suddenly spun around and walked away. He

stopped just under a camera, turned, and said, "Damn it, let's just try it again."

"It won't work. God damn it, it won't work. How many times do I have to tell you that. I can't play the goddamn scene." The actor stood there glaring at Frank, glaring at Stuart. I didn't know him, but I had heard he was not the easiest guy in the world to work with. He was, though, a perfectionist, and when things went right for him, they went right for everybody around him.

Frank shouted back. "Jimmy, just calm down for once in your life. Let's give it a try once more. Maybe Charlie can finally figure out what's wrong. Something sure as hell isn't right, but it beats me if I can figure it out. Let's run through it again."

"It's a waste of time," the actor said. "But if you want it, I'll do it. It's your damn money."

Frank looked around. "Where's Katie?" he yelled. His voice got very calm, and very deadly. "We can't begin without Miss Summers. Would someone be so good as to inform her that we are about to begin again and would she be so kind as to join us?"

A young girl raced away, toward a mobile trailer abutting a distant wall. She knocked at the door. It opened, and Katie, in costume and makeup, appeared. Winnie Argoth was with her. The girl said something to Katie. Katie nodded and started across the floor toward the set. She said something to Frank. He nodded and gestured toward the set. She moved onto it, joined the other actor. I never noticed where Winnie Argoth went.

"Okay," Frank said, "let's run it. No cameras, please. We're going to let the actors run the scene without cameras."

They moved through it. On the page, and even reading it aloud, the scene had rung true. Watching them now, it didn't seem true to me; it didn't seem fine at all. Maybe it was the actor. Maybe another actor could have breathed life into it. But he sure as hell wasn't, or couldn't. It was patent that he didn't like the scene and wasn't comfortable with it and was barely trying. Against what he was doing, or not doing, there was not a thing for Katie to do but to walk through and try to make the best of it.

I thought I saw what was making him unhappy, what was wrong. And if it was wrong with this scene, then it was wrong with the other one, for though they were separate, what happened in the second grew out of the conflict in the first. Watching the struggle, I began to see where I had gone wrong, and I was sure I knew how to make it right. But this one wouldn't be that easy. It would require some basic restructuring not just in the two scenes but in five or six others. They were all interrelated, and you couldn't change one without it affecting all the others. It would take a couple of days to do it, but it could be done.

And then I heard the loud bellow. "What the fuck is he doing on the set?"

I turned to look. Winnie Argoth was glaring in my direction, pointing toward me, standing and roaring at Charlie Stuart. And a lot of other eyes were turning and trying to follow that pointing arm. I had thought I was pretty well concealed in the shadows, not that I had thought it necessary to conceal myself, only that I wanted to be as unobtrusive as possible.

Frank turned and stared at Winnie. He snapped, "Miss Argoth, will you please shut up. We are trying to make a picture."

Winnie swiveled, glared back, turned away deliberately, as if he and his words meant nothing to her, turned back to Charlie Stuart, and bellowed again, "I don't want him here. Get him the fuck off this set. Off the goddamn lot."

Both Katie and the actor had stopped what they were doing. They were peering out, trying to see what was causing the commotion. But, blinded by the glaring lights in front of them, all they could make out were shadows, if even that.

Winnie started to advance on me. Charlie trailed in her wake. Watching them approaching, I thought of Nicholas, her flunky. She stopped abruptly a foot away from me, glared, and said too loudly, as always, "What the fuck are you doing here?"

Charlie said, trying to calm her, "He's a friend of mine, Winnie. I invited him."

Winnie spun on him. "I don't give a shit if he's your lover," she said. "I want him the fuck out of here. Now, if not sooner."

"He's not making any trouble, Winnie," Charlie said, placating. I wasn't saying anything. I was just watching and hoping that Katie couldn't see and didn't know what was going on.

"Screw you," Winnie said. "He's making plenty of trouble. That's the only fucking thing he knows how to do. I don't want my Katie to know he's here. She's got enough problems as it is." She turned back on me. "Get lost, husband," she said. "Take a fucking hike."

I looked at her, and then I grinned, though I didn't feel very amused. I just wanted to enrage her a little more. I said, as mildly as I could, "I seem to get on your nerves."

"Fuck you," she said. "Get lost."

"I don't think so," I said. "After all, I'm a guest."

"I don't give a shit whether you're the goddamn king of England," she said. "I don't want to see your fucking face around here."

I looked over at Stuart. "Charlie?"

"Take a little walk with me, Harry," he said. He took my arm and started to lead me away.

Winnie Argoth smirked. That's about the only word for the expression that came over her face. She watched us for a second with that mien of mastery and victory, then turned and started toward the set. Katie and the actor were still on it, peering into the lights, trying to see through them. Winnie walked past Walter Frank, walked directly to Katie.

I heard Katie ask, "Was there some trouble out there? I heard you yelling."

Winnie said, "Don't worry about it. It was nothing. Just some creep who didn't belong on the set and was making trouble. I got rid of him."

Walter Frank said, and his voice was acid, "Miss Argoth, would you kindly move your ass off the set. We would all like to get on with our work, if you don't mind. We're waiting."

Winnie smiled at him. "I wouldn't mind at all, Walter. You just go ahead." She walked slowly past him under the cameras and turned to watch.

Charlie Stuart led me out of the set through the wide doors, out into the corridor. "I'm sorry, Harry," he said. "I didn't know it was like that between you and Winnie."

"That's all right, Charlie," I said. "Not your fault."

"I asked you to come."

"You didn't have any way of knowing."

"Well, anyway, you saw the scene."

"I saw it."

"Can you figure out what's wrong?"

"Yeah, I think so. I think I can fix it. But it'll take a couple of days."

Relief went through him. "Thank god," he said. "Take all the time you need. Only, you know, the sooner the better, right? Look, now I'd better go and talk to Walter. You know, tell him it's going to be all right."

"You do that," I said. "You tell him you know how to make it right."

"You bet," he said, and hurried away, back through the door onto the set.

17 Two days had been my guess. It took me three. It was not that the changes were more difficult than I had thought. It was that the screenplay was now something out of the past. I was tired of it. I had used it up, and it had used me up; I had gone on to other things, and so I wasn't much interested in it any longer. It took me time to force myself back and recapture the mood and the other time, but once I did, the changes came easily. I turned the new pages over to Stuart. He read them, pacing around my office. He looked pleased, but he wasn't sure of his own reactions by then, and he wasn't sure, because he hadn't seen what was so wrong with the way they had read before. He took the pages out to Burbank, had them typed and run off, and turned the copies over to Walter Frank, who read them, grinned happily, and called Stuart a genius. The actor who had started the whole thing was handed a copy. He read through it, said, "I told you from the beginning. Now, for chrissake, it's right and it'll play."

I didn't know any of that until the evening, because Charlie didn't bother to call and tell me. It was Katie. She got home and found me out by the pool. She looked and smiled and said, "You write good, Miller."

I said, "Really?"

She said, "Everybody says so."

I said, "But they don't say Miller. They say Charlie Stuart. Right."

She laughed. "Right." She said, "You know, you could write screenplays. I mean, under your own name. I've read a lot of them now. You write better."

"Thanks," I said, "but no thanks. One member of this family in the movies is quite enough. Besides, I like going my own way, doing my own thing. I like writing books, and I don't like writing screenplays and all the crap that goes along with it. I like being just plain Harry Miller."

"Do you think that would change? Do you think you could ever be anything else?"

"No. But too many people would think I was taking a free ride on your coattails. I wouldn't like that. I wouldn't like people calling me Mr. Summers."

"Nobody would ever call you that."

"You'd better wake up, Katie. Some people already are."

"Nobody who counts."

"No," I said, "nobody who counts. To the people who matter, I'll always be Harry Miller."

"And," she said, "I'll always be Mrs. Harry Miller." She looked at me. "Would you like some company in the pool?"

"I'd love it. Why don't you take off your clothes and join me?"

My agent called from New York. He'd read the manuscript. It was better than he'd hoped for, after all the delays. "What kept you so long?" He told me I'd be getting a call from Sy

Marshall. He had already talked to Sy, and Sy thought it had the makings of a good book. We might even make some money out of this one.

Sy Marshall called a little later. He liked it, too. He had nice things to say about it. Then he asked what I'd think about making a few changes.

I said it was just a draft, anyway, and I was already planning on a lot of changes. Just what kind of changes did he have in mind, in particular.

"Nothing major," he said. He'd have his notes typed up and sent off to me in a day or so. When I got them and had time to go through and think about them, we should talk more. But did I think I could have my own rewrites and revisions, and whatever we agreed to in his, finished in time so they could bring out the book early in the new year?

I said, "That would depend." But I didn't see any reason why not.

He said oh, by the way, he was putting through an authorization for payment of the rest of the advance. He didn't see any reason to wait for the final manuscript; this version was good enough. We should be getting the check as soon as business got around to it. He figured I could probably use the money.

I said I appreciated that.

He said no sweat. Then he laughed and said, "Don't worry, we haven't suddenly lost our minds and decided this was be kind-to-authors week." The subrights people had read the manuscript and said it was going to go for a nice piece of change on the reprint market. He asked if I was planning to be in New York anytime soon, because it sure would be nice to sit down and have a drink and talk about any ideas I might have for the next book.

I said I wasn't sure when I'd be coming East, but I hoped it would be pretty soon. Meanwhile, I had already begun thinking about another book, but I wanted the ideas to take on a little more solid form before I talked about them.

·   ·   ·

We went to Garland's house one night for a buffet supper, Katie and I and a lot of other people, including Winnie Argoth. We filled our plates and found a couch, and Katie sat in the center, and I sat on one side and Winnie sat on the other. It was the first time I had seen her or heard her voice since that day on the set. I had not mentioned that to Katie. What would I have said? I had not been on the set before, had deliberately stayed away both because I thought my presence might be a distraction, and that she didn't need, and because the set was her turf and I felt I didn't belong there, which was the same reason I had rarely gone backstage at the ballet, had always met her either outside or just inside the door. She would not, then, have taken kindly to my going out to the set without telling her or, once there, without sending some word that I was there. It had been better, I thought, just to ignore the whole thing.

Winnie didn't talk to me, and I didn't talk to her, but it was more than that. Even in that silence, the hostility between us was palpable. Katie sat between us, rigid, frozen, not looking at either one of us. Most others, if they noticed or felt something, pretended it wasn't there or stayed clear. But Suzie, from across the room, kept her eyes on us and watched and nodded to herself.

Later, she got me alone and said, "So the war's out in the open at last."

"If you want to call it a war."

"Don't let that dyke win," she said.

"She won't. Not if I can help it."

"Katie's not blind. She sees it now, you know."

"I know."

"Say something to her."

"What? Winnie's very good and very careful. Katie'd think I was being paranoid. You know she thinks she owes everything to Winnie."

"The bitch is good at that. But don't give up, Miller. Katie needs you. And you need her."

After dinner, we went down to the screening room to see the rough cut of the musical. It was too long, of course. But that would be fixed in the final editing. The dances were very good. Katie and Terry Markoff could be proud of what they'd done. Katie was wonderful. She walked away with the picture in less than a dozen scenes. The picture itself, it seemed to me, was a bore, an overextended and overblown soap opera. But who was I to voice an opinion when everyone else around, all experts in the business, were enthusing about how marvelous it was, even in the rough version, and what a smash it was certain to be? (As it turned out, unfortunately, I was more nearly correct. The critics panned it, echoing my unspoken view, had kind words only for the dances and more than kind words for the redheaded newcomer, Katherine Summers; audiences just sort of drifted in when there was nothing better to do or see. The film eventually made a little money, I heard, but not much; it all depended on who kept the books and which books you got a chance to examine. It disappeared after a couple of months from the theaters and then began appearing on television every once in a while when there were empty time slots to fill. The most anyone seemed to remember about it was that it was the picture that introduced Katherine Summers, and I imagine that someday that will be one of those items of trivia about the movies to amaze your friends with.)

Katie was silent most of the way home. She sat far away on the edge of the other seat, almost pressing against the door, let me drive, watched me. When she broke the silence, it was to say, "I hate it."

At first, I thought she must be referring to the picture, and I tried to frame some soothing and reassuring phrases. Not about what she'd done in it—by then she was beginning to accept the fact that she was good, even if not as good as everyone was telling her—but about the picture itself.

Before I could find the right phrases, she said, "You have to stop it, Harry. I won't have it anymore."

So she wasn't talking about the picture, after all. I kept driving and didn't reply.

She said, "I'm going to do something about it. I'm going to make you two get along if it kills me. You don't have to love each other. I don't expect that. But you have to get along. I won't have two tigers around me growling at each other like juveniles all the time. I just won't have it."

What she was going to do, though I didn't know it, was put the two of us together and force us to come to terms, force us into at least a truce, and possibly even a friendly one. That was her aim.

It took some doing and some arranging and some time. She went on location twice, for a week each time, before she could find the right moment. And since she didn't mention it again during those weeks when she was home or when we talked in the evening while she was away, I thought and hoped that she had decided to forget all about it. Besides, I had other things to do. I had gotten Sy Marshall's lengthy memo, and we had argued for a couple of hours over some of the changes he wanted until finally I agreed to some and he agreed to forget some. I was well and deep into the revisions and was not dissatisfied with the way the book was now shaping up. It seemed to me to be becoming richer and fuller and better all the time.

The one thing I wasn't looking forward to was the three weeks Katie would be on location in Colorado, and those weeks were fast approaching. I was hoping I could finish the revisions sometime early while she was away, send them off, and then join her in the Rockies. I didn't care about the picture, but we would have some time together in a different setting, and there would be at least one weekend when we might go off somewhere by ourselves.

The night before she was to leave, and she would be leaving early the next morning, she had to work a little later than usual on the set. I was upstairs, moving through the revisions, when I heard the front door open and close. Without looking up, I shouted, "Katie? You home?"

She shouted back, "Home," and I heard her feet racing up the stairs. She darted in, kissed me, and looked at the paper in the typewriter. "Are you still working?"

"Almost done now. Just a little more and then I'll come down and make us a drink and we can have dinner."

"You don't have to bother," she said. "Why don't I fix dinner tonight? You can work until you're finished."

She went out and I kept working, and a little later I heard the doorbell and then the sound of voices. I wasn't paying any attention. I figured it was probably a delivery man, nothing very important.

I finished. I didn't bother to change, went down in what I usually wore while working, old chinos, a little too stained and in need of a washing, a faded polo shirt, and sneakers with no socks. Katie was in the kitchen. I could hear her moving around, could hear the clatter of pots and pans, the sounds of food being prepared. It didn't sound terribly organized, but then Katie was never terribly organized in the kitchen, and it was a surprise whenever she announced that she wanted to do the cooking.

The glass doors to the patio were open. I glanced through them as I was passing by. Winnie Argoth was sitting on one of the lounges, relaxed, at her ease, sipping a drink. For just an instant, I froze, then continued on into the kitchen. Katie had an apron on, had some chickens quartered and seasoned, was doing a few others things.

I watched her until she became aware of my presence. She smiled. "Hi," she said. "You finally finished."

"You didn't tell me she was coming," I said.

"Behave, Harry," she said, and she was annoyed by my tone and manner. "She's a guest."

I shrugged. "I'll behave. You can count on it. I'll be a good little boy."

"Now, you just stop that," she said. "Go fix yourself a drink. And you can pour me a glass of wine. And then go out and keep her company. I won't be a minute."

I poured the wine and gave it Katie. She put it on the counter near her, distracted, and I doubted whether she even noticed it. I made myself a drink, strong. I walked slowly and with obvious reluctance out onto the patio. Winnie looked up. She gave me one of her smiles. I said, "Hello."

She said, "Why, husband, you're still around."

I said, "Of course. Where else would I be?"

She said, "Katie said you were writing. What? Letters?" She laughed.

I took a deep breath. I took a deep swallow of my drink. I said, "Why don't we cool it."

"Cool what, husband?" she said. She was enjoying herself. She looked around. She said, "Katie's got a nice house."

"Yes," I said.

"Enjoy it, husband," she said, "while you still can."

"I intend to," I said, "for a long time."

"Don't kid yourself," she said.

Katie came out through the glass doors, too late to hear any of it. She carried her wine with her. She sat down and sipped it. I finished my drink and started away to refill it. Winnie held out her glass to me, asked me to get her another, told me what she was drinking. Bourbon straight, with one ice cube. I thought it was too bad we didn't have any poison around the house the color of bourbon. I made her drink, double, made a double for myself, and then added a little extra; I drink, but usually not very much, and when I get drunk, which isn't very often, I can become obnoxious. That didn't seem like such a bad idea. I took the drinks back out to the patio and handed Winnie hers. I sat down next to Katie.

Katie looked at me; she looked at Winnie. She said, "This has been going on long enough. Too long, if you ask me. I want you to really get to know each other."

"We know each other," I said.

"Harry," she said, staring at me in warning.

"Sorry," I said.

So we sat there talking, or rather Winnie and Katie talked, Winnie doing most of the talking, and I listened, or didn't listen, and stared off at the flowers beyond the pool, examined Charlie Stuart's massive plant, which was threatening to become a malignant growth that would take over the whole yard. Katie tried to include me in the conversation, but that didn't work very well. She sighed and went back into the kitchen to check on the dinner.

Winnie said when she was gone, "You can't win, husband."

I wasn't going to rise to it. I said, "I didn't know I had anything to win. I didn't realize I was in a fight."

"You fucking well better know it, husband."

"Such language from a lady," I said. "Why fight with me? I'm not worth it."

"It's about time you knew that," she said.

"Then why fight?"

"You're in her goddamn way, that's why," she said. "I'm looking out for her. I'm doing what's best for her, even if she doesn't know it yet. You hang around, you'll hold her back. And I'm not going to let that happen."

"So you told me. Before."

"Well, I'm fucking well telling you again."

"Why don't you tell Katie?"

"I don't have to. She'll find out for herself."

"Then why bother?"

Katie came back to tell us dinner was ready. The tension was too thick. She looked from one to the other of us. "Will you two please stop this," she said. "There's only one thing I want, and you can give it to me, both of you. I want you to like each other."

"Sure thing, sweetie," Winnie said sweetly.

I didn't say anything. I finished my drink and got up and went to make myself another, stronger than before, and then I joined them in the dining room. Katie looked at the drink, and she didn't like it at all. She said, "You don't need that, Harry. We're having wine."

"Great," I said. "I'll have both."

She stared at me. She said, "I have the wine cooling. Would you get it, please, and pour?"

"Of course," I said. I put my glass down beside my plate, went into the kitchen, took the wine out of the refrigerator, uncorked it, carried it into the dining room, and poured glasses for everyone.

I picked at my dinner, hardly tasting it, and I alternated sipping wine and scotch. Katie picked at her dinner and watched me. Winnie ate everything on her plate, asked for more, and told Katie she was a marvelous cook and if she weren't such a great actress, she could make a fortune cooking. She talked a lot. She laid it on to Katie. She tried to pretend I wasn't there, which suited me, except when Katie was occupied out in the kitchen and out of hearing. Then the knives came out, blunter and more savage.

I took it for a while, said almost nothing, and retreated into the wine and scotch and into a private world of thoughts, trying to turn my mind away from the table to the pages that still needed to be worked on and that were waiting upstairs. But maybe it was too much booze and too much wine and too close proximity to Winnie Argoth in the house where I lived, or, more likely, it was a combination. We were having coffee then, and Winnie was at her effusive best, telling Katie what she was planning, what she thought, what she should begin thinking about.

She said, "It's time we start planning for your next picture."

Katie said, "It's a little early for that. We've still got a long way to go on this one."

"It's never too early," Winnie said. "I have an idea that just maybe we ought to think about doing another picture with Charlie Stuart."

Katie was surprised.

"Maybe I was wrong about that little runt," Winnie said. "I used to think he was one great big fucking nothing. But he's hot now, and he's going to be hotter when this picture comes out. A guy who can do what he's doing on the picture and write the script at the same time and see the whole thing, well, there has to be more to him than any of us figured. In this business, you can be wrong sometimes. Everybody is. But me? Not often. But even Winnie Argoth can be wrong."

If ever there was a moment to open up and reveal the truth about that screenplay, this was the moment. But that screenplay was Charlie Stuart's dream, and more than his dream; in its way it was the peak of his life. And the truth, the concealment of it, and so the lie, was my bargain and my promise. I could not go back on them, no matter the cost. And I would never permit those who knew, only Katie and Garland, to do what I refused to do. I do not give my word cavalierly, and when I give it, I am committed. So I kept my silence, even though had I spoken, the future might, not might but would have been drastically altered. I looked at Katie, who seemed about to say something, and shook my head. She looked back and sighed, and her lips tightened. So she did not ignore me and my wishes and say what she wanted to say.

"You are so right, Miss Argoth," I said instead.

She turned slowly and looked at me. And her eyes told me that she'd had a little too much to drink, too. She said, "You say something, husband?"

Katie looked at her, startled perhaps by the venom. She looked at me. I ignored the look. I said, "I said I agreed with you for a change, Miss Argoth. I agree that even you can be wrong."

"Not so you'd know it, husband," she said.

"Really? I thought only God was perfect. Have you now assumed the guise of the divine presence, Miss Assgoth?"

Katie said, "Harry."

I ignored it.

"What's with you, husband?" Winnie said.

"With me? Why nothing, Miss Assgoth. Nothing at all. I was just commenting."

"Well, you can keep your goddamn comments to yourself."

"Of course. I must remember that. It's so original. But, just one thing. May I ask you a question? Or would it be out of line for me to ask you anything? After all, in front of the queen, or is it the king, a peasant must hold his silence."

She glared. She waited. Katie sat rigid. She put out a hand to stop me. I ignored it.

"Tell me, Miss Asshole," I said, "do you have any other clients? I mean, besides Katie? What I mean is, you spend so fucking much time with Katie that I can't imagine you have any other clients. What I mean is, you spend so fucking much time with her that I'd think if you had any other clients, they'd begin to get just a mite pissed off and walk out and find another agent. Or maybe they've done that already. Is that it? So, Miss Asshole, what I'm asking is, do you have any other clients, or do you just intend to hitch your wagon to Katie's star and take a ride on her gravy train?"

Katie whispered, "Oh, Harry, shut up. For god's sake, shut up."

Winnie thrust back her chair. She rose, towering, threatening in her attitude. And not a little stunned, I think. She screamed across the table at me, "I'm not going to sit here and listen to any more of that kind of crap from you."

"Good idea," I said. "Great idea. One of which I heartily approve. But you still haven't answered my question."

"Fuck off, husband," she said. She turned and strode out

of the room. Katie looked at me, hesitated, turned and ran after her. I heard the front door open and close. I wasn't sure whether I felt good or bad. Probably good. Probably drunk, too. I told myself it was about fucking time.

The front door opened again. Katie came back and stood in the doorway to the room. She was furious, all the way through. Her eyes were cold and hard. Her arms were crossed on her chest, as though holding herself, as though trying to hold something in. She stared at me. She said, "How could you?"

I said, "How could I, indeed. How could I not."

She said, "She's my friend."

I said, "Your friend, indeed. With that kind of friend, as the old saying goes, you need no enemies."

She said, "She was a guest in this house."

I said. "Your guest. Not mine. You invited her. Not me."

She said, "I need her. She's responsible for everything I am. For everything I'm becoming."

I said, "Bullshit. She's responsible for nothing. Whatever you are, it's because you've done it. Whatever you become, you're the one who's making it happen. Not her. Not anyone. Just you."

She said, "Winnie says—"

I said, "Winnie says . . . I'm getting goddamn tired of hearing what Winnie says. Winnie says, and you listen like a good little girl. Winnie says, and you do like an obedient child. Winnie bends over, and you kiss her ass. Grow up, Katie. She's a goddamn parasite, and she's sucking the blood right out of you." I wasn't as drunk as I thought, or maybe I was just getting sober fast. Maybe I should have stopped. Maybe I should have stopped at the very beginning, but I don't think so, and I couldn't, and, after all, maybe it had to be said, finally. I said, "I don't want that fat, ugly bitch in this house again."

We were both standing, and we were staring, or glaring, at each other across the distance of the room. She said back.

"I'll invite anyone I choose to this house. It's my right. It's my—" and she stopped suddenly.

But there was no need for her to finish the sentence. I finished it for her. "It's your house. Isn't that what you were about to say?"

Maybe it was the way I said it. Because she looked at me as though she hardly knew me, as though I was a stranger who had wandered in from some terrible place and had forgotten to wipe his shoes. She said, "Yes. That's what I was going to say. It's my house. I pay for it. Everything in it belongs to me. I bought and paid for everything. I'll have anyone here I want to have."

"It's your right," I said.

"Damn right it's my right," she said.

"Only you have to make a choice." She looked at me. I said, "You'll have to choose between Winnie Asshole and me. You can't have both. Not any longer."

That got to her. She hadn't expected that. She took a step back. She seemed shaken. She said, in a whisper, "I can't."

I said, "You'll have to. Either Winnie or me. You can't have both. Not after tonight."

She said, "I can't. Don't make me."

I said, "Okay. You have." I walked past her, swerving to avoid contact, and walked up the stairs and into the small room that she had made into an office for me. I slammed the door.

Later, I heard her come up the stairs, felt a slight hesitation outside the door, felt and heard her continue on, into the other bedroom.

I slept on the convertible sofa that night, though I didn't sleep. It was the first night since we had been together that we had not shared the same bed when we were in the same place.

In the morning, very early, I heard her moving around the bedroom. I heard her go down the stairs. She didn't pause before the closed door. I heard the doorbell. The limousine had come to pick her up, to take her out to the airport and to the plane that would fly her off to the mountains of Colorado for three weeks. I stood in the window and watched. The driver came out of the house with her luggage. He stowed it in the trunk. After a minute, Katie came out, walked to the car, and got in. She never looked back at the house. Maybe if she had, things would have been different. I don't know. But she didn't. And then the limousine was gone.

Part Two

*

18   The house was empty and quiet, too empty and too quiet. A few morning birds were calling to each other somewhere up the hill. The early-morning scent of the flowers drifted in through the windows. Our morning humming bird was darting in and out of its feeder. I went downstairs. Everything was neat and orderly and put away. Katie had cleaned up the residue, the physical residue, anyway, of the night before. I wandered around the empty, silent house, and then I went down to the basement, got a couple of suitcases, and brought them upstairs. I packed them with the things that were mine, as much as they would hold. I stowed my typewriter in its case, filled a briefcase with manuscripts and notes, and then carried it all back downstairs and set everything beside the front door. I called the airline and booked a seat on the three o'clock flight to New York, called a cab, and arranged for a pickup about twelve-thirty.

There was just one more thing, and I was not looking forward to it. But it had to be done. I called Suzie. She knew that Katie was going on location that morning, so maybe it wouldn't sound like a strange request, and maybe she wouldn't ask any questions. I asked if she'd mind stopping by sometime before twelve to pick up the keys to the house and sort of watch over things for the next couple of weeks.

She asked if I was going somewhere.

I said yes.

She said, "Colorado? Why didn't you go this morning with Katie and the rest of the cast?"

I said, "No, not exactly Colorado. Actually, I'm heading for New York."

Maybe it was something in my voice. She said quickly, "For how long? When are you coming back?"

I thought of a lot of things to say, and then I decided just to tell the truth. I said I didn't know.

She started to swear. She said I was a goddamn fool. She said I ought to have my fucking head examined. She said, "What the fuck do you think you're doing?" She said a lot more. She said, "Don't you go anywhere. Don't you move, god damn it." She said she was coming over right away.

While I waited, I took out some stationery and wrote a note to Katie. I no longer remember exactly what I wrote, but I remember it was a sad note and one filled with rage.

I had just finished writing it when Suzie showed up. Before she was even through the door, she was shouting, raging. "Just what the fuck is going on around here?"

I said there'd been a big blowup the night before.

She said, "For chrissake, you guys have had fights before."

"Not like this one."

She looked at me. "About the bitch?"

I nodded. "About the bitch. While she was here for dinner, and later."

"Oh, Jesus Christ," she said. "You laid her out. You finally laid her out."

"I laid her out," I agreed. "The noble knight vanquished

his foe. The only trouble is, the noble knight killed himself in the process. With a little help from his lady fair."

"Oh, Jesus," she said. "But you can fix it."

I shook my head. "I don't think so, Suzie. Not this time."

"Oh, Jesus, Miller, don't say that. Stay and fix it. You can do it."

I shook my head again. "Not that easy, Suzie. I wish it were. Maybe in time. Not now. We both need room, and we need time away, to try to look at the pieces."

She said, "Okay, Miller, so you need time and space. Katie's away. You've got three weeks. Stay here, put the pieces together, and when she gets back, it'll be all right again."

I said, "Not possible, Suzie. This is Katie's house. I can't stay here."

She stared at me and she swore, and she said something about stupid pride and how it always got you into trouble. She must have said at least a dozen times that Katie loved me and I loved Katie, that Katie needed me and I needed Katie, and that Katie would be lost without me and what the hell was I going to do without her.

I let her go on like that for a while, and then I said it was getting late and the cab would be there any minute to take me to the airport.

She said, "Screw the goddamn cab. I'm driving you. Nobody's going to drive you but me."

The cab came, and we sent it away, and then Suzie drove me out Sunset to the freeway and then down to the airport. On the way, she ran out of things to say, and so we didn't talk much for most of the trip. I checked in, checked the luggage through, and then we stood near the ramp to the plane. She kept looking at me and trying to find something else to say, and I wouldn't look at her. Suddenly she grabbed me and kissed me and held on and started to cry and said, muffled and hard to follow, that I should take care of myself and think a lot and come back, god, come back. When she let go, she turned and ran away from me and out of the building.

It was a lousy flight. It was taking me where I wanted to go and where I didn't want to go, where I belonged and where I didn't belong. And I kept remembering another flight six years before and how on that one I had been filled with anticipation and not a little fear. Then I had been coming home. That plane had gotten in early; the sun was still not up. There had been no trouble finding a cab, and there was almost no traffic on the road in from Kennedy. It was just a little after six when I reached my building, and I had climbed the stairs and opened the door and tried to be quiet as I walked into that dark apartment. Katie had moved in a month before I had gone away and had stayed there all the time I was gone. I had walked into the bedroom that morning, and she was still asleep, way over on the side of the bed that had always been hers. I had sat down on the bed beside her that early morning and watched her sleep and then touched her hair and touched her face, and she had come awake and started to laugh and cry and hold me. And she had whispered, almost angrily, "Don't you ever leave me again, Harry Miller. Or I'll kill you. With my bare hands."

I had said, "If I ever leave you again, you have my permission."

I stayed in a hotel for a few days. I had lunch one day with Frank Lester, my agent, and another day with Sy Marshall. They both asked how long I was staying around. I said I wasn't sure but that I thought it would probably be for a while and that the first thing I had to do was find a place to live. Neither one of them asked any questions, but I guess my face was answer enough. They both recommended real estate agents who might be able to help, and they both said that as soon as I was settled and as soon as I was finished with the last revisions, we had to sit down and talk about the next book.

I suppose I was lucky. I found a place after a hunt of only a couple of days. It was a third-floor walk-up in the Village, on Charles Street, just a block from where Katie and I had lived. Even the apartment was much the same, though we had lived on the second floor. There was a nice-sized living room with a fireplace and a view out over the trees and the quiet street, a small kitchen, a small bedroom, just large enough for a bed and a dresser, and a miniscule bathroom that you had to turn sideways to get into. It would do, even though the rent was a lot more than Katie and I had been paying for about the same thing. But then, rents had gone up a lot over the years. I scoured the secondhand shops down on the Lower East Side and bought enough furniture to fill the place and didn't really care that the pieces were old and a little scarred and didn't match.

I began to write and found I could and that it didn't hurt quite so much if I could just concentrate on the pages and the ideas and blot everything else from my mind except the world I was trying to create and fill with people. I finished the revisions fairly quickly, and that was done, and we had another lunch and talked about another book. I talked through the long afternoon, and by the time we left the restaurant, Sy and Frank and I, all a little fuzzy in the head from too many martinis, had agreed that this was the one I was going to write, and we'd even pretty much agreed on what kind of advance I was going to get.

I started going back to some of the old watering holes at the end of the days and ran into a lot of old friends. They seemed surprised to see me. Wasn't I supposed to be in Lotus Land? They wanted to hear all about the golden hills, and were there really dollar bills lying around waiting to be picked up? I assured them there weren't, that it was just as tough to make a buck out there as it was back here.

Somebody said one night that he'd heard rumors that Katie was in the movies. I said, "For a change the rumors are true."

He said, "What ever happened to her dancing?"

I said she wasn't dancing anymore because she'd had a bad accident, and that had finished that.

Somebody asked if I'd run into Phil Garland out there. I said sure, and we'd become great buddies again, and Phil was doing just great. He said that's what everybody said, and leave it to old Garland, he could fall into a shithole and come up smelling like roses.

Somebody asked if Katie was with me, and I said no and tried to leave it like that. But you can't ever leave it like that, and I guess if anybody wanted to know, all they had to do was look at my face. Somebody else said he had always thought we had a good thing going. I said I thought we had, too, but you know how things happen.

Somebody else said, "That's Southern California for you." I said no, it wasn't L.A., and, actually, L.A. wasn't such a bad place when you got used to it.

Somebody else said, "Yeah, there's nothing wrong with L.A. that a hydrogen bomb wouldn't cure." That hadn't been particularly funny the first time I'd heard it, and it was a lot less funny now.

But you can't very well sit around a New York bar defending Los Angeles unless it's late at night and you're very drunk, and if it's that, nobody wants to listen to you, anyway. What you really can't say, because nobody wants to hear it, is that there's not much wrong with California, or even Hollywood, for that matter, that's not wrong with most other places. It's just that out there everything happens under a microscope, with the whole world peering through the lens. Nobody much cares what goes on in the private lives of people in Detroit or Philadelphia or Dallas or most other places. There aren't any reporters and gossip columnists camped out by the doors of the people in the auto industry or the space industry or most other industries, because nobody finds all that much glamour there, and the faces and the names aren't terribly familiar. Nobody sees them every day up there on the movie screens or on the television sets. Nobody comes to identify with and become envious over the successes and spitefully malicious and gleeful over the failings and failures and foibles of those someplace else. But there are just as many people who had made it big and made it fast in those other places, and what goes on behind their closed, private doors is no different. It's just that the press and the public don't seem to care as much or zero in as close and hard and those other people don't seem to be fair game. But there are no fewer good people and bad people out in Los Angeles than there are anywhere else and in any other business. Winnie Argoth and Charlie Stuart and some others I remembered were not unique to the movie business. There are people like them in every business. And Phil Garland, after all, used to be a newspaperman and a damn good one. And there are people like Karl Vogel, who was a nice man and a good and tough businessman who just happened to have found his niche in the movies but who would probably have been just as big a success in whatever business he chose. And there were people like Walter Frank and Billy Fielding and a lot of others who knew their craft and were good at it and went about their work and their private lives with some circumspection and so nobody commented. You could have found the scandals anyplace if you looked hard enough, but when they happened out among the quick successes and the carloads of money, they always seemed to be somehow different and exotic, somehow peculiar to the West Coast.

It wasn't possible to say anything like that in a crowded bar early in the evening, and so I rarely tried. But then, in those bars, there were people I knew and liked and enjoyed being with, and so I showed up and drank with them and talked about a lot of things and had a lot of laughs. It was almost like old times, almost as though I'd never been away. Except that there was a missing piece, a pain that never went away.

I kept a watch on the calendar, and so I knew when Katie was coming home from Colorado. A dozen times that night, I reached for the phone, but every time, I stopped before I picked it up. The next night, and three or four times after that, I did dial the number and listened to the ringing. When I heard her voice say, "Hello?" I found I couldn't say anything, so I cut the connection.

That same week and a couple of times the following one, my phone rang. But every time I answered and said, "Hello?" the connection cut off. For an idle moment, I wondered if she was trying to reach out to me, too, and was, like me, unable to make the final stretch. Probably not. Just somebody dialing a wrong number.

One morning after I'd been back in New York for some months, the mailman brought a registered letter from a Los Angeles law firm. I signed the slip and opened it, and then I got a little sick. I called a friend who happened to be a lawyer and said I had to see him right away. He made some free time for me that afternoon.

He looked at the papers, read them through quickly, read them again, and said, "Boiler plate. The usual thing." He looked at me. He said, "I thought you had a good thing."

I said, "We used to."

He asked what I wanted him to do.

I said whatever he had to do.

He said, "Do you want to contest it?"

I said, "Not if it's what she wants."

He said he'd make a call to the lawyer out there, talk to him, and see what had to be done to resolve the whole thing amicably. He asked if there was anything of mine that Katie had that I might want.

I said I'd probably left some clothes behind, because I hadn't had room to pack them. There were also some papers and some books. A lot of the books were Katie's, so she'd probably have to go through and sort them out. If she could do that and pack them up and have them sent to me, collect, that would be fine.

He asked about alimony.

I said I didn't think that was likely to come up. Katie had a lot more money than I ever would, and a lot more potential. But if she wanted anything, she could have it.

He said he would see what he could do and would let me know.

He called a couple of days later. He'd talked to Katie's lawyer. Katie would pack my clothes and books and papers and send them off as soon as she could find the time. There was no argument about that. If there was anything else in the house that I wanted, all I had to do was ask and she'd get it to me. She didn't want any alimony. There was one thing, though, that had belonged to both of us that she'd like to keep, if I had no objection. She'd like the MG.

I said of course. It was really hers, anyway.

He asked whose name it was registered in.

I said I thought we had joint ownership.

He said then I'd probably have to sign a quitclaim and some papers transferring ownership solely to her. He'd get back to the lawyer, and they could work that out.

A few weeks later, United Parcel made a large delivery. Several big boxes, prepaid. My clothes, cleaned and pressed and neatly folded. All the papers I'd left behind, even scraps that I'd been meaning to throw away. Boxes of books. It was a while before I got around to unpacking and putting them on the shelves. She'd done a good job sorting them out. As far as I could see, she hadn't missed anything that had been mine or that might have some value to me.

But among them I discovered a copy of the first book I'd written. It wasn't mine. It had been hers. She had bought it and read it before we even met, and one day, after we'd known each other a little time and had fallen in love and she had come to live with me, she had pulled it out from the among the things she was unpacking. She had laughed about it and then asked me to autograph it. I had. I'd written, "To Katie Summers, the only reader who counts. Harry Miller."

I held on to the book for a week or so, waiting for the ache to subside, and then I wrapped it up and sent it back, with a note that said only, "I think this belongs to you."

A little while later, the divorce decree arrived.

There was a call late one afternoon from a publicity lady at the studio's New York office. They were holding a private screening of a new movie, and Mr. Charles Stuart, the producer and writer, and Mr. Philip Garland, the producer, had both asked particularly that I be invited. I thanked her. She asked if she should put me on the list for two seats. I told her one would be sufficient.

The night of the screening was one of those dreary, stormy New York nights when you really don't want to go out. I had a bad cold and debated for a time, then thought, What the hell, I really ought to go and see what they'd finally done. I walked through the rain over to Sixth Avenue, found a cab going uptown and rode it to the studio's offices, rode the elevator to the right floor, joined the people moving past the girl at the desk, pointed to my name on the invitation list, watched her scratch it off and hand me the thick press package, then walked into the screening room and found a seat toward the back.

While I waited for the lights to go down, I thumbed through the program and the rest of the mimeographed material. There was a nice photograph of Katie, and her biography was pretty factual, mentioning her dancing and how an accident had set her on the road to a new career and how she was destined for the top. It was all pretty flat.

The lights went out, and the film started to roll. Right away, there was Katie's name, on the same card, in the center, with the other two stars. The rest of the credits rolled. Charlie Stuart had a card by himself, saying original story and screenplay by . . . , and he shared a card with Phil Garland, produced by . . . The first few scenes moved nicely, the pace was good, and Walter Frank had gotten in what I intended. Katie's first scene started. The camera moved in on her. I got a very empty feeling. I got up and walked quietly out of the room. The girl at the desk looked at me peculiarly. I walked past, rode the elevator down to the street, and went outside. I walked the long way downtown through the rain.

Frank Lester called. Amazing things happen all the time, he said. He'd just had a call from the Coast. Somebody wanted to buy one of my early books for the movies, and the offer was a very nice one. If we agreed to take it, it would probably mean that the paperback people would take another look and we might get an offer for the reprint rights, which nobody had been interested in before. What was particularly nice about the whole thing, he said, was that they weren't interested in an option. They wanted to buy the film rights outright. Did I agree that he should accept?

"Of course," I said. "We can use the dough."

What would I think about going out to do the screenplay? He said they'd expressed an interest in my doing that.

I said, "No, thanks." What's the old expression? Take the money and run.

He said maybe I should think about it. It would mean a lot more money.

I said I didn't have to think. I didn't want to get involved. I was too busy on other things, and I'd had my fill of the

West Coast. By the way, I said, he hadn't told me yet which book they wanted to buy and who was doing the buying.

He named the book. He said the guy was Charlie Stuart; you know, the guy who produced that new picture, the one with your . . . your ex-wife.

The book was the one Stuart had had in his office the day I met him for the first time, the one he'd read. So, I thought, sometimes Charlie keeps his promises. He even made the film. It wasn't bad, or so I was told, because I didn't see it. It wasn't the book, though, but then, movies never are.

A few years before, I would not have believed it, but my destiny had now become ineluctably bound to those California hills and the dreams that took root in that strange soil even while I stayed far away. I had lost much to them, too much, and now it seemed I would gain something in return. It was poor recompense, but it was recompense nevertheless.

Frank Lester called. The novel I had started, had put aside while I became Charlie Stuart's ghost and had then taken up again and finally finished, was at last published. The reviews were good, and the initial reports from the stores seemed to indicate that it was going to sell a few copies, enough that we might do better than earn back the advance. Then a paperback house bought the reprint rights for more than anyone expected. And finally, Lester said, the movies got interested, three companies bid against each other for the film rights, and the winning bid was high enough so that, while I was not likely to become as rich as Katie, I probably would never be poor again, either. The producer who got the rights was somebody I'd heard of but hadn't met while I was living out there; his reputation was for making good films and sticking pretty close to the source material. He asked if I'd like to go out and work on the screenplay and that way make sure nobody did violence to my book. I didn't have to think about it. I said a polite thanks, but no, thanks, I trusted him to take care and see that the right things were done, and I'd just as soon take the money and stick to what I was doing and knew something about.

The book came out. I took a copy, autographed it: "To Suzie Willens. Promises to keep and miles to go before we meet, Harry Miller." I packed it up and sent it to her in care of Garland.

On a blustery winter day, the clouds low and ominous, with the threat of heavy snow, I saw Suzie again. It had been more than a year since the divorce, and I had not heard directly from her or from anyone else. She called. She was at the Plaza, and she was just passing through. She'd only be in New York a day or two. Could we have lunch?

I'm not sure what I felt when I heard her voice, but I knew I wanted to see her. I said, "Sure. Where would you like to go?"

She said, "Anywhere, someplace nice where we can sit and have a drink and talk."

I named an expensive French place in the fifties. "On me," I said.

She said, "You've come a long way. It used to be you could barely afford a hamburger, and then it had to be dutch."

I said, "Times change."

She said, "Don't they," and I didn't like the way she said that. She said she didn't feel particularly French, and anyway, she'd probably be eating too much of that kind of food over the next couple of months. How about just hamburgers, like we used to?

I said, "Sure, if that's what you'd like. How about Joe Allen?"

She said, "Any relation to the one in L.A.?"

I said, "One and the same. And to the one in Paris. Only the one in New York is the original."

She said okay, that sounded good, and she'd meet me there about one.

I grabbed a cab uptown and got there first. The snow hadn't started falling yet, but it would. That was obvious. Joe Allen was crowded, as it always is at lunchtime, but I'd called ahead, and somebody must have recognized my name, or maybe I just looked fairly presentable and not like an out-of-work actor when I walked in, because I didn't have to wait long for a table off to the rear in the big room. I had just sat down when I saw Suzie come in. She had a mink draped around her shoulders, a coat whose cost I would have hesitated to guess at but which must have cost Garland a little of his profits from the picture. Back in L.A., Suzie wore jeans or pants most of the time. Now, under the mink, she was wearing one of those Rodeo designer originals; another piece of Garland's profits. Pretty soon, there wouldn't be any more. From the distance, she looked spectacular, as always. She stood there for a moment, looking around. I stood up and waved, and she spotted me and came forward.

Up close, she looked terrible. She'd let her hair grow, and it was very highly styled, and it didn't become her. But that wasn't it. Her face was drawn, and there were dark circles under hollowed eyes. She had lost weight, too much, and even her once great breasts seemed to have shrunk.

I came around the table, put my arms around her and held her and kissed her, and she turned her head a little so that she could kiss me. I said, "Suzie, this is great. You look wonderful."

She slid into the seat across from mine and shed the coat like a skin she was just as glad to get rid of, letting it rest across the back of the chair. She looked at me. She said, "You're a lousy liar, Harry Miller. But then, you always were. I look awful. And you don't look so great yourself."

I said, "I've been working too hard."

She said, "Sure." She said, "Jesus, I've missed you. Get me a drink, will you, Miller? Vodka. Russian. On the rocks."

I flagged down a waitress who was passing and ordered the drinks. She asked if we were ready to order lunch. I said, "Later."

I said, "What are you doing in New York, Suzie? I thought you hated the place."

"Just passing through," she said. "On my way to Europe. The grand-tour kind of thing, you know. I'm leaving in the morning, early."

"Phil going with you?" It was a dumb question. I knew it as soon as I asked it.

She looked away, looked back, but didn't answer for a minute; then she shook her head hard. "No," she said. "The train pulled into the last station, and it was time for Suzie to get off. Actually, Suzie got thrown off." She made a vague gesture. "You like my farewell presents? The kiss me and say good-byes?" She touched the mink. She touched the sleeve of her dress. "And a lot more," she said. "And the trip, too. He picked everything out."

It's hard to know what to say. I said, "I'm sorry, Suzie. Really sorry. I thought . . . well, you always said it was going to happen one day."

"I did, didn't I," she said.

The waitress came with the drinks, put them in front of us, and walked on to answer somebody else's hail. Suzie looked at her glass, took it, swirled it a little, lifted it, and made a little motion with it. "To old times, Miller," she said. "To old times and better times. They were that, weren't they? For both of us."

We drank. She looked at me. "Thanks," she said.

"For what?"

"For keeping your promise. I keep my promises, too. I read it. I liked it."

"Thanks." I took another drink. "What's for you now?"

She said, "Go to Europe. See everything."

"I mean, later."

"Who the hell knows?" she said. "Who the hell cares?" She shook her head, dismissing that. She looked at me. "Aren't you going to ask me?"

She said it too fast, too abruptly. I didn't have time to prepare for it. I think I said, "Ask what?" It was dumb.

She said, "Don't play stupid games with me, Miller. You know exactly what I mean."

"You're right," I said. "I know. Okay. How is she?"

"Lousy," she said.

"I'm sorry," I said. I meant it.

"She walks around like a fucking zombie," she said. "The only time she's alive is when she's working. So she's working all the time."

"I know what you mean," I said.

"She wants you back," she said.

"Did she tell you that?"

"Don't be an ass, Miller," she said. "Don't act dumber than you already are. Of course she didn't. She didn't have to. It sticks out all over her, like measles."

There wasn't anything for me to say, except the things I wouldn't say, or couldn't say.

She said, "It sticks out all over you, too. I knew it would. I didn't even have to see you to know."

"I didn't think it was so obvious," I said, trying to be light and not succeeding very well. "I'll have to go to the doctor."

"You do that," she said. "You just fucking well do that. Only make sure it's a head doctor."

"We're divorced, Suzie."

"Who gives a fuck about that?"

"A lot of the world. The courts, for one. Me, for another. Her, for a third."

"What's the matter, you can't say her name anymore?"

I shrugged.

"Her name's Katie. Remember?"

"I remember."

"You sitting there trying to tell me you don't love her?"

I thought of a lot of answers. I said, "I wouldn't tell you that. You know me too damn well."

"Get off your ass, Miller. Get on a goddamn plane and get back out there. Before it's too late."

"It's too late now, Suzie," I said. "It wouldn't work."

"Bullshit," she said. Then, "She's getting married."

That hurt. I looked at my drink, swirled it around in the glass, took a swallow, finished it, and looked around for a waitress. One was just passing. I flagged her and looked at Suzie. She shrugged. I ordered another round.

Suzie said, "Didn't you hear what I said?"

"I heard."

"That's all you have to say?"

"I didn't know," I said.

"Don't you want to know who to?" she demanded.

"Not particularly," I said. "Not to somebody I know, I hope."

"Somebody you know," she said.

"You want me to guess?"

"Sure," she said. "Guess, you bastard. You think I'm going to make it easy for you?"

"Garland, I suppose," I said.

"Garland?" She seemed surprised. She laughed sourly. "Are you out of your fucking skull?"

"It seemed logical," I said.

"Bullshit, logical," she said. "Oh, maybe he gave it a thought after you ran out. I could tell. He never said, but the way he looked at her . . . Well, maybe he thought about it for a second. He sure as hell tried to get her in the sack. That I know for sure. Like I know she told him to go to hell. But marry? Don't make me laugh. Your old asshole buddy doesn't marry anybody. He likes 'em young and with boobs out to here, but only as long as he likes 'em and only as long as they make no demands."

"Then who?"

The waitress came back with the drinks, put them in front of us, and asked something about food, gesturing toward the chalked menu on the blackboard. I looked at Suzie. She shrugged. I said, "Two hamburgers."

She said, "French fries?"

I looked at Suzie. She shook her head. I told the waitress, "No, just the burgers, rare." She went away. I looked back at Suzie. I said again, "Who?"

She said, "Fat little Charlie Stuart, that's who."

It was almost as big a shock as hearing that she was getting married. Maybe it was a bigger shock. I said, "You've got to be kidding."

She said, "No joking, Miller. He's been drooling after her since the first time he saw her. You knew that."

"Sure," I said. "But she thought it was funny."

"Well, it's not so funny now, is it? He's been around all the time since you blew, taking her places, throwing gifts, all kinds of crap, at her. Flowers every day, for chrissake. You never saw anything like it. He's always around, always telling her he's there just in case. He's always telling people what he's doing is helping her get over a bad thing. You know what happened, Miller? She got used to him. It doesn't take much, you know, when you don't give a good goddamn about anything. So now the little prick is even building her a house. As a wedding present. A goddamn mansion on top of a goddamn mountain. You got to stop it, Miller. You got to stop it before it's too late."

So Charlie Stuart was finally building his castle on his mountaintop because he'd finally found the person to share it with and all his dreams were coming true. I said, "I know the place." She looked at me oddly. I said, "He drove me up there one time. He's owned the land for years, probably since before you were born. He was always talking about building a big house up there."

"You've got to stop it," she said.

"Why me? I'd have thought what's-her-name would have seen to that little matter." Even then, I still had trouble saying that name.

"That cunt," Suzie said. "She's all for it. She thinks it's the greatest thing since God made apples. I mean, what the hell, why wouldn't she? Charlie Stuart's no threat to her. He thinks she's the second coming, for chrissake. All she has to do is ask and he'll bend over. Anything she wants, he'll do. All she has to do is say it's good for Katie."

"I see," I said, and I did see.

"So you're the only one can do it," she said, and leaned toward me. Her hand brushed her drink. It spilled across the table. She didn't pay any attention at first. The waitress was at the table with the hamburgers. She looked at the wet table, put the plates to the side, whipped out a cloth, and wiped the table. She looked at Suzie. Suzie said, "Bring me another." The waitress put the hamburgers in front of us and went away. Suzie turned back to me. "You got to go out there and stop it, Miller," she said. "She loves you, for chrissake."

I shook my head. "If she wants Charlie Stuart," I said, "then I think she ought to be allowed to have Charlie Stuart. I won't interfere. She's a big girl now, Suzie. She's all grown up. She makes her own decisions."

"Bullshit," Suzie said. The waitress was back with her drink. She took a swallow. She said, "She doesn't know what she wants, so how the hell can she make a decision? What she wants is you, for chrissake. That's what she really wants."

"I don't think so," I said. "Not now. Not anymore."

"Yes, anymore," she said. Then, "What is it with you guys? I never saw anything like it. You want her, she wants you, and neither of you will move one inch off your asses. Goddamn pride. Both of you. You take your goddamn pride and stick it. Look where it got you."

We went around with that for a while, but it wasn't any

use, and we both knew it. We ate our burgers and had yet another drink, and then some coffee, and talked about other things. What she ought to see and do in London and Paris and Rome and how they were nice in the winter when there weren't many tourists. That kind of thing. When there wasn't anything more to talk about and we'd finished our coffee and the place had pretty well emptied out, she put on her mink, and we went outside. It had begun to snow very hard, the start of the blizzard the weather man had said was coming. A cab was just letting some people off in front of a restaurant down the street. I ran and grabbed it before it could get away. I held the door and put her in and told the driver to take her to the Plaza. She leaned out from the seat, and we held each other tight and awkwardly for just a second, and then I let her go and shut the door and stood there watching the cab vanish into the blinding snow.

I used to go the White Horse every once in a while. It was not far from where I lived, and it held a lot of memories of the time when I had first come to New York and had a little fling with a lot of writers who were young like me in those days and so hung out at places where more famous writers used to congregate, maybe in hope of picking up by osmosis some of their talent or something. It never changed. There were always a couple of guys down at one end of the bar arguing about what Dylan Thomas had said to Jim Agee the night they were both drunk and started to throw punches and about just who had pulled them apart and what had happened then. It had all taken place before my time, and before theirs, and the story had obviously been embellished and had taken on the aura of myth, and there were moments when I wondered if it had ever really happened.

It was there that an old friend from the paper discovered me late one night. I don't think he had come looking for me; it was just that the White Horse was near where he lived and it was a place he often stopped into for a drink on the way home. He spotted me at the bar, came over with a grin, and said, "Hey, Harry, you buying the drinks tonight?"

I said whatever gave him that idea?

He said, "Man, you should be. You're off the hook."

"What the hell does that mean?"

"Your ex-wife got married today. To some big producer out there. It came over the wire just as I was leaving."

Katie got nominated for an Academy Award for our picture, which I had never seen, or at least not more than the first few scenes. I stayed home in front of the television set that night and watched. The camera kept flicking to her through the evening, and it focused close and held on her while they were announcing the nominations and getting ready to open the envelope. She was sitting next to her husband, Charlie Stuart. He looked very proud. He was holding on to her arm, but that was rather clumsy, because she had her hands clasped in front of her chin, was leaning forward on them. Winnie Argoth was sitting on the other side, looking very self-satisfied. Katie, in a long green dress with a high neck, looked very beautiful and very grown up, as though she'd matured a lot, as though the little girl was gone and the woman had finally come out. She looked as though she didn't smile very much anymore, but that could have been my imagination, because nobody smiles much at those things while waiting, and nobody smiles much unless they win. She didn't win.

(It wasn't until three years later, and two more nominations, that she finally did win her first Oscar. I was out of the country then, but I read about it, and for the first time since she'd returned the book that was really hers and I'd sent it back, I communicated. I sent her a short note, offering congratulations and saying I was sure she deserved it. I sent it care of the studio, since I didn't know what her address was any longer. I got a note back, which surprised me, forwarded by Frank Lester from New York. It said, "Thanks for the note. But you should never forget what Phil Garland said about people who win the Oscar." I was happy to see that she hadn't lost that self-deprecating, sardonic edge.)

If it wasn't her night, then, that April, it was Charlie's. He won the Oscar for best original screenplay and made a very humble acceptance speech, saying he couldn't have done it alone, that he'd needed a lot of help from a lot of people, and he couldn't possibly name them all, but they knew who they were.

And Charlie was up there a second time, along with Garland then, to accept the award for best picture. It was a singular experience. He waved his second statuette and this time went on at length about dreams and how you have them for years and don't think anything is ever going to happen with them and then one day they come true, which was the magic and the glory of Hollywood. That got some nice applause. Garland waited and then waved his, which, of course, was coming to him as coproducer and joint owner of Stugar Productions, and laughed and said something about how this proved that even old newspapermen sometimes turn honest and earn a little respect. That got applause and some laughter, and the television announcer cut through to explain that Philip Garland had once been a war correspondent for a New York newspaper before becoming a Hollywood executive and producer.

Somebody, I never found out who, but I suspected it was Suzie, sent me a clipping from one of the L.A. papers a year or so later. It was a review of *A Doll's House* being done downtown at the Mark Taper. There was a picture of Katie as Nora. The critic was respectful, perhaps a little more than that, and spent three paragraphs noting that this was Miss

Summers's first major stage appearance, though she had been in several workshop productions, and that she had brought remarkable insight to a very difficult and challenging role. She had, he said, demonstrated a growing power and a talent for the stage that might, in time, equal her talent on film.

I thought I saw Katie once, coming out of the Carlyle as I was on my way up Madison in a cab. I turned to stare out the back window and saw the slim woman with red hair standing just under the marquee. I couldn't be sure, and I didn't stop the cab.

I did not, naturally, live a monastic life. I met a lot of women and girls, at various places and through friends, took them places, and tried to readjust myself to the pavanne of the dating, or mating, game and to its changing mores and morals. Nothing ever really worked out, though, and I don't think I ever saw any of these women, or girls, more than half a dozen times. Sometimes one of them would start to get ideas, and when she did, it was time to break things off. But I had fun with them, at times, enjoyed the company, enjoyed the talk, enjoyed some of them in bed. But something was always missing, and usually the relationships just faded away on their own, to, I think, a mutual feeling of relief. It both amused and annoyed me, when I thought about it, that more than half the women I spent time with on any intimate basis, and to whom I was most attracted, had red hair.

For a couple of seasons, I went on the college lecture circuit, talking about my books and about the books of other writers. It was intriguing and stimulating to spend time around young and eager minds and to engage in the kind of intellec-

tual combat it's hard to find anywhere else. The fees were
good and going up. But a lot of the kids seemed to know that
I had been married to Katherine Summers, and reticence is
not a particularly strong attribute of the young. So at some
of the colleges, during the question periods and later at the
cocktail receptions, a lot of questions were asked about her.
What was she really like? Was she as beautiful in person as
on the screen? Were the stories about her dancing career and
the accident really true or just the usual Hollywood hype?
Was she really as much a lady as the columnists and publicity releases said, or was that just the usual garbage? And
more and more. I answered yes and yes and no and no and
maybe, and yes, she used to be, but I haven't seen her in a
long time, and so you know as much about that as I do,
which nobody really believed.

After a couple of seasons, I decided to quit the circuit.

For the first few years, Katie made a couple of movies a year;
then she cut back to just one, and I heard she was devoting
more time to stage acting. If all her movies weren't especially good, some of them were among the best the years
they were released, and she herself never got a bad notice,
got increasingly good ones, the critics regularly noting an
increase in confidence and assurance from film to film, and
she kept getting nominated for Academy Awards and won
two.

I joined the lines at the box office to see some of them but
somehow never made it to the ticket window. One night,
though, I caught that first musical on television. My palms
got a little sweaty, and my stomach turned over. I stayed
with it through her death scene, which was not easy for me
to watch, and then I lost interest and turned the set off. But
the rest of the night was bad, and I was surprised by my
reactions. It had only been a movie, after all, and I had only

watched an image frozen on film a long time before, and as she had said, it wasn't really her up there, it was the director.

I went off to two small wars and wrote about them for a syndicate that was willing to send me and that paid well and distributed the dispatches widely. About one of them, I wrote a book, which I thought was pretty good and captured a lot of the feeling of what it had been like, but the book sold not at all, and Sy and Frank and I all came to the conclusion that nobody wanted to read books any longer about small wars in small countries far away where it was hard to tell the good guys from the bad; there continued to be just too many of those wars, and we had all had enough when we were trapped in one of them of our own.

Mostly I wrote. It was something I had to do, had always had to do, and it was a way of coming to terms with my life, or maybe of escaping from my life by creating other worlds and other lives. I averaged about a book a year, or a book every eighteen months, and found a niche somewhere between the popular, slick novel and the serious literary effort. Some of those books sold well and made money; after a while, an author's name gets to be recognized, and if he's fortunate, he begins to accumulate a following that grows steadily, if not spectacularly. The sales of some of the books, especially in the paperback editions, got a nice boost when the movies took an interest, bought the rights, and turned the books into films. I had nothing to do with any of those movies. I went to see them, though, usually at the urging of the producers, and if I could vaguely recognize in them some of what I had tried to write about, I had little judgment about them and felt divorced from what was happening up on the screen.

The critics were generally kind about what I wrote, though some complained about my tendency to long, run-on sentences and an overuse of adjectives. Others thought they saw an increasing control and maturity and depth and hard edge. I don't know. I suppose that comes with time and experience, just as the bad habits become ingrained. As I once said to Katie, never ask a writer to explain his work.

I lived in Paris one year and in Venice another and traveled a lot, though I always returned to that small apartment on Charles Street. I suppose I could have afforded more and better, but I liked it and it was home, and you have to put down roots somewhere.

After a few years, I didn't go to the old watering holes quite so often and didn't stay quite so long. The faces were getting younger, or I was getting older, and there were fewer of the old friends around. Worst of all, the younger crowd was beginning to treat me as some sort of doyen, an elder stateman of a kind, and I found little pleasure in pontificating about things I really knew little about and didn't care much more about.

But I was not exactly reclusive. I made an effort to see old friends when I could and when I was in New York and made some, though not many, new ones. I went to a lot of places, and I did a lot of things I'd always wanted to do because I had nothing to hold me and there had to be some ways of filling the passing years.

When I was younger and had less knowledge and experience, and so thought I knew more, and so was more cynical, I believed that nothing lasts forever and that time heals all wounds. As I grew older and became, beneath a hard surface, more of a romantic, I came to understand that the old truths were not truths at all. Time heals nothing. It only puts a thin tissue of scars over the old wounds. The tissue can easily be abraded, and the old pain can once more rise achingly, and without bidding or conscious thought or reason, to the surface. All time does is dull the pain, not kill it. All time does is teach that the pain will always be there but that it is possible to learn to live with it and come to some kind of terms with it.

It was nine years before I went back to the corrugated brown mountains and hills of Southern California.

Part Three

*

19

A couple of weeks before my new book was scheduled for publication, Taurus Productions bought the film rights. Taurus Productions was Phil Garland's new company. He was not with the studio as one of its top people any longer; he had left either at his own choosing, if one cared to believe the press releases, or he had lost out in one of those recurring power struggles. It didn't really matter which, since he had been rewarded with a lot of money and an independent producing company on the Burbank lot whose films would be partly bankrolled and released by the studio under a long-term deal. Over the years, I had talked with him a few times and had seen him now and again when he was in New York. He had been forever saying that one of these days he was going to buy the rights to one of my books and turn it into a film. He had even bid for but never won the rights to a couple. He had said when he did get those rights, he was going to dragoon me back to work on it.

Now he had actually bought the rights to one. He called

once the deal had been settled. "When are you coming out?" he demanded.

"I'm not," I said.

"It's your book," he said, "so don't give me any of that crap that you don't care what we do with it."

"I don't," I said. "Not particularly. If somebody wants to find out what I had to say, he can always buy the book. And read it."

"Goddamn New York writers," he said.

"You used to be one."

"I got over it." Then, "Look, at least do me a favor, Harry. I think you owe me one."

"Okay, Phil. What?"

"Come on out. You don't want to work on the film, that's your problem. But meet with the screenwriter. I've got a top guy lined up."

"I thought you wanted me," I said, laughing.

"Screw you," he said. "I knew you were going to say no. So I lined somebody up to be on the safe side. What I want you to do is talk to the guy. Let him pick your brain. Let him bounce a few of his ideas off your head. I want him to get the feel. I mean, I don't want the usual crap. I want to make a good picture, a real quality thing. You understand?"

"You don't need me for that," I said. "A book's a book, and a picture's a picture. It's yours now, and his. I wouldn't want to get in the way."

"You wouldn't be getting in the way, for chrissake," he said. "You know the goddamn thing backward and forward, inside out. You wrote it, didn't you? I mean, you didn't hire a ghost." He laughed at that. "Not like some guys I could name," he said. "So you could only be a help. I've got a lot staked on this thing, Harry. Do it for me, as a favor. You owe me one."

He wore me down. Perhaps, anyway, it was time I made the trip, just a brief one. It was just a city, after all, and whatever memories and pains were tied up in it were old ones. A lot had changed over the years, and there wasn't much chance I'd run into anyone in just a few days who might rip open some of the scar tissue. So at last I agreed. He was delighted. He'd arrange everything. He'd have the plane tickets delivered by messenger, first-class, of course. Everything would be on him, or Taurus, anyway. I wouldn't even have to bring cash if I didn't want to. Just charge everything and give him the bills. Where did I want to stay? The Beverly Hills? The Beverly Wilshire? Name it and they'd have a suite for me, a bungalow, if that's what I wanted.

"What about Chateau Marmont?" I said.

"The Chateau? Jesus, what is it with you New York guys? But if that's what you want, that's what you'll get. You want a bungalow?"

"What for? A room will do just fine."

"If that's what you want, we'll arrange it for you. The best they have. I'll have a car and driver meet your plane. He'll take you wherever you want while you're out here."

I said that was dumb. The last thing I needed was a chauffeur. If he'd just rent a car and have it waiting for me, that would suit me just fine.

He sighed and said something more about dumb people from New York who looked down their noses at gift horses. He said they'd make the arrangements and the car would be waiting. All I'd have to do was check in with the rental people and then drive away.

I made an early flight, left on one of those incredible New York mornings after a snowstorm, the air brittle, tearing into the lungs, the sky blown clean and deep blue, the snow pristine, drifting in tall mountains, the city untouched and unlived in. I flew into palm trees and searing heat and a gentle, dry breeze.

Driving out of the airport, I decided not to take the freeway but drove up LaCienega instead, toward those distant dun-brown mountains, past the ever dipping locusts in the oil fields. Not very much seemed to have changed. Some of the old stores with the same signs were there along the road, and a few new ones, some of the old restaurants and a few new ones along Restaurant Row, a few new, tall buildings and a lot of the old low ones, and, in the hills, as I approached, it seemed, perhaps, a few more houses crammed in closer together.

Out of a sudden and in ways reluctant impulse, I made a right on Fountain, went down toward Hollywood, turned a corner and drove slowly, and passed the first house we'd lived in when we'd arrived. It was still there, a little seedier, needing a new coat of paint and some repairs. Some kids were playing on the sidewalk in front; they were young enough so they could not have been born the last time I'd seen it.

Naturally, there was a message waiting at the desk when I checked in. Call Philip Garland as soon as I was settled. I unpacked, took a shower, and then called. We chatted for a few minutes about the flight and how little the city seemed to have changed, how most things don't ever really change much. He said he'd set up a meeting with the screenwriter out on the lot for the next afternoon. Was that all right with me? If it wasn't, he could always change it. Maybe we ought to all have lunch and then the writer and I could take it from there.

I said whatever he wanted was all right with me. I was at his disposal.

He said, "Lunch it'll be. I'll make the arrangements." Then he said, "Why don't we have dinner tonight?" I could come out to his house about seven.

I said that would be fine. It would be nice to see him again. Did he have the same cook as in the old days?

He had to think about that. Then he said, "Oh, her. Hell, no, she went and opened a restaurant out at the beach." But, of course, he'd put money into the restaurant, and it was doing great, so it had been a sound investment. He had a new cook these days who was, if not as good, pretty good.

I spent the afternoon around the pool, swimming a little, relaxing in the sun, falling asleep for a while. There weren't too many other people there, just a couple of boys in their mid-teens who'd climbed in over the fence, a couple of teenage girls, and some women in their early twenties. The last time I'd been there, while we were living in L.A. and I'd dropped in on a friend from New York who was staying there, none of the girls swam or sunbathed without tops, even if their bikinis barely covered what they had. Now there didn't seem to be a top in evidence anywhere. Some things change, I guess. But the view was pleasant, and provocative.

On the way out to Garland's house, again out of some kind of strange and unbidden impulse, I made a detour and drove a little way up the hill. The house was still as it had been when I'd left, neat and trim and well cared for. Some new people lived there. The garage doors were open, and there was a Jaguar parked inside. A little girl, about eight, with long light-colored hair, holding tightly to the hand of a woman in her early thirties with hair somewhere toward dark blond, was just coming out the front door. The two of them walked toward the garage. I slowed for just an instant. I didn't know the woman and couldn't, of course, have ever seen the child before. I drove on up the hill a little way, made a U-turn in somebody's drive, and headed back down. The Jag was just pulling out of the drive. I slowed and let it go ahead, then followed it down to Sunset. It turned left. I turned right.

The inside of Garland's house had changed a lot. The modern furniture had all been replaced with period pieces, though of what period it would have been hard to say. It was expensive stuff, though. The whole place had been redecorated. It seemed strange and, perhaps because of remembered absences, not quite as welcoming as it had once been. Garland had changed a lot, too. Gone were the suits and the close haircut and the eastern manner. He had become Californian at last. He was wearing jeans, expensive ones, with the designer's name sewn on the back pocket; he was wearing a silk shirt open halfway down the chest, revealing matted gray hair and a medallion hanging on the end of a chain; the medallion was of a bull. His hair was a little lighter than I remembered, not gray, and a little longer and more carefully styled, and he'd grown a mustache and a small beard. He looked younger and healthier and satisfied with himself and his life and his possessions.

We had drinks and a nice dinner, though it didn't measure up to the dinners I remembered. We repeated a lot of the old shared stories, which over the years had become tired and not a little boring. He asked a lot about the wars I'd been to. What were the real stories, the ones I hadn't been able to write? He didn't seem to believe me when I told him I'd written the real stories, at least as I saw them. It had been a long time since he worked for a newspaper and written stories himself, and maybe he'd just forgotten the way it was.

He had a girl in the house, of course. She was tall and slim and very pretty and blond, and naturally she had enormous breasts. Her name was Vicky. She fit in with the new decor and was, I suppose, just as permanent. She had little to say. She sat and drank, sat and ate, and looked and acted very bored, acted as though she hadn't the slightest idea what we were talking about and couldn't have cared less.

She wandered off at one point, and it was then that I said, perhaps because I didn't like it there anymore and I didn't particularly like Phil Garland anymore, not the way I once had, "I ran into Suzie a few years back. In New York." I had never mentioned it to him before; it had just never seemed appropriate.

He looked blank for just an instant. His face screwed a little as though he were trying to remember, as though his mind were trying to come up with an image. Maybe it succeeded, and maybe it didn't. He said, "Oh, yeah, Suzie. How is she?"

I shrugged. "I only saw her that one time. She seemed all right. She was on her way to Europe."

"She was a good kid," he said. "I imagine she's making out all right. Her kind always land on their feet."

There wasn't anything more to say.

Late the next morning, I drove out to Burbank. Garland took me around his new offices, which were bigger and a lot plusher than the ones he'd had when he was a studio executive. The decor was very modern, all glass and steel. He introduced me to the screenwriter, a guy in his fifties who'd been around for years and had turned out a lot of good scripts and won a couple of Oscars in the bargain. We had lunch in one of the private dining rooms, and they talked a lot of movie gossip. I listened and didn't say much.

Garland left us after lunch, saying he'd see me again, a couple of times at least, before I went back to New York. The writer and I adjourned to his office, which was small and filled with books and scripts and papers and dust and a new word processor; I still used a typewriter. At first, he seemed to want to talk mainly about New York gossip, and he had a lot to say about how much better living was in California than in the East, where you could never depend on the weather. He'd heard it was snowing back East. I said it had snowed but it had stopped by the time I left.

We ran through that, and then he started to talk about how he saw the book as a screenplay. He had a lot of ideas, and he said again and again, "See if you can visualize this," and some of what he was asking me to visualize strayed pretty far distant from the lines I'd developed in the book. He acknowledged that and said, "You understand, of course. When you write a book, you have all the time and

272)   RICHARD HAMMER

all the space you want to build characters, tension, all that
kind of thing. We have to collapse, foreshorten, indicate,
sometimes even combine characters. You understand that,
of course. And we only have a hundred twenty minutes at
the outside to play with, so naturally it's impossible to do
everything."

I said I understood.

He said, "The important thing is to get your ideas across.
What you were trying to say in the book."

I agreed.

"So a little collapsing and tightening, a little of this and
a little of that, if it works, it's okay."

I agreed.

He picked up a copy of the book. He had it all marked
up with a transparent yellow crayon. He pointed out things
he wanted to keep in and things he wanted to take out,
things he thought might be changed because of motion-
picture requirements. He asked if I had any objections.

I assured him I had none. I assured him that I trusted him
to do the best job possible.

He said, "It won't be the book, of course."

I said of course. It would be a motion picture.

He said, "But we won't do violence."

I said I didn't think they would.

When there wasn't anything more to talk about, I wished
him well and hoped that he wrote one hell of a screenplay
and that the movie was a good one and big box office and
that he got himself another Oscar out of it. He laughed and
looked happy, especially since he now realized that I wasn't
going to make any trouble for him. He wished me well and
said he was sure he'd see me again, certainly at the premier
or one of the screenings, and if he ran into any problems,
he hoped he could call on me. I assured him he could,
anytime. He said he really envied me the leisure to write
books, and one of these days . . . We shook hands and said
nice things to each other and said good-bye.

I drove back across the mountains to the Chateau Marmont. Garland had said I could stay a week if I wanted, more if I felt like it. I thought I'd check with the airlines and see if I could get a seat on a plane back East the next day.

I parked the car around behind the hotel, circled the building, and walked under the balcony and into the lobby.

Charlie Stuart was sitting on the edge of a chair, watching the door.

20

He jumped out of the chair, rushed toward me, grabbed my hand, and wouldn't let go. He kept pumping it up and down, beaming with what I assumed was pleasure. "You son of a bitch. I heard you were back."

"Hello, Charlie," I said. "It's been a long time. It's nice to see you again."

He rushed ahead. He said, "I read you were here. This morning, in the trades. You know, in that comings-and-goings thing. I was just glancing over it, and there was your name, bold as brass. I said to myself, 'Charlie, for chrissake, Harry's back. Get off your ass and go see him.' Let me tell you, it wasn't easy. I called every damn hotel in town. The Hills, the Wilshire, the new ones, since your time, all of 'em, and you weren't in any of 'em. I said, 'Use your head, Charlie Stuart. New York guys, they stay at the Chateau.' So I call over here, and bingo, I hit the nail on the button." He let go of my hand then, backed off a step, and looked at me closely. "Jesus," he said, "you look good, kid. Like your old self."

"You look pretty good yourself, Charlie," I said.

"Couldn't be better," he said.

As it happened, he didn't look bad. He'd aged some, but hadn't we all, and he'd stopped using Grecian Formula or whatever it was. His hair had gone pure white, but it was still well styled and recently barbered, and it went well with his tanned face. He was dressed as I remembered, in those golf slacks, beltless, this time maroon, and an alligator polo shirt, white. He'd lost a little weight, had slimmed down enough so that his belly didn't ride out over his pants and press tight against his shirt as it once had. But there was something. I recognized it, by the slightly sweet aroma that couldn't hide behind the expensive after-shave lotion and the breath spray and by the slight cloudiness in his eyes. Charlie Stuart had had a couple of drinks, and it wasn't quite cocktail time yet.

We stood like that in the lobby for five or ten minutes. I ran out of things to say to him in thirty seconds. There were things I wanted to say and things I wanted to know, but I didn't want the answers from him, and there are only a limited number of things you can really say to the man who's married to the woman you're in love with. But he didn't run out of things to say and things to ask. "I've got a million questions," he said again and again, "a zillion." He wanted to know how I was and what I was doing and what the wars had really been like, because they'd run my dispatches in one of the local papers and, of course, he'd read them and he'd been worried as hell about me over there where people were shooting at anything that moved, they'd all been worried, though he didn't specify who the all were, and wasn't I getting a little old to be taking such stupid chances. The parade marched on, endlessly, streaming past so rapidly that he never waited for an answer, and I don't think he expected one. Finally, he stopped and took a breath and said, "For chrissake, will you listen to me. You can't get a word in edgewise. Look, let me tell you what we'll do.

We'll go someplace nice and quiet and you'll let me buy you a drink and we can do some more talking, only this time you'll do the talking and I'll do the listening."

I said, "Sorry, Charlie, but I'm really beat. The long flight. You know, jet lag and that kind of thing, and I've been on the go ever since I hit town. Another time."

He grabbed my arm and held tight, trying to pull me along with him. "No other time," he said. "I haven't seen you in a dog's age, and I'll be damned if I'll let you get away now. Come on. You're never too tired. What do you say? The Polo Lounge? Right?"

I tried to argue. He insisted. He got louder, loud enough so that the people at the desk and a few people passing through the lobby turned to look. There wasn't any other way to quiet him and get him out of there. I sighed and said, "Okay, but just one drink."

He was happy. We walked out to his Cadillac, got in, and he drove away, talking incessantly, still not waiting for answers. Just before Beverly Hills, he suddenly braked, swerved over into the right lane, narrowly missing a collision with the front end of another car, and turned sharply into a road. I had been on that road before. I knew where he was taking me.

I said, "Charlie. This isn't the way to the Polo Lounge. The Beverly Hills is straight down Sunset."

"You think I don't know?" he said. "But, what the hell, we can always go there. All of a sudden, just like that, I got a better idea. There's something I want to show you. And we can have our drink in private, nice and comfortable."

I said, "Charlie, why don't we just go to the hotel? We can do this another time."

"Not on your life, kid," he said. "This you got to see."

He was driving, and he was determined, and short of wrenching the wheel away from him or opening the door and jumping out of a fast-moving car, it didn't look as though I had any choice.

The road seemed a little wider than I remembered, and a little smoother, but nobody had been able to do anything about the curves. Stuart wheeled the car around them and through them, barely slowing; he knew the road, and he was confident.

So I came at last to the castle he had built on the top of his mountain, the castle of his dreams that he had built for the lady fair of his dreams out of the success of his other dream. It was long, very long, a low flagstone front, with a brownish-red roof. It stretched along the lip of the plateau, a line of cedars growing on either side of a massive front door. We went almost to the end. He pressed a button somewhere under the dash. The garage doors swung up. He drove into the garage and pulled into an empty space beside a black Mercedes convertible. There was another empty space on the other side of the Mercedes.

He got out of the car, took a step toward a door in the garage wall, then stopped. "Hell, not that way," he said. "I want you to take in the front. I want you to see the whole thing." He took my arm and led me out of the garage, pushing a button just before we emerged. The doors swung shut behind us. We walked along the front of the house. Just before we reached the door, he backed off and pulled me across the roadway so I could look at the front. "Doesn't look like much, does it?" he said. "Just like a one-story thing spread out along the road. Right?"

I said even with one story it looked pretty impressive.

He said, "You ain't seen nothin' yet. Hey, you remember what it was like back when? Nothing up here but a lot of scrub and junk? Deer and crap like that? The deer, we still see 'em now and again. Not like we used to, but they still come around. But, let me tell you, we've made a few changes. Come on."

He dragged me back across the road to the front door, fished in his pocket, and came out with some keys. He unlocked the door, pulled it open, and then we were inside.

He was right. I hadn't seen anything yet. We came out onto a long, wide balcony. It hung out over a vast living room whose floor was two stories below us and whose ceiling was one above. There were oversized sofas and oversized chairs and oversized tables, of wood and stone and glass and marble, and they were dwarfed by the room. There was a massive stone fireplace. There were paintings on the wall, by some of the most prized modern masters. There was a painting over the fireplace. Of Katie. In a long green gown. Looking off into the distance. Looking a little sad. She had a strand of pearls around her neck. She had drops of dark jade at her ears. I looked away from the portrait and saw directly facing us, across the room, a wall entirely of glass. I stood there on the balcony trying to take it in and unable to do so. It was overwhelming. I would not have wanted to live there.

"Come on," Stuart said impatiently. "You ain't seen nothin' yet. This isn't even the beginning." He waved a hand over the vista. "I had this place built right into the side of the mountain. No stilts like some of these hill houses. Nothing like that. Pilings what I did. Pilings driven so far into the mountain they'll hold for a million years no matter what. I had the whole side of the mountain dug out and faced and reinforced, so from here down the mountain's the whole back wall. Of course, we faced it, but it's right behind the wall. You know how far down we go? Three more floors below the living room. Three goddamn floors. And you see that wall?" He gestured toward the glass wall. "That thing goes all the way down, right to where the house ends at the bottom." He laughed with pleasure and pride. "You think that's just a wall, right, like a picture glass window? Only you're wrong. It ain't. You push some buttons—I've got 'em hidden in the floor—and that thing slides open, and you walk right out onto the terraces. There's terraces outside every room on every floor. Even the goddamn kitchen's got a terrace, for chrissake."

He tugged my arm, pulled me along the balcony, passing a stairwell with a spiral staircase leading down, stopped before we reached a door at the end that lead who knew where. He turned to face the wall and pushed a button. A door opened, and we stepped into a rosewood-paneled elevator, rode it down to the living-room level, and stepped out. The room was even larger and more impressive being in it than looking down on it. He stood there looking out at it as though seeing it for the first time, through my eyes, seeing it with renewed wonder, seeing it as the master of it all, the culmination of a dream of decades.

He led me around the room so that I would see everything. He stopped before and pointed out each painting, reciting the pedigree, telling me where it had been bought and even how much he had paid for each. There were niches on either side of the fireplace. In one stood two Oscars. "Katherine's," he said. "You knew she won 'em?"

"Yes," I said.

"She should have had two, three, more," he said. "She got screwed. You know what the politics are like out here."

I nodded.

On other shelves in the niche were Golden Globes and several other lesser awards. They were all Katie's.

On the other side of the fireplace was his niche. On one shelf were Golden Globes and the other honors he had taken. On a separate shelf were his two Oscars. "Mine," he pointed with not a little pride. "You know I copped them."

"Yes," I said. "I watched that night."

"You did? Wasn't it something?"

"It certainly was."

"I never expected it," he said. "It came as a total surprise. I was sure one of the other jokers was going to take it, you know, one of those guys who'd had a zillion nominations but never the big banana itself." He was lying and he knew it, and he knew I knew it and he didn't care.

We finished a cursory tour of the living room. He said

he'd show me the rest of the house later. Right now, he said, he could sure use a drink. What about me?

I said sure, that's what he brought me up here for.

He laughed and said, "What're you drinking?"

I said, "Scotch."

He said, "Just like old times. I remember. On the rocks, right?"

I said, "Right."

He walked across the room, under the overhanging balcony, touched something on the wall and it swung open. A vast bar appeared. It would have been the envy of a lot of saloons I'd been in. It was stocked with just about anything anyone could possibly have wanted and a lot of things I'm sure nobody would ever have thought to ask for. He opened a refrigerator, took out some ice, took two glasses from a vast array and put the ice in them. He searched among the bottles racked up behind the bar, found one, and took it down. He looked around. "Black Label okay? You want something else, name it. We got it."

"Black Label will be fine," I said.

"It ought to be," he said, "after the swill you used to have around in the old days. Jesus, I never could understand how you drank that crap."

I shrugged. "You drink what you can afford."

"Bull," he said. "Sometimes you got to live good even when you think you can't. It's good for the soul. And it says the right thing to the people you got to deal with." He poured the scotch into the glass. Too much.

I said, "Go easy, Charlie."

He laughed. "What the hell," he said, "I treat my friends right." He reached for another bottle. "Jack Daniels," he said. "Strictly a Kentucky sour-mash man, that's me. Always was, always will be." He filled his glass right to the brim, looked over at me, and when he thought I was looking the other way, he poured some more into another glass, concealing the movements, and tossed it down quickly, straight. I watched. I was a little surprised. In the time I had known him, he had not been much of a drinker, only a drink now and then when we finished work or on social occasions.

He carried the glasses across the room, spilling a little of his, which was too full. He handed the scotch to me and said, "What do we drink to? Old times. They were pretty good, those days, when you look back on 'em."

"It depends on how you look," I said, "and how far back."

He gave a little laugh. "They were pretty damn good, if you remember 'em right," he said. "So let's drink to the old days. Then we'll have another and drink to new times and better times. What the hell, I can think of a dozen things we'll drink to when we get to it." He raised his glass and downed almost half of it in one swallow. I took a sip. He looked around pridefully. "What do you think of my house?"

"Very impressive."

He snorted. "What the hell kind of word is that? Impressive, hell."

"What would you like me to say?"

"What you really think, for chrissake."

"That's what I think, Charlie. It's very impressive."

He took another drink, not as deep. There was still a little, but not much, left in his glass. "Let me tell you about this place," he said.

I said, "Charlie, let's just have our drink and then you can drive me back to the hotel. You can tell me all about it some other time. Right now I'm pretty beat."

"No way, kid," he said. "We got plenty of time. I got you up here, and I sure as hell don't intend to let you fly the coop just like that. So just relax. Have your drink. Have another. I was going to tell you about the house, right? You remember what it was like before, I mean, when I took you up here in the old days and there wasn't a thing around?"

"I remember."

"Well, all the years I owned it, I knew I was going to build something special up here. I told you that. The thing was, I never had a real picture in my mind, just that it had to be special, something like nobody ever dreamed up before. But when I decided to build—you know, I was doing it as a wedding present . . .?"

"So I heard," I said.

He went on. "I decided I'd get the best. Didn't matter what it cost. I mean, I called those guys down at Taliesin. You know what that is? Frank Lloyd Wright, for chrissake. They sent some guy—he was supposed to be a cracker-jack—up here to get the lay of the land. He was up here three, four, days, maybe a week. Then he went back down there and drew up a set of plans. Only they weren't right. Not what I had in mind. I told him that. I sat down with the guy and explained just what I wanted. I mean, by then I knew. He went away and came back with a whole new set. And they still weren't right. But he was getting close. So I sat down with the guy and those plans, and I took out a big black pencil and started sketching in over his drawings. I thought the guy was going to have a heart attack right there, on the spot, until he finally got my drift. Once he did, it was clear sailing. So I guess you could kind of say I designed the house myself."

I nodded. Like he'd written a movie himself.

"Let me tell you," he said, "I didn't pinch one penny. Not on this place. You couldn't guess how many rooms we've got. Not in a million years. Hell, I'm not sure myself. All I know is an army could get lost in here and we'd never know they were around. When we first moved in, we used to get lost wandering around. Katherine would go looking for the kitchen or something and end up in the steam room or someplace and start yelling for help, only nobody could hear her. Let me tell you, we've got a kitchen like you've never seen. I mean, it's copied straight out of the best restaurant in town. And crappers. When I was growing up, I was so damn poor we didn't even have a crapper of our own; we had to share one out in the hall with three other families. So when I decided to build this place, I said the one thing we were going to have was plenty of crappers. No matter how many people we had here, nobody was going to have to stand in line to take a leak." He laughed suddenly, looked into his glass, raised it and emptied it, and started for the bar. "You ready for another?" he asked.

"I'm fine," I said. I wanted him to stop drinking. I wanted him to stay sober so I could get out of there. Before she came home. And I wanted to be there when she came home. I took another sip of my drink.

He poured himself another full glass and went on talking. "You know, when I was a kid, I used to think crapper was a dirty word, what you weren't supposed to say in front of nice people. I found out that ain't so. You know where crapper comes from?"

"I know," I said. I had told him one afternoon. I wasn't going to remind him.

He ignored that and went on. "You won't believe it, but it's true, so help me. There was this Lord Thomas Crapper in England, he was the Earl of Ipswich or something, some kind of big shot, anyway, in the East India Company more than a hundred years ago. He used to spend a lot of time out in India, and he got pretty damn disgusted with the way they did what they were supposed to do. I mean, right out in the street. And there weren't no proper places for the fancy British, either. So he figured there had to be a better way. I mean, I guess he thought it was one thing in England, where you had servants and things to empty out the shit pots as long as you never saw what they did with it. But it was another thing when there was shit everywhere you looked and there were people doing the shitting. Now, this Lord Crapper was a scientific kind of guy, so he started experimenting, and pretty soon he came up with this bright idea. What he did was invent the kind of crappers we have now.

So that's where the word comes from, so it ain't a dirty word, after all. Right? So, what do you think of that?"

"I think it's very interesting, Charlie," I said. What I had told him so long ago was that the guy who had invented the flush toilet was a Thomas Crapper who was no earl, no nobleman, just a sanitary engineer.

"Jesus," he said, "you're just full of enthusiasm tonight."

"You know me, Charlie," I said.

"Yeah, you bet I know you. Come on, there's something else I want you to see." He turned and hurried back to the bar first, refilled his depleted glass, something he would do too often. Then he walked directly toward the glass wall, stopped just before reaching it, moved his foot a little, and pressed with his toe. A wide panel of glass slid slowly to one side. "Come on out," he said, and he went out onto the terrace without waiting. I followed. While we had been talking, dusk had settled in over the city. I had forgotten how quickly daylight died and night came. The lights down below in the distance had gone on and were shimmering.

He pointed out, waving to take in everything. "The last time you were up here," he said, "it was daytime, right? Just look at it now. Look at all those lights. Look at all those colors. It's like having your own private collection of diamonds and rubies and emeralds all spread out in front of you on black velvet. You can look anytime you feel like it, and you don't have to worry that some bastard's going to come up here and rip you off."

The view was, indeed, breathtaking, as it had been the first time I was there, perhaps even more breathtaking with the sun vanished into the distant Pacific. I looked out toward the ocean. There was a lighter, hazy, fluffy bank drifting above the lights of Santa Monica. The fog was beginning to gather and move in on the land. I pointed it out to Stuart and said maybe we ought to think about leaving. He waved that away.

I walked along the terrace with him. He said, "You know

what's down there at the bottom? A pool, of course. Straight down. We had that leveled off and filled in so we could have the pool and it wouldn't just hang out over nothing. But we've got our own private sauna and steam room there, too, and cabanas and all that crap. It's all right there just for us. You look down, you can see it."

Moving close to the redwood railing, I leaned against it and looked over and down. Into a pool, lit from the bottom with recessed lights. Stuart's hand suddenly clutched my arm and pulled me back. "Jesus, Harry," he said, "watch it."

I looked at him.

He said, "I mean, one slip and over you go."

I laughed. "You sound worried. I'm not about to slip, Charlie. I value my life too much."

"You think I want to see you splattered all over the bottom down there? How the hell would I explain it?"

"I wouldn't worry about it."

"That's what everybody says. But, let me tell you, we almost had a dumb kid go over a couple of months ago. We were having a big bash, and this kid got really smashed. I mean, I don't know whether she was drinking or smoking or snorting or popping or what, but she was up to the gills, let me tell you. The next thing we know, she's climbing the railing there, like she's going to walk a tightrope and maybe do a swan dive into the pool. Jesus, I don't know. But it took three of us to pull her off and bring her back into the house. Let me tell you, I would've hated to find out what would've happened if she'd done whatever she was thinking of." He shivered suddenly and took another deep drink. "Jesus," he said, "all of a sudden it got cold. The temperature must've gone down twenty degrees. Come on, let's go back inside."

I followed him back into the house. He pressed with his toe, and the glass panel slid shut. He looked at my drink, took it out of my hand, ignored the protest, carried it to the bar, refilled it, refilled his own, brought them back toward the center of the room and handed me mine, and took a drink of his. He stepped back a little and stared at me. He said, a little blearily, "Harry, I want a favor."

Everybody, especially in California, wanted favors. I shrugged. "Sure, Charlie. If I can. Shoot."

He said, "Harry, I want to tell you, we're proud of you. Katherine and me both. We're really proud."

"Thanks," I said.

"I mean, you've really done good since you pulled up stakes and walked out of here without so much as an I'm going and I'll see you sometime to me or anybody. Well, we forgive you that. It's water over the dam, like they say. But you've done good, real good. I mean, all the books you wrote. That kind of thing. Jesus, I mean, I've read every one, from cover to cover. They're good. Believe me. I mean, I've got 'em all in the other room, in the library. Had 'em all bound in leather. Just waiting for your autograph."

"That's nice," I said. "That's more than I have."

"Doesn't mean a thing," he said. "Just shows what I think. I mean, I love 'em. So we're proud of you for them and for the prizes and all that. I mean, those prizes for a writer, they're like the Oscars for people in the business, right?"

"Right."

"So now I got a favor to ask. I mean, back when you needed it, I did a favor for you. Right?"

"Right."

"I mean, if it hadn't been for me, you'd never have got off your ass back then. Right?"

"Right."

"So now I want a favor back. Okay? You got a new book coming out. Right?"

"That's right. Any time now."

"I want it, Harry. I don't want it. I need it."

"Charlie . . ." I tried to stop him. He wouldn't be stopped.

"I'll level with you. I wouldn't ever bullshit you, kid. I never have, and I never will. I need your book."

"I'm sorry, Charlie."

"Don't say you're sorry. Do it, for chrissake. I need it. You want to know why? I won't bullshit you. You think I'm a big shot, right, everything coming up roses, the king of the mountain, sitting on top of the world, everybody bowing and scraping, yes, Mr. Stuart, whatever you say, Mr. Stuart? A few years back, that was the truth, that was the way it was. You go to the movies, Harry?"

"Not much."

"You seen any of my pictures?"

I shrugged. I hadn't.

"The last four. Poison. Absolute poison. Didn't make a dime, not a nickle. They lost a bundle. I lost a bundle. All of a sudden, I got leprosy. Guys see me coming, I've known 'em all my life, they run the other way. Nobody wants to know Charlie Stuart. Nobody answers their goddamn phones. Even the goddamn secretaries don't want to talk to me. I come up with an idea for a picture, and, believe me, I got plenty, nobody wants to hear it, and there's not a soul will put up a dime. And then some bastard, and I'll bet it was that shitass friend of yours, my fucking former partner, some bastard starts spreading the rumor that I never even wrote the goddamn picture that won me the Oscar. Can you believe that? And what can you do about a fucking rumor? But you, Harry. It's different with you these days. You got a name these days. People, they read your books if they read at all. They made what, two, three, movies out of your books. Jesus, I made one myself. Remember? And it was damn good, if I say so myself. It's like they can't sell enough tickets the lines are so long. So Harry Miller writes a new book, everybody wants to make a movie out of it, because everybody knows that out there in the sticks they're going to want to see it. Even if they never read the book, they know the name, and they want to see the movie. Like the old days, almost. So if Charlie Stuart's got the rights to Harry Miller's new book, Charlie Stuart's in the driver's seat again."

"Charlie, Charlie," I said. For the first time, I felt sorry for the man. I wanted him to stop. But I felt something else, too. There was something about all this that didn't ring quite right, quite true. He was putting on a performance, but it had a false note to it, and I couldn't figure out why.

He kept on, riding over me. "What do you want?" he demanded. "You name it, you can have it. You want a big price? I'll match anybody's offer. I'll top it. Jesus, kid, I read the goddamn galleys. Somebody, I won't tell you who, let me borrow them. I mean, I know what it's worth. You want a piece, some points? How many? Just say the word and you can have them, and gross, not net. You want to be involved? You're involved, whatever you want to do. You want to write the screenplay, make sure it comes out your way, you can write the screenplay. Hell, we'll do it together, you and me, like the last time, like the old days. We'll do it. It'll be like it used to be."

I raised a protesting hand. He ignored that, ignored everything, as though he had to get it all out and said.

"Jesus, Harry, we could do it. The guys with the bucks, they'll line up and shovel them at us. The studios, they'll fall all over themselves to give us a distribution deal, on our terms. Directors, actors, everybody, we'll have to fight them off. Do me this one favor, kid, and I'll never ask another. I mean, this could be so big, even Winnie Argoth would forgive and forget just to get involved."

"You're exaggerating, Charlie," I said. "Nobody cares about books. Nobody knows who the hell writers are. This isn't the day of *Gone with the Wind,* and even then I'll bet there wasn't one person in a hundred who knew the name Margaret Mitchell. For god's sake, Charlie, people don't go to the movies because they're based on books by Hemingway or Faulkner or Tolstoy or anybody else. They haven't the foggiest idea who wrote the damn books, or the films. In fact, if you really get down to it, most people think the actors are making up the lines as they go along."

"Don't you believe it," he said. "Books are still where the movies come from, and they're still what the yokels want to see."

There was another thing. It took a minute for it to enter and be absorbed. I looked at him. I slowed down. I suppose I could have said a word then and stopped him. But I wasn't about to do that. I said, "What about Winnie Argoth?"

He said, "If I had my hands on the right property, she'd forget what happened. She'd be buddy-buddy again. I mean, when everything's said and done, Winnie never takes her eye off the main chance."

I said, "I thought you were buddies. I thought she was one of the family."

He didn't look happy. He said, "Not for a long time."

"Oh?"

"Not since the time she and Katherine had their big blowup. I mean, it was like World War Three. I mean, lawsuits and lawyers and threats and people saying crap like you never heard. It was like half the town was choosing up sides. I warned her. Jesus, I warned her. Don't say I didn't. I told her to go down there and apologize, even if she had to get down on her hands and knees and crawl. I told her Winnie was the best in the business. I told her Winnie was only thinking about her welfare. I told her nobody crosses Winnie. I told her her whole damn career could go down the toilet, for chrissake. But does she listen? Not her. Jesus, I'm married to the woman, and she never listens to me. I know this town; I know this fucking business inside out. But that woman goes her own way. She goes out and does whatever she likes. Well, look where it got us. You think she wouldn't be bigger if she was still with Winnie? You think she'd only be making a picture a year if she was still with Winnie? You think she'd be wasting her time downtown with those goddamn stage actors if she was still with Winnie? If she was still with Winnie, she'd be making double, triple, four times, on every picture and twice the points.

She'd be turning away projects. But you can't tell her a goddamn thing. She thinks she knows it all."

I said, "What exactly happened, Charlie?" It was something I had to know.

He shrugged. He took another long drink. He said, "Beats the hell out of me. It happened right here, maybe a year, maybe a little less, a little more, after we moved in. I was in here. I don't remember what I was doing. The two of them, they were in another room. The library, I think. All of a sudden I hear a lot of screaming. I mean, I thought this house was soundproof. It was supposed to be. I paid for it. But they were yelling so loud it cut right through like the walls were cheesepaper. I mean, I ran into the room, and they were standing there, and I thought they were going to start throwing punches any second. I didn't know Katherine even knew half the words she was using. I mean, she was telling Winnie to get the hell out, only she said it a lot stronger than that. She was telling Winnie to take a flying jump off the goddamn mountain. She was telling Winnie if they ever saw each other again, Winnie had better damn well cross the street and hide in a doorway, because if she didn't, she'd wake up in the fucking hospital, or maybe the cemetery. And Winnie was giving as good as she was getting. Well, almost. But what it was all about? Beats the hell out of me. I couldn't get it out of her. All she said was that it was a long time coming, too goddamn long. The thing was, Winnie wouldn't talk to me again after that. She wouldn't even answer the damn phone when I tried to call. And she looks at me like I'm not even there whenever I run into her, which, let me tell you, isn't often. And she put out some bad words about me, too, damn it." He sighed. He shook his head. He said, "The thing is, I could have straightened it all out if Katherine had let me. But she wouldn't. But I could straighten it all out now if I could just go to her and say, 'Winnie, I've got this hot thing, this tremendous thing, this blockbuster, and I need your help to put the package together.' She'd jump. Believe me, she'd jump, and it'd be like the old days again. So, Harry, you got to help me out. You got to do me this one favor. I'll never ask another."

There was, of course, no way I was going to do him a favor if the end result was what he hoped. But it didn't matter, because he was asking a favor I couldn't grant. I shook my head. I said, "I'm sorry, Charlie. I can't." He started to say something. I held out my hand to stop him. "It's not available."

"You sold it already?"

"I've sold it."

"Oh, Jesus." He deflated. His entire body seemed to shrivel. He seemed on the verge of collapse. But there was something else. Something in the attitude. A sudden listening. I thought I even sensed a kind of relief, though after all he'd said, that would have been hard to credit. He turned away, stumbled, righted himself, made it across to the bar, poured himself another drink and gulped it down fast, poured yet another, held the glass and looked into it. His color had gotten very high, the flush radiating through the tan of his face, sweat standing out on his forehead. He looked up and tried to focus on me. He attempted to form some words, moved his lips, but it was as though his mouth were frozen. He tried again, still had a little trouble, finally found his voice. He articulated very slowly and carefully, trying to form the words and get them to come out right. He said, "Who bought it? Maybe you could put a word in and we could work it out."

I shook my head. "Phil Garland."

"That prick."

"I thought you guys were partners. Used to be partners, anyway."

"Used to be. That's it. Son of a bitch. Never turn your back. Won't live long enough to regret it. Bastard, he's the one started the stories. Sure of it. Know it. Denied it. But he was the one."

I didn't care then whether that had been the issue between them or whether it had been something else. It didn't matter. I wanted out of that house, that castle of his. And I knew I was trapped. He was so drunk that there was no way he could drive or that I'd even consider sitting in a car with him. I wondered where the phones were. If I could find one, maybe I could get a cab.

I hadn't heard the car, hadn't heard the garage doors open and close, hadn't heard the door on the balcony open and close. All I heard, without warning, was a voice calling from up there on the balcony.

"Charlie? I'm home. Are you down there?"

21

He didn't answer, and he didn't move. I moved, out of the light. I turned my back, tried to calm myself, stay cool. I heard the feet coming down the spiral staircase, soft tapping.

"Charlie?" A pause. "Oh, we've got company again."

I turned slowly and looked at her, trying to keep my face still, without emotion. "Hello, Katie."

She was very good. The reaction lasted only a split second, just a little hesitation, a little stiffening, not enough so you'd notice unless you were watching for something. There was no way of knowing what lay behind it.

"Hello, Harry," she said. She was wearing a white silk blouse, the top three buttons undone. She was wearing old, faded jeans, not designer ones, the bottoms turned up a couple of times. She was wearing ballet slippers, only with hard soles, and no socks or stockings. Her hair was loose, hanging down over her shoulders and around her face. She was, as always, beautiful. There were changes, differences. And they weren't just from the apparent fatigue, and they weren't just from the passing of too many years. If there was still a vulnerability about her, she had managed to conceal it. Something said she could be tough and unrelenting to a degree that had not been present before and that she knew herself and knew what she could do.

Almost without pause, without reaction, with no emotion visible, she said, "I assume Charlie's around somewhere."

I motioned with my head toward the bar. She turned. Stuart was leaning on the bar, watching us closely. His eyes might still be a little glazed, his body might be swaying unsteadily, but he was watching, and on his face there was a calculating look. I wondered, then, was this why he had brought me there, the real reason? Maybe he had been serious about the rest, or maybe it had been subterfuge and he had been performing, had been trying to find a way to hold me and occupy me and so prevent me from noticing the passing of time, prevent me from leaving until this moment, until he could watch this moment.

Katie looked at him. In that glance and in her voice, there was the kind of weariness that said she had long since passed beyond anger, that she could not find it any longer, could not even find pity. She said, "All right, Charlie. Put the glass down. You've had too much already."

"Had a drink," he said. "So what? I'm entitled."

"One?" she said.

"Maybe two," he said.

"Or five or ten or twenty," she said.

"I'm entitled," he said.

"Yes," she said, "you're entitled. You're entitled to drink yourself into a sanitarium, or into the cemetery, if that's what you want."

With an ostentatious show, made more ostentatious by his inability to hold himself steady, he raised the glass from the bar, his hand never having left it, always holding it, brought it slowly and deliberately to his mouth, and took a sip. He watched her over the rim, calculating, challenging.

"Put it down, Charlie," she said.

"You tell me 'bout your day, I'll put it down," he said. He was having trouble articulating. "You always promise you'll tell me 'bout your day. You don't do it. Not no more."

She turned to me. "I'm sorry, Harry."

I shrugged.

"You should have come another night," she said. "But it wouldn't have made a difference. It would just have been like watching the same film over and over again." She looked back at Stuart. "Go to bed, Charlie," she said. "I'll call Samuel. He'll help you."

"No Samuel," he said slyly.

"Then I'll call Marie."

"No Marie," he said slyly. "No cook. No gardener. No nobody. Just Charlie Stuart and his beautiful loving wife and his best friend. That's all."

"Where are they, Charlie?" she said.

"Fired 'em. Told 'em to get lost. Told 'em didn't need 'em no more. Told 'em they wasn't no good in first place. Told 'em they was all robbin' us blind, like we didn't know it. Told 'em we knew it and they should get lost."

"That's the third time, Charlie. You can't keep doing it. I don't have the time to keep looking for people and then have you fire them. And I don't have the time, or the desire, to take care of this place by myself."

"Got to," he said. "Don't want nobody here. Just Charlie and Katherine and best friend."

"Go to bed, Charlie," she said.

"No, siree," he said. "Gonna sit here and watch show." He stumbled out from behind the bar, holding tight to his glass, trying to balance it. He weaved across the room, toppling and stumbling a few times, managing to keep himself upright. I didn't think he was going to make it. I was sure he'd fall and lie there in his own pool until somebody came and picked him up, and it didn't look as though anybody in that room was about to do that. He made it to a chair somehow and collapsed into it. He raised the glass and took an unsteady sip, spilling a little on that white alligator shirt, a wet stain spreading across the front, low, near the pants. He took another sip, then brought the glass down and let it rest, unsteadily in his lap, one hand cupping it. He grinned inanely. He watched us. He said, "Gonna see the show. Want to watch the show."

I looked at Katie. She was watching him. There was no emotion in her face.

"What show is that?" I said.

He tried to laugh. His face was frozen, and the sound wouldn't come out. "You know," he said archly.

"You'll have to tell me," I said.

A sound came out. Perhaps it was a laugh. He looked at me and grinned and winked, or tried to wink.

"I'm sorry you have to see this," Katie said.

"I am, too," I said. "It wasn't my choice. I didn't want to be here."

"I didn't know you were back," she said.

"No way you could."

"He knew."

"He said he read it in the trades. This morning."

"I wouldn't know. I don't read the trades."

"He said he read it there."

"And, of course, he went to see you immediately. And he forced you to come up here."

"You could say that."

"No explanations, Harry," she said. "Please, no explanations. I'm tired of explanations."

"Bravo," Charlie said. He clapped his hands. Some of the whiskey slopped on his pants. "Oops," he said, and tried to mop it up with an ineffectual hand. " 'Scuse me. Didn't mean to do that." He grinned. He raised the glass and sipped at what remained. "Please continue," he said. "Don't stop show on my account. Show begins. Want to see."

She looked at him. "Go to bed," she said.

"No," he said, shaking his head several times. "Won't go. Want to stay. Want to see how show comes out."

"Ignore him," she said.

"Does this happen often?"

"Often," she said.

"How long has it been going on?"

"Too long."

"Why? He didn't used to drink, at least not like this, at least not when I knew him."

"Ask him."

I looked toward him. His eyes were glazed. He was trying to focus them on us. He was grinning that silly grin. I looked away.

"I didn't want this to happen," I said.

"I suppose it was bound to, sooner or later," she said. She seemed resigned. She didn't seem to care.

"Not necessarily," I said.

"Yes, necessarily," she said. Her voice was suddenly too loud and the tone too sharp. She took a breath, shook herself, then looked at me, I think for the first time. "How are you, Harry?" she said. "I haven't asked."

I shrugged. "Okay," I looked at her. "And you?"

She didn't answer. She looked away.

"You look fine," I said. "The way I remember. You haven't changed."

"You always were a lousy liar," she said. "You ought to take acting lessons. Of course I've changed. We all change. Nothing ever stays the same."

I didn't say anything.

She said, "You've got gray in your hair."

"And a bald spot starting on the top," I said. "Like a monk."

"You're doing well."

"So-so."

"A little better than that, I think," she said.

"Not so poor anymore."

"None of us are," she said. "In some ways, at least. You haven't married." It was a statement, not a question.

"No," I said.

"No prospects?"

"None."

"Make me a drink, please, Harry. It's been a long day."

I walked across to the bar. "What do you drink these days?" I asked.

"Scotch," she said, "and water and ice."

When she drank, that's what she used to drink, mostly water and ice with just the aroma of scotch. I made it stronger and brought it to her. She took it, making sure our hands didn't touch. She nodded and then took a sip. She looked around. "God," she said, "how I hate this place."

Charlie came back from whatever country he had been lost in. He looked up and blinked a couple of times. "Didn't used to hate house," he mumbled. "Used to love it. Built house for Katherine. Present for Katherine. Wedding present."

"You built the house for yourself, and you know it," she said.

He shook his head. It kept going from side to side as though he couldn't stop it. "Not so," he said. "Not so. Took you up mountain. Wasn't nothing here then. Loved it. Said so. Loved house when Charlie built it. Didn't love Charlie. Never loved Charlie. Loved house. Katherine don't hate house. Can't hate house. How can she hate house? Beautiful house. Wonderful house. Only house like it in whole world." He was off and spewing it out now, and nobody could have stopped him. I looked over at Katie. Her eyes had been watching me. She turned away before I could catch the expression in them. She watched him. He was going on and on. "Katherine loved house. Know it. Can't say she don't. Can't ever say that. Charlie's gift. The one thing. Has to love it. Katherine. Katherine. Don't let me call her Katie. Tried. Wouldn't let me. Don't let nobody call her

Katie. Nobody but Suzie. Good old Suzie. Like Suzie. But Suzie don't like Charlie. Suzie says she'll kill Charlie if he don't take care of Katie. Only won't let Charlie call her Katie. Only Katherine. Why won't let Charlie call her Katie? Best friend used to call her Katie. How come not Charlie? Married to Charlie now, not best friend. So why not Katie? Won't let me do it." He stopped just like that. He started to cry, the tears streaming down his cheeks. He sat there crying and not bothering to wipe the tears away.

"Go to bed, Charlie," Katie said wearily.

He put his head against the back of the chair, going flaccid all of a sudden. His eyes closed. He started to snore. The glass fell out of his hand, what little was left in it running out in a little stream on the floor.

I picked up the glass and put it on a table. I looked at him. "I think he's asleep," I said.

"Yes," she said. "It happens that way." She took a deep breath. She noticed the glass in her hand and raised it and took a sip. She made a face, looked around, and set it down on a table. She looked at me. "Do something for me, Harry."

"Anything," I said. I hadn't meant to say that, or if I had, I had meant it to come out lightly. It didn't. But she didn't appear to notice.

"Would you put him to bed?" she asked. "I can't face it. Not tonight."

"Sure," I said. "Where do I take him?"

"Oh, you wouldn't know, would you? Down the elevator." She made a gesture toward it. "Push the second button. Then down the corridor. You can't miss his room."

"Do I get him undressed?"

"Don't bother. Just dump him on the bed. He'll undress himself when he wakes up."

I went over to the chair and heaved him out of it. He came out heavily at first, and then more easily, not resisting. He opened his eyes for just a second. "Show over?"

"The show's over," I said.

"Missed the end. Damn. How'd it come out?"

"Dull, Charlie. Very dull."

He grinned an inane grin. "Where you taking me?"

"To bed, Charlie. You can sleep it off."

"Good friend," he said. "Good friend always helps Charlie. Need some sleep. That's what I need. Sleep. Feel better when I wake up."

He closed his eyes again and tried to settle back into the chair. I pulled his arms, hauled him back out of it, put one arm over my shoulder, and half dragged, half carried, him to the elevator. He leaned against me, asleep, snoring, while we rode down. There was no trouble finding his room. The door was open. Everything in it said a man lived here, a rich man. The carpet was thick and deep and blue. So was the spread, and so were the drapes that hung across the glass wall. The military brushes on top of the custom-made dresser were expensive. Everything was masculine. There wasn't a feminine note to the room. No sign of Katie. No sign that she had ever been there. I lowered him gently onto the bed. He spread out on his back, snoring, not moving. For a moment I stood over him, looking down. The king in his castle. Charlie Stuart on his mountain peak.

22

When I got back upstairs, the window wall was open. Katie was out on the terrace, leaning against the railing, the drink in her hand. She was staring out into the distance. I got my drink and went out and stood beside her. There wasn't much to see. The fog was thickening, a dense gray blanket covering everything, isolating us up on that mountain.

"He's asleep," I said.

"Of course," she said, not looking at me.

"Katie," I said.

"Could I have a cigarette, Harry?" she said.

I reached for a pack in my pocket, pulled it out, stopped. "Since when do you smoke?"

She shrugged. "Now and then," she said. "Sometimes it helps."

"Like a drink."

"Like a drink."

I held the cigarette out to her. She took it, and I lit it for her. She took a puff, didn't inhale, looked at it with distaste, dropped it on the terrace floor, and stepped on it. "I suppose I'll have to clean that up in the morning," she said. "He made certain of that." She looked out at the fog. "It's getting thicker," she said.

"Yes," I said. If I didn't leave very soon, I'd probably have to spend the night. I didn't want that. I ought to go and call a cab, I thought. Maybe one would still be willing to take a chance and drive up and down the mountain. I didn't move.

"I like it up here when there's fog," she said. "The only time. I'm all alone then. Nothing can touch me. I come out here and stand alone and just look out at the fog. The rest of the world doesn't exist. It's vanished somewhere down under that gray cover. That's when I feel safe. Nothing can hurt me then."

So the vulnerability wasn't gone. Just hidden, and maybe not too deep, and maybe, at times like this, it came back to the surface.

"I don't think it's going to last," she said suddenly. "There's a breeze. I can feel it. Sometimes it's like that. You think you're going to be fogged in forever, and then the breeze comes, and the fog just disappears." She turned her back to the railing, leaned against it, and turned her head a little to look at me. She looked away. "Are you happy, Harry?"

No games, I thought. Not now. "No," I said.

"You should be," she said. "Look at all the things you've done. All the books you used to say you'd write. Now you've written them. I've read then, Harry, and they're good. They get better, each one. You should be proud, Harry. You've done well with your life. People look up to you. They know you. You're . . . you're invulnerable now. You should be happy."

"If that's what it takes to be happy," I said, "you ought to be delirious."

She didn't answer. She stood there staring at the reflections in the glass wall, the two of us against the gray desolate backdrop. She still didn't look directly at me. She said, finally, "We made a mess of things, didn't we?"

"Yes," I said.

"Do you remember? We played a silly word game once. If only . . ."

"That was after you broke your leg and the world was closing in and there didn't seem to be any way out. If only . . . a million of them."

"A million of them," she said.

"Do you ever miss it?" I asked suddenly, from nowhere. "The dancing, I mean."

"Every hour of every day of my life," she said.

"But you had a second chance," I said. "Not many people get that. And look what you did with it."

"No," she said sharply, angrily. "You can't go back. There aren't any if onlys and there aren't any second chances. What's over is over; what's done is done. You can't repair things. You have to live with what you've done. You have to go on, and on, and on. If only? That's a fairy tale. And I won't." She put her hands behind her and shoved herself away from the railing, a violent movement, and took a quick step toward the inside. "I'm hungry," she said. "Suddenly I'm very hungry. I'm starving." She looked back. "Have you eaten?"

I felt the hunger pangs. I hadn't eaten since lunch, hadn't thought about food until that moment. "No," I said. "I'd forgotten about food."

She stopped. "Damn. He fired the cook."

"You must have a kitchen," I said. "I'm sure the cook didn't take it with her."

"I haven't cooked in years," she said, "and even when I did, I was no damn good. You remember."

"You were okay," I said. "And I still cook."

"For all your lady friends? Wine 'em and dine 'em and screw 'em."

I laughed. She had said those exact words a long time ago, after I'd cooked a meal for her the first time and we'd gone to bed together for the first time. "For myself mostly, these days," I said.

"I'll bet," she said. "You never were a monk, Harry." She smiled a little. "Well, you can cook for me again if you want. Let's go down and see what Cook left behind."

She led me down a flight of stairs beyond the living room, down another flight and along a corridor, through a room and another until we came out into the kitchen. As Charlie had said, it was right out of a restaurant. I went to the refrigerator and, opening it, looked inside. "Were you planning a party?" I asked.

She gave me an odd look and shook her head. "Not unless Charlie set something up and didn't tell me. Why?"

"Take a look," I said. She walked over and looked. The refrigerator was completely filled, a couple of large steaks, some chickens, a large rib roast, and a lot more. It didn't look as though there were room to put another thing in there. "If you're not planning on entertaining half of Hollywood," I said, "you'd better put that stuff in the freezer before it spoils."

"Why do you imagine she bought all that?" she said.

"What would you like?" I asked.

"You choose," she said. "God knows, there's enough to choose from. What am I going to do with it all?"

Something simple and something quick, I thought. I looked around and found the eggs. I looked at her. "You must have herbs," I said.

"We must," she said. "But I wouldn't know where. I can't remember the last time I was down here. This is Cook's private preserve." We both looked around. I spotted a herb garden growing just inside the window.

"Cut some," I said to her. "I'll make an omelet." She cut while I mixed the eggs and then watched while I blended in the herbs, watched as I hunted through the refrigerator and came out with lettuce and other things. "You set the table," I said, "and I'll make a salad."

"First," she said, "I have to find the dishes. Where do you suppose she keeps them?" She opened several cabinets before she finally found them. She looked at them. "I don't think I ever saw these before," she said. "Well, they'll have to do." She took down plates and salad dishes, went hunting through drawers until she found the knives and forks, through other cabinets until she found glasses. She carried everything to the table at one end of the kitchen, near the glass wall, and set the table. "There must be wine somewhere," she said. "Look in the refrigerator, will you, Harry?" I looked. There were a couple of bottles of average California chablis. I took out a bottle and held it out to her. She looked, made a face, and said, "That's probably what she uses for cooking. Or maybe they drink it down here. I suppose it will have to do." She found a corkscrew and opened the bottle, carried it to the table, and poured some into the glasses while I finished the salad, made a dressing, tossed and served it, and then cooked the omelet.

We sat down, Katie across from me. Déjà vu. Except that Charlie Stuart was sleeping a floor below us and this was his house and she was his wife. We ate and we talked lightly, about nothing important, nothing that could possibly matter or mean anything or start anything, skirting and being careful never to come too close. But no matter how careful you try to be, one thing leads to another, and pretty soon you find yourself where you did not intend to be.

Without realizing it, we began to edge in. We touched on her work. She sighed. I said something about how she must be tired. She said it had been a long day. I asked if she was in the middle of a new picture.

"Just finishing," she said. "I spent the morning looping. Then I had to be downtown this afternoon. We're rehearsing a new play. Did you know I'm acting on stage these days?"

I said I had heard. I said somebody had sent me the reviews when she did Nora.

She laughed a little. "Oh, god," she said. "They were so careful and so kind. I really wasn't very good. But it was the first time, really, and I liked it. You know, I've done five or six plays since. Now I try to do at least one every year."

"And, of course, they want you."

She looked at me with surprise. "What ever makes you think that?"

"You're a big movie star, Katie."

"Don't you know, they don't trust people from the movies."

"Too temperamental?"

"Yes, too temperamental. And a lot of them expect too much money and too much attention. And a lot of them don't know their way around a stage. It's not easy. It's hard work. It's the closest thing to dancing I know."

"That's why you do it?"

"No," she said, "and, I suppose, yes. I like the stage. A film belongs to the director, and maybe the editor. We just do what the director wants and it's frozen forever and you can never change it. And if there are a dozen takes, the director and the cutter decide which one they want. On the stage, what the audience sees is what you have to give, at the moment you give it. You can grow and change and keep finding new things, new dimensions, from performance to performance. I like that. And, of course, I'm getting older. Don't make that face, Harry. It's true. I'm not a kid anymore, at the beginning. And there are a lot of young kids coming up. They're fresher, and they have a lot more motivation than I ever had for films, and so they get offered the parts I might have had a few years ago. Nobody even thinks of me for them anymore. Of course, some of them are willing to do things I won't and never would think of doing. I mean, they don't think anything of taking their clothes off, if that's in the script or if the director thinks he wants it.

Well, I won't do that. Who'd want to see my body, anyway? I mean, my god, what is it with these people? What's so terrific about seeing a naked body walking around, or lying with some guy on a bed? I mean, we all have bodies, and we use them, but I don't see a lot of people taking off their clothes and walking around the streets in public. So why should I do it in a film just because some director thinks maybe it'll excite someone or draw a few people into the box office? My body belongs to me, and I decide who I'm going to take my clothes off for and when. Maybe that's cost me some parts. But I don't care. Somebody I used to know said it did. But if that's the way it's going to be, they can have it. But it's more than that. I've grown up, Harry. I know things don't last forever and you can't go on doing the same thing year after year. I've only got a few years left to do what I do now on film. After that, even if they offered me the kind of roles I do now, I'd just look like an old fool trying to stay young. That I'll never be. But there are things I can try on the stage, things I can act and things I can grow into. I mean, there are roles you have to be older and more experienced before you even dare to think about. Maybe someday, if I ever get good enough, I might even get a chance to act in New York."

"That would be a nice way to come home," I said.

She made a face.

I looked at her and smiled and said, "And I wouldn't say you're exactly over the hill as far as films are concerned, either. You're good. That's what everybody says. You're one of the best."

"What do you say?" she asked.

I shrugged. "I'm no judge. Films aren't my thing. You know that."

She studied me for a moment. "Have you ever seen me?"

I didn't answer. I didn't want to lie.

She said, "I didn't think so. I've read your books."

"It's not the same."

"No? Why not? There's more of you in your books than there is of me on the screen. But you know something, Harry? I knew you'd never go. I bet Suzie on that. She was sure you'd see everything I ever did, and more than once."

"You still see Suzie?"

"Of course," she said. She seemed puzzled. "Why wouldn't I? She's my friend. My best friend."

"I didn't know where she was. I wondered if she was back here."

"Not exactly," she said. "I don't see her as much as I'd like. It's harder now. She's in Vegas, so we only see each other when she's in town or we're over there."

"Oh," I said, "she's in Vegas." I had an unpleasant image, and it must have been reflected in my face. I said, "There's no justice."

She looked at me and shook her head. "Oh, Harry," she said, "she owns a store, high fashion. That's all. Whatever gave you any other idea?"

I shrugged. "Even so, there still ain't no justice." I took a sip of the wine. It was better than I expected, or maybe it just sat well after a few tastes. "I haven't seen her in years," I said, "not since I ran into her in New York and we had lunch."

"I didn't know," she said. "She never told me."

"No reason to, I guess," I said. "It was right after she and Phil Garland split. She was on her way to Europe."

"He's your friend," she said, "so I won't say anything. But you can have Mr. Philip Garland, with my compliments. And you can keep him."

"You used to like him."

"Maybe. But that was a long time ago."

"Before Suzie?"

"Before Suzie and before a lot of things. I suppose he'd be tolerable if he'd only grow up instead of growing down. But he's one big pain."

"A successful pain, though."

"It depends on how you define success," she said. "Successful at his business? I suppose so. Successful at being a person? Hell, no."

"You could say that about a lot of us."

"All right," she said. "I won't criticize anymore. Besides, he's the reason you're out here, isn't he? I mean, he's bought your new book."

"So you knew that?"

"Naturally. Everybody knows. Do you think there are any secrets in this town? And whatever would he want to keep that a secret for?"

"Did Charlie know?"

"Of course Charlie knew. He was the one who told me. He read it in his damn trades."

"He reads everything in the trades, doesn't he?"

"They're the first thing he reads in the morning. Before he looks at the *Times*. Before he has his coffee. Before he does anything. Are you going to write the screenplay?"

"No."

"You should."

"Why does everyone keep saying that? As though screenwriting is the only kind of writing that means a damn. No, I'm not going to write the damn screenplay. The reason I'm out here is because Phil asked me to come out to talk with the writer he hired. Why he wanted it beats me. It was a damn waste of time, for everyone. But what the hell. So Charlie knew."

"Just what are you getting at? Did you think he didn't?"

"He said he didn't." I said that very deliberately. "He brought me up here to see his castle, and then he said the reason he really brought me here was to ask me a favor."

"What favor?" She had an unreadable expression.

"He asked me to sell him the rights. He said he'd made a bunch of lousy pictures and now nobody would talk to him and nobody would back him in making another picture. He said his only way back was to get the rights to a hot property. He said my book was a hot property, and he begged me to sell it to him."

She shook her head sharply. She was angry, very angry. She said, "He wouldn't know what to do with it if you handed it to him on a silver platter, all tied up with a gold ribbon."

"I don't get it."

"You don't get it? God, are you blind, Harry. You're supposed to be a writer. You're supposed to have insights. And you don't get it."

"No," I said. "Charlie's made some good pictures. At least that's what they say. He knows how to make movies. He's got his damn Oscars and he's got his damn money to prove it. And maybe if I hadn't sold the rights to Phil, I might even have considered it."

She laughed. It had a bitter edge. "You can say that? You, of all people?"

"Why not? I owe the man something."

"You owe him nothing."

"Not true. I owe him plenty. When you come down to it, you could say he saved us when it didn't look like we could be saved. We were as low as it was possible to sink, and he pulled us out."

"Really? Do you really believe that? Do you think he did it out of love, because he's such a sweet, wonderful man?"

"Maybe you've forgotten what it was like then."

"I forget nothing," she said. "It's merely that I know Charlie Stuart. Oh, how well I know him. Do you really want to know about him? Because if you do, just listen to me and I'll tell you. Oh, my god, how I've been longing to tell somebody. You came along at the right time, Harry. It's time for the truth, time to stop pretending, to put an end to the lies. It's late and I'm tired, tired to death with the pretending and the lying and the covering up. So don't try to shut me up. Wonderful Charlie Stuart. Do you know what he really is? Charlie's a talker and Charlie's a user and

Charlie gives nothing back. Don't give me that look. I'm telling the truth about him, for once. I'm tired of covering for him and lying for him. Oh, Harry, you're such a fool, such a goddamn fool. If you'd only think about it for half a second. Did he really save us? Don't you remember? I'd begun working for Terry on the picture. Don't you remember? I wasn't making much, but it was enough. So we didn't need his money. We would have made out without it. And just what was it he gave you? A few dollars? He even cut corners there. You told me so yourself. You looked it up, and it was less than the guild minimum. And those few dollars were all you ever got. All right, so he threw in a little more, but only when he knew you'd given him the gold mine. Look at what he got. He got his picture. The one he'd been talking about for years, for so long that everybody laughed whenever he mentioned it. You gave it to him, and you gave him his goddamn Oscars and all the rest. Did he ever so much as thank you? Did he even offer to share a little of the credit with you? Like hell he did. He took it all for himself. Every bit of it. And you, you were such a goddamn nice guy, and such a goddamn fool, you made everybody promise never to tell the truth, to let him have it all. So who besides Phil Garland, your dear friend, and me and Charlie ever knew it was a lie? Everybody thought Charlie had finally done it. Everybody thought there must be more to Charlie than they'd ever thought. You gave him that, and you gave him this goddamn castle in the sky, and you gave him a lot more. Oh, my god, the things you gave him. You made it all possible for him. And you still think you owe him something? You owe that man nothing. Nothing."

"Katie," I said, "Katie."

"Don't Katie me, Harry Miller." She was boiling over now, and nothing was going to stop her and put it back in the bottle. "You don't know," she said. "You don't know the half of it. Do you have the slightest idea what that man really is? He's a taker who gives nothing. He's a user who won't be used himself. And he's a loser. Oh, yes, he's a loser. That's Charlie Stuart. The big-time producer, the big-time screenwriter with his Oscars sitting up there on the shelf. Don't make me laugh. He's written one screenplay in his life, and he didn't even write that, and now, probably thanks to your friend Phil Garland, because it wasn't me, oh, no, it wasn't me, because I keep my promises, half the people in town know he never wrote it; the only thing they don't know is who wrote it for him. He's produced three or four movies that were worth anything at all, and the only reason they were was because he at least had the sense to surround himself with good directors and good actors and good technical crews. Oh, they came to him, all right, and they worked for him, all right, until they finally saw exactly what he was and how he was using them. My god, all that man ever was in his life until you came along was a sycophant, a man who said yes to anyone who'd ever let him say yes. Phil Garland told you that, told us that, right at the very beginning. Didn't you pay any attention? Didn't you listen to him? Didn't you know that by the time you came along, he'd even run out of people who'd let him say yes? He was an old bore, that's all, sitting in that silly little office out on the lot pretending he was busy, pretending he was somebody. And everybody ignored him. The only reason anybody ever gave him anything was to get him off their backs. That's all Phil Garland was doing when he sicked him on you. Didn't you understand that? Well, Harry, you made him important. You made him something he never was and never could be, not if he lives a million years. You even made people think he was somebody. My god, he even started to believe it. Oh, don't stop me, Harry. Don't you even try. Because I haven't even started yet. Charlie Stuart. My god, that man took something from everybody he ever met who'd give him half a chance. If somebody had an idea, he took it and said it was his. It didn't matter what; you just name it and he took it and pretended it was his, and after a while I think he even began to believe it was his. He used anybody who would let him, and after you gave him what you gave him, there were plenty of people who would give him anything. He just told them he was doing them a favor, and, my god, they bought it. Oh, you ought to know about that. It was just fine for him, as long as it lasted. Only it couldn't last, could it? He's so damn transparent. When you really get to know him, you can see right through him. It just takes the time and the desire to look, and I suppose most people at first didn't have the time or maybe they just didn't dare. I don't know. But eventually, oh, yes, eventually people started to take a good look, and they began to see him, and they began to realize that he was just the same old Charlie Stuart. He hadn't changed. He was still the phony who was just big talk. He was still just Charlie Stuart, the loser, the man who wanted to say yes to anyone who wanted to let him. When they saw that, they knew they didn't need him anymore. Do you really want to know why he kept on producing? Do you really want to know why people kept giving him pictures to do, even if the pictures were less and less important and the budgets were smaller and smaller? Because of me, god damn it. Because of me. Because he was my husband and they thought if they did something for him, it would please me and then maybe I'd do something for them. But after a while, he couldn't even do the lousy films right, not when he had to do things on his own without someone to back him up and give him ideas and tell him what to do and how to do it. People stopped doing that when they knew he would just take the credit and tell them to take a jump when it was all through. Buy your book? Turn it into a picture? Don't make me laugh. Even if you gave him the chance, he'd wreck it. Unless you were fool enough to write the screenplay for him, and even then he'd probably make a botch of the whole thing. So now that little man sits up here and feels sorry for himself. He sits up here and he drinks and feels sorry for himself. Nobody loves him.

His wife doesn't love him. Well, he knew that when I married him. Nobody understands him. The trouble is, everybody understands him only too well. Nobody appreciates him. Because there's nothing to appreciate. When he gets too lonely, he gets into that damn car of his and he drives down to one of his old hangouts or to his golf club, only he doesn't play much golf anymore. He just sits around and he gets drunk with his old buddies and he tells them his sad story. Maybe they don't care, or maybe they drink with him and commiserate because he's just old Charlie, the loser, and their old drinking buddy, or maybe they do it because they think they have to be nice to him because he's married to Katherine Summers."

She stopped. She took a deep breath. She pushed her hair away from her face. She picked up the wineglass and drank some. She glared at me.

"Don't say anymore, Katie," I said. "You don't have to." I wanted to do something, anything. But there wasn't anything I thought I could do, so I just sat there.

"Like hell I don't," she said. "It's about time I got it out. I should have done it a long time ago. Don't stop me now, Harry. Don't you dare even try. Oh, yes, I'm feeling sorry for myself. You bet I am. I have reasons. Too many. Oh, do I have reasons. Do you have any idea what that son of a bitch does now when he gets drunk? Do you want to know why that son of a bitch really asked you to come here? That little bastard decides he wants to watch a show. He's going to put it on his way. He's going to produce it, and he's going to stage it, and he's going to do everything with it, and then he's going to watch it. It's going to be a great big Charlie Stuart Production, for Charlie Stuart alone. He invites one of his old drinking buddies up here, and they're all settled in, nice and comfortable and half-drunk or all drunk by the time I get home. He arranges everything. Oh, he arranges them. He wants to see how long it takes after I get home before his dear old buddy starts coming on to me. He nudges and he urges, and he's not even very subtle about it. He sits there and he watches and he waits. He wants to see what I'll do. I think he even hopes and prays that something will happen. He's absolutely convinced I must have a million lovers. I won't sleep with him, so I must be sleeping with someone. Isn't that right? But do you want to know the truth, Harry? I'm the faithful little wife. I've never strayed. Not once. God knows I've had opportunities. God knows I've thought about it. God knows I've even wanted to. And god knows he's given me plenty of reason. But I haven't. Don't ask me why. Maybe I'm a fool, too. But does he really think I'd let one of his drunken friends put a goddamn hand on me? Do you know what I do? I just go to bed. And that drunken sot sits there and actually looks disappointed. That is, if he hasn't passed out by then."

She stopped and glared at me, shook her head. "And you, you're an even bigger damn fool," she said. "He wants to buy your book? He begged for it? And you didn't see through that? He brought you up here, and he set you up, and you never even guessed. He's so damned sure that I'm still in love with you that he must have thought one look and he'd have his wish at long last, he'd finally see his goddamn show. Well, if you hang around here much longer, he just might get his wish at that." And she stopped. She held on to the wineglass, her knuckles white around it. She didn't look at me.

"Why the hell did you marry him?"

"Why?" She turned and stared at me. She was furious. She said, "You ask me that? You? I was alone, you bastard. I was frightened. God, I was frightened. Every man I met tried to get me into bed. The first thing. Practically before we even said hello. Maybe they thought they were doing me a favor. I don't know. I don't care. They couldn't understand why I said no. They were certain I must be putting on an act. Do you want to hear about the guy who tried to rape me? Not one. More than one. Do you want to hear about the black eye and the bruises? Do you want me to tell you all about that? But then there was Charlie. Good old Charlie. He was always around. He was kind then. He was sympathetic. He didn't make any demands. He kept sending me flowers, presents, all kinds of things. He said all he wanted was to take care of me. He said all he wanted was to protect me. And he was becoming very important then, and I thought finally, Well, maybe if I marry Charlie, people will leave me alone. I won't have to worry, and I won't have to fight, and I won't even have to think. And there were people telling me to do it, do it, it will be the best thing, the right thing. Oh, it seemed so easy, so easy."

"And she didn't object?" I didn't have to put a name to the she. She knew. She laughed a bitter laugh.

"Are you kidding?" she said. "She was all for it. She was the one who was always telling me to do it, do it, it was the right thing, the best thing. She practically threw me into his arms. Charlie Stuart. He was no threat to her. Never. He'd do anything she wanted. She didn't even have to ask. If he thought something would please her, he couldn't wait to do it. He thought the world wouldn't spin if she didn't turn the key. So she was all for it. She pushed me down the aisle. Only, maybe the way I was then, she didn't have to push very hard. But she had Charlie Stuart in her pocket, and she was sure that Mrs. Charlie Stuart would be a nice little girl and never ask a question and never have a doubt and she could call the tune and I'd dance to it forever."

"But it's not like that anymore," I said. "So why do you stay with him. You could walk out anytime."

"Why?" she said. "Because he needs me. It's as simple as that. Just look at him. That poor drunken sad loser. What would he have left if I walked out? But it's more than that. I don't want to go back down into that zoo again. I don't want to be alone down there again. I couldn't face that. So I need him, and I'll put up with him." She shook herself. She turned and looked directly at me, and the expression on her face was not pleasant. Suddenly, abruptly, she pushed herself back from the table, got up, turned away, and stood by the window, looking not out but at the reflections. She said to the reflections, "You'd better go now, Harry. You'd better go before I do what he's been waiting for me to do. You don't belong here. You never should have come here. Go, Harry. Now. Or we'll both be sorry."

For a moment I didn't move. I sat there, looking at her back, looking at the image of her face reflected in the glass. "I love you, Katie," I said. "I always have. I always will."

She spun around. She was angrier with me now than she had been with him, perhaps angrier than I had ever seen her. "Then why the hell did you walk out on me?"

"You didn't give me much choice," I said.

"No?" she said. "Did you give me one? You could always have said something. Why didn't you?"

"It was too late by then," I said. "You wouldn't have listened. I don't think you'd even have believed me."

"Not then. At the beginning. All the time. Why didn't you ever say anything, tell me anything?"

"Would you have believed me?"

"I'd have listened to you."

"With everyone else—Garland, Vogel, the rest of them—throwing you in her arms?"

"You were the one who was important. You knew that. All you had to do was say something, anything. But no, not you, you kept your damn mouth shut and just let it happen."

"And you?" I said. "You were so damn convinced that everything she did was right, everything she was doing was for you. It wouldn't have mattered what I said."

"It would have mattered."

"You had to find out for yourself."

"You could have helped," she said.

"I don't think so."

"You don't think so? God damn you, Harry Miller. You don't think so. You don't think. You don't do. You just sit there and let things happen, watch them happen. But you don't do anything to stop them or make them happen. You just sit there and watch, like you were outside and they didn't affect you. Maybe you pray or maybe you hope, but you never get off your ass and do anything."

"And if I had?"

"Oh, my god, if you had. Yes, I had to find out for myself, but you could have helped. Yes, it took a long time, too long, oh, how long, but you could have helped." She looked away, looked back. "If you'd said anything, anytime, it might never have happened. If you'd stayed, it wouldn't have taken so long, and none of the rest would have happened. If I'd had you . . . But no, not you. You couldn't do any of it, you couldn't even do that. You couldn't even call, not once, not ever."

"You're right. I should have. I even started to, dialed the number a couple of times, at the beginning."

"But you didn't follow through. You couldn't, could you, Harry?"

"I couldn't."

"Go away, Harry," she said. "Please go away."

She was right. There wasn't anything more to say. "I'll have to call a cab," I said. "Where do you keep the phones?"

She looked out through the windows. The fog was still thick, but it looked as though it were starting to drift away. I imagined I could see little points of light dimly struggling to come out high above it. She said, "They won't come up here when it's like this. Not until the fog lifts. You can borrow one of the cars. If you drive carefully, and, oh, my god, you're a careful driver, you never take chances, if you drive carefully, you'll be all right. I'll pick up the car in the morning."

She turned quickly and started from the room. I followed at a little distance. I wanted to reach out, to touch her, but I didn't. We retraced our steps through rooms and up stairs, back to the living room. She stood there, looked around, saw her purse where she had dropped it. She went to it, dug around, came out with a set of car keys, and dropped them on a table. She said, "Here," and didn't look at me.

I picked them up. When I had them in my hand, I looked at them. They had a remembered feel. I looked at her. "You still have the MG."

"Yes," she said, "I still have it. It's got a new engine, new seats, a lot of new things. But, yes, I still have it."

"You never sent me the papers to sign it over."

"I never got around to it."

"So it's still in both names."

"Yes, I suppose so," she said. "Go away, Harry." She motioned, then said wearily, "Up the stairs. The door to the garage is at the end of the balcony." She turned away.

I took a step, stopped, turned, and took a step and came up behind her. I put my hands on her shoulders and tried to turn her around. For just an instant, she started to turn, then stiffened and pulled away. She turned then and glared at me. "Oh, you dirty bastard," she said. "Don't you dare touch me. Don't you dare put your hands on me. You walk out on me, and all these years you never say a word, never give an indication of anything, and now you think you can just walk back into my life and it will be like nothing ever happened. Get the hell out of here, Harry. Don't you ever dare come back."

I went then. From the balcony I looked down on her. She was standing in the middle of the room, not moving, just standing there, looking small and defeated. It was not just that vast space that made her seem so. She didn't belong here. Maybe only Charlie Stuart belonged here, in a castle of dreams on a mountaintop. She belonged more, I suddenly thought, in that rundown place of Wolf Rabinowitz than here. I hesitated, started to turn back, and then did not. I walked slowly along the balcony until I reached the door at the end, opened it, and went into the garage. The MG was parked there, in the space next to the Mercedes, dwarfed by it. I stood for a moment looking down at it. It was still without its top. Memories flooded through me. I climbed in, put the key in the ignition, felt around under the dash until I found the right and unfamiliar switch, and pressed it. The garage doors swung up and open. I turned on the ignition. The motor turned over and caught, no hesitation, and it gave off a remembered sound.

And then I turned it off. She was right, of course. All my life I had been the passive observer. I had stood back from the action, watching it, commenting on but rarely a part of it, always somehow a little removed, never participating, never doing anything, making no move to change or influence events, to try to stem a tide and turn it back. That was always for others. I had thought it enough merely to watch from the fringes and so maintain an objectivity that would permit me to write the truth about what I had seen. Maybe that had been enough once for a career.

But it had been a delusion, and it had made a mess of my life. What was worse, infinitely worse, it had made a mess of other people's lives, too. Katie's. Long ago, in difficult times in dangerous places, I thought I had come to understand that objectivity is impossible and that, finally, I did not know the truth about anything, for one man's truth is another man's lie. When I had learned that, it had been time to leave the paper, and I had. But now I knew that I had merely replaced one kind of objectivity with another. If I could not know the truth, then I could not act on a sureness, and so I had done nothing. But nothing is a solution to nothing. It is not, as Lucretius said, as Lear said, that nothing will come of nothing. Too much comes of nothing, and what comes is unbearable. To stand aside and watch the events and the actions and refuse to intervene, to think that the wisest and safest course, because it is impossible to know the right course, is to do nothing and so let things go as they will is to abdicate all responsibility as a human, all responsibility to those we hold dear. So it is not nothing that comes of nothing, but pain and loss and too much more, and in the end, even doing nothing is an action, a refusal to do what one should. Only the dead can truly do nothing.

I yanked the keys out of the ignition, shoved them into my pocket, got out of the car, and started to move fast across the garage toward the door. I could not right the wrongs I had done by doing nothing, and I could not undo the damage of all the years of saying nothing. But I could try.

I reached the door, put my hand on the knob, and started to turn it. It turned under my hand even before I had a good grip. The door opened. She was standing there, her hand on the knob, a little out of breath. She looked then as I remembered her from long ago. We faced each other, not moving for a moment.

"Where are you going?" she said.

"Back," I said. "I was going back for you. I'm not walking out again. Not this time. Not ever again."

She looked at me closely. She nodded slowly, her face serious. There was something else there, too. I nodded back. She started past me, reached out as she went by, and her hand touched mine for just a moment. She moved toward the car. I followed.

"Get in," she said. "The other seat. Let me have the keys. I want to drive."

She had thought she knew me so well, and indeed she had. She had been sure she knew what I would do, or would not do, and so if anything were to be done and anything saved, it would be she who would have to do the doing and the saving.

I shook my head, took out the keys and held them. "Not this time," I said. "You get in. I'll drive."

She stood for a moment beside me, next to the car, staring up. She studied my face, then smiled just a little and gave a slight nod, just the barest movement of her head. It was enough. She reached out and touched my face with her hand, then turned and walked around the car and got in on the passenger side.

We drove away from there then, through the fog that was lifting so that we could begin to see a few points of stars overhead. We started down the mountain.

Behind us, we left the king, asleep in his bed in his castle, wandering through whatever realms were conjured in his dreams. We had seen him through the distorting lens of our own disappointments and different expectations, and so, perhaps, we had never really understood him. Charlie Stuart was a man of his time, and he dreamed dreams fitting to this strange and unreal place on the rim of the vast ocean. He had dreamed of a picture, a castle, and a woman. The picture would be his Holy Grail, and he would be Galahad; the castle would be his Camelot, and he would be Arthur; the woman would be his Guinevere, and he would be her champion, her Launcelot du Lac. The picture would be his and his alone, and it would make him famous and gain him the respect and the envy he had never known. The castle would be on the highest mountain, and it would be like no other. The woman would be his lady fair and would share it all. In this unreal yet all too real world in which he had lived so long, he had made his dreams come true. I had written the script for him, yes, but he had taken it and made it into that picture, and he had made it well, and so he had possessed his Holy Grail. And from it, he had built his castle, his Camelot, on top of his mountain, where nothing had stood before. And I had stood aside and without struggle and without thought had let him take the woman to share it, which was the most valuable prize of all.

No matter the rumors that were being spread, no matter the later failures, the picture was there, and he would always have the reality of it and the knowledge that he had made it happen and without him it would not have been. That could never be taken from him. And when he woke in the morning, it would be in his castle. That, too, was real, and that, too, would still be his. What would no longer be his was that final prize. I was taking her back, or she was returning to me, so he would have to make do with what remained.

But Charlie Stuart was a dreamer, and dreams die hard. Perhaps he had other dreams now, and perhaps somewhere he would find the resources to pursue them.

I didn't know and I didn't care. I had Katie again, and we had each other, and that was real, that was not a dream. We had climbed that mountain with Charlie Stuart, and now we had come down from it and left him there, with his dreams.